Edie's Books

PARANORMAL

Dragon Blues
Cattitude
The Fat Cat, a Cattitude short story
Dead People
Dead People in Love, a Dead People short story

SCIENCE FICTION ROMANCE

Galaxy Girls
Mixing It Up, a Galaxy Girls novella
The Kiss, a Galaxy Girls short story

Cattitude

Edie Ramer

Published by Blue Walrus Books

ISBN: 978-1-939328-28-1

Copy-editing by Blue Otter Editing
Proofreading by Judicious Designs
Formatting by Author E.M.S.

Published in the United States of America.

One

A muffled shriek from the office next door rudely jerked Belle awake. Curled on the desktop, she recognized the voice, yawned, and settled back down to finish her nap. Less than a tail length away, Max continued typing, his human hearing inferior to hers. A moment later, footsteps tapped toward their office, fast and angry.

Belle opened her eyes to a slit. This was her castle, and she needed to be vigilant.

A tall, blond woman entered, carrying the hot drink that she and Max shared a liking for. She shot Belle a glare, then plastered a smile on her face and changed her walk, her body swaying catlike, steam snaking up from the drink.

Max didn't turn from his computer, but the fur on Belle's spine lifted. Caroline's poor-widowed-me demeanor didn't fool Belle. Beneath the flowery perfume, she detected the stench of a predator.

"I brought you coffee." The woman's chirpy voice reminded Belle of a bird—one she wanted to catch and bite its head off. Ignoring her, Caroline set down the mug and hovered over Max.

Frowning at his computer screen, he thanked her. Only when she leaned her hip against the desk did he turn his head.

Belle sat, her claws extending.

"Your cat's giving me the evil eye."

That wasn't all Belle wanted to give her.

Max reached past Caroline's hip to stroke Belle's ear in

1

the perfect spot. She meowed and pushed the top of her head against his palm, marking his skin with her scent. Peering at Caroline through slitted eyes, she conveyed her thought: *He's mine. Leave him alone.*

If Max found someone to love who loved him back, she wouldn't mind. But his cousin's widow wasn't worthy of him. In Belle's four years with Max, he hadn't brought home one woman worth a bowl of sour milk.

"Belle doesn't give the evil eye. She's a sweetheart, aren't you, Belle?"

Belle purred her agreement, her body rumbling and vibrating. She dropped onto the desk and rolled over, exposing her belly, her vulnerable spot.

I'm a sweetheart with people I like.

"That's my baby."

Yes, I'm your baby.

Caroline sighed and looked sad, with her eyebrows and shoulders drooping. "Max, you know I don't like to complain—especially after all I owe you—but your baby peed on my new book of fabric samples."

His eyebrows drew together. "Belle? She's never had a pissing problem before."

"Then she's doing it on purpose." Caroline's voice sharpened. "The last time it was a hairball on my scarf."

Belle rolled onto her belly in order to keep an eye on her enemy, this woman who invaded her castle and was a liar. Not about the peeing and the hairball, but Belle suspected she lied about something much worse.

"It's not anything I've done to her." Caroline flipped her hair behind her shoulder and arched her back, reminding Belle of a strutting turkey spreading its tail feathers. "Animals love me."

Dumb animals, Belle thought, her whiskers twitching. Animals like dogs and Max's dead cousin, Emery.

"I'll pay for the samples." Max's tone was clipped and his eyebrows drew together.

Caroline recoiled, then flapped her hands as if she wanted to fly backward in time and swallow her words. "You've done too much already. I won't take another penny from you. You've been my guardian angel since Emery's accident. Without you, I don't know what I'd do."

Belle knew. Find another man to take care of her. A man who wasn't Max.

"Forget about it. It's no big deal." Max stroked his fingers along Belle's jaw.

Her body rumbled with purrs and she rubbed her teeth against his fingers. *More, more. I want more.*

"You spoil that cat."

"We all deserve a little spoiling." Max stopped petting Belle to gesture at the coffee. "You don't have to do this. You're decorating the house, not waiting on me."

Caroline set both buttocks on the desk, and Belle's claws extended again. This was her desk to sit on. No one else's.

The blond leaned toward Max and gazed at him beneath lowered eyelids. "Next time I'll remember not to bring you any."

Smelling stray pheromones, Belle hissed.

"Eeek!" Caroline jerked off the desk.

Max chuckled.

"See? She's jealous." Caroline glared at Max. "And you encourage her."

He stopped laughing, but his shoulders shook. "Sorry."

She opened her mouth, then gave Belle the same glare as when she entered the room, pressed her lips together and stomped away.

Belle butted Max's arm to show her approval, then a bug scurrying across the floor caught her attention. She leapt off the desktop in a long arc and landed a foot from the door. The many-legged insect scuttled into the office Caroline was using, inconveniently located next to Max's.

Belle followed the bug. Though it was going into the enemy's camp, she was fearless.

"Stay away from me, you damn cat," Caroline said in a low voice. She was bending over a large desk covered with swatches of material. Her gaze darted to the doorway, as if to make sure Max was out of eyesight and earshot. "Come any closer and you'll be roadkill."

Belle turned her attention from the bug to the bigger and more dangerous being.

"That's a good idea." A small smile formed on Caroline's face. "Roadkill cat. It's what you deserve for using my office as your litter box." The smile disappeared, her features hardening. "And for coming between me and Max every time I'm making headway. If you wandered outside and something happened, who would think of blaming me?"

They didn't blame you when Emery fell off the trail while you were hiking. Belle's stare held Caroline's gaze. *Did they?* When Caroline didn't say anything, she repeated the mental command. *Did they?*

"After all," Caroline murmured, "no one suspected me when I pushed Emery off the trail."

Adrenaline surged through Belle. She knew it! She swiveled her neck one hundred eighty degrees, but Max wasn't there. If only he understood cat language. Of course, if people understood cat language, then cats would be queens and kings of the world and life would be orderly and sane.

"Why did I tell you that?" Scowling, Caroline grabbed a stapler and waved it in the air. "Get out or I'll staple you to the wall."

The bug landed on the desk in front of Caroline. She made a sound like a squeaky door and slammed the stapler on it.

Belle zipped out of the room, quivering with triumph. Her curiosity was satisfied. Once again she'd been right.

If she suspected that Caroline would hurt Max, she would have to do something about it. But what Caroline wanted from Max, he wasn't going to give her. No matter how much coffee she brought Max, he loved Belle more than Caroline.

Which was just as it should be.

The door to the main house was open, and she dashed through it. Late last night, she'd heard Ted, Max's brother, clomping into the house. He worked in a bar, whatever that meant. Humans did odd things.

She'd see if Ted was awake. Next to Max, Ted gave the best back rubs.

Her tail swaying in the air, she padded along the hall, past the kitchen and the big room where they watched TV, past the bedroom Max's sister, Tory, used when she visited. The rest of the time, the bed belonged to Belle.

Wasn't every soft place in the house a potential napping spot for her?

Ted's bedroom door was open a couple inches. She stuck her nose into the room. His scent wafted to her nostrils and she heard the creak of the bedsprings. She nudged the door open wider and flowed through, then took a flying leap, landing on the bed with a thump.

The lump beneath the covers didn't stir. Only Ted's neck and head stuck out, facing the wall. She sniffed the back of his head. Yesterday morning, she'd smelled a woman on him, but not this morning. In the four years she'd been with Max, she'd smelled a lot of different women on Ted. Once in a while, she smelled one on Max, too.

She didn't mind sharing—much—but if she smelled Caroline on him she'd have to do something. Caroline might push him off a trail, too, and who else knew how to massage her on the perfect spot?

Ted turned over and opened his eyes. "Hey, Belle girl."

She meowed. Anticipating his caresses, she kneaded the blanket with her front paws, her purr reverberating. He laughed and reached out.

"Ted!" Max called from the hall.

"What?" Ted's hand stilled.

Yes, what? She cocked her head as Max strode into the bedroom. Ted pulled his hand from her back and pushed to a sitting position.

"It's Mom. Her car broke down. She's on the expressway, just past the truck stop."

Groaning, Ted threw the cover aside, on top of Belle. "Shit. That's the second time this month. On her next birthday, I'm enrolling her in AAA."

Belle wiggled out from under the cover in time to see him pulling on his jeans. She needed to see everything. She needed to know everything.

"You think she'll use it? With two sons nearby?"

Ted smacked his forehead. "What the hell was I thinking? The smart thing to do is move a thousand miles away, like Tory."

"I moved into the next county." Max's voice sounded dry to Belle with her ultra-sensitive hearing. "She followed me."

"You're the oldest." Ted shoved his feet into his shoes.

"Yeah." Max's voice lowered to a rumble that reminded Belle of far-away thunder before the storm began with wind gusts and bursts of lightning. "The oldest."

Belle jumped off the bed and rubbed her cheek against his pant legs. Rose, Max's mother, was always calling him to ask for help. Last week it was her toilet, the week before her condo roof was leaking.

Belle purred her understanding. It was too bad the rest of the world wasn't as resourceful as her.

He bent to pet her. "At least Tory only wants money from me. That's easy."

Ted snorted and sat on the bed to tie his shoes. "Easy for you."

"Tips lousy last night?"

"Don't start. It's better than doing a job I hate."

"One college degree wasted." Max straightened. "Come and work for me. Don't make me ask again."

Ted stood. "You mean leech off you, like everyone else. No thanks."

"This isn't a pity job. I need you."

"Later, okay? After we take care of Mom and I've gulped down a gallon of coffee."

They strode into the hall, Max first. Belle thought about following. Instead, she lifted her back leg in the air and groomed herself. Satisfied with her cleanliness and beauty, she put down her leg and stretched. Time for a nap.

She jumped on Ted's bed again, his scent still fresh, the sheets still warm. After circling once, she curled into a ball, her head on his pillow, her eyes closed. Eating, drinking, purring, bathing, exploring, playing, putting her scent on anything that moved and didn't move, and, finally, uncovering murderers. She'd had a full morning and needed her rest for the afternoon.

Anything could happen, and someone had to watch over her house and her humans.

Even though the car's heater blew full blast, cold crept into the pores of Sorcha Anders' skin. "Blackmailing Deavers? Are you nuts?"

Fletcher turned the eight-year-old Taurus with the dented right front fender onto a street lined with narrow duplexes and yellow-green lawns. The northwest Milwaukee neighborhood looked as dreary as Sorcha felt inside. The early morning sun hit Fletcher's thin face, showing his white teeth in a crooked grin and his dark brown hair tumbling onto his forehead.

He looked like a poet. Sensitive, troubled, and doomed.

"The whole fucking world believes Deavers is the genius of the hotel industry." His harsh laugh grated on her ears. "If they only knew the truth. Just think of the half mill as our share of Deavers' big stock bonus. It's not like he'll miss it. I bet his wife spends more on shoes every year."

They pulled into the narrow driveway, slowing for cracks the size of a Sumo wrestler's arm. Their landlord's car blocked the garage. Biting her lip, Sorcha glanced at Fletcher. He swore, then shrugged, emotion flashing on his face, hot and cold.

Sorcha touched his arm. He was a fool, but he was her fool. "I've got a bad feeling about this."

He leaned over and kissed her cheek. "You can't con me, baby. You never get premonitions about yourself. The only thing that's going to happen is we'll get a few bucks in our pockets. Deavers is lucky I went to him instead of the tabloids. He'd be laughed out of town if we told them he buys hotels on the advice of a psychic."

"It's not wise to put the squeeze on Deavers," she insisted.

"He's just a man." Fletcher's voice thinned with irritation. "If it weren't for his daddy and granddaddy, he wouldn't be any higher up the money chain than you or me."

He got out of the car, slammed the door, and stomped toward the back of the house.

Sorcha rubbed her arms, her jacket sleeves riding up. With a sigh, she slid out of the car and grabbed the paper bag filled with groceries from the back seat. Hugging the bag to her chest, she started down the driveway. A shiver ran through her, even though the weather was warming. About time.

She frowned at a brown patch of grass. It was April, and she wanted spring. Spring always chipped away a little at her depression. The SAD disease, the doctors called it. The most appropriate medical term she'd ever heard.

A popping sound, as if a balloon burst, came from the back of the house. Her forehead scrunched. Had Fletcher fallen? He never watched where he was going, and the landlord's kids never picked up anything. A lawsuit waiting to happen, Fletcher liked to say with a laugh. But getting hurt didn't amuse Sorcha.

"Fletch, are you okay?" The bag was slipping, and she hefted it up. It was heavy, potatoes and cans on the bottom, eggs, bananas and bread on the top.

Fletcher didn't answer. If he were hurt, he'd be swearing by now. Sorcha hadn't heard the door slam, so he must be waiting for her, his anger already evaporated. She hurried around the back of the house—and tripped over something lying across the sidewalk.

Her hands parted as she fell forward, the grocery bag dropping, and she heard the plops and thuds of the food items she'd carefully chosen. Dammit, the eggs were going to break.

Her knees connected with softness instead of concrete. Her palms hit the sidewalk and slid, the hard sidewalk stinging her skin.

"Don't scream."

Instead of glancing up at the muffled voice, Sorcha looked at her jean-covered knees. Oh God, she was kneeling on Fletcher. His soulful brown eyes open, he stared past her without blinking. And what was that leaking from his head? Oh God oh God oh God.

She scrambled backward.

"Don't move."

She peered up at the man in front of her. He wore black slacks, a black sweater, and a black ski mask.

"Mr. Deavers," she whispered, recognizing his medium height and build and the pouch over his belt buckle.

"I didn't plan on killing you." He nodded at Fletcher's body. "He said you were getting your hair done today."

"My hairdresser's sick." She felt as if she were in a dream. No, a nightmare. How else could she explain kneeling on the cold sidewalk, a three-pound bag of potatoes at her side and Fletcher sprawled in front of her, blood pooling beneath his head?

"That's too bad. I was hoping to keep you as my consultant after he was gone. He said you didn't have anything to do with the extortion plan. In fact, he seemed quite proud of himself. Was that the truth?"

She nodded, her head light, as if it might fly off her neck. This wasn't happening. It couldn't be happening. It must be a nightmare.

He stepped closer. "I don't suppose I can trust you not to tell the police?"

Her gaze dropped from his masked face to Fletcher's still features. She touched his cheek, and her heart raced. His face was warm! Was he alive?

Then she looked into his unseeing eyes and knew her hopes were false.

"No answer? Doesn't matter, I wouldn't believe you anyway. As much as I value your special talents, I'm afraid I'll have to manage without them. If I'm in jail, they won't do me much good, will they?"

Her hand curved over Fletcher's cheek. *Fletch, how will I live without you?*

In her peripheral, the black shoes moved another step closer.

"I'm not a bad man." Deavers gestured toward Fletcher. "He's scum. He deserved to be eliminated."

Anger roared through her mind. Fletcher was the only person who'd ever loved her, and this animal had taken him from her.

And she was next.

Looking up, she took her hand from Fletcher's cheek and reached sideways for the bag of potatoes.

He aimed the gun at her head. "You're too pretty to die this way. I'm sorry, but I have to do this for the sake of my children. I can't let them be humiliated. Why don't you close your eyes? I'll feel better if—"

She slammed the potatoes in an arc, knocking the gun from his hand and hitting his left knee. He staggered and grabbed his knee, muffling a moan. Still holding the bag of potatoes, she stood in one fluid movement and smashed the bag onto the side of his head. Then she turned and ran.

Two

"What took you? I could've been killed." Rose scurried out of her Lincoln Town Car onto the sparse grass verge, looking fearfully at the cars speeding along the expressway, her nose wrinkling as if the smell of exhaust offended her sensibilities.

Max tightened his mouth and reached inside the car for the switch to release the hood. His mother was always afraid of something. To her, every cloud had a black lining.

"We came as soon as you called," Ted said, behind Max.

"Can you believe it?" Her voice squeaked with indignation. "A *man* stopped. He knocked on the window, trying to get me to open it, saying he wanted to help."

"You should've cracked the window open." Ted lifted the hood. "He could've been the man of your dreams."

"He could have been a rapist. You're being foolish. There is no such thing as a dream man."

Ted bent to examine the engine. "Not even Dad?" he asked, his voice muffled.

Max stuffed his hands into his jean pockets, forcing himself to watch Ted handle this instead of shoving him aside and taking over. A semi raced along the slow lane behind him, its draft tickling his neck.

"Your dad left," Rose said.

Max shifted his gaze to her. "Dad died," he snapped.

She shot him an accusing look, as though it were his fault.

The old heaviness settled in his chest. Rose's lips curved down, her face unsatisfied, her eyes squinting against the sun. Her navy pants and light blue jacket covered those fifteen extra pounds she was always talking about losing. Her hair looked neat, her only wrinkles showing around her eyes and mouth.

He supposed a man her age might find her attractive. Yet she'd never dated since the day that started with sunshine until late afternoon when the storms swooped in and—

"He was killed." Bitterness edged the flat words. "It's the same result. He's not here, is he? This is a silly conversation. I don't want to talk about it anymore."

"Found it!" Ted said. "A loose spark plug wire."

"Are you sure?" Rose tapped her fingers on her upper lip. "Maybe you should let Max look at it."

About to bend under the hood for a look, Max pulled back. "I'll get the pliers."

Ted glanced up, his eyebrows lifted. Max read the question in his eyes. He nodded, giving Ted the message that he was letting him take care of this. That he trusted him.

He turned away. In a couple weeks, Ted would be handling everything. He just didn't know it yet.

As Max reached into the back of the Jeep, a tug on his sleeve stopped him.

"I don't want to hurt Ted's feelings," Rose whispered, clutching his sleeve, "but I'd feel safer if you took a look."

"Ted will do just fine."

"If *you* say so." She sighed and let go of his shirt. "At least you'll be there to supervise. I don't know what I'd do without you."

Another semi roared by. Rose squeaked and jumped back onto the grass. His mouth tight, Max grabbed a pair of pliers from the toolbox he kept in the back of the Jeep.

"I suppose Caroline was at the house." Her voice grew louder and more petulant. "She's after you. And don't roll your eyes at me. Ted, you tell him."

"It's true," Ted said. "You're single, heterosexual male with a few bucks in the bank. You might as well paste a target on your chest that says, 'Come and get me.' They've been coming for years."

"Jealous?" Max strode toward the hood.

"Not over Caroline. She's too old for me. More your type, anyway. Beautiful, smart, and needy." Ted snickered. "A damsel in distress."

"I wouldn't call her beautiful," Rose said. "She uses too much makeup."

"Needy?" Max handed him the pliers. "Is that what you think I go for?"

"C'mon, look at yourself." Ted gestured with the pliers. "You're always there for Mom. You're supporting Tory. You bankrolled Caroline's design business. Even gave her an office in the house."

"Only until she gets her business going and can afford her own place," Max said.

Rose and Ted both snorted, sounding freakishly alike. "Yeah, right," Ted said. "Like that's gonna happen. And, hell, you even rescued Belle when she was a kitten."

Max frowned. Ted made him sound as if he had some kind of save-the-world complex, when the opposite was true. It was duty. Someone had to make sure everyone was taken care of. And he was the oldest. In a wolf pack, he'd be alpha.

If something needed to be done, he took care of it. He had the money, so why not? Better that than buying flashy cars or an oversized house with rooms he'd never use.

Besides, he had other plans for his money. Plans that would saw off the yoke around his neck.

Let Ted take a shot at being the alpha. It would be good for his backbone.

"Anyone would've done the same thing," he said.

"Yeah, if the person was Sir Lancelot." There was an edge to Ted's voice as he stuck his head under the hood. "Or King Arthur. That's even better. The king waiting for the perfect queen."

"You're wrong." Max smiled grimly. Arthur had earned his kingship. Max had his thrust upon him. Now it was time to abdicate.

He'd fulfilled his promise to his dad.

He'd made his plans.

In two weeks he'd be breathing in the perfumed smells of

island flowers instead of the stink of diesel exhaust. In two weeks, the yoke of his family would be off his shoulders.

Speeding along the freeway heading out of Milwaukee, Sorcha glanced in her rearview mirror and spotted Deavers' silver sedan three cars back. Following her. Closing in on her. Preparing to kill her.

She tried to care, but blackness spread inside her, despair slithering into every cranny, chomping on every cell, threatening to overwhelm her. Fletcher, she thought, what am I going to do without you?

Tears streamed down her cheeks. She saw the future for everyone else. Why hadn't she seen it for Fletcher, the only person who'd ever loved her?

A thought started as a whisper and ended as a scream. *She should have died with him.*

The SUV in front of her slowed. So did the car in the right lane and the one in the left. She lifted one hand from the steering wheel to wipe tears from her face. A patrol car was parked on the shoulder of the road behind a white station wagon, lights blinking.

She flicked on her signal lights and turned into the right lane. In her rearview mirror, she saw the silver car change lanes. A shudder shook her. Cold pierced her bones.

"Damn you," she whispered. Deavers wasn't a professional killer. He was something more deadly—a desperate man. He'd always seemed so nice, smiling when they met for their sessions, as if she were the most important person in the world, but underneath she'd sensed the roiling darkness. If she stopped the car, she feared what he would do.

In the back window of the station wagon, children's heads bobbed. A vision flashed in her mind. Two small girls lying on the floor, their mouths and eyes open in death, crimson blood flowing into their blond hair.

A cry wrenched out of her throat, and the vision dissolved. Her foot pressed down on the gas pedal.

The two parked vehicles were a blur as she sped past them. Her fuel gauge showed a quarter tank of gas, which should get her into the next county. And then...she would die. She knew this the way she knew evil lived in the world and so did good.

Her tears dried. An eerie calm settled in her, and she almost smiled. All her life she'd been frightened. Of her visions, of other people. Now, with death as close as her shadow, she felt...nothing. As if she were already dead and gone.

Would dying be worse than living without Fletcher? Or for the first time in her thirty-one years would she be at peace?

Belle dreamed she was climbing a tree in the jungle outside Max's house. A squirrel fled from her, jumping from limb to limb. She leapt after it. They were both flying. The hunter and the prey. Finally, they reached the top branches. She stretched out a paw and—

Something grabbed her ribs. Awake instantly, she yowled. *Hands.* That's what it was. She smelled a flowery scent. *Caroline.*

Long fingers covered with toweling tightened around her ribs. Belle lashed out with her four legs, her claws catching on cotton threads. She screeched. The towel wound twice around her, restricting her movements, covering her face and blinding her. She stopped squealing but kept trying to struggle free.

"There's one cat too many in this world." Caroline's mutter penetrated the two layers of towel wrapped around Belle's ears. "And I'm going to take care of that. You'll never pee on anything of mine again. You'll never steal Max's attention from me again. Without you constantly stealing his attention, I know he'll fall in love with me."

Belle's useless struggles stilled. Caroline had killed her husband. Now it was her turn to die.

But she wasn't dead yet. Beneath the toweling, she kept

her eyes open, her ears listening, her senses alert. Her body ready, she waited for a chance to escape.

An up-and-down motion started as Caroline hurried through the house. Caroline clasped Belle to her chest, her heartbeat reverberating against Belle's head, pounding almost as fast and loud as Belle's own heart.

The outside door opened. Beneath the folds of material, Belle welcomed the chill air. Then the door closed behind them, and the up-and-down motion began again, this time faster. Caroline was running.

She was afraid Max was coming home, Belle thought.

Max. He would save her.

If he returned in time.

If he didn't, she would have to save herself.

Belle sensed when Caroline started toward the woods. Her breaths rasped and she panted like a dog on a hot day. The smell of trees and damp grass grew stronger, overpowering the stench of her perfume.

Caroline stumbled. Instead of letting go of Belle, her grip tightened. Belle tried flailing her legs. But the snugly wound towel restricted her limbs, and she stopped. She needed to save her energy.

What was Caroline planning? To kill her, yes. But how?

Caroline caught her balance, and the up-and-down motion started again. She held Belle almost in a lover's embrace, except the blond woman loved only herself.

From the curving country road came the rumble of a car going driving the road. Belle pictured the thicket of trees surrounding Max's house. Sometimes when Max was working outside, washing his car or doing something on the house or lawn, she roamed through the trees and tall grasses, chasing birds and squirrels. She was the queen, the lioness.

Now she was the prey.

No! She refused to let Caroline kill her. If Max didn't come back in time to save her, she'd find a way to save herself.

They seemed to walk for a long time. Every once in a while, Caroline laughed wildly, a sharp edge to her voice that reminded Belle of a squirrel she'd once seen running around madly, its odor diseased. Through the towel, Belle felt Caroline's hands shaking. Another car zoomed by, the engine louder, and Belle smelled exhaust through the towel. The road must be a few feet away.

"Here it is," Caroline said. "No, it's the wrong place. It'll be better around the curve."

The curve of what?

She walked again. Her fingers dug into Belle's ribs, making her squeal.

"Yes, this is the place."

The place for what?

Caroline boosted Belle higher, her hold firm, but her hands trembling. Whatever was going to happen was happening soon.

Belle tensed, ready to take action. A car approached, its engine roaring too loud. It came closer. And closer. And close—

Caroline tore off the towel and, with her strong arms that lifted weights in Max's exercise room, heaved Belle into the road.

Belle's legs flailed the air, trying to stop her flight path straight toward the car's windshield. All her senses expanded. She heard the squeal of tires. She smelled the dust and the trees and the car exhaust. She saw the terrified face of the woman driver. She saw the front of the car, the rust spots and the dented fender. From behind her, she heard Caroline crash back into the woods.

Belle's mouth opened, and she cried out. *I want to live! I want to live!*

Sorcha slammed her foot on the brake pedal, her hands clenching the steering wheel. The car zigzagged, tires squealing. A cat was flying toward her car as if someone had flung it, but who would do that? What would be the sense? Even the homicidal megalomaniac chasing her across the Wisconsin countryside killed for a reason.

For a second, Sorcha thought she'd miss the cat. Then the car swerved and the small, gray creature smashed against the windshield.

Sorcha stared into the cat's green eyes, the same shade she saw in the mirror every day. The next instant, the cat flew backward.

The car followed the cat, slamming into the bottom of a deep ditch. Sorcha's head thumped against the windshield, and the driver's door flew open, the airbag deployed.

She tumbled onto the hard ground. The cat lay inches away, its eyes staring like Fletcher's after his breath had stopped forever.

A cry of anguish escaped Sorcha's throat. Why the cat? Why not her? Without Fletcher, what was life to her?

"If you're listening, God, let the cat live. Take me instead." Her fingers reached out to touch the cat's front legs and her voice rose to a scream. "Take me!"

Let me live. As the life force seeped out of her body, Belle stared into the woman's green eyes. The woman's fingertips touched her left front paw. *I want to live,* Belle thought. *I want to live, I want to—*

The wind kicked up, swirling, whistling in her ear. A glittering ring of light surrounded her and the woman. The ground beneath Belle's body heated. A jolt of energy passed from the woman's fingertips to Belle's leg, traveling through her muscles, blood, and bones. The woman's eyes widened, and Belle knew she felt the jolt, too.

Then everything went black.

Three

"I can't believe Mom agreed to join triple AAA," Ted said. "Bet she still calls you next time it happens."

Max took his eyes off the S-curved road to catch Ted's grin. They'd turned onto Camel's Back Road leading to their home. One side was a wall of trees. On the other, a steep ditch led to another thicket of trees. He switched his attention back to the road ahead. He never knew what might be around the curve—another car, a bicyclist, wild turkeys, deer, fox, or a skunk. In the four years since he bought the house and eleven acres, he'd seen it all.

"She won't call me." Not when he was half a world away, she wouldn't.

"What're you smiling about?" Ted asked. "Your load getting a little lighter?"

Max took one hand off the steering wheel to wipe it over his smile. "Your shoulders look wide enough to carry some extra weight."

"*Moi?* I'm having too much fun for weight lifting."

"You can have your fun and make some money, too."

"Like you?" Ted's tone said Max was as much fun as a gray day.

Max steered the Jeep around the last curve before his driveway. "Like me." *The new me.* When they reached home, he'd tell Ted about his plans—

A woman staggered out of the ditch, dark hair curling wildly around her head and shoulders, her mouth open in a plea. Looking straight at the car, she stumbled onto the road.

Max stomped on the brakes. Jesus! He was going to hit her! The tires squealed and he steered to the right. As if her feet were nailed to the pavement, the woman stood in the middle of the road, her body swaying.

The car stopped inches from the ditch. Max punched his seat belt release, shoved the door open, and jumped out. He was halfway to the woman when Ted's door slammed shut.

The woman faced him, her green eyes wide and dazed. Her forehead was bruised, her cheek scratched, and her jacket sleeve torn. With her small-boned frame, she looked breakable, as if a heavy breeze would take her down.

"You okay?" Max asked, reaching her.

She slumped forward. He caught her, holding her upright. Her arms wrapped around his back. Her mouth opened and a mewling sound came out. She blinked at the noise, her expression surprised and scared. Closing her mouth, she pushed her face against Max's brown leather jacket.

Ted slipped a blanket over her shoulders, tucking the ends between her shoulders and Max's chest. "I tried calling 911, but my cell's dead. Hand me yours."

"Shit." Max grimaced.

"You forgot? I'll see if there's one in her car." He started to run.

"Don't go inside if you smell gas," Max yelled.

"Think I'm stupid? Damn, her car's totaled." Ted stared into the ditch that bordered Max's property. "She say if anyone was with her? I better check."

"Were you alone?" Max asked as Ted clambered into the ditch. He sniffed the air for gas fumes but only smelled the woman's hair, honey tinged with lemons.

Still silent, the woman shuddered in his arms. He patted her back. "It's okay," he murmured. "It's okay."

The hum of a car engine carried to Max. "We need to get off the road." He drew the woman to the shoulder, her feet tripping as if she'd forgotten how to walk. A silver car drove around the curve and slowed to a crawl. Sunlight sparkled on the tinted windshield, and Max saw a man's silhouette. Good, Max thought. The driver could call 911 or go for the authorities. And if Ted found someone injured in the car, they might need another—

The engine revved. The car raced away. Max bit back a curse, aware of the woman hanging on to him as if he were her lifeline.

"I didn't see anyone else." Ted hiked out of the ditch, brandishing a small black purse. "No cell phone either. Here, take her purse. I'll run home. It'll only take a few minutes."

A few precious minutes. Max shook his head. He knew better than Ted what could happen in seconds. In less time than to finish a last breath. "We'd have to wait another ten minutes for an ambulance. I'll take her to St. Joe's. She's not talking. Could be in shock."

Her fingers clutched his back, and she made another frantic mewl. He curved his hands around her shoulders and used just enough pressure so she raised her head and peered up at him.

"Are you okay?" He lowered his tone, calm and reassuring, fighting his instincts to lift her like a baby and run with her to his Jeep. "What's your name? Can you talk?"

A mewl of distress came from her throat. Her green eyes were dazed, and she shook her head.

The wind whistled through the elm trees. The woman's loose jacket rippled, and so did she. Max didn't know whether she reacted to the cold breeze or the shock of the accident, but he folded his arms around her and drew her against him again.

"You'll be okay. I'll make sure of it, I promise."

She made another sound in her throat like one of Belle's meows.

"Hand her over." Ted held out his arms. "I'll check her out while you drive. I took the CPR class last summer, not you."

Cradling the woman against his chest, Max glowered at Ted. No woman was safe from a twenty-four-year-old man's libido. Not even a woman who looked as if she'd walked out of a fairy tale with a sad ending.

"You drive," he said, his tone firm. He took a step to the side, drawing the woman with him.

Her feet dragged and her fingers dug into his back muscles through the layers of his jacket and shirt. She made a sound of protest.

Max lowered his head, his mouth brushing the thin shell of her ear. "Don't worry, I'll stay with you until the doctors release you."

"You don't have to take care of the whole world," Ted said. "She doesn't even know your name."

"Max." He looked down at the top of her curling dark brown hair. "My name is Max."

Her face lifted, her green eyes staring into his. She opened her lips, and a froglike croak came from her throat. Her lips pressed together, then opened again. Another croak came out. Her forehead furrowed, and her lips pulled back from her teeth. She looked less dazed than a moment ago and more frustrated.

"Is your throat sore?" Ted leaned forward, his face lit with interest. A kid solving a puzzle. "You want water? Can you talk? Speak English?"

She didn't glance at Ted, but her forehead cleared. She continued to gaze at Max, as if memorizing his face, feature by feature.

He felt caught by her stare, unable to break eye contact. He studied the oval face, the too large eyes, the thin nose and wide mouth. She wasn't beautiful, she was just...lovely.

Patting her back, he wished he knew what the hell she wanted from him. At this moment, whatever it was, he'd give her. Anything to make her feel whole and healed.

He shook his head. These bizarre thoughts were coming from adrenaline. He didn't even know her name.

A gray streak whipped by in his peripheral, and he tore his gaze from the woman. Squinting at the trees edging the ditch, he frowned. Belle? Impossible. He hadn't let her out. Scrutinizing the area, he saw only the wrecked car and the trees thick and high, blocking the sun.

A squirrel. Must've been a squirrel.

"C'mon, let's go to the hospital," Ted said.

The woman burrowed her face into Max's jacket, her head just under his chin.

A perfect fit, he thought, and his arms tightened around her.

Belle jerked her head away from Max's chest. Wasn't it bad enough she was inside this human body? With these clumsy arms that didn't propel her forward when she wanted to leap and run? With this ugly, furless skin? And now Max wanted to take her to the hospital. How could he do something so horrible?

Three years of sitting on Tory's lap, being petted while they watched Tory's favorite TV show, *The Love Chronicles*, had taught Belle what happened in hospitals. People would poke and prod her and stick her with needles. Plus, she might fall in love, lose her memory, be murdered by someone disguised as a doctor, and maybe have a baby. A *human* baby.

No! She was not going to let that happen.

Belle's arms dropped from around his back. Her palms slammed into his chest, and he lurched backward. The blanket slid off her shoulders and pooled around her ankles. She leaped, twisting to face the ditch and thicket of trees. The heaviness of her new body made her land with a stagger. Then she followed her feline instincts and sprang forward.

"What the hell—" Max shouted.

Belle lurched. Her human legs didn't want to obey her. She tried to force them to move faster, but it was like wading through snow. Crouching to avoid low tree branches, she darted into the trees at a fraction of her normal speed.

This was her environment. As fast as Max was, he wouldn't catch her unless she let him, even with her clumsy limbs.

"Get back here," he called. "I'm trying to help you."

"She looks pretty damn healthy to me." The amusement in Ted's voice carried to Belle. "If she wants to go, let her."

"I'm not leaving until I find her," Max said.

Crashing noises came from the trees near the road. Max. She put her hand over her mouth to stop a cry from coming out. She'd never thought she'd run from him. Never thought he'd be the one who would make her heart thump in fear.

Her human feet made noises, too. She glanced down at them. They were covered with soft-soled tie shoes like the ones Max and Ted wore. Maybe if she walked on the balls of her feet, she wouldn't crunch with every step. She'd be quiet...like a cat.

For two steps she tried, but walking this way was slower than stalking an ant. The crashing noises moved to her left. Close. Too close. Spying a tree with low branches, Belle grabbed the closest branch and pulled herself up. Her arms ached, as if they didn't want to do this. She set her mouth and commanded them to obey.

This human body was so clumsy. No stretch, no agility, no energy.

Belle hated it. Where was her agile cat body? She wanted it back.

Max smashed through the woods, leaves crunching beneath his shoes, branches cracking. Belle changed her opinion that dogs were the clumsiest creatures. Her muscles straining, she pulled herself up to another branch, then another.

None of the branches had leaves. If Max looked up...

Biting back gasping breaths, Belle hung on. Max walked below her, peering down at the ground, as if looking for tracks. Stopping directly beneath her, he glanced around.

"Where are you?" he shouted.

Belle clasped the branch, its bark rough on her soft human hands. She couldn't go to the hospital. She had to stay here, find her cat body, and claim it back.

Don't look up. Don't look up. Don't look—

She stopped her silent commands. The last time she'd wanted something so fervently was when Caroline had flung her into the path of the car. Her frantic plea had worked, but look what had happened. If it worked this time, she might change into a bird.

Belle shuddered. Being a bird would be worse than being a human. Cats *ate* birds.

Max raised his head—a movement that made Belle swallow a whimper—and he called out, "If you come right now, I'll help you. I won't let anyone hurt you. You have my word on it." He cocked his head, listening and waiting.

Belle clung to the branch, afraid to breathe. Her hands were growing colder by the second. She wanted to drop into his arms and let him take care of her. But she was a cat, not a puny human who let Max do everything for her like his mother, sister, and sometimes Ted. Sure, she let Max feed and water her, but look what she did in return. He didn't see any mice in his house, did he?

She didn't need Max to fix this. She'd fix it herself.

He turned, dried leaves crunching underneath his heavy feet. In a moment, he disappeared from her view but not her hearing. The smashing sounds moved toward the road, and she bit her lower lip, swallowing the urge to call out to him. Moments passed, and her hands grew numb. Two birds landed on the branch above her. A squirrel scampered down the tree next to her.

Her muscles tightened and she stopped her breath, her eyes narrowing in on her prey, her muscles tightening, in hunting mode. A lesser animal would've given into the urge to leap at it. Exhaling, she forced her muscles to relax slightly and adjusted her grip on the knotty branch. Then she waited.

The woman with her cat body had to be nearby. She knew it. And she wasn't going away until she found her.

Four

"That wind's wicked." Ted hunched his shoulders. "She wants to stay, let her."

Max smacked his fist into his palm. If he was cold in his leather jacket, how cold must the woman be in her cloth one? He tossed the keys to Ted.

"Take the car. I'll get home when I get home."

Ted shook his head. "I knew you'd say that. You can't resist a stray."

"Go. Get out of here." Max gave Ted a dismissive nod.

"You really think I'll leave? We could have an escaped serial killer on our land."

"Or an injured woman."

"You don't know her or why she's afraid of going to the hospital."

"A lot of people have hospital phobias."

"A lot of people have criminal records."

Max tried to entertain the idea, but his mind shut down, rejecting it. He'd held her small-boned body in his arms, felt her trembling alarm. Something had traumatized her. She needed help. His help.

"She was in an accident," Ted said, "yet she's running away. What does that tell you?"

"No other car was involved. When did you find the stick that's up your ass?"

"About the same time you pulled it out of yours." Ted held his palms out and stepped back, laughing. "Amazing how fast everything can change. Just this morning I was thinking how boring my life was becoming."

Max glanced behind them at the silent woods. She was in there somewhere. Alone and scared and cold. "When I find her, you can thank her for her entertainment value."

"*If* you find her." The smile in Ted's eyes disappeared before his mouth pressed together, a sternness that didn't suit his fun-loving character.

"Not if. When." Max strode to the side of the road and grabbed the black purse Ted had dropped.

"What're you doing?"

Max ignored the question. He rummaged inside the bag and fished out a navy wallet. He opened it. No photos, three grocery store cards, a debit card and a driver's license. He slid out the license.

Ted breathed over his shoulder. "Sorcha Anders. A nice Scottish name. And thirty-one, just the right age."

"Too old for you," Max snapped.

"Maybe I was talking about you."

Max gave his grinning brother a look that should have made him burst into flames.

"Or maybe I was talking about me," Ted continued. "What's seven years?"

"You ever shut up?"

Ted laughed. "You're jealous. I don't blame you. What woman would want an older, worn-out man like you when she could have a young stud like me?"

"You're talking like an ass." Max rifled through her money. A ten, a five, three singles. A coupon for fifty cents off a brand of cheese. No insurance cards, no photos. A private woman. He should feel guilty for invading her privacy, but he didn't. In those few moments when she'd clung to him, they'd bonded. She'd trusted him to help her. Even though she'd run from him, he wasn't turning his back on that trust.

It was illogical, but he saved his logic for business, not people.

"Didn't I say you needed a damsel in distress?" Ted asked. "Man, was I right."

Shoving the wallet into his back pocket, Max said, "Either you help look for her, or get back to the house and stay the hell out of my way."

"Your mind's made up?"

Max thrust past Ted, slipping into the woods. The time for talking was over. The time was action was now.

I'm a cat! Sorcha looked at her trembling, fur-covered legs. This was insane. It had to be a reaction from the accident. Things like this didn't happen.

But the two men stomping through the woods toward her sounded all too real, like ten men, thanks to her new, super-powered hearing. She dived into a pile of dead leaves. Her quivering body shook leaves off the top of the pile and she peeked out at the men.

She'd already tried to climb a tree, her claws catching on the rough bark. Halfway up, she'd glanced down, her claws had retracted, and she'd tumbled to the ground.

Why wasn't she dead? She'd seen the cat's eyes glaze over, the life force leaving the small body. She'd wanted it to be her, not the cat. That's what she'd prayed for.

Half of her request had come true.

The older man tramped a step ahead of the younger one. She'd heard him try to get the cat inside her body to say his name. Max. A strong name for a strong man. One look at the determined set of his chin, and she saw he was in charge. The kind of man who knew what he wanted and where he was going. The kind of man who made her want to run the other way, as far and fast as these four furry legs would take her.

The younger one looked like he was more fun. He smiled often, the dimples in his cheeks indenting. Max had no dimples. The younger man's chin was rounded, his nose high-bridged. Max's chin was square and stubborn and his nose...impressive. He looked like whatever he put his mind to, he'd accomplish.

No one would have called Fletcher impressive. Or accomplished. He wasn't even an effective blackmailer.

A plaintive meow escaped her throat.

Immediately, the footsteps stomping through the forest

stopped, then changed direction. Turning in a slow circle, the younger man reconnoitered the area.

"Is that you, Belle?"

Belle. She glanced down at the dainty body covered with medium-length gray fur. A southern belle, or perhaps a silver bell. So that's whose body she occupied. She'd worn secondhand clothes before, but this was the first time she wore secondhand fur.

The younger man hiked toward her, and she burrowed beneath the dead leaves. Both men seemed helpful, staying to search for her. Well, not her. For her body—currently occupied by the cat, but they didn't know that. And if they found her instead, what would happen? Would they think she was their cat and take her back to the house?

She couldn't let that happen.

Someone had thrown the cat at her car. She hadn't seen the person, but by the rate of force, she was positive the cat had been flung directly at her windshield. Someone had been trying to kill it.

If she went back in this cat body...

Not too long ago she'd wanted to die. The only person who had ever loved her was dead. Why should she care if someone killed her in the cat form?

But she did. Maybe it was the cat body that didn't want to die. But she cared terribly.

A strangled sound came from her throat.

"Is that Belle?" another voice asked, deeper and more commanding.

Inching her head out of the leaves like a worm, Sorcha peeked at Max's granite face, about ten feet away. Her heart fluttered so fiercely her whole body quivered. He scared her. He was too masculine. Too positive. The kind of man who would never understand a person like her.

"I thought I saw her out here earlier," he said.

The younger man shrugged. "Could've been any cat."

"If you find a stray, bring it in."

"Taking on another needy creature?"

"Stuff it." Max turned and strode away.

Ducking back beneath the leaves, Sorcha shivered. She

couldn't let either of them find her. She had to get away.

Sorcha used her claws to push leaves to the side, then saw the younger man's feet pass over her head. "Sorcha," he called. "C'mon, Sorcha, don't be afraid. We'll make sure no one hurts you."

No, she thought, even though she knew he was calling the cat that was using her body. *I'll make sure no one hurts me.*

After all, the last man who'd promised to take care of her was murdered. She had to do a better job than that.

The younger man disappeared into the trees, his footsteps squishing on wet leaves. Sorcha poked her head up and climbed out of the pile of leaves. Ignoring an urge to lick herself clean, she leapt away from the two men and ran.

"Sorcha," Max called. "Sorcha."

Belle watched from her tree branch. Sorcha must be the woman whose body she was temporarily using. Not a bad name, but not as good as her own. Not a bad body, either, as far as human bodies went. For a human, it seemed sleek. But not as sleek as she was accustomed to.

Her chest ached with an unaccustomed emotion. The way she felt when she couldn't go outside with Max. Only this was many times worse.

A short while ago, she'd thought she was going to die. The car had hurtled toward her and every fiber of her being had protested. She'd wanted to live!

Now she had her wish. But at what cost?

"I'll make sure you're taken care of," Max called. He stopped below her. If she lost her grip and fell, she'd land on his head.

She was tempted. This was her human. Her Max. Her chosen person above all others.

"Sorcha? You don't know me, but I promise not to harm you."

A yowl wanted to come out of her mouth, but she

swallowed it. What about Caroline? Could he promise her that Caroline wouldn't hurt her? Even in this human body, Belle didn't trust her.

Belle clung to the branch, the bark digging into her flesh-covered fingers, the knobby wood rough against her ribs and stomach. Her muscles, tired from holding so tightly for so long, trembled. As a cat she could stay here for hours. But she wasn't a cat anymore. That was the problem.

"I want to make sure you're all right." Max tramped on, still calling. "I won't take you to the hospital or report you to the authorities. I promise."

Belle watched his back, his squared shoulders, his lean hips and strong legs.

Why hadn't she noticed these things about him when she was a cat?

The wind gusted, cutting through the tree branches with an icy edge. Belle's teeth clicked together. She wished for her warm fur back. How could humans stand this hairless skin?

She could see nothing good about being a human.

"I'm going back." Ted stood under her tree now. "I'm cold and hungry. The woman doesn't want to be found. The best thing we can do for her is go home so she can be on her way."

Max turned back and crashed around the tree next to hers. "There was a bruise on her forehead. She might have a concussion, and her car's totaled. There's no bus stop nearby. You go, but I'm not leaving until I'm sure she's okay."

Now they both stood under Belle's branch. She clenched her jaw to keep her teeth from clattering like chatty chipmunks. Max had said he wouldn't make her go to a hospital. Should she let go and return home with them?

The answer was a big fat NO. She was a cat turned into a human. It was Max's fault for letting Caroline into his home. His fault for not seeing what Caroline was. A murderer. It was bad enough Caroline had killed her husband, but she'd gone too far when she'd tried to kill Belle. Max would have to suffer a lot longer to make up for that.

But what if Caroline tried to kill Max?

Belle froze, her hands numb, her breath sucked in. Then she remembered that Caroline didn't want to kill Max. She wanted something else. To marry him.

Belle hissed.

A crack exploded in the air like a bang of thunder. The branch! It wobbled for an agonizingly long instant, then lurched downward. Belle cried out, hanging on, her thighs and hands tightening.

Max looked up and saw her. He raised his hands, ready to catch her.

Another crack. Two words she'd heard Ted say often went through her mind, words she'd never thought of in her cat body. *Oh shit.* Belle stared down into Max's I'll-take-care-of-you blue eyes and let go of the branch.

The next instant she was flying, but for the first time in her life the act of falling frightened her. She spread out her limbs for the air to catch her belly and slow her, but these front limbs were so much smaller than the back ones. And where was her tail for balance? Instinctively, she knew she wouldn't end up on her feet.

Max caught her, holding her to his chest, staggering back. "Oomph."

Ted slapped him on the back. "I always knew you were a hero."

Belle slumped against Max's chest, clutching his wide shoulders. Her heartbeat thumped inside her ears as loud as Ted's music. Her mouth was so dry she could have lapped up half her water bowl.

Only as her heartbeat slowed did she pay attention to Max's arms curving around her back and beneath her thighs. Max had held her so many times, but everything felt different now.

Why hadn't she noticed before this how hard his chest felt? How strong his arms were? And he smelled different, like a man. Not just human, but *male.*

She felt different, too, like...well, she wasn't sure. A woman?

Yech. This was terrible.

She'd rather have a hairball in her throat.

Five

Max closed his eyes and breathed in the honey-flavored scent of the woman in his arms. Sorcha Anders. He tossed the name around his mind, liking the softness of it. But there was nothing soft about her clinging arms.

"Nice catch." Ted slapped his back. "You're a hero."

"Yeah, right." A horny hero. Must be a side effect of adrenaline.

"Are you okay?" he asked.

Her face buried into his leather jacket just as she'd done when he held her after the accident. His muscles bunched and he swung her around, her feet missing Ted's head by inches. Ted jerked back with a surprised look that would have made Max laugh any other time.

"I'm taking you home with me." His breath ruffled the dark curls on top of her head. "If you don't want to go to the hospital, I won't force you. Rest awhile, and I'll see what I can do about your car. Okay?"

She didn't answer.

They passed the ditched car. The driver's door hung open by one hinge, the windshield smashed, the front end resembling a giant accordion. Looking at the wreck, he felt amazement and horror. Why she wasn't dead or hurt badly, he didn't know.

It almost made him believe in a higher power. Something he'd stopped doing as he'd watched his father die among the wreckage of their old house on the day his fourteen-year-old life had turned upside-down.

But if there were a God, why the accident at all?

"You sure you won't go to the hospital?" he asked with more urgency.

Her arms clutched tighter, as if she never wanted to let him go. As if she was frightened for her life.

"It's okay," he said. "You'll be okay. I won't let anything or anyone hurt you."

Ted strode ahead of them and opened the Jeep's passenger door. Max bent to set Sorcha inside. She clasped her hands around the back of his neck, her arms locked.

"You have to let go so I can drive you home."

She made a sound like the one Belle made when he didn't give her a treat or pet her on demand. Behind him, Ted snickered.

"I'll drive. Looks like she's become attached to you. Must be your animal magnetism."

Max shot Ted a glare that made him grin wider. A mewling sound came from Sorcha, and his attention swiveled back to her. Her green eyes stared at him, not beseeching but...demanding. Almost angry.

"Get in," Ted said. "It's getting colder by the minute."

Giving up, Max slid onto the passenger seat, the woman cradled in his arms. During the two-minute drive home, he breathed in her honey scent with every inhale and tried not to think of her hip pressed against the front of his jeans. When he gazed down into her wide eyes, she stared back at him, not blinking once.

She and Belle would get on well. Two of a kind.

Ted parked the Jeep in the garage, then jumped out to open the door leading to the house. Max carried Sorcha over the threshold like a bride. Her driver's license put her at five foot five, her weight at one hundred twenty, but she felt lighter. Too light. She needed someone to fatten her up.

Not him. He would make sure she was all right, call someone to tow away her car, then send her on her way.

His steps lengthening, he strode along the hall, past the guest bedroom.

"Where are you putting her?" Ted asked, strolling behind them.

"My bedroom."

34

Ted laughed. Sorcha's head lifted, her green eyes searching Max's face.

"There aren't any sheets on the bed in the guest room," Max said, his voice as soothing as if she were a sick child. "You need to lie down."

More snickers came from behind him. Max reminded himself his brother was at the age when a woman in one's bed had one conclusion.

"Max! Max! What is it?"

He glanced behind him and saw Caroline sprinting along the hall. He automatically noted the bouncing breasts beneath the yellow sweater, the long legs in the beige slacks, a worried expression on her flawless face.

Damn Emery. He wished his cousin were in front of him so he could ask how the hell he'd been so clumsy, falling off the trail and leaving his young wife alone and broke. A man needed to take care of the people who counted on him. Even if he had to die to save them.

Max had learned that lesson from his father. Learned it the hardest way possible.

She stopped next to Ted, but her gaze fixed on Max and the woman in his arms. Her long fingers splayed over her breastbone, her breathing hoarse. "What's wrong? Who is this woman? Why are you carrying her?"

Sorcha's body stiffened. Max nodded at Ted. "You tell her. I have to get Sorcha to bed."

Caroline gasped. Max swept around. Right now, Sorcha needed him more than Caroline.

"There was an accident," Ted said. "In front of the house. Her car's totaled. She's not talking, but she seems okay—"

"If she's okay, what's she doing here?"

Max stepped into his bedroom and closed the door on Caroline's rising voice. The tension seeped out of Sorcha's body, her shoulders loosening, her muscles relaxing. The covers of his bed were already thrown aside, and he laid her on the sheet. Her head fell back against his pillow, her dark curls spreading out. She stared at him, her green eyes open and trusting.

"I won't harm you. You're safe here."

She continued to stare.

The door opened. Ted walked in, a glass in his hand. "Water?" he asked.

She pushed up on one elbow, her hand reaching for the glass. Ted sat on the side of the bed. Standing on the other side, Max crossed his arms over his chest. What the hell was his brother up to now?

"I'll hold it for you," Ted said. "You look a little weak."

He slid his arm around her back and held the glass to her plump lips as if she were a child. Max watched Ted through narrowed eyes. A child was the last way Ted saw any attractive woman.

Instead of swallowing, Sorcha drew back. Her tongue poked out and she appeared to taste the water, lapping it. Ted tilted the glass bottom, spilling water into her mouth. Her head curving back, she sucked down the water, her slender throat working.

"Good girl," Ted said.

Max folded his arms. He knew what Ted was really thinking, but he trusted him not to act on the thoughts.

Hell, he was having the same thoughts and wasn't acting on them. She was disoriented and not talking. Though something about her attracted him, he preferred women who were able to say simple words like, "Hi," "Thanks," and "Oh my God, Max! You're the world's best lover!"

Ted took away the empty glass from Sorcha's mouth. "Caroline's changing the sheets in the guest room."

"Hmmm?" Max kept his gaze pasted on Sorcha's face.

"For Sorcha. She doesn't like the idea of another woman being in your bed. Remember what I said earlier?"

Max shook his head but couldn't deny Ted's words. And he couldn't deny his money was part of it. Caroline prided herself on being impeccably dressed, and her income, with only two decorating jobs so far, wasn't going to buy five-hundred-dollar designer shoes.

He uncrossed his arms. Caroline had come to him a week after the funeral, saying she missed Emery so much, despite all his faults. She wanted to make her decorating business a success, and if she could just get a start...

Then she'd started crying, saying Emery must've had a premonition, because before they'd started on the trail he'd said if anything happened to him, Max would take care of her.

In Max's head, he'd seen his father's face growing paler by the second and heard his last words to him. *"You'll take care of them,"* he said, his voice raspy and fading. But for the next words, his voice grew strong. *"Promise me."*

Looking into Caroline's watery eyes, he'd told her Emery was right. He'd take care of her. She'd laughed and cried and hugged him. He'd smiled grimly and thought someone should hit him on the head with a two-by-four.

His glance landed on Sorcha as she licked a drop of water from her lower lip.

Now he had a new dependent. This one in his bed. But this one wasn't family or connected in any way. As soon as she could talk or even write and tell him where to take her, she'd be out of his house. He'd have his life and his bed back.

Ted got to his feet. Bending over Sorcha, he tucked the blanket around her shoulders. His hands lingered on the blanket, and Max tensed. Only when Ted straightened and stepped back from the bed did Max's muscles ease.

Muffled footsteps came from behind him. He heard Caroline's voice but didn't turn.

"I made the bed," she said brightly. "You can move her now."

Sorcha turned her head and watched Caroline. The wary gleam in her eyes reminded Max of an animal watching a predator.

"Thanks," he said, "but you shouldn't have bothered. She's settled where she is."

Caroline exhaled heavily out of her nose. She stepped toward the bed. "It's no trouble. She'll feel better with the new sheets than in your old bed. Won't you?"

Sorcha shrank away from Caroline. A mewling sound emitted from her mouth and alarm flickered across her face. She sat up, the cover falling to her lap. Her hands came up with her fingers bent, claw-like.

"You're frightening her." Max held out his arm to stop Caroline from moving closer to her.

Caroline glared at him over her shoulder. "Why would I frighten her? I'm a woman. If she's scared of anyone, it's you and Ted."

"Ya think?" Ted jabbed his thumb at Sorcha. "Take a good look at her face. You're scaring the crap out of her."

"I don't believe—"

Max curved his hands over Caroline's upper arms and hauled her away from the bed.

"What are you doing?" Caroline's voice raised two octaves.

"I'm moving you away from her." He released her shoulders and stepped between her and Sorcha. His temporary guest was slumped back onto the bed, watching them, and he had the impression she was waiting to see which way to jump.

Caroline's lips tightened. "I'm just trying to help."

"You can't force your help on people who don't want it."

She laughed wildly. Without another word, she spun around and rushed out of the bedroom.

"That was a hell of a show." Ted grinned. "I think she's pissed at you."

Max turned back to Sorcha, bending over her. "You okay? If you can't talk, nod your head for yes or shake it for no. I won't leave until I know you're okay."

Her lips trembled. Seconds crept by before she dipped her head up and down.

A blaze of achievement shot through him. "Are you ready to go to the hospital?"

She shook her head emphatically.

"Are you hungry?"

Another shake.

"Tired?"

A nod.

"We'll go and let you sleep. You understand I'll have to wake you every hour, in case you have a concussion?"

She frowned, her displeasure evident.

This was becoming one of the easiest conversations he'd

ever had with a woman. Who needed words? Her expression said it all.

"If you object, I'll have to take you to the hospital."

Her soft lips formed a pout. She lifted one shoulder in a gesture he took for agreement.

"Want us to call anyone?" Ted asked.

Max nodded at Ted. Good question. When he turned back to Sorcha, she was shaking her head.

"We'll leave you then," Max said. She seemed to understand everything he said. A bit of his worry disappeared. "If you need anything, just call out."

She relaxed against the pillow, her eyelids closing. The blanket was still at her waist, and he leaned over her and pulled it over her shoulders. When he straightened, her breathing was already even, her lips slightly parted.

"Great sleeper," Ted murmured. Max shoved Ted by his shoulders, pushing him out of the bedroom. As they reached the hall, Ted's voice grew louder. "That reminds me. Where's Belle? She usually greets you like a dog."

Max glanced around. Where was Belle?

"Maybe she saw you carrying Sorcha and was jealous." Ted chuckled. "Caroline sure the hell was. Did you see her face when you kicked her out of the bedroom? She looked like she wanted to bite you."

"She was scaring Sorcha." Max glanced behind him, one last look to make sure she was all right. In her sleep, Sorcha's lips curved up. "I couldn't let her do that."

"Listen to yourself." Ted cuffed his shoulder. "You just met her and you've got it bad."

"I'm making sure she's okay." Max cuffed Ted's shoulder back, fulfilling the Eleventh Commandment in the Brannigan family: Thou shalt not hit your brother unless thou shalt want to be hit back.

"Yeah, sure." Ted rubbed his shoulder.

Max's hand twitched, but he refused to rub the sting of Ted's fist and let him know it hurt. "She hasn't said one word to me."

"To do what a man and a woman do best, who needs words?"

"You're bad, brother. Bad to the core."

"Yeah." Ted poked his elbow into Max's ribs. "And you know why I'm bad? 'Cause the girls love it." Grinning, Ted strutted into his bedroom before Max could jab his ribs. "When you check on Sorcha, don't wake me. I need my beauty sleep."

"Waking you is the last thing I plan on doing." Max scowled. Maybe Sorcha was one of those women who liked bad boys. What she did out of his house was her own business, but in it she was under his protection, and he was making damn sure no one was going to hurt her.

Six

Guessing she'd run an eighth of a mile, Sorcha stopped to lap water from the ditch. It tasted like mud, but she was thirsty. And hungry. The cat's stomach was emptier than her and Fletcher's joint bank account. She wondered when the cat last ate.

A bird landed on the ground nearby. Sorcha froze, watching it. A robin. Never before had she noticed how big robins were. How the meat packed tightly against their bones.

Her claws extended, and she gazed at them with horror. What was she thinking? She was a vegetarian, for God's sake. She couldn't eat a bird.

The robin saw her. Its wings flapped and it flew away. Sorcha watched it disappear into the trees. *You don't have to be afraid. Even if I could catch you, I wouldn't eat you.*

A voice in her head mocked her. *Oh yeah? Cats are carnivores, you know. You're a cat now. You can't fight your nature.*

The voice sounded like Fletcher. He'd disparaged her vegetarian diet often, eating Big Macs in front of her and ordering steak when they ate out.

A car cruised along the road, the hum of its engine growing louder. With these cat eyes, she saw colors hazily, as if looking through a cloud. But gray was still gray—unless it was silver, like the car Deavers was driving.

She darted into the ditch. Deavers must still be looking for her. A ragged meow tore out of her throat, and she shivered.

The car rolled toward her about ten miles an hour. She imagined Deavers peering at the sides of the road, searching for her. If he saw a small, gray cat, it wouldn't mean anything to him. Still, she stayed in the ditch until the car snaked around another curve.

A mewl came out of her throat, and the sound made her jump. She mewled again. This time she didn't jump. Her whole world was upside-down. She was a cat, for God's sake.

Raising her head to the sky, she yowled. She'd asked to die instead of the cat. She hadn't asked to *be* the cat.

Turning tail, she dashed through the thicket of trees alongside the road. She felt sorry for the cat in her body. Did it know its life was in danger? As was hers, she reminded herself. Someone had tried to kill the cat and might try again. She needed to suspect every person she ran into.

Despair filled her. She was trapped in the body of a small cat, but inside her was enough unhappiness to fill the Grand Canyon. When she'd moved into the duplex with Fletcher, he'd promised her she'd never be alone again.

As usual, he lied.

Belle opened her eyes, stretched, yawned, and frowned. Her head rested on Max's pillow. She felt the familiar softness and smelled his scent, but why had the pillow shrunk? Why were the colors brighter and the scents duller? Why didn't she feel her tail? Or her whiskers brushing against the pillow?

A torrent of answers poured into her mind. She was human! It wasn't an awful dream. She touched her nose and felt a bony protrusion. Horrible, horrible, horrible. With a bad feeling in her human stomach, she lifted both hands in front of her eyes.

Even more horrible than the nose. No lovely paws with the strong claws she extended and retracted at will. What good were these thin, breakable things on the ends of human fingers? And her lovely, lovely fur, protecting her from heat and cold. Helping water slide off her body. These tiny hairs on her arms spaced so far apart provided no protection at all.

Her full bladder informed her of a familiar need. She tossed aside the covers and sat up. Her legs, covered in dark pants, slithered over the side of the bed. Her feet, encased in white socks, reached the floor. She wiggled her toes, testing her range of motion, to see how they worked. Earlier, in the flare of danger, she'd walked on these two feet instead of four. Humans did it all the time.

Holding her breath, she pushed off the bed. If humans could do it, so could she.

For a second, she swayed. Then her balance steadied. She started to walk out of the bedroom to go to her box in the basement, but the sight of the woman in the mirror above the dresser stopped her.

Her hand reached toward the smooth surface, and the hand of the other woman reached, too. Their fingers touched, but Belle only felt cool glass. She cocked her head, frowning. The other woman cocked her head, frowning. Belle leaned closer. The other woman leaned closer.

Belle's hands curled into fists on the dresser top, too low to show in the mirror, but Belle spotted the arm muscle flexing in the mirror.

It was the woman from the car. The woman who'd reached out and touched her. The woman who'd traded bodies with her.

She'd known this before, but now she saw it. Now she believed.

The woman in the mirror was...her.

She staggered back and gulped air. She wanted to curl up in a corner and think about this until she was ready to slink out. But the pressure in her belly worsened, reminding her that, human or feline, she needed to pee.

Slowly, she turned to the door on the other side of the bedroom. Raising her chin, she headed toward it. Humans didn't use litter boxes. They used bathrooms. She could do this. She was a cat, and cats could do anything they decided to do.

Belle had seen Tory use the toilet many times before she went away last year. It looked easy enough. Two minutes later, she returned to the bedroom, the toilet flushing in the other room. She stepped on a pair of Max's jeans and debated whether to take another nap. The door opened and a blond head poked into the room.

"How are you?" Caroline asked.

The hairs on Belle's arms bristled. She perched on the edge of the bed but kept her feet on the carpet, ready to jump up and claw Caroline's face.

Maybe she shouldn't wait. Maybe she should just do it. After all, Caroline had tried to kill her. Because of Caroline, she was in this clumsy human body.

Caroline stepped inside the room and headed toward her. As she passed the dresser mirror, she glanced into it, changing her mouth from a straight line to a smile. The smile remained when she stopped in front of Belle.

"Now that you're rested, you must be eager to go home."

Belle stared at her. She pictured claw marks on Caroline's face and a silent purr rose in her throat.

"Do you understand English?" Caroline's voice raised and she curved toward Belle.

Belle's fingers cramped into the claw position. If Caroline moved an inch closer, Belle would go straight for her eyes.

When Caroline straightened, Belle felt disappointed but kept her fingers curled.

"You can't expect Max to take care of you forever."

Yes, I can. Belle stared into Caroline's eyes. They were dark blue now, but Belle had seen them change to the color of mud when she took out the round glass circles.

The blue eyes blinked. The smile disappeared. "Don't you have people who are worrying about you? A husband?" She glanced at Belle's fingers, and reached for her left hand. "You're wearing an engagement ring. There must be someone who— Ow! Why, you bitch!" Caroline jumped back, holding her bleeding hand to her mouth.

Belle smiled and put her hand back on her thigh. Finally, she and Caroline were communicating.

"I'm telling Max. Don't think you can get away with—"

"What the hell's going on here?" Max strode into the room, two lines carved between his eyebrows. The same look as when Belle nibbled on leaves of his plants.

Caroline waved her hand in the air. "She scratched me!"

"Is that right?" Max stood next to Caroline and frowned at Belle. "Did you scratch her?"

Belle set her mouth. She didn't like the way his voice sounded. If he wanted to talk to her, he should do it nicely or she wouldn't respond.

"Look," he said, his tone the same as when he tried to talk Ted out of being a bartender, "you can't stay here if you're going to scratch people."

Belle glared at him. This was her home. He couldn't make her leave.

"I think she has mental problems." Caroline put her hand on his shoulder.

Belle's fingers curled again. She wished she'd scratched Caroline harder and deeper.

"What did you do that made her scratch you?"

"Nothing!" Caroline snatched her hand back. "I reached down to look at her engagement ring, and she sprang up and scratched me."

He rubbed his forehead. "She's disoriented."

"She's engaged." Caroline gestured toward Belle, who thought how easy it would be to move forward two inches and bite her fingers.

But she remained still. Max wouldn't like it if she bit Caroline in front of him.

She'd wait until he was gone.

"Someone should notify her fiancé as soon as possible," Caroline continued. "He's probably worried sick."

Max took Belle's left hand and her fingers uncurled. She'd always liked his hands and fingers. They were warm and held her firmly. She wanted to lie on her back and let him pet her chest and stomach, but she didn't think humans did that.

Humans missed a lot of good stuff.

"Do you have a fiancé?" he asked.

She shook her head.

Caroline made a noise like she was coughing up a hairball. "She's wearing a diamond. Of course she's engaged. She's lying her head off."

Still holding her hand, Max stared into her eyes. "You're not engaged. Is that the truth?"

She nodded. She knew what engaged was. On *The Love Chronicles,* the humans got engaged and married all the time.

"You must have a home. There's an address on your driver's license. Your car's totaled, but I can drive you there."

She shook her head. *This* was her home. She was never leaving. Ever.

"You can't stay here," Caroline said. "You're taking advantage of Max's generous nature. He doesn't owe you anything."

Spit from Caroline's mouth hit Belle's face. Belle's muscles tensed and she scooted closer to the edge of the mattress. If Caroline spit on her again, Belle would make her sorry.

Max's grip on her hand tightened. "Caroline, I appreciate your concern, but it's my decision to keep her here until she's well enough to leave."

Caroline's cheekbones flushed the same color she painted her lips. "I'm sorry. I appreciate so much all you've done for me. I guess I'm trying to make things a little easier for you in return."

"She'll be okay soon and out of here," Max said.

Caroline smiled weakly. "Maybe I should stay until that happens."

"Better not. She seems to have taken a dislike to you."

Caroline backed up, keeping her mouth in a smile. "Don't hesitate to call if you need me for anything." She swiveled and strode past Ted, who stood just inside the doorway.

Belle and Max stood with cocked heads while they listened to Caroline's footsteps tap on the wooden hallway floor. Then Max dropped Belle's hand, and Ted strolled into the bedroom.

"What'd I miss? A catfight?"

"Go back to bed," Max said. "You're not helping." He bent over Belle, his tone coaxing, the way he talked to her when she was a cat, and he was ready to sit back and pet her, his eyes half-closed, his body relaxing, a slight hum in his throat as if in that second he felt like everything was good.

Of course it was good. She raised her head. It was good because he was petting her.

"I want to help you," he said, "but if you don't give me any information, I'll have no choice but to go to the authorities. Someone might be frantic about you. Even if you don't have a fiancé"—he glanced at her ring, then back into her eyes—"you might have a family. A mother or father."

She looked down at her lap. What if someone were looking for Sorcha? What if they found Belle and wanted her to leave with them? If she refused to go, Max couldn't make her go.

"Maybe you can write. You want to give it a try?"

She shook her head.

"Are you hungry? Do you want food?"

She shook her head again.

He straightened. "I'll leave you for now. If you want anything, I'll be in my office. Take the hall straight down until you reach the door. That's the office wing. Don't knock, just walk on in."

She nodded. If he only knew, she could find her way through the house with her eyes closed. And why not? It was hers.

"I'll give you until after dinner." His voice grew stern. "Understand?"

She didn't nod and didn't look at him, her eyes on his shoes. He only talked to her with this hard voice when she ate a plant or chased a bird. She didn't like it. Not at all.

His shoes made a circle, and he walked out of the bedroom. Ted's shoes followed.

"Want me to close the door?" Ted asked. "Keep away unwanted visitors?"

She lifted her head. He was grinning at her, as if he

knew—but of course he didn't. She nodded, and her lips curved. She guessed she must be smiling. As soon as the door was closed, she clapped her hands to her cheeks and opened her mouth.

"Waaa," she said. No, that wasn't right. Maybe she needed to shape her mouth differently, the way humans did, and move her tongue around. "Haaa." No. "Taaa. Caaa. Raaa. Maaa." Yes! She had it!

Going to the mirror, she looked at herself while making the word again. So that's how she held her lips. Together but not too tight. "Mmmaaa. Mmmaaa. Mmmaaa." Still not *Max*. She needed more sounds.

A TV sat on the end of the dresser, about the size of one of Max's large books. She picked up the thing that Ted used and poked at buttons, the way she'd seen him do so many times. On the fifth button, the screen lit up. A man came on, and she felt a spurt of recognition. Beau from *The Love Chronicles*.

Clapping her hands, she sat down to listen. Since she was still stuck in this body—she shuddered—it appeared necessary for her to speak like a human. Who better to teach her than the characters from Tory's favorite TV show?

She stared at Beau's mouth. Other animals would find human speech hard to learn. Dogs, for instance. But she was a cat, gifted at birth with a vocal range that went from a roar to a hiss, a purr to a yowl. Learning human speech would be a piece of tuna.

Seven

Sorcha hid in the woods all afternoon, watching the road. Twice she saw a gray car drive up and down slowly, the person inside searching for someone. This was a rural road, lightly traveled. It had to be Deavers. Besides the gray car, only a dozen cars and SUVs, a Sears van, and a cable TV truck had sped past. After a while, she nodded off until the roar of a school bus engine woke her.

Rustling sounds came to her ears, something coming through the trees. She lifted her nose and sniffed, smelling another animal. A bear perhaps? Did bears eat cats? As her heartbeat tapped a hip-hop dance, a raccoon jumped out from between two trees and dashed straight toward her.

Sorcha squealed and took off, running so fast she felt as if she flew. About a quarter mile from Fletch's wrecked car, she lost the scent of the raccoon. She kept running but more slowly. From the pads of her four feet to her tail to her whiskers, she trembled. She wasn't sure if raccoons ate cats but didn't want to find out the hard way.

Another quarter mile or so she came upon a cast iron fence. She followed it...and followed it...and followed it. A smell floated by her nose. Turkey. Smoked. Her human mind said *yech.* Her cat body said *yum.*

Saliva gathered in her mouth and she looked at the bars of the fence. Could she squeeze through? Somehow she had to get into the grounds. She'd been ready to die only a few hours ago, but the needs of this new body were too strong to resist.

Licking her mouth, she spotted the gates. They were

open, which meant they couldn't have dogs. Or maybe they had ones that let themselves be trained by their humans to stay inside an unlocked gate.

She sniffed, then wondered where this disdain came from. She liked dogs. Didn't she?

She was so confused.

Oh, Fletcher, if you're in heaven watching me, I hope you realize what you caused. A thought wiggled into her mind, like a worm in an apple, that maybe Fletcher wasn't in heaven. She sniffed again, this time with sadness. The hell she believed in was life on earth without Fletcher, the only person who'd ever claimed to love her.

The curved driveway was long and concrete. In the distance, she could see the outline of a structure. She squinted but it didn't get clearer, as if these cat eyes needed glasses. Although the cat brain had to be much smaller than her human one, it seemed to be holding all her human knowledge. She'd read somewhere that humans used a small percent of their brain. Too bad no one except herself knew for sure how true this was.

Was the cat inside her body having similar problems adjusting? How wonderful it must be for the cat to be a human. It probably never wanted to be a cat again.

The smell of smoked turkey grew stronger and she detected a hickory taste. Her body wanted it with the same urgency that made her gobble a package of chocolate chips on the night before her period. She dashed toward the smell, whipping along the driveway like a racehorse.

A dozen yards away from the house, she slid to a stop and stared, her hunger forgotten in her amazement. It looked like a small castle. She imagined what Fletcher would say: *Some folks throw money around like it's candy. See anything in their future, honey? We could use some of that sweet stuff.*

And she could never lie to Fletcher. If she saw or felt something, she told him. And she always saw or felt something. Sometimes it was the blackness of death, purple of sickness, red of anger, pink of passion, or green of money. Sometimes it was a series of pictures she didn't understand—but the family members did. As they drove away afterward, Fletcher would be chortling while she clasped her head, trying to turn off the pictures of other people's lives.

They were turned off now. Looking at the house, she felt nothing, saw nothing. The only emotions she'd felt since she'd become a cat were her own.

Her grief and sadness diminished. Her heartbeat skipped. She wanted her hands back so she could clap them together. Her tail went up, waving in the air like a victory flag. No more visions, no more emotions, no more blinding headaches.

She felt light-headed. As though a gorilla had sat on her shoulders her whole life and had suddenly leapt off and disappeared.

"Here, kitty."

Sorcha squealed and darted into the evergreen bushes bordering the front of the mini-castle. Green needles brushed against her thick fur. A piney smell penetrated her nostrils. Quivering, she pressed against the rough brick.

"Don't be scared." Through the branches, Sorcha saw patches of blue denim as someone knelt in front of the bushes. The voice was pitched high and sounded like a child's. "You can come out. I promise not to hurt you. Here, kitty, kitty."

A face pressed to the ground, peering at Sorcha through an inch gap between two of the bushes. A girl. Small face and nose, big ears and eyes. "Come out, kitty. I'll give you food. I left my sandwich on the porch. Wait here, I'll get it."

Food. Sorcha stretched her neck to see the girl better.

The face disappeared. The girl scampered away. A moment later she was back, waving a sandwich in front of the bushes. The smell of turkey wafted into Sorcha's nostrils.

A hum reverberated inside her. She tried to stop but it got louder.

"Are you purring?" The girl's voice sparkled. "For me or the sandwich?"

Sorcha's front legs began doing an odd dance, patting

the ground in front of her one foot at a time, as if she were kneading bread. She'd never had much to do with cats but it was something this small feline body needed to do. The same way she needed to move her hips when she played a Beyoncé song.

"I can leave it here." The girl slid backward on the grass.

Sorcha's kneading slowed.

"I'm at the sidewalk now. You can come out and eat."

The voice sounded farther away. Sorcha stopped her kneading and pressed against the brick wall. The smell was calling to her to come and eat it. Her body urged her to go. Her mind argued to stay. It was the same way she felt before every client's reading.

Still shaking, she took a tiny step forward. Was she walking into a trap? Her cat ears heard the wind slap against the leaves. If the girl moved, surely she'd make more noise than the wind, giving Sorcha time to run back to the wall.

She took another step. Another. And another. Still huddled between the two bushes, she stopped, needles bunching against her fur. She stretched out her neck. The half sandwich lay on the ground inches away. Like bait for a fish. Sorcha peered around instead of rushing forward, even though her empty stomach protested.

The girl sat cross-legged beneath a maple tree, her elbows resting on her knees, her hands cupping her cheeks. She beamed at Sorcha.

"It's okay." The girl's voice pitched high and gentle in the singsong way people spoke to babies. "I promise not to hurt you."

Sorcha darted out the last few inches, grabbed the bread with her teeth, ripped off the top layer, tossed it aside, then bit into a slice of shaved turkey. Carrying it in her mouth, she dashed back between the long-needled branches to her refuge against the brick. She tore at the turkey, chewing and swallowing with gusto.

It wasn't enough. She raced for another piece, taking it back with her. She did this again and again. And all the while she watched the girl through spaces between the bushes, because she never completely trusted anyone. Not even Fletcher.

After gobbling half the meat, she was sated, her stomach puffed out. She made one last run. This time she grabbed the bottom slice of bread with the shaved turkey piled on it and dragged it back with her into the bushes.

"I'll get you water." The girl scrambled to her feet and ran off into the overlarge house.

The ground was hard and cold but Sorcha curled next to the turkey-covered bread. She never napped during the day, not since she was a child, but like eating meat, it was another need she couldn't fight.

She closed her eyes. Visions came but they were her own: Fletcher lying on the sidewalk, his eyes like glass. A sad-faced CEO chasing her, crashing her car into a ditch. A cat switching bodies with her.

One thing was certain, she'd reached the bottom. It couldn't get any worse than this.

A cat! A cat! Gwen ran into the house, the words humming a happy song in her mind. This morning when she'd awakened, she'd tingled all over. She'd thought maybe the feeling meant something good was going to happen today. Maybe her mom and dad would come home from Greece.

But Katie, her nanny, had been grouchy, her eyes red. She said she was up until three in the morning studying for her calculus class. Gwen had sat huddled in the chair, feeling guilty because Katie had to get up to make her oatmeal—that Gwen didn't even like—then take her to her private school, a twenty-five-minute drive.

School was okay. She thought of herself like wallpaper, the kind that blended in and wasn't noticed. If no one noticed her, they wouldn't know she was a freak.

But the tingle remained with her. When Brandy Newhauser, the most popular girl in school, had sat next to her at library, Gwen had held her breath. Maybe Brandy was going to talk to her. The thought had made her heart thump inside her chest and her breaths catch in her throat. If Brandy talked to her, what would Gwen say back?

Turning her back to Gwen, Brandy spoke to the girl on her other side, who'd said something back that made them both giggle. Gwen had felt let down and relieved at the same time. Even though she was smart in school, the only time she said anything that made people laugh was when they were laughing at her.

When she'd reached home, Katie had made turkey sandwiches and steamed broccoli and carrots. Ewww! "Another diet?"

Katie put her hands on her wide hips. "Are you saying I'm fat?"

"I don't think you're fat," Gwen said and grabbed the sandwich. Katie's laptop, books, and papers were spread over the table, so maybe she wasn't dieting but just making something easy. "Is it okay if I eat outside?"

"It's cold." Katie sat again, sliding a book closer. "I don't want you to catch anything. Your parents will blame me."

"People don't catch colds from cold air but from germs on doorknobs and stuff."

"I know that. I'm in college." Katie gave her a don't-be-a-smartass scowl. "What about your vegetables?"

Gwen gave the brocs and carrots a glance. "When I get back I can eat them."

"You better." Katie nodded toward the door. "You can go, but stay near the house. It'll be dark in a little while. I don't want to chase you down like last time."

Gwen nodded and hurried away before Katie could change her mind. As she left the house, the tingle grew stronger. Almost like a tickle in her tummy.

Something good was going to happen. She knew it.

Then she found the cat. It ate her food. Now she'd get it water.

As she barreled back into the kitchen, Katie glanced up from her book. "Eat your vegetables," she said. "No vegetables, no dessert."

"Okay." Gwen snagged a bowl from the cupboard. When

she spooned veggies into it, Katie's eyebrows rose at her choice of container but she didn't say anything.

Gwen sat at the table and scarfed down her veggies. Katie looked at her once.

"Your face is flushed."

Gwen's nerves buzzed a warning. "I'm okay."

"Are you feeling all right?" Katie reached out and put her hand on Gwen's forehead. "You feel cool."

"I'm okay." She chewed faster. The quicker she swallowed, the less she tasted the broccoli.

"Don't eat too fast," Katie said, but she was frowning at her notebook computer, her hands already on the keyboard.

Gwen watched the clock on the microwave. It took her three whole minutes to finish the vegetables. "Okay, I'm done." She jumped off the chair, planning her next moves.

"Rinse off the bowl and put it in the dishwasher."

"Okay." Gwen yanked the faucet on and rinsed off the scummy broccoli pieces. She slammed the faucet off, then opened the dishwasher just behind Katie.

"You're being helpful tonight. Thank you."

Gwen jumped. Katie was turned around in her chair, looking straight at her. She even smiled, something she hardly ever did. Fear paralyzed Gwen's vocal chords. She put the bowl in the dishwasher and slid it closed.

"Have two cookies," Katie said.

"Can I eat them outside?"

"No, it's cold out there and your color's too high. I'm not taking any chances." Her mouth thinned and she turned back to her book.

Gwen wanted to scream. Instead, she grabbed two cookies from the jar. "I'll take them into my room."

Katie nodded. "Don't make a mess for Bonnie."

"I won't." Gwen liked Bonnie. Too bad Bonnie wasn't her nanny and Katie her cleaning lady. Then she'd make a big mess for Katie.

Gwen stomped up the front stairway to her room. She tossed the cookies in her desk drawer, then tiptoed to the back stairway. With every footstep, the boards under the carpet creaked, making Gwen wince. She reached the first floor and scuttled past the library, the study, and the dining room that no one used.

When she reached the open kitchen, she dropped to her knees and crawled, afraid to look inside, as if her gaze would draw Katie's eyes, holding her breath in case Katie heard her over the music. Finally, she reached the other living room wall and her breath gushed out.

Scrambling to her feet, she glanced around at the cream furniture, walls and carpet. Gwen's mother called it the "white room." Gwen had told Bonnie the cleaning lady that it was the "boring room," and Bonnie had laughed until she wiped tears from her cheeks.

An empty crystal candy bowl sat on the coffee table. Perfect. Gwen grabbed the bowl and tiptoed out. Maybe the cat would come out for water and let her pet it. If she did, it would be the best thing ever.

Eight

Max looked at the woman in his bed. With her creamy skin and dark hair she reminded him of Sleeping Beauty. Since he was no prince, he resisted the urge to bend down and kiss her. He was stepping backward toward the hall when her eyes opened.

They were the same green as Belle's. She saw him, smiled, and held out her arms, as if to a lover.

He leaned toward her, drawn as though an invisible hand pulled him. Her eyes rounded, her pupils expanded. Her tongue darted out, licking her lip. He pulled himself up and put his arms behind his back, locking his hands together.

"We'll be eating in an hour. I came to ask what you wanted on your pizza."

She stared at him, a vulnerable look in her eyes.

He cleared his throat. "You've had pizza before, haven't you? Everyone's had pizza."

Blinking, she shook her head.

"Are you a vegetarian? I can order a vegetable pizza."

She slapped her hand over her mouth, muffling a giggle.

"I guess that means no."

Her hand dropped but the smile remained. She shifted, her hair sliding on the pale blue pillowcase.

As if she'd pressed a switch, his genitals grew heavy. Not good, not good at all. Sorcha had been in a serious accident this morning. And he didn't know her. She might be engaged. She might be insane. She might be confused. Anything to explain her odd acceptance of her situation.

Nothing confusing or odd about the reactions of his body. It was responding to an attractive woman in his bed, but he wasn't letting it control his mind. He stepped back. "I'll order you what I'm having."

She nodded.

"It would be a lot better if you could talk." He turned to leave.

"I talk." She spoke slowly, her voice husky.

He snapped around. "Could you talk before this?"

She shook her head and bit her lip. "I don't know."

"You don't know? Is it shock? Trauma?" He waited. She'd tell him the problem, he'd take care of it, send her on her way, and his life would go back to normal.

Belle's brain ached from talking. Meowing was so much easier. Humans made everything difficult, even communication. So few words, so many meanings.

"You want to tell me about yourself?" Max asked.

She put a hand on the bruise on her forehead, just like Annette in today's TV show. "Amnesia." She'd practiced saying it while watching the show, the *mmm* sound easier than the *nnn*. "I have amnesia."

"Amnesia?" He looked at her with disbelief. "The only people I've heard of with amnesia are actors in bad TV shows. If you're afraid of someone, tell me. I'll protect you." His gaze shifted to her ring. "No matter what. You have my promise."

She nodded. Of course he'd protect her. She'd never thought anything different.

"Do you want to tell me?" He moved closer, bending, the same concentration in his blue eyes as when he was reading one of his travel books.

"Pretty eyes," she said.

He snapped back. "You don't need to flirt with me. I already told you I'll protect you."

"You have pretty eyes," she repeated. He also had a pretty face and body, but she decided not to say that.

What had she done wrong? Max told her all the time how pretty she was. *Pretty Belle. Beautiful Belle. Pretty kitty.* She always liked it. Didn't humans like to be called nice things?

"Well, thanks." He shoved his hands in his pockets and backed up. "I'll order the pizza. You like garlic bread?"

She shook her head. She liked meat. Lots of meat.

"We'll probably eat in about a half hour." One corner of his mouth flicked up. "Don't go anywhere."

She shook her head. Where would she go? This was her home.

As soon as he left, she stretched, holding the position for a long moment. Then she rubbed her cheek against the pillow. It was soft and smelled of Max. Now her smells mingled with his, her cat body and her human body.

A knock rattled the door. A mewl came out of her mouth, the unfamiliar words forgotten for a second. The door opened before she remembered how to purse her lips and where to stick her tongue to tell whomever it was to come in. Unless it was Caroline. Her she would tell not to come in.

"You're decent? Too bad." Ted strolled inside, clothes draped over his arm. "Max said you're eating with us tonight. I thought you'd like a change of clothes." He tossed his armload of garments on the foot of the bed. "They're my sister's exercise clothes. They should stretch or shrink to fit you. Tory won't mind if you wear them."

Belle nodded. Tory liked her. Tory had wanted to take her to New York, but of course Belle couldn't go. This was her home. Why would she want to live anywhere else?

"I'll leave now." Ted glanced at his watch. "You have enough time to take a quick bath or a shower and change."

Watching him leave, Belle felt sick inside her stomach.

Bath? Shower?

No, no, and no!

She wasn't going to do it. She refused to do it.

But if she didn't, they'd smell her. Cats groomed themselves all the time, but they didn't wash away their scents. Any animal knew scents were good. Water was for drinking. Inside the body, not outside.

Her mouth set. She threw back the covers, rolled out of bed, marched into the bathroom, knelt by the bathtub, and turned on the faucets the way she'd seen Max do so often. Anything a human could do, a cat could do—no matter how disgusting and unnatural.

But she'd better find Sorcha and get her body back. Fast. How many more indignities could she stand?

"Are you there, kitty?"

Sorcha woke. In her human body, she would've jumped up screaming. In this cat body, she knew immediately she was hidden in the bushes, it was morning, and there was no way anyone could see her unless she allowed it.

That was not going to happen.

"Here's water and food for you."

Well, maybe...

"Please, I'll scoot back to the tree, like yesterday. I promise I won't touch you until you're ready."

Sorcha listened to the girl's footsteps recede. She peered through the sharp-needled branches but saw only bright sunlight. The tiny squeak of athletic shoes sliding against grass stopped. Something slithered against bark and she guessed the girl was sitting on the ground.

The smell of tuna wafted to Sorcha's nostrils, like a gift from God. Whisker by whisker, paw by paw, she crept out. The girl had placed two bowls at the edge of the grass, a couple inches farther from the bushes than last night's leavings.

Was this on purpose? Was the girl luring her out a little more each time?

Sorcha peered across the length of grass so smooth and green it could have been a carpet. The girl sat in front of a giant tree, her arms around her knees, watching Sorcha as if she were something precious and special.

Sorcha had never felt special and precious in her life. Not even with Fletcher.

Pushing that unsettling thought aside, she lapped up the

water. All the while she drank, she watched the girl. Braces sparkled on too-big teeth, arms and legs as narrow as sticks, and ears like Disney's Dumbo.

Sorcha tensed, waiting for a vision of the girl's future.

Nothing.

So it wasn't a fluke, this nothingness. It was here to stay.

An unfamiliar emotion filled her, and it took a few seconds to identify. Happiness. So that's what it felt like, as though she'd swallowed sunshine.

She took a bite of tuna—yummy!—then did a little dance, her four legs bending up and down, a humming sound coming out of her throat.

The girl jumped up and sprinted toward her. "Are you having a fit?"

With a squeal, Sorcha dived back into the bushes.

"Sorry, sorry, I'm sorry. I didn't mean to scare you. Look, I have to go to school. Come out and eat. You're a good kitty. Come."

Sorcha stayed where she was. Fletcher was dead. How could she dance? What was this new body turning her into?

Even as she asked, she knew the answer. It was turning her into a cat.

Nine

Max woke up in the guest room with a stiff erection, a stiff back from the too soft mattress, and his mind stiff, too. Stiff with determination.

He wasn't buying Sorcha's amnesia story. But something was behind her resolve to stay in a stranger's house, and he planned on finding out what it was. Maybe something to do with the ring on her finger. Maybe an abusive relationship. She didn't seem like the kind of woman to let herself be abused, not with her stubborn refusal to do what she didn't want to do. But he'd heard it could happen to anyone.

He used Ted's electric razor, which didn't give as smooth a shave as his own. Rubbing his jaw, he frowned at his reflection. Two lines were etched between his brows. Frown lines, not smile lines. He looked like a man who didn't enjoy life.

That was going to change soon. But not today. In addition to Sorcha, he had Belle to worry about. He hadn't seen her since yesterday morning. Sometimes she disappeared, but she usually managed to sleep curled against his back.

Was that Belle yesterday in the trees? If so, why hadn't she come to him? And how had she stolen out of the house?

Yesterday hadn't been one of his stellar days. Today would be different. Today he'd get Ted to agree to his plan, relocate Sorcha, find Belle, get his agenda current and back on course.

If something happened to delay him, he had the sick feeling inside that he would never go. Never achieve the dream he'd had since he was a kid.

Some days he felt as though they'd been buried the day his dad died.

He tilted his head toward the ceiling. "I did it, Dad." His voice sounded loud in the bathroom though he spoke quietly. But he was speaking loud words. "I kept my promise. Ted and Tory are grown and ready to be unleashed. Now it's my turn."

Lowering his head to frown at his reflection, he waited a moment, as if expecting a reply.

"Stupid," he said. He left the bathroom and headed toward his bedroom.

His knock was forceful. So was the second. The third. No answer to any of them.

Maybe she was sleeping, though she'd slept most of the afternoon yesterday and went to bed right after she'd eaten all the anchovies and half the sausage off the pizza. He knocked again. No answer. He brought up his hand again, and this time he stung his knuckles pounding.

"Sorcha?" he called. When no one answered, he pushed the door open.

The sheets and covers on his bed were more rumpled than usual, but Sorcha's slender body wasn't tangled in them. He glanced around the room. When he'd checked on her last night, he'd picked up his clothes from the floor and piled them on the padded chair in the corner. She'd added her jacket, slacks, and top to the pile, and it looked like the leaning tower of laundry.

The door to the bathroom was open and he heard running water. Why didn't she answer him? Last night she'd mentioned she was dizzy. Could she have fallen and hurt herself?

He hurried across the room, calling her name.

Bliss. Belle reclined in the tub. Yesterday's bath had been too short. Just as she'd discovered how wonderful the pulsing water felt, Caroline had barged in to get her. The blond woman had made her dress in Tory's exercise clothes. Then Caroline had said if she was well enough to get out of bed and eat, she was well enough to leave.

Belle had considered picking up the lamp on the dresser and conking Caroline on the head. Instead, she'd pretended to be weak and dizzy, like Annette in *The Love Chronicles*.

Closing her eyes now, she purred. Warm water jetted out at her back, her sides, and her two human breasts. This strange body sang with pleasure.

She stretched, her head back, concentrating on the experience. A knocking sound came but she ignored it. This was too delicious to—

"Sorcha? Are you all right? Sorcha?"

Max! Jolted out of her languor, Belle's eyes opened. She sat up straight, water splashing. For an instant, she forgot how to talk like a human, and a startled noise came from her throat.

"Sorcha!" Max rushed into the bathroom.

She gawked at him.

"What are you..." He stared at her breasts, then backed up. "Uh...sorry. I didn't expect... I wanted to see... Umm." He swallowed, the lump men had in their throats going up and down. Backing over the threshold, he pulled the door shut. "If you want breakfast, help yourself." His voice sounded thicker than she'd ever heard it. "I'll be out looking for my cat."

Belle glanced down at her breasts. Was something wrong with them? They were puffy and inconveniently big, tipped with pink. And only two of them. That couldn't feed many babies at once.

She cupped them in her hands and felt a tingle. Her breath gasped at the feeling, like when she rubbed against the rug and Max touched her and she sparked. But this was a different kind of spark. Not in way that pained her, but in a good way.

Did Max know about the tingle? Was that why he'd stared?

Did he want to do this to her?

She dropped her hands and stood. Her mind swirled with all the new sensations. She decided to get dressed in Tory's clothes, then go outside with Max to look for the real Sorcha and get her body back.

The cool air chilled her skin, warm from the water, and she grabbed the towel to wrap it around her body. But though the towel was warm, she shivered.

"I'm a cat," she whispered fiercely at the ceiling. "It doesn't matter my skin is completely hairless, not one speck. Inside, I'll always be a cat."

Sorcha lifted her head. Without buildings to block the sound, the wind carried the voice to the bushes where she hid. "Belle," the man called. "Belle." And again and again and again.

She recognized the voice. The man from yesterday, calling for his cat.

"Belle," came the voice. "Belle, Belle."

Sorcha quaked. Most of the time, she was cozy in her hideaway between the bushes and the brick mansion, but every once in a while a gust of wind sliced through the branches. Even though it was April, winter didn't let loose of its tight grip on Wisconsin.

If she went to the man calling for his cat, he would never guess she wasn't his Belle. She would be warm. She would be fed and watered. Maybe she would see the cat inside her body. Maybe they could switch back.

She whimpered, curling against the wall.

The she remembered why she couldn't do that. Someone had thrown the cat at her windshield, trying to kill it, just as Deavers tried to kill her.

What if she went back and the cat killer tried again?

Her body chilled, as if ice built up within her.

She wasn't ready to face a killer again. Not now. In her earlier despair, she'd been ready to die. Perhaps it was leftover determination from the cat that changed her, made her cling to life. Even in this small, four-legged body.

At least for now.

The wind buffeted Belle. Without fur covering her skin, she quaked with cold. She wanted to go home and huddle next to a heat vent, but humans didn't do that. Instead, they piled clothes on their bare skin. Besides, she had to find the cat and get her body back.

She trotted to the trees that lined Max's property, convinced Sorcha would have hung around, eager to find her human body. Belle opened her mouth to call out to Sorcha—and heard Max's voice.

"Belle!" he called. "Belle!"

Every cell in her body sprang to attention. She fought an urge to run toward his voice. Instead, she stepped back. If he heard her calling Sorcha's name, he'd make her go to the hospital for sure. He thought she was Sorcha.

Would Sorcha realize Max was calling her? Would she go to him?

Not sure if it would work, Belle sent out a silent command: *Come to Max. Come to him or come to me. Come now!*

She waited a moment, listening. The wind gusted. Leaves rustled. From a distance, she heard the muted sound of a truck. Then Max's call again. "Belle! Belle!"

Her teeth chattered, and she turned back to the house. She'd look for Sorcha later, when Max wasn't outside. Besides, her stomach was giving her *feed me* messages.

The wind blew against her back, propelling her forward. The door handle was cold under her palm. She turned it the wrong way. Turning the knob the other direction, she told herself it was okay to make mistakes. In the four years she'd watched humans, they made mistakes all the time.

The kitchen looked odd without the morning paper spread over the table and the cereal box and empty bowl left on the counter. She nodded her understanding and approval. Of course Max had left without eating. He thought she—the cat—was missing and it was more important to find her than to eat. He loved her.

She loved him, too, but she wasn't letting that stop her from eating.

She tossed Sorcha's jacket over a chair back and hurried

into the pantry. For almost her whole life she'd been lusting after the tuna in the cans inside. Even though she couldn't read words, she grabbed a can from the second row, recognizing the shape and the mermaid design.

Two things about being human were good, she admitted, walking to the can opener on the counter. First the bathtub and now the tuna.

Squinting at the opener, she started pushing and pressing buttons. A small roar came. She jumped back, her hand opening. The can crashed to the countertop and bounced to the floor.

"Eeep!" She slapped her hand over her mouth. Taking a calming breath, she bent and picked up the can to try again, ignoring the wild beating inside her chest, like bird wings flapping. The machine was supposed to make that noise when it was working. She could figure it out. After all, she was Belle.

Max's cousin, Emery, used to sing parts of a song to Max. "Anything you can do I can do better." It turned out he was wrong, because if he was so wonderful Caroline wouldn't have pushed him off a hiking trail.

But in her case, it was true.

Ten minutes later, Ted walked into the room, his hair mussed, his eyes half-lidded, bristles on his jaw, looking like he'd just rolled out of bed.

"What's all the ruckus?"

Belle jumped again. Her hand dropped from the top of the machine, and its noise stopped. This time, she kept her grip on the can of tuna.

"I'm trying to open this thing."

"Jesus." He strode to her and grabbed the can from her hand. He pressed it against the rim of the can opener, slammed down on the silver handle, and the motor droned. The top popped off, he released the handle, the motor silenced, and he held out the can to her.

"You really do have amnesia, don't you?"

Busy pulling tuna out of the can with her fingers and stuffing it into her mouth, she didn't answer. Tuna. Was there anything better?

Ten

Bob Deavers drummed his fingers on his ebony desktop and watched his half brother enter his office in the Evanston corporate office. Phil's quizzical smile was like a big question mark hovering over the top of his full head of hair and boy-next-door-meets-teen-idol face.

Bob stood and stepped around the desk, holding out his arms. Phil looked surprised but came toward him. A simple man, eager to believe in goodness. Easy to manipulate.

They hugged awkwardly, pounding backs and stepping quickly away.

"How are the kids?" Phil asked.

"The best." Bob gestured him to one of the two leather chairs and took the matching chair next to his. More friendly and less intimidating than sitting behind the desk. "My P.A. sent you the latest pictures, didn't she?"

Phil nodded at their photos on the desk. "Tell them Uncle Phil said hi. Melanie, too."

"Will do." Bob worked to keep his smile in place. The last time his wife had seen Phil, she'd cooed over him like he was a kitten she wanted to take home. With her supermodel looks and his toned body and glossy hair, they made a striking pair. No room for short, chubby husbands who paid Melanie's exorbitant bills without questions or complaints.

He caught himself rubbing his hands together and put them on his thighs. Time to get down to business.

"Did you get that loan for your fitness center?"

"Uh, no. I—"

"You still need the money?"

Something flashed across Phil's face. Desperation? Bob knew all about desperation. It drove a man to do terrible things.

"Doesn't everyone?" Phil's voice wasn't quite steady and he laughed a breath too late.

The tension eased from Bob's muscles. He leaned toward Phil. "Maybe I can help."

Phil's fingers clenched and unclenched. "You said my plans were worthless."

"I didn't say worthless."

"You said your financial advisors told you it was an unstable investment and advised you not to put money into it."

"And you remembered that word for word." Bob lowered his head and shook it, rubbing his hand through his thinning hair. "I must've hurt your feelings. Will you accept my apology?"

"Yeah, sure." Phil crossed his arms over his chest.

Bob frowned. Phil wasn't buying his contrition. As if Phil knew he'd kept it on his desk for a week before calling him with his line of bull. Family was always the hardest to fool.

Everyone but his father and brother bought his act. And his wife, who only cared that he pay her bills and didn't complain when she flew off to Europe and New York to mingle with the rich and slightly famous.

But his kids... If they doubted him...found out that he was a fake...found out he'd murdered a man...

The thought lodged a fist-sized knot in his chest, and he sought out the photo of Lorna and Danny on his desk. They both had dark blond hair like their mother and smiles like his. If they saw through his façade to the insecure wimp his father had more than once said he was, he might as well cut his throat.

He tore his gaze from the photo and sucked in a breath. Phil was looking at him curiously, waiting for him to go on.

His stomach tightened. Time for the show.

"Let me tell you a story. I married above myself." He held up a hand. "No, no, don't lie. I know what I look like. I know what she looks like. Women like Melanie only marry men like me for our money and our power."

His throat tightened and unexpected emotion slammed into him. Phil frowned with concern. Good, Bob could use this. He looked Phil straight in the eyes, knowing that his next words were going to be the sorry truth.

"It's just like Mother and Father."

Phil recoiled. Bob reached out and gripped his wrist, compelling him with the force of his gaze to listen. "You know it's true. He was short, balding, overweight, and twenty years older. Don't tell me she married him out of love."

"Looks aren't everything." Phil jerked his arm away easily. "Mom said she was astounded that out of all the women your dad could've had, he chose her."

"Then why did she run off with your father?"

"Because yours was cheating on her for years. She was miserable."

Rage surged up inside Bob and he rose to his feet. "So miserable she abandoned me?"

"Your dad wouldn't let her take you. Besides, you were thirteen. She thought you were old enough to handle it."

"Handle it? I hated her." The words bellowed out of him and he leaned forward, in Phil's face. "She was pregnant, that's why she left. Pregnant with you."

Phil's eyes and entire face puckered inward. Troubled, contrite. Bob should strike now, seal the deal. But he couldn't speak, gasping for breath, his body shaking after saying the words that had been locked up inside him for decades. Decades of pain, decades of anger. Stuffed inside him like rice in a turkey. Stick a fork in him and out it spewed.

He dropped onto the chair, sucked in one last breath, and exhaled, letting out the last of the poison. Then the words poured out. "I didn't ask you to come here to go over all that old stuff, but maybe now you can see why I was so easily duped."

Phil's frown deepened. His expression wary, he nodded.

"I've been seeing a psychic." Bob held up his hand. "A

friend raved about her, and his business was taking big leaps, one right after another. While he was leaping, I was stumbling. A hurricane had flattened the hotel in Mexico. And I don't want to talk about the one on the Gulf. My father was still CEO and threatening to kick me out of the decision-making positions."

He stopped, taking another emotional break. Dammit, this pain wasn't supposed to happen. He was supposed to fake it, not feel it. Bending forward, he gazed down at the muted carpet between his feet in their shiny black shoes. Even Phil with his marshmallow heart was going to get sick of him whining.

A pat came on his back. And another. Phil commiserating. Funny, the pats were working, the hurt easing. In that second, Bob felt more affection for Phil than he'd done in his life.

But not enough affection to change his mind.

He raised his head and peered into Phil's face as he frowned with concern, sympathy written all over his open face. "I saw the psychic, followed her advice and started hitting bull's eyes. Every single time." Speaking about it made him dizzy. Everyone had admired him, looked up to him. Even his father. Something Bob had thought would only happen after the earth split open and fires razed the land.

Why the fuck did Fletcher have to ruin everything?

"My father stepped down and chose me to succeed him. That's when I made a huge misstep. Sorcha told me if we had sex she could make better choices for me. I knew it was wrong—I'm married; she was engaged to her manager—but I couldn't turn her down. I couldn't pass up her promise of bigger and grander success."

In his imagination he saw it unfold as he said, as if his lies were true. As if Sorcha hadn't been polite and deferential at every meeting.

"After a few months, she demanded that I divorce Melanie and marry her. That came as a shock. Up to then she seemed fine with our relationship and the gifts of jewelry I'd given her. I tried to be tactful and told her I couldn't divorce Melanie because of the children. If we divorce, she gets custody of the kids. It's in the prenup. She'd whisk them away to New York faster than I could hug them good-bye."

Unhappiness and sympathy crossed Phil's face. He was melting like warm chocolate.

"Sorcha went psycho," he continued. "She threatened to tell Melanie. I told her that I'd tell Melanie myself rather than be blackmailed."

"Good for you." Phil gave him another pat on his back.

"She backed down, but a week later she called and said she'd had a vision about me. She wanted to meet me one last time. We'd always met at my office, but this time she insisted I come to her place in Milwaukee. When I got there, she and her fiancé were in the backyard. She took one look at me, whipped out her gun, and shot him."

Phil gasped. Bob bent toward him, holding Phil's gaze with his stare.

"She set it up so it would look like I did it, and then she ran. I raced after her. I don't know what I was thinking." He wiped his hand over his face, as if he were troubled. "I found her car in a ditch but she wasn't around. I don't know what happened to her."

"Maybe she's hurt." Phil frowned. "Or dead."

"Not dead. She called me yesterday and said Melanie and the kids will be next unless I pay her one million dollars." He lowered his voice, put in it all the anguish he felt, all the fucked up emotions he'd suffered through for years, never being good enough, smart enough, lucky enough. Then it had all turned around, and suddenly he was at the top of the heap. The one everyone looked up to. Even his father. And it had been euphoric, as if Sorcha were his personal fairy godmother. One sweep of her wand and he was golden.

Until Fletcher had ruined everything with his greed.

"She means it. It would ruin me, but I'd pay her. God knows I'd do anything for my kids." His voice vibrated with sincerity. "But I know it wouldn't be the end. She'll come back again. And again. Until I had nothing left. When that happens, she'll kill them." Tears tracked down his cheeks.

It was partially the truth, part of the reason he'd shot Fletcher. "After that, she'll kill me and I won't care."

"Go to the police. Tell them."

He shook his head. "I can't. They won't find her. And somehow, some way, she'll kill Lorna and Danny. I have no choice. I have to kill her first."

Phil's eyes widened but something besides surprise showed in his face. Dismay.

Bob plunged ahead. "I'll pay you a half a million dollars to find her and do whatever it takes to get rid of her forever. I'll give you twenty-five thousand as an advance. Right now. No waiting." He held out his hands, pleading with everything he had, as though Lorna's and Danny's lives really depended on it. "For God's sake, Phil, they're your nephew and niece. Don't do it for me, don't do it for the money, though I'll give it to you anyway. Do it for Lorna and Danny."

Emotions fought on Phil's expressive face and his eyes blinked fast. Teetering on a ledge, about to fall off in either direction. Kill or Don't Kill.

Bob leaned into his space. "Do you want to see them murdered? Because if you don't help me, that's what will happen. The next time you see them will be at their funeral."

His grimness growing with each step, Max hiked a quarter mile in each direction, calling Belle's name. Then he walked along the roadside. If a car had hit her...

Finally, he trudged home. In his office, he grabbed the phone and called the Humane Society. The only cat dropped off last night and this morning was a black and white male. However, if he wanted a gray cat, they had a half dozen—

He interrupted, leaving his number in case someone brought in a small gray female. He didn't want a substitute. He wanted Belle.

Next he called the non-emergency number of the county

sheriff's office and gave his information in case any reports of a dead cat came in. He hung up and glanced out the window, in the hope that maybe—

A movement caught his attention. Sorcha? Where the hell was she going?

He grabbed his jacket and a moment later stormed out the back door. She was only a few feet away from the tree line that hid the house from the road.

"Sorcha!" he yelled. "Sorcha, stop!"

She kept walking. He called again. She slowed, hesitated, and turned.

He kept his eyes on her face until he caught up to her. Her mouth was closed, her full lips firm, her eyes unreadable. "What are you doing?" he asked.

Her chin went up. "Ted said your cat was lost. You helped me, so I decided to help you find her."

The way she spoke as though she considered every word, pronouncing each syllable carefully, made him suspect English wasn't her first language. "Belle won't come to a stranger."

She shrugged and turned toward the trees.

He reached out, catching her jacket. She looked at his fingers on her sleeve as if she were considering pulling out a knife and cutting them off.

"We have to talk." He released the jacket.

Her chin lifted another inch. The wind painted her cheeks a bright pink and whipped her dark hair into chaos, one strand swirling across her face and into her mouth. She made a face and spat it out.

Max shoved his hands in his jeans pockets. "You can't stay here without notifying the authorities. Someone has to be looking for you."

"No one's looking," she said too quickly. "I can too stay. I *will* stay."

"You're wearing a diamond ring." The size of a pin top, but a diamond all the same. "It's on your ring finger. You're probably engaged."

"That's what *she* said."

"She?"

74

"Caroline." She sniffed as if she smelled raw sewage. "She's wrong. I'm not engaged."

"You don't know. You've lost your memory."

She glanced down, then up at him through her thick lashes. "I wouldn't forget love."

"People forget all the time."

"Not me." She stared into his eyes. "Once I loved, I would never forget."

A howl of frustration filled in his throat. He swallowed it. He was supposed to be making his life easier, getting rid of responsibilities, not adding new ones.

"You need to see a doctor. If you've lost your memory—"

"What would a doctor do?"

"Talk to you, jog your memory."

"You can talk to me."

He laughed. She smiled, her scorn apparently forgotten. His laughter caught and he shrugged. "All right, you can stay. For a few days." What would another day or two matter?

She turned and started walking toward the trees.

"Where are you going?" he asked again.

"To look for your cat."

He watched until she disappeared behind a white pine. Only then did he stride back to the house. He needed to find out if anyone was looking for Sorcha.

He had the feeling that, like a stray kitten, the longer she stayed in his home, the harder it would be to put her out.

Eleven

Behind the bushes in front of the mini-castle, Sorcha heard a woman call her name. The voice was familiar. It called her name again, and she shivered. It sounded like her voice on the answering machine.

She mewled. It must be Belle calling her. Belle wanted Sorcha to come to her so they could trade bodies.

Sorcha backed up until her tail hit rough brick. Her heart was beating like an electric hammer. Fletcher, the only person who didn't treat her like a freak, was dead. By now, Deavers had bought himself an ironclad alibi. If she went to the police, they'd arrest her instead of him.

Better to remain a cat for a little while longer. If someone was searching for her, it couldn't go on forever.

Although, thanks in part to her, Deavers was a very rich man. According to Fletcher, rich men did whatever they wanted to do.

"Sorcha!" Belle called. "Sorcha!"

Sorcha remained where she was, her eyes open and unblinking, her senses alert, listening and waiting. Just like a cat.

At his computer, Max looked at the subject line of his sister's e-mail to him. *Sorcha.* He swore. Ted must have emailed Tory. Why did his entire family think everything he did was their damn business?

He clicked on the message line, but moved the arrow to the delete button, ready to press down.

To: Max Brannigan
From: Tory Brannigan
Subject: Sorcha

Ted told me about Sorcha. I think it's so cool that you're taking care of her. Just like a plot from The Love Chronicles!:-)))

Ted told me you're keeping her in your bed! IMHO, you must be in love with her. It's so not you!

If you need any advice on dating, give me a call. You've been out of the dating scene for a while and I've been seeing a lot of guys. Maybe you should call me and let me talk to her. I'll find out if she likes you:-) I'd call you, but I used my minutes and you know I'm trying to hold down expenses:(

That reminds me, could you send me another thousand (2 would be better)? I'm trying to budget, but everything costs so much over here. When I'm a star in a Broadway hit, I'll pay you back every penny.

XXXOOO
Tory

Max pressed delete. His cell phone rang. Looking at the caller ID, he hesitated. His mother. What did she want now?

He thought of letting the call go to voice mail. But that would delay Rose, not stop her. He picked up the phone.

Ted had told Tory about Sorcha. Which one had told Rose?

"Yeah?"

"Is that how you answer your phone?"

"I knew it was you."

"You only answer my calls with rudeness?" Her voice rose. "How do you think that makes me feel?"

"I'm busy, Mom. What do you want?" He swiveled to look out the window. Usually, his eyes searched the skies, as if seeking his freedom. Now he searched the distant trees for a glance of one slender woman or one sleek gray cat.

A sniff came to his ear. "I talked to Caroline this morning and she told me about that woman. You should've called me. This isn't a puppy you've picked up off the street. I don't believe that story about amnesia for one second. It sounds like something out of that soap opera Tory watches. If the woman refuses to see a doctor, there's a reason for it. She must be wanted by the police. Have you thought of that?"

Two weeks, Max told himself. Less. One week and six days from now he'd be gone. "Maybe she's an axe murderer."

"You think you're funny. Let's see who's laughing after you're killed in your bed."

"You'll be laughing, right?"

"I'll be crying. She'll be laughing. If you don't care about your own safety, think of Ted's. This woman could be trouble."

"It's my trouble, my business."

"Isn't that just like a man? Even though you're my oldest, you'll always be my baby. If you hurt, I hurt. You need to take her to the hospital. Right now. At the very least, call the police and tell them about her."

"Mom, I love you but I'm hanging up."

"Max!"

He set the phone down as Ted sauntered into the room, his hands in his pockets. "I caught that. Mom found out, huh? Who told her?"

"I don't want to talk about it." He gave Ted the glare he couldn't give his mother.

Ted raised his palms, hunching his shoulders as if he were ducking a blow. "Fine with me. You want any pizza? If not, I'll finish it off."

"Go ahead, eat the pizza." Max glanced out the window again. Still no Sorcha. Where the hell was she?

An image of her in the tub flashed into his mind. He shut

it off. Later. He'd take it out later. Right now, he needed to focus. She had a head injury and she'd been gone for over an hour. She could be sick.

And what about Belle? Where the hell was she?

"Jeff called." Ted slid into the chair facing the desk. "He wants me to manage the bar."

Max sat up straight. "You turned him down?"

Ted shrugged. "I don't know what else I'd like to do. May as well—"

"I want you to take over Brannigan Enterprises."

Ted shook his head. "I won't leech off you. You've done too much already. I'll still help you out part-time, but you don't need—"

"You're not listening. I don't want you to work for me. I'm handing you the business."

"Jesus, you can't mean that." Ted sat back in his chair, his expression as shocked as if Max's skin had turned blue.

Max stood and peered out the window. Sorcha was walking toward the house, her head held high, her hips swaying. Relief made him stiffen instead of relax. Like a hunting dog spotting a tasty rabbit, he thought, then dismissed it and shifted his attention to Ted.

"You're the first I've told. In less than two weeks I'm out of here. You and Tory are old enough to be on your own. Now it's my turn to follow my dream."

"Well, shit." Ted rubbed the stubble on his jaw. "We were holding you back? All these years?"

"It was my decision. I did what needed to be done."

"What are you going to do?"

"Travel." Max stepped back to his desk, opened the top drawer, pulled out the brochures, tossed them on the desk. "I always wanted to travel, and now I'm going to do it."

Ted picked them up with a dazed look of a boxer who'd staggered out of the ring after an unexpected punch. "Australia? Half a world away." He glanced up, his brows drawing together. "You can't get much farther from home."

"Don't practice your Psych 101 on me. If you don't want the business, I'll sell every piece of real estate we've got."

"You'd do it, too." Ted dropped the colorful brochures

onto the desktop. "Go ahead. I wouldn't be able to do half the job you do. Hell, I'm the screw-up of the family."

Something hardened inside Max, a ball of anger. "I was fourteen when I took over." His voice came out rough and raw, but not as rough and raw as the emotions that heaved inside him. "Going to school during the day, making decisions at night. Mom carrying them out, leaning on me, depending on me. I didn't know anything. If I could do it, you sure the hell can."

"But look how well you did. You were born to do this."

"I was scared as hell. Every day, every decision. And every night I prayed I did the right thing."

"It worked, didn't it? You're made out of hero material. Dad couldn't have done better."

The ball of anger inside Max exploded. He slapped his hands on the desktop and leaned forward, resting his weight on his palms. "You don't know what you're saying. Dad saved us. All of us. If not for him, we'd all be dead."

Ted stared. "What're you talking about? He—"

"Died during a tornado, yes. Died saving our lives."

His jaw dropped, Ted shook his head, his words apparently flown out of his mouth along with a few brain cells.

"Dad hustled Mom and Tory downstairs," Max said. "I pushed you after them. Mom yelled at us to get her jewelry. The storm was worsening, the rain clattering against the windows, the wind whipping against the house. I started to run for her room. Dad caught me and said to forget the jewelry." Nearly twenty years later, he could hear his dad's voice. Urgent and commanding with a thread of fear. He'd never seen his father afraid before that day, and he'd turned back.

Too late. Before he'd taken two steps, a giant's roar had shaken the house, shattering it. Changing their lives forever.

"I was thrown to the floor." His father had cried out his name. He heard it in his mind now, heard the fear and desperation. *Max! Max! Max!* "The house was falling apart, shit swirling. The ceiling blown apart, the refrigerator crashing to the floor. Dad shoved me down and jumped on top of me, his body protecting me from the house." The house that seemed to be alive, attacking them. Killing his father. "He saved me." Saved him as blood leaked from a sliced vein in his leg and he slowly died.

"Why weren't we told his?"

Max shrugged and pushed upright from the desk.

Ted huffed out a mirthless laugh. "Mom. She didn't want us to know about the jewelry. Didn't want us to blame her."

"The jewelry doesn't matter." Max made a dismissing gesture. He felt drained after his outburst. Drained of emotion and energy. "It's time you knew Dad was the real hero. He died for us."

"I guess heroism runs in the family. Now I've got to emulate him as well as you." He shook his head, his eyes still dazed. "That will never happen."

"Emulate one person. Yourself." Max sank into the chair.

Ted leaned forward, his hands clasped, his elbows resting on his spread thighs. "I've handled the apartments and real estate side of the business, but the three times I tried to pick out stocks I lost money. Not like you. Even when the experts strike out and the experts on TV are squawking about double fouls, you're throwing the ball to just the right stock pick."

"I can buy and sell stocks wherever I go," Max said, "but I can't buy and sell Wisconsin real estate when I'm in Sydney or Perth. You're the business major. You handle it."

Ted's brows drew together. "After what you said, I feel like I have to do it."

"You don't have to do anything. Manage the bar if that's what you want. I'll put the real estate end up for sale." Max sat back in the chair, unable to get worked up about it anymore. "It's not the best market right now, but we'll do okay. You can handle the sale, right?"

Ted scowled. "I can handle it, but you know I can't let you do that."

"Sure, you can." He stared into Ted's eyes. "Do what calls to you."

"The only thing that calls to me right now is pizza." Ted's

jaw set, his expression mulish, the way he'd looked as a kid intent on climbing to the top of the tree and refusing to listen to Max. And damned if he hadn't made it, clinging to the branch and laughing, afraid as hell to let go. "I'll do it. I'll take it over."

"You sure?"

"Don't mess with me. I said I'd do it." His jaw unlocked and a smile tugged the corners of his lips. "Jesus, I can't believe I just said that. I don't know what Mom's going to say."

"They won't have a say in it. I bought Mom and Tory out a year ago. I put their money in stocks and silver bars. I can do the same thing with my share—or I can be your silent partner. Your choice. I'm not handing this over to you with baggage."

Ted wiped pretend sweat off his forehead. "That baggage would make me run like the pit bulls of hell were snapping at my heels. I wouldn't want to do what you've done."

"I didn't have a choice." Max leaned back in his chair, gazing at a print of a sailboat on the wall behind Ted. He'd told Ted so much, why not tell him this one thing more? "When Dad was dying, he made me promise to take care of all of you."

"Shit. You couldn't say no. Not after he saved your life."

"No, but you can. Tory's going after what she wants. So am I. Why would I hold you down?"

"Don't worry about me." A light gleamed in Ted's eyes, his face brighter than when he'd come into the office, the most important thing on his mind leftover pizza. "I'm good with people. More outgoing than you. I might even be better than you are."

Laughter nudged the darkness inside Max, shrinking it, though not completely gone. Never completely gone. "I'll put money on it."

Ted's laugh held a trace of self-consciousness. "What about you? You're not staying in Australia forever, are you? Where else are you going? A cruise around the world? Europe? Asia? Alaska? China?"

"All the above." The tension eased from Max's shoulders.

Telling Ted hadn't been so hard. It had even been therapeutic, seeing what happened the night of the tornado through the eyes of an adult instead of a young, hormone-driven teen. "I'm taking a year, maybe two."

"Mom's gonna flip."

"Why do you think I haven't said anything sooner?"

"What about the house? Why let Caroline fix it if you aren't staying?"

"I'll be back. Besides, you'll be here with Belle."

"Me and the cat. Thanks." Ted shook his head, but he grinned. "I don't know if I want to stay here, but I sure as hell know Belle would hate to be anywhere else."

"I can't believe she hasn't returned." Max looked out the window. Sorcha was walking to the back door. "She never liked staying out too long. Any moment, I expect to hear her scratching at the door, yowling at us for not letting her in immediately."

"What about Sorcha?" Ted asked.

Max watched Sorcha disappear into the house before he turned back to Ted. She was a complication he didn't need. "We'll find out where she lives."

"We have the address from her driver's license. Want me to take care of it? It can be my first official duty as manager of Brannigan Enterprises."

"No," Max said sharply. If Sorcha had a fiancé waiting for her, Max wanted to see him, question him. There might be a reason she didn't want to go back. "We'll both go."

"This afternoon?"

"Let's give her one more day." Max got up, hungry for pizza after all. Maybe at the end of the day, she'd tell him the real reason she didn't want to go back to her former life. It was possible she did have amnesia.

But more likely not.

He should think of what he'd do to her when the truth came out, but he must've had more of his brother in him than he'd thought because the image of her in the bathtub popped into his mind and he could only think of one thing. One very enjoyable thing.

Twelve

Caroline pushed away from the wall and hurried to her desk. If Max and Ted glanced into her office on their way to the kitchen, they would assume she'd been working the entire time.

Max was leaving. He was leaving. Shit, shit, shit. Her whole life was shit.

It was all Emery's fault. If he hadn't lost all his money, she'd never have given into the impulse to push him off the hiking trail. And if he'd told her he'd stopped paying his insurance policy, he'd be alive today. Divorce would've been inconvenient, but she wasn't a psycho.

Like her mother always said, "A girl's gotta do what a girl's gotta do."

The worst part about killing Emery was finding out she was still broke. When Max had agreed to fund her interior decorating business, she had wept real tears of joy, confident she'd have him wrapped around her finger by the time the year was up, along with a four-carat diamond ring.

After a lifetime of lousy luck, good luck was finally turning her way. Sure, Max had said he was doing this in Emery's memory, but just because she was a real blond it didn't mean she was stupid. When a man gave a woman money, he wanted something in return.

And now he was leaving.

This was screwing up her plans. She'd thought she'd been making headway with him. That he'd been giving her time to grieve.

Why did rotten things always happen to her?

Her breaths shortened and she felt light-headed, dizzy. She forced herself to breathe slow and easy until her mind cleared and she felt solid. Solid on shaky financial ground. After a childhood of barely scraping by, living in kitchens with cockroaches, buying gowns for the beauty pageants in consignment shops and Goodwill, her mother altering them to fit her, she couldn't stand being poor again.

Poverty shrouded her soul. She couldn't sing or fly or love with the threat of poverty hanging over her head like Lizzie Borden's axe. There had to be some way to catch Max before he flew out of reach. Unattached multimillionaires weren't falling on the ground like dead leaves. The ones that fluttered by were looking for beauty queens in their twenties, not their thirties. It wasn't fair, but in the poker game of life, money trumped beauty.

In her head she heard her mother say, "Whatever it takes, baby, I know you'll do it."

She set her jaw. Damn right she'd do it. She pictured Emery, blood splattered on the hard ground, his arm and leg at awkward angles, his neck twisted.

She would think of something. In the end, she always did.

This time, nothing was going to screw it up.

Belle set the can of tuna on top of the newspaper. Looking down, she saw drawings of people and animals. She moved her tuna to get a better look, then traced her finger over the figure of a cat and dog, wondering what they were saying. She knew the marks inside the cloud above the cat and dog were letters that formed words. How many times had she stretched out on Max's lap, letting him pet her while he read? Even Ted read, although not as much as Max.

If she stared at the letters hard enough, maybe she'd learn how to read, too. If humans could read, it wasn't that hard.

She told herself that out of bravado, but as she stared at the letters, something happened. It felt as if she knew them already. Not from Max but from Sorcha, stored in this body's brain cells. If she looked at them a bit longer, or if someone started her off, she would pick up the knack of reading faster than it used to take her to throw up a hairball.

"You don't know how to read, do you?"

Belle's head snapped up. Max leaned against the doorway, watching her. Gladness welled up from her stomach to her throat, plugging words from coming out. She'd missed him. After dinner last night, Max had disappeared into his office and was still there when she went to sleep in his bed.

For four years, she'd slept with him and now she was sleeping by herself. She didn't like it. Not at all.

Where was Sorcha? She wanted her cat body back.

"Can you read?" he asked again.

She swallowed too fast and tuna caught in her throat, though it was nothing compared to a hairball. She coughed and grabbed the glass of milk she'd poured for herself. For a moment she'd forgotten she was expected to answer when he spoke to her. "No."

He straightened and strolled into the room. "Tuna? For breakfast?"

Belle nodded. Why did everyone think tuna for breakfast was odd? It was delicious.

"Is this a craving? You're not pregnant, are you?"

Belle choked. "No!"

"You honestly can't read?" He flattened one palm on the table and leaned over her.

She nodded. Did he think she lied? Well, when necessary, of course.

"If you're here long enough, I'll see that you get help."

"I'll be here." Forever. She'd be here forever.

Max continued to gaze at her face. Unblinking, she stared back into his blue eyes, the same color of the sky when the sun was the highest.

"What else can't you do?"

She shrugged. Admitting she couldn't do something soured the tuna in her stomach.

"Do you remember how to drive a car?"

Belle blinked several times. The only time she went in

the car with Max was to the vet, imprisoned inside a carrier, yowling the whole time. But she'd seen people drive on TV. You stuck a key in a hole, turned it, stepped on a pedal on the floor, and the car moved forward.

She'd learned how to use the can opener. How much harder could driving a car be?

"Maybe."

"What about—" His lips clamped together, and he moved backward.

Why did Belle have an idea he was going to say "sex"? Maybe because the people in *The Love Chronicles* talked about it a lot. In fact, they talked about it a lot on all the TV shows she'd seen. When she'd been a cat, sex was boring. Now she looked at Max and thought *hmmm*.

She rose from her chair and stepped toward him. Was that what those tingles were about yesterday morning when he saw her in the bathtub? His gaze lowered to her breasts now, as if he were remembering, too, and the tingles started again, like fireflies dancing over her skin.

Did she want to have sex with Max?

But cats didn't have sex with humans. Humans had sex with humans. If she had sex with Max, it could change her. Not her body, but the essence of cat that remained inside this human shell.

She stopped and wrapped her arms over her breasts, not liking this. She was used to doing whatever she wanted whenever she wanted. Now she wanted Max. But she couldn't have him.

Being human was awful. How did they stand it?

The silence stretched into moments. A current of energy crackled between them, like invisible lightning. Then Ted stumbled bleary-eyed into the kitchen.

Max felt the tension ease, like a flame sizzling down. But it didn't go out completely, the heat simmering inside him. Sorcha sat at the table, her lips pressed together, giving nothing away.

"You remember anything?" Ted asked Sorcha.

"I can drive. Maybe."

"We know that. You drove your car into a ditch. Anything about your past and who you are?"

She shook her head, but her eyes flickered and she avoided Ted's gaze. Max wondered what caused the flicker.

"We'll find out something today." Ted strode past her, touching her shoulder. He opened the refrigerator door and took out the orange juice. "Max and I are going to your apartment."

"Apartment?" She frowned at Max, then back to Ted. "How do you know where it is?"

Standing in front of the open refrigerator, Ted took a long swallow from the orange juice container.

"Your driver's license," Max answered for Ted. "You have any objections?"

She shook her head, but her teeth worried her lower lip and her head bent slightly, her expression and silence shouting out her nervousness.

"You don't mind if we use your keys to go inside?" He watched her closely.

She stood, shaking her head so hard her hair lashed out.

"Maybe I'll have you home by tonight," Ted said. "You want to come with us?"

She walked backward until the cupboards stopped her. Her arms crossed over her chest so tightly Max thought they must hurt her breasts.

His jaw setting, he strode from the kitchen. Whatever he and Ted found, he'd think twice before making her go back. As uncomfortable as it was having her around, if she needed his protection, she had it.

She just needed to tell him. He couldn't protect her if he didn't know why she wanted to hide out at his place.

Again the image of her in the bathtub popped into his mind. Naked breasts bobbing, pink-tipped nipples pearling, soft mouth open in an O of surprise.

He willed the image from his mind. He'd do this for any woman, he told himself. Any woman at all.

Thirteen

Belle watched a red monster sing on the TV about people liking his smile.

Humans wanted everyone to like them.

She sat alone in the big room that Tory called a media room and Max and Ted called the man cave. Max and Ted used it mostly to watch games where men tackled each other or hit balls with their hands or wooden sticks. Tory used it to watch *The Love Chronicles*.

A noise like thunder came from the front of the house. Bonnie, the cleaning lady, was roaring through the house with the vacuum cleaner. Belle hunched her shoulders and dug her fingers into a soft pillow shaped like a football. Before she turned into a cat again, she planned to take the vacuum cleaner apart and throw the pieces in the garbage.

On the TV, the monster's friends ran to him, calling, "Elmo! Elmo!"

Belle aimed the remote control at the screen. She pressed but nothing happened. Sometimes her fingers didn't work right. She pressed again, but still nothing happened. She hissed and stood. *The Love Chronicles* wasn't on any of the stations. She might as well leave, as soon as she got this stupid thing—

"Let's sing about the letter B!" the red monster said in his squeaky voice.

Belle's finger froze just above the power button. *The letter B. The monster knew the letters?*

She flopped back onto the couch. Crossing her legs, she gave the monster and his friends a mental command: *Teach me the letters. Teach me to read. I want to know everything.*

The three-story apartment building straddled the edge of the worst part of Milwaukee, giving off a stench of poverty and desolation. Max felt as grim as the neighborhood at the thought of Sorcha living here.

Her name wasn't on the tags for the apartments, so he rang the manager. An emaciated man with a barbed wire tattoo around his neck and a prison pallor told Max he'd been the manager for only two months and he'd never heard of any Sorcha Anders.

Two minutes later and fifty dollars lighter, Max and Ted were being invited into 207B by a woman as plump as the manager was thin. She barely gave Max a glance, her gaze fixed on Ted, a smile creasing her apple cheeks. She was a foot shorter than Ted and a few dozen years older, but she looked at him as if he were a cheese Danish she wanted to devour.

"Mrs. Havenhoch," Max began—

"It's Ms., not Mrs." She patted the tops of her large breasts, not taking her gaze from Ted's face. "You can call me Maria. Come in, come in. Jimmy called and told me why you came to see me. It's not often handsome young men come visiting."

They entered a room crammed with overstuffed furniture and knickknack-laden tables. It wasn't an oasis in a desert, but the scent of poverty that clung to the hallway walls was overcome by an aroma that jump-started Max's salivary glands.

"I just made chocolate chip cookies." Maria pointed at two chairs in the living room. "Sit. I'll bring a plate. Do you want coffee, too? I grind my own."

"No—" Max began.

"Yes," Ted said at the same time.

Maria bustled into the kitchen. Max glared at Ted. He wanted to get the information and get out. He didn't have time for cookies and chitchat.

Ted dropped into a chair. "You're jealous. She likes me better than you. I'm the handsome brother."

"Yeah, but I'm the rich one." Max reluctantly sat, feeling like a leashed dog.

Ted snickered, yanking that leash, when Maria hurried back, carrying a loaded tray. She set it on the coffee table. "Cream or sugar?"

Ted jumped up to help pass a cup of black coffee to Max and take one for himself. Before sipping, Ted wolfed down a chocolate chip cookie and started on the second. Unable to resist, Max chewed one more slowly. It tasted like it came directly from Aunt Bee's Mayberry oven, but that wasn't reason enough to waste their time. He was a busy man with things to do, women to relocate, cats to find.

He swallowed. "You know Sorcha Anders?"

"Do I know Sorcha?" Her eyes rolled and she sat on the love seat, resting her chubby feet in pink fuzzy slippers on the hassock. "Didn't she live next door to me for two years? No matter how much I fed her, she never gained an ounce."

"Then you know where she went when she left here."

A yellow flag of caution rippled across her fleshy face. "Why are you asking?"

Max reached for his wallet in his back pocket. Money again.

Ted leaned forward and aimed his hundred-watt smile at Maria. "She was in a car accident and lost her memory. She's staying at our home and we'd like to hook her up with her family."

"Amnesia?" She looked enthralled. "I never met anyone with amnesia."

Max took his empty hand out of his back pocket and picked up the coffee cup. A thin trickle of steam curled up to his nostrils, the smell of chicory almost as enticing as the Aunt Bee cookies.

"We're trying to help her recover her memory," Ted said.

"Of course, I'll help. What do you want to know? She's a nice girl, never too loud, always ready to hold the door and help carry groceries." Her plump shoulders lifted. "She was sad, though. She had the gift, but to her it was a curse."

"What gift?" Max set his coffee cup down.

"You don't know? She's clairvoyant. That's how she earns her living."

"Jesus," Ted said. "You mean she claimed to be a psychic?"

"She *is* psychic." Maria's abundant bosom swelled. "Last May, almost a year ago now, she had a vision of me counting dollar bills, yelling 'Yahoo!' Well, she told me on a Wednesday and I only play bingo on Fridays. I don't buy lottery tickets, not ever, but I did that day. Won five thousand dollars."

Ted whistled. "Nice."

"And I yelled, 'Yahoo!' just like she said. I tried to give her five hundred. Ten percent, that's fair. But she wouldn't take any. Said all the cookies and cakes and pies I shared with her were worth more than money." She sniffed, her eyes watery.

"She's right." Ted swiped the last cookie from the plate.

Max picked up his coffee cup before Ted snatched that, too.

"That's not what her boyfriend thought," Maria went on. "As soon as I left, I heard him giving her hell for refusing my money. But she never came and asked for it. At least she had that much backbone."

"Boyfriend?" The coffee lost its flavor and Max returned the cup to its saucer.

Maria's mouth twisted with disgust. "She's such a pretty girl, but she hardly went out until she met that man. She knew he was using her, but she didn't care. When a woman gives her heart to a man, sometimes she gives away her brains, too."

Max frowned. That didn't sound like the Sorcha he knew.

Ted leaned toward Maria. "If she was clairvoyant—"

"She couldn't see for herself," Maria said before he could finish. "It's probably a good thing. I don't want to know what's coming. Except for money. Sorcha knew that, and it's why she told me about the money. She's a good girl."

"Do you know where she moved?" Max asked.

"Somewhere on the northwest side." Maria flapped a

chubby hand toward the front window. "She said she'd stop by sometime, but I didn't need to be psychic to guess that wasn't going to happen. People come, people go." Some of her cheer deserted her, like a puffer fish losing its puff. "It's the way of life."

"You know the boyfriend's name?"

Her lips pursed, her forehead rippled. "She wasn't going with him long before she moved out. Some dog name. Stay. Sit. Fetch. Something like that."

Max stood, giving Ted a look that brought him to his feet, too. "Thank you for your cookies and coffee." Max handed her a business card. "If you remember anything else, call me."

"I remembered one thing." She pushed herself up from the chair inch by excruciating inch, the struggle silencing her. Max held out his hand to help her, but she shook her head, her breath panting.

"Are you all right?" Ted asked.

"I'm old on the outside, but here..." She tapped her head. "Up here I'm flirty and thirty. Kris, three doors down, has a story about Sorcha. If you wanna talk to her, I better go with you. She's got a small son and wouldn't let two strange men in her place. Cory loves my cookies. I'll take some with me."

Max glanced at his watch. Ted had been helping him out part-time since he'd been a junior in high school but Max still had a lot to show him. And they needed to go to the bank, and he had to make an appointment with his lawyer. Make it legal. Get the papers signed by both of them. In just one week and five days, he would hop on a plane and fly far away from Wisconsin. He should leave the apartment now.

But he stayed rooted where he stood, waiting for the plump, poky woman. Someone needed to take responsibility for Sorcha before he sent her on her way. Even if he ended up handing her to the fiancé.

Unless the fiancé was the reason behind her memory loss. Maria said he was a user. It wasn't a big step from user to abuser.

Carrying a container of cookies, Maria led them along the

hall and knocked on the neighbor's door. They waited in silence, listening to the muted sounds of traffic from the busy street outside. No one answered. Maria knocked again. Max heard a siren wail. Still no answer.

Reaching over Maria's head, Max knocked hard enough to sting his knuckles. Once, twice, three times.

"Looks like no one's home." Ted smacked Max's arm. "We may as well go. Maria, will you tell your friend—"

The stairwell door clunked open and childish laughter spilled out. They all turned toward the sound, drawn by the pure joy. A dark-haired female pixie stepped into the hall, followed by a smaller version, male, about four years old. The woman blinked at them, the laughter in her face dimming. The boy still giggled as he dashed past her.

"I won!" He spotted Maria. "Cookies!"

He ran to her, his hands out to take the container, ignoring his mother's demand to walk. "Hi, Maria, is that for me?"

"Honey, I told you not to ask for cookies." His mother came up behind him, pulling his arms down.

Maria introduced them and explained why they were there. Max gave Kris his card. She held it as if it were a present from the devil, holding it away from her body with her fingertips, her nose wrinkled. Then her mouth set, the corners down, as though she'd made a decision that she didn't like.

"Come inside." She stuffed the card into her jean pocket. "I owe Sorcha."

Kris and Cory's living room was the twin of Maria's, but theirs seemed roomier with only a couch, a TV, and a child-sized chair. Toys littered the floor, and a blue-and-gold throw didn't disguise the couch's shabbiness.

Maria gave the cookies to Cory, then glanced at a flamingo clock on the wall. "I've got to go. *The Love Chronicles* is on and I hate to miss it."

After Maria bustled out, Kris told Cory to eat the cookies in the kitchen. She gestured to Max and Ted to sit on the couch.

She remained standing, her lips clamped together like a

locked door. Finally she took a deep breath, her slight breasts lifting and falling. "I never believed in psychics or seeing the future, but Sorcha saved Cory's life." She held up a closed fist and opened it, as if she were letting a moth fly free.

Tension gathered in Max's body, his spine not touching the back of the couch. Next to him, Ted leaned forward.

"She was moving out the same weekend Cory and I moved in last October. We passed in the hall, she looked at Cory, and she went white. I swear I never saw anyone lose color like that before. I thought she was going to faint, but she pointed at Cory and said, 'He's the one.'"

Swallowing, Kris glanced toward the kitchen, adjacent to the living room, where the small boy sat at the table devouring a cookie. She dragged her gaze back to them.

"She said she dreamed she was in an operating room and doctors were taking the appendicitis out of a small boy. She saw the boy's face. Cory's face."

"That must've been creepy," Ted said.

Max wanted to clobber him for interrupting, but the pixie was nodding her head.

"I thought she was wacko. I hustled Cory away, but two months later, he had a pain in his stomach that wouldn't go away. At first I thought it was the flu, but then I remembered what she said and took him to the ER." She rubbed her arms, as if trying to warm herself. "It still scares me how close he was to death."

"Freaky," Ted said.

"Do you know where she lives?" Max asked, but she was shaking her head.

"I tried to find her. I wanted to thank her, buy her a bottle of wine or something. But no one knew where she moved." She walked to a desk in the corner that wasn't much bigger than the one Max had in grade school. Scribbling on a scrap of paper, she said, "Here's my name and phone number. If she needs a place to stay, she can live with me and Cory."

"There you go, Max," Ted said. "That's your solution."

Max took the scrap of paper. "I'll let her know, but she'll stay with us until she gets her memory back."

Ted's eyebrows arched. "I thought you didn't believe she had amnesia."

"I don't believe it and I don't disbelieve it."

"You're a fence-sitter," Kris said.

Ted shouted out a laugh.

Max gave him a look that should've stopped his laughter but didn't. "I'm keeping an open mind."

Still laughing, Ted wagged his finger at Max. "What you're keeping, brother, is Sorcha. You sure that's not what you wanted all along?"

Turning his back on Ted, Max thanked Kris and asked her to call if she remembered anything that might help Sorcha. Ted thanked her, too, telling her to come over and visit Sorcha anytime.

"My car's in the shop. Maybe next week."

"Next week she might be gone." Ted shrugged, his easy come, easy go attitude firmly in place. "Bye, Cory," he called, waving.

The small boy waved back, his rounded chin smeared chocolate-chip brown.

Max and Ted walked out of the apartment building in silence, Max frowning as he crossed to his Jeep.

A clairvoyant? A victim? A woman on the run? Who the hell was the woman in his house?

Fourteen

"Here, kitty." Gwen peered into the gap between bushes, straight through to the brick wall of the house. Twisting her head, she looked from side to side, but only saw sharp-needled branches and no cat. She bit her lower lip to keep from crying out. Where would it be?

All day at school, only thoughts of the cat kept her from hating her life like usual. She'd thought of a hundred names for the cat, but couldn't pick one until she found out if it was a boy or a girl. When she and Katie had returned home, Katie had clomped to her room to change into her pants with the elastic waist and a sweatshirt. Gwen had raced to the kitchen and opened a can of salmon. After emptying it into one of her mother's china dessert bowls, she'd hurried outside.

Even if the cat wouldn't come to her yet, she loved it. Maybe today would be the day the cat loved her back.

First she had to find it.

She crawled along the front of the house, looking around the thick branches for a spot of gray fur, poking her hand between the gaps, trying to tempt the cat with the good china and the salmon. "Here, kitty, here, kitty." Sharp needles scraped the backs of her hands, and all she saw was darkness.

What if the cat had left? What if it had a home to go to? Someone else who loved it?

"I can love you better," she whispered. "I can love you lots. Lots and lots and lots."

She got to her feet, careful not to dump the bowl and its

smelly contents, then hurried around to the back of the house. Covered rose bushes and white wrought iron benches circled statues of dead gods and goddesses that stared blindly at Gwen. The rose garden, her mother's landscaper called it. "My garden," Gwen used to call it. Last summer, she'd spent fifty dollars of her own money to buy a bird feeder and bird feed. Katie had said it was educational and even braved the pollen and plant smells to help put it up.

Then Gwen's mother had flown home for a dentist's appointment, said it looked tacky, and thrown it in the trash. A week later, she'd left again.

Now Gwen hated the rose garden. When she was older, she'd have her own garden. Everything would grow wild in it, and she'd have birdhouses and bird feeders everywhere.

"Kitty," she called. "Where are you, kitty? I've got food."

Beyond the garden was a swimming pool, covered until it got warmer. In summer, Katie sat on the side and watched Gwen swim laps, counting to make sure she got enough exercise. The chlorine made Katie's hair feel like straw, so she never went in. Even on the hottest days, Gwen didn't stay in the pool long. Swimming wasn't fun by herself.

She looked past the pool, trying to spot the green-eyed, gray-furred, best-looking cat in the world. The lawn stretched out a quarter mile, according to her father, trees looking like sentinels ringing the property.

On one side was a house where adults with no kids lived. Gwen knew because she'd snuck over there a couple times. She'd even seen them playing in a big pond by the house last July Fourth, splashing and laughing. That night they'd set off fireworks, and she'd watched from her bedroom window.

In the back was a marsh, and the other side was a farmer's field. Last summer he'd planted corn. The year before he'd grown cabbage, and when the wind blew toward their house it carried a stink that made Katie close all the windows in the house.

Where would the cat be? The trees? Her neighbor's? The marsh? The field?

She shuffled back to the front lawn, her shoulders slumped. The cat was gone. After four days of hope, she was alone again.

"Here, kitty. Here, kitty." Her voice was flat, empty of hope. Last night, she'd knelt three feet away while the cat gobbled her food. She'd told herself today was the day the kitty would let her pet it, but that turned out to be a big fat lie.

Sagging against the big maple, she slid onto her butt, not caring about the bark digging into her back. At school today, no one had sat with her at lunch. Katie had only said a dozen sentences to her since breakfast. Her mother and father hadn't called her in ten days. If it weren't for the short notes the new lawyer in charge of their money e-mailed each week, she wouldn't have anyone who cared enough to ask how she was doing. And the lawyer only did it because she got paid.

Was there something so wrong with her that her own mother and father didn't like her?

"Even the cat doesn't like me," she said aloud. She held back the tears that wanted to gush out of her eyes. When she cried her eyes got red and so did her nose. Combined with her big ears, she looked like an ugly, skinny clown.

Carefully, she set the bowl on the short grass. Then she rolled stomach-down on the cold ground and hit it with her fists, again and again.

"Why can't I be like everyone else?" she cried out. "Why? Why doesn't anyone like me?"

Something nudged her thigh. Her fist in the air, she whipped her head around. The cat looked at her with those wide green eyes.

"Kitty?" Gwen stayed in that awkward position, her neck cricking, afraid if she moved the cat would dart away.

The cat rubbed her head against Gwen's thigh and meowed. The kind of meow that said, "I like you."

"Kitty?" Gwen twisted into a sitting position. "Kitty?" She held out her arms and stopped breathing. Would the cat come to her?

She sent a prayer to God. *Please, let the cat come to me. Please.*

Never taking her gaze off Gwen's face, the cat took one dainty step at a time toward her. Slowly, as if it had never done this before, the cat climbed onto Gwen's lap.

Gwen breathed again. Inside her chest, her heart warmed, growing bigger, glowing brighter. Slowly, carefully, she brought her hand up and put it on the back of the cat's neck. Just as slowly, the cat lowered its body onto Gwen's lap. Gwen stroked the length of the cat's back once. When it didn't object, she petted it and petted it. The cat purred, the small body vibrating against Gwen's thighs and tummy.

Only then did Gwen cry. For the first time in her memory, another living being was offering her comfort and affection.

"I love you," she whispered. "I will always love you."

As if it understood her, the cat purred louder.

Phil lied.

He lied to the small boy who opened the door at the duplex where Bob's blackmailer had resided, allowing him to believe he was a reporter. He lied to the boy's harried looking mother who told Phil that her son had nightmares every night since finding the dead body. He lied to the elderly neighbors who claimed to have witnessed a chubby man in a ski mask fleeing in a dark car with muddy license plates.

And for all his lies that he said with a smile and the twisted stomach and the bile rising up his throat, he found nothing.

Dread and regrets and a wonky stomach accompanied him to the motel parking lot. He wasn't cut out for this. He wasn't a reporter. He wasn't a detective. He sure the hell wasn't a murderer.

Even the thought started his stomach twisting and turning, doing a sad, bad dance with only one ending in sight and it wasn't going to be pretty. He rushed out of the car to his room, but didn't make it and threw up his energy shake into the bushes.

In the bathroom, he brushed his teeth so hard his gums bled. Then he unrolled his exercise mat, dropped to the carpet, and did fifty push-ups. His arms not even quivering, he rolled onto his back, sucked in deep breaths for a few seconds, then did sit-ups, the old-fashioned kind, from his head on the floor to a straight sitting position. Fast and furious and ferocious, anything to make him stop feeling and stop thinking. To make his mind a blank.

He didn't count, continuing past the time his muscles strained and his arms trembled and sweat rolled down his face and upper body. Only then did he drop to the mat, and with the right side of his head mashed against it, he allowed the tears to flow.

Because he didn't know if he was doing this because it was the right thing to do. Saving his niece and nephew. Or if he was doing this because of the money. Because God knew he needed it.

If he'd told Bob the truth, that he needed it to help his parents, Bob would never have offered to fund him. Even now, Bob blamed their mother for deserting him. Maybe she should have fought harder for custody, but his mother wasn't a fighter. Still beautiful in her mid-fifties, she liked to say that she was a lover.

To Phil, she was just a love.

A love who needed a hip replacement.

And Phil's father needed his rotary cuff repaired.

And the last time his father's gym had made a profit was two years ago. They were living on their savings, cutting back wherever they could, and one of the first things to go had been insurance. They'd filled out what seemed every state and federal form request for health insurance available and each one was rejected. They hadn't fallen between the cracks, they'd tumbled into the health care system black holes.

The business had been on sale for nine months, but no one wanted to buy a gym that didn't rely on machines for exercise. Phil had tried, with no luck. No one would loan him money and neither would his half brother.

But now his mom and dad would get their operations

before they were crippled beyond repair. He'd save the gym. And it wasn't like he'd be an assassin. He'd be an avenger, a vigilante, killing a blackmailer and a murderer. He'd be saving the lives of his nephew and niece.

He'd be a hero.

A hero who killed a woman.

He cried out, a bellow of pain and denial and anger at himself and the world and most of all God. Then rolled onto his belly and started another fifty push-ups, his tears dripping onto the mat.

Only when his tears dried did a question enter his mind.

Why had Bob worn a ski mask and smeared mud over his license plates?

Fifteen

Turning into his driveway, Max saw a slight figure race out of the trees and swerve onto the middle of the blacktop toward the Jeep, dark hair flying behind her. Sorcha. He stomped on the brakes and rolled down his window.

"Are you trying to get yourself killed?" he snapped.

She glanced past Ted and looked straight at him. "I missed you."

Ted laughed. Frustration gnawed on Max's nerves. What the hell was he going to do with her?

"Get in." He gestured toward the backseat. "Drive to the house with us. What are you doing out here anyway?"

"Looking for your cat." She scrambled inside, leaving the door open.

"You have to shut the door," Ted said.

"Oh." She reached for the handle and pulled.

"Another thing you forgot?" Ted asked.

She shrugged and sat in the middle of the seat, visible in the rearview mirror. She glanced around with a crease on her forehead, as if she were adjusting to a new experience. Max tore his gaze from the mirror and stepped on the gas pedal.

Every day he believed her amnesia story a little more. Simple things like closing the door and eating with a fork seemed new to her.

"Belle doesn't know you," he said. "If she won't come to me, she sure the hell won't come to you." Next to him, Ted pressed the garage door opener.

"Cats like me," Sorcha said. "We understand each other."

"I never understand cats or women." Ted unhooked his seat belt and peered back at Sorcha. "Maybe you can teach me."

Max pulled into the garage. "Maybe not." He heard his voice, hard and sharp-edged.

"You got a problem?" Ted asked.

"Sorcha's injured. She doesn't remember who she is. I don't want you taking advantage of her while she's a guest in my house." He pushed open the car door and jumped out. Subject closed.

Inside the kitchen, Max headed straight to the refrigerator. Ted dropped off a bag on the table and followed on his heels. Max took out the carton of milk and stepped back, Ted stepping forward. The refrigerator dance, Max thought. He wasn't surprised to see Sorcha grab a can of tuna from the pantry.

"You need other food besides tuna and meat," he said.

"Why?"

He gulped from the lip of the carton, then wiped his mouth with the back of his hand. "It's not healthy to have a limited diet."

Ted took the sub leftover from yesterday. "What are you? The nutrition police?"

Max gave Ted a look that should have soured Ted's stomach. The can opener whirred. Max put back the milk and grabbed a wrapped ice cream sandwich from a box in the freezer. On impulse, he grabbed another one.

Leaving the can's lid in the opener, Sorcha grabbed a fork and sat at the table. At least she was using a fork now. Yesterday Caroline had told her she should use a plate, and Ted had asked, "Why dirty one?"

Caroline had stepped back, her brows up, her mouth opening and closing but no words coming out, looking as shocked as if Ted had asked why break the Ten Commandments. Max had turned away to hide a grin. With her casual manners, Sorcha fit in with him and Ted, accepting what they did without a frown or a raised eyebrow and in return not caring what anyone thought of her. Like a guy with strange eating habits in a sexy body.

Max handed her the ice cream sandwich. "Try this."

She turned it around and examined it from every angle, her eyes narrowed with suspicion. He took it back, ripped off the wrapper, and handed to her again.

"Eat."

"What is it?"

"Something good."

"Chocolate and ice cream," Ted said. "Something all women like."

"I'm not all women."

His cheek stuffed with a quarter of the sub sandwich, Ted nodded. "That's for sure."

Max agreed silently. Sorcha wasn't like any woman he knew. If he were a UFO enthusiast, he'd wonder if she was an alien. He bit into his ice cream sandwich, chewed, swallowed. She watched him with her green eyes that reminded him of Belle. "See," he said. "It's good."

Still watching him, she sank her teeth into the corner, taking a tiny bite. Her eyes flared wide. She swallowed. Took a bigger bite. As she tasted, a purr came from her throat. In less than two minutes, she was licking residues of chocolate off her fingers.

"That's wonderful!"

"Knew you'd like it," Max said, watching her suck the tip of her middle finger.

Leaving the can of tuna on the table, Sorcha jumped up, crossed to the freezer, and took out another ice cream sandwich. "Chocolate and ice cream?" she said with her mouth full. "I've heard about them."

"We should've bought more tuna and ice cream instead of books," Ted said.

"Books?" She bit off a giant bite of the ice cream sandwich, then ate greedily.

Max forced himself to turn away. He upended the bag on the table and books tumbled onto the wood top. "For you. Children's books to learn how to read."

"I learned the letter B today! And the number nine." Sorcha rushed to the table, her mouth full with the rest of the ice cream sandwich. Chocolate streaking her hand, she grabbed the top book. Her mouth formed a moue, as if she held a dead animal. "What's this?"

"A favorite. *The Cat in the Hat.*"

"That's silly. Cats don't wear hats."

Ted laughed. "No, they don't."

She dropped the book and grabbed another one. "A dog?"

"A red dog. Clifford. The saleslady said his books are a big hit."

"I don't like dogs." The book thumped to the table.

"Try this one," Ted said. "It's about a train who thought it could."

"Oh." She took the book and held it reverently. "I think I can, too."

Max stood and pushed away from the table. "Ted can teach you how to read. All right with you, Ted?"

Ted glanced at the microwave clock. "Sure, why not? I've got an hour before I have to leave for work. We can get a start."

"Give your notice," Max said.

"Yes, boss. Where you going?" He swiveled to watch Sorcha get up from her seat. "If you're getting another ice cream sandwich, get me one, too."

Instead of walking to the freezer, she turned to Max, her arms raised, her face glowing. She took a dancing leap forward and her body smacked against his. Her arms hugging him, she rubbed her face back and forth against his shoulder.

For a second, he stood as still as a tree, inhaling her honey scent and taking pleasure in the soft thrust of her breasts against his chest. Then he cupped his hands on her shoulders and pried her an inch away.

"I don't need payment for helping you out."

She frowned into his eyes as if she was trying to figure out a puzzle. "It's not payment. I only do what I want to do."

He propelled her back another two inches and stepped to the side.

"Didn't you like it?" she asked, her voice wounded.

"That's not the point. It's not appropriate. You're in my care and I'm not going to take advantage of your gratitude."

Ted made a sound of choked laughter. Max glared at him, glad for the excuse to rip his gaze away from Sorcha's bewildered face. In another second, he might forget his reasons for pushing her away.

She was a complication, and this was the wrong time for complications. The worst time.

"I hope you're enjoying yourself," Max said to Ted, his voice gruff.

Ted glanced out the window. "More than you're going to be in another minute. Guess who's got company?"

Max strode to the window and spotted the redheaded woman climbing out of the beige car. He groaned and Ted laughed again. From the corner of his eye, he caught a movement next to him. He didn't have to look down to know Sorcha stood inches away. He already sensed her, the cells of his body reacting to her nearness.

"You're going to meet my mother," he said.

"I have to warn you." Ted came up on her other side and dropped his arm around her shoulder. "Don't take it personally, but I don't think she'll like you."

She shrugged. "Maybe I won't like her either."

Ted laughed.

Max grimaced. This was going to be as much fun as having his taxes audited.

Sixteen

"So." Rose stood inside the kitchen, her shoulders straight and her head angled back. Even though she was shorter than Belle, Rose looked down her nose at her. "You're the woman who smashed into the ditch and is claiming to have amnesia."

"That's me." Belle scratched her nose, not caring if Rose liked her. Rose never liked her, and that was okay because Belle didn't like her back. Rose always stuck to Max like a refrigerator magnet. She didn't seem to know that grown kittens needed to go off on their own. "I went into the ditch. I have amnesia."

Max rested his hand on Belle's shoulder. "Mom," he said in the same tone of voice he used when he caught Belle nibbling his plants.

"Don't you want to get your memory back?" Rose asked, not taking her eyes from Belle's face.

"I like remembering."

"Then you need to see a doctor. Immediately. Staying in an unfamiliar environment with strangers is going to inhibit your memory."

Belle took a backward step, and Max released her shoulder. Rose better not try to make her leave. Even without her claws, she could take Rose down.

"Mom, this is none of your business," Max said.

Her head high, Belle went to her seat at the kitchen table. Ignoring Rose had always worked when she was a cat. She put her elbows on the table, picked up her fork, and dug into the can of tuna.

"You're my son," Rose was saying. "What you do is always my—" Her voice rose. "What are you doing?"

Belle pulled the fork out of her mouth. Was Rose talking to her?

"She's eating." Ted's voice shook as if he wanted to laugh.

His mother glared at him before turning her I'm-mad-at-you face to Belle. "Apparently you've forgotten your manners." Her gaze took in the ice cream wrappers on the table. "Along with the need to clean up after yourself."

Chewing her tuna, Belle nodded.

Ted clamped his lips together but a laugh snorted out of his nose.

Max's eyebrows met. "Mom, stay out of it."

"This is pathetic. She can't lie around the house all day eating bonbons."

Belle glanced at Ted. "Bonbons?"

"Chocolate," he murmured. "I think."

"I'd like to eat bonbons."

Rose sniffed. "Is she mentally retarded? Caroline said she wasn't quite right in the head."

"That's enough," Max snapped. "There's something you should know. In eleven days I'm leaving and traveling around the world. I'll be gone a year, maybe two."

Belle stopped eating, her breath stuck in her throat.

Rose staggered back two steps, a hand over her left breast. "What?" she gasped out.

"I've kept my promise to Dad. The kids are in their twenties and on their own. They—"

"They certainly are not! Tory can't get a job as a walk-on. And Ted—" She pointed at Ted, her hand shaking. "Ted's a bartender living on tips."

"Good tips," Ted said.

Belle breathed again. She didn't say anything but she stared at Max, a voice in her head shouting, *Nooooooo! You can't go away.*

"I'll continue to take care of the investments for the company and in your names. I'm also putting a lump sum into Tory's bank account that should last at least a year," he said. "As for Ted, you'll be happy to know he's taking over the real estate side of the business."

Rose's lips quivered. "What about me?" she asked, her voice small and thin.

Belle sniffed. Rose always thought of herself above others. Though Belle agreed with that attitude in regard to herself, Rose was the mother of Max, Ted, and Tory. Shouldn't she think of them first? Besides, Rose was human, not a cat.

Another reason to want her cat body back. When she had babies someday, they wouldn't need her time and attention for years and years.

"I'm giving you a lump sum, too, but you don't have to worry." Max's mouth curled down on one side. A smile with no warmth. A winter smile. "If you need financial help, I can transfer funds into your bank account no matter where I am."

"Your father would want you to stay."

Belle grabbed the table edge to keep herself from running to Max, throwing herself on his chest, and demanding he stay.

He had to stay. He was her human.

But she couldn't tell him not to go. Everyone had to do what they chose. Even if they should be staying home and taking care of her.

"Dad would want Max to live his own life." All traces of laughter fled Ted's face.

"What do you know? You were only four when he died. I was his wife." Rose faced Belle, her arms stiff at her sides, her mouth distorted. "You! It's your fault. He's doing this because of you."

"That's enough." Max stepped in front of Belle, shielding her from his mother. "I want you to leave."

"Max. You can't—"

"Right now. You're hysterical and you're rude."

Gasping, she twirled. Her coat spread around her legs and she scuttled out the door, making little crying noises.

"Shit," Ted said.

Max's face looked like a rock. "I knew she wouldn't take it well."

Belle nodded. Rose deserved to be scratched, but if she had scratched Rose, Max would have been angry.

Humans were funny that way.

"Don't worry." Max nodded at her, putting distance between them. "I'll make sure you're taken care of too."

She looked away from him. She wasn't worried about him or anyone else taking care of her. Her sadness came from the black hole growing inside of her when she thought of him leaving.

She turned to Ted. Later she'd think about Max leaving. "Are you going to teach me to read?"

He opened the book on top of one of her discarded ice cream sandwich wrappers. She remembered what Rose had said and grabbed the wrappers.

"Should I put this somewhere?"

"The trash goes under the sink." Max stopped beneath the arch leading to the hall. "The tuna can goes into the recyclable bin in the garage. Ted will show you."

Ted stood. "I'm in charge of garbage, too?"

Max laughed but there wasn't any humor in his voice as he strode from the kitchen.

Ted showed Belle how to rinse out the can, then took her into the garage to show her the green bin in the corner. "Bonnie already did dishes, but the next time we have a load I'll show you how to use the dishwasher."

Speechless, Belle stared at him. Cats didn't do dishes. Cats didn't take out garbage. Cats did whatever they wanted.

She didn't like being human. Not one bit.

Except, perhaps... She marched back into the kitchen, straight for the freezer, and took out an ice cream sandwich. Ice cream and tuna. She held back a human-sized purr.

"Get one for me, too," Ted said, "and I'll teach you how to read."

She nodded at Ted. Even without Max, she would be fine. She still had her home, with or without Max living in it, and nothing was going to make her leave. Nothing.

But despite her thoughts, a small ache formed in her

chest and she hesitated over the wrapped chocolate and ice cream sandwiches, not hungry anymore, the air from the open freezer cold on her skin and her open eyes. And inside, the small ache grew cold, too.

Raindrops plopped on Gwen's head and she leaned forward to protect the kitty on her lap. "I don't care about the rain. But if I don't go inside, Katie will come out after me."

The cat stared at her with her big green eyes. As if it understood every word Gwen said.

"I don't think cats like rain. You wanna go inside? I'll make sure Katie doesn't find you."

The cat still gazed at her, unblinking, trusting. Gwen's heart felt as if a balloon was blowing up inside it, making it bigger and bigger and bigger. "I love you," she whispered.

The cat rubbed the side of her face against Gwen's arm. Then the rain pelted down harder, like wet bullets, and the cat was getting splattered even though Gwen bent over her. She stood, holding the kitty as if it were something precious, something more special than all her mother's jewelry.

Lightning flashed and thunder rumbled like the sky was angry. The clouds thickened, blocking out the sun. On the second floor, a light flicked on in Katie's sitting room. Good, she wasn't studying in the kitchen. Easier to sneak the kitty into the house.

For once, Gwen didn't mind having a nanny who ignored her. For once, it was a good thing.

Twenty minutes later, she was in her own room, changed into dry clothes. She sat on the bed and scratched the cat's ear. It rolled over on her bedspread, showing its belly.

"You're a girl," Gwen said, petting the soft belly and chest, feeling tiny nipples. "What should I name you?" She frowned. What would she want to be named if she were a cat? Then she knew. She'd read a book where a father called his daughter Princess. Not like her own father, who she saw in ten-minute snatches about four times a year.

The cat meowed. Gwen realized she'd stopped petting her, and she started again, her hand sliding down the fur-covered belly. "Princess. How do you like that name?"

This meow had a different sound, as if the cat laughed.

The next second the cat twisted to her feet, leapt off the bed, and scampered under it. "Where—"

The bedroom door opened. "Who are you talking to?" Katie demanded.

Gwen put on her most innocent face. "Myself."

"Just so you don't start answering. Then you'll be in trouble." Katie hooted at her own humor, but her gaze darted around the room. As if she *knew*, Gwen thought.

Gwen grabbed her laptop from the table next to her bed. No way could Katie know. She was probably checking to see if Gwen had snuck in a rock band or something. Like that was going to happen.

The screen powered on and Katie frowned at it.

"Is your homework done?" Katie asked.

"I'm doing it now," Gwen said. Inside her head, she screamed at herself. *Stupid! Stupid!* What if Katie wanted to see what she was doing?

Katie opened her mouth. Her nose wrinkled, her forehead crinkled, and a giant sneeze whooshed out. And another. And another.

"Has Bonnie been dusting in here?" She stepped into the room and ran her fingertip along the top of Gwen's dresser. She let go of her nose and glared at her dust-free finger. She sneezed twice as she backed into the hall. "You don't have any of those plug-in fresheners, do you?"

"No!" Gwen said. As if she'd spend her money for air fresheners when she could spend it on cat treats and cat toys.

"Something is making me sneeze. If you run into any questions, you come to my room. Remember, no TV until your homework is done." Not waiting for a reply, Katie closed the door behind her.

Gwen exhaled, her shoulders relaxing. The cat crawled out from under the bed and hopped back up next to Gwen, her ears perked and her head cocked. Gwen patted her lap, but the cat lay at the foot of the bed, staring at the door.

The lit laptop monitor drew Gwen's attention. She opened her Word program, then clicked on her journal and typed.

I found a cat and named her Princess. I love her, and I know she'll love me. I'm the luckiest girl in the world!

Seventeen

Caroline model-walked through the upscale hotel bar decorated in granite and bamboo. From the corners of her eyes, she saw men shift to follow her movements, their gazes traveling over her body. She held her head high, pheromones sparking from her skin like invisible fireflies. She wasn't the most sexual woman in the world, but she had her needs.

Why shouldn't she feed them? It wasn't likely any of Max's friends would see her and report to him.

Besides, she was hungry. A hunger that gnawed at the base of her throat and the pit of her belly. She could've picked up Chinese takeout or had a pizza delivered, but she wanted something more tonight. Something better. Something richer. Something that would prove she was still beautiful and desirable and didn't have to worry that she soon might not have money to pay her rent.

A woman who wasn't bordering on the edge of poverty.

For this to happen, something had gone wrong in the world.

It was hell to be a woman with a takeout budget and a lobster appetite.

And Max... He'd said he was leaving. She couldn't allow that and would think of something to stop him. But for now, she needed to take care of herself. It was impossible to think when the hunger stuck its claws into her belly and threatened to swallow her whole.

Sitting on a barstool, she glimpsed her gleaming reflection in the tinted glass behind the bar counter. Blond and slender and nearly perfect. An image of a woman who deserved lobster.

In a snap, the bartender stood across the bar from her front, adoration softening his expression. He was cute with curly hair and white teeth and wide shoulders, but though his admiration was sweet enough to gobble up like her favorite Swiss chocolate, she smiled politely and ordered an appletini. Tonight she wasn't looking for cute. Tonight she was looking for rich.

The gnawing in her belly was driving her, whipping her hard.

She glanced at her reflection again and caught movement behind her, a silver-haired man striding to the bar. He pulled a ring off his finger and slipped it into his pants pocket before he took the stool next to her. She didn't turn but kept her gaze on his wavy image. Short hair, tall and fit, a gleam of gold on his wrist, and a look about him that whispered her favorite word. *Money.*

Her skin warmed, her pheromones flared.

The gnawing in her belly subsided and she turned to him with a smile.

Tonight she would have lobster.

And perhaps, if he told her how lovely she was enough times, another hunger would be satisfied.

Max would never know.

Sorcha curled up against Gwen's side, letting herself be petted. She was warm, fed...and loved. It was a tangible thing, the love this gangly, big-eared girl was giving her in whispers, in giggles, in petting, in kisses. Like a starving child at a table weighted down with food, she couldn't get enough of Sorcha.

And all she wanted in return was for Sorcha to be there.

Even Fletcher, the only man who considered her talents a gift instead of a curse, had used her talents for his benefit. People had thought she was crazy to stay with him, that she hadn't known what he was. Of course she'd known. Love never blinded her, it just made her look the other way.

Outside the bedroom window, a bolt of lightning lasered a bright path through the dark night. Inside, a bolt of grief stormed through Sorcha's mind.

Fletcher was dead. She would never see him again.

She meowed plaintively.

"Is something the matter?" Gwen bent her head and nuzzled her nose in Sorcha's neck, then kissed the top of her head. "I wish I knew what you were saying. Then I could make it all better."

A purr hummed from Sorcha's throat, her small body reverberating with it.

This wasn't right. She was a human, for God's sake, not really a cat. What had happened to her and the cat wasn't possible. It was against...well, *everything.*

But just for tonight she would succumb. Just for tonight she would let herself be a cat.

And tomorrow? Tomorrow she'd cast aside her fears and do something to fix it. Because that's what humans did.

Thunder boomed and the ground cracked. Belle glanced up from her book in time to see a flash of light in the darkness outside the window. She thought of Sorcha and frowned. Why hadn't Sorcha come to her? She'd walked outside for hours calling Sorcha's name. Max had walked early this morning and in the evening calling Belle's name. He'd phoned the sheriff's office and the Humane Society in the morning and after dinner again. No one had found a gray cat about four years old—dead or alive.

Belle hoped Sorcha was safe.

She hoped Sorcha was dry.

She hoped Sorcha would come back soon.

In the meantime, she'd discovered something she liked more than catnip, more than eating tuna, and even more than ice cream sandwiches.

Reading.

After she'd read the books Max had bought just for her, Ted had gone into his room and brought out a book about Harry Potter. He'd complimented her on learning so much so quickly, then ruined it by saying her memory was coming back fast. She'd turned up her nose and taken the Harry Potter book, which he'd said was the first one.

Five chapters in, she was turning pages fast, bending forward in the chair, her breaths shallow, her entire attention focused on the words and the story.

"You're reading Harry Potter?"

She started, Max's voice shocking her head up, her jaw open, her heart hammering. The only other time she'd been surprised by a human was the day Caroline had grabbed her. Caroline had snuck in, but Max didn't sneak anywhere. He always strode in boldly.

"Harry Potter is wonderful," she said. "He had a bedroom in a room beneath the stairs. The Dursleys are mean to him."

"You learned how to read that well already?" He frowned, and she wondered if he thought she was faking, like Annette on *The Love Chronicles*.

"I'm not faking anything." She scowled at him. Yes, she was lying, but he should still believe her. He should believe everything she told him.

He remained standing over her, his expression hard instead of soft. She liked soft much better than hard. "Your memory could be coming back."

"Or it could be that I'm very smart." Or brilliant. She'd always suspected she was brilliant. Or perhaps she was tapping into the body's brain cells. Though Sorcha had vacated the body, maybe some of her knowledge remained. Maybe that was why she was catching on so quickly.

She shifted in her chair, then shifted back. She wanted her own knowledge, not Sorcha's.

He grinned and she sucked in her breath, feeling as if she'd been kicked in the heart.

His smile never made her feel this way when she'd been a cat.

Bending down, he grabbed one of the books she'd set

apart. "Did you read this?" He showed her the cover, a cartoon cat in a hat, tall with stripes.

She made a face, though she was glad to talk instead of think. "It's a silly book, the worst ever."

His eyebrows climbed up his forehead and his body relaxed, an odd look on his face that she couldn't place. A good one, not bad. "Sure, it's silly, but everyone loves *The Cat in the Hat.*"

She waved her hand in the air. She didn't care what everyone liked. Everyone was human and didn't know better. "Cats don't wear hats," she said.

He laughed harder than she'd ever heard him in all the years she'd lived with him. Looking at him, she felt the kick in her heart again. She swallowed a scream that said, *No, no, no! I should not feel this way about him.*

"What about a book about a dog?" he asked.

The horror made it easy for her to ignore the kick and remind her that Max was not perfect, though this stupid body seemed to disagree.

"I don't like dogs."

"You remember that, too?"

She glared at him. She supposed it wouldn't be appropriate to give him a warning nip. "I don't remember anything."

One corner of his mouth quirked up. "You look so offended."

She wasn't sure what he meant but she nodded. From his face, offended was a good thing to look like.

"If you change your mind, I saved one of my favorite dog books." His mouth straightened, and his mood changed. "I wish I could forget I'd read it, so I could read it all over again."

His eyes darkened, touching a spot within her heart, making her ache for him and want to say something that would warm his eyes and curl up his mouth again.

"Why?" Her voice sounded funny to her own ears, and she couldn't think of one thing to say that would make him smile. "Why does it make you sad?"

He shook his head and backed up, his face closing. "Just

thinking. It was a favorite of my dad's. I'd better get back to work. I have a lot to do." He gave a sharp nod and left.

She watched him turn into the hall, the ache still heavy in her chest. Frowning, she sat and returned to reading Harry. It stopped her from thinking about what had just happened. It stopped her feeling sad because Max was sad. It stopped her from thinking of the kick in the heart because he'd laughed.

Most of all, it stopped her from thinking how un-catlike she felt when Max was around.

This was not good, not good at all.

Eighteen

Belle read until a crick started in her neck. Standing, she stretched her neck as high as she could, the way she had when she was a cat. She wondered what time it was—then slapped her hand to her mouth.

Cats never cared about time. What was happening to her?

Her fingertips went numb and the book fell to the floor. She started to walk away, but hesitated, thinking of the book on the floor. Rose wasn't here to watch her, so she didn't have to pick up after herself. Humans did that, not cats. Not even dogs did that.

She turned back. She couldn't mistreat Harry Potter. He got enough of that from his uncle, aunt, and cousin. She whipped through the pages until she found where she'd left off, and a yawn came over her, along with a wave of tiredness. She put the open book facedown on the table. In case she found Sorcha tomorrow and changed bodies, she'd try to finish the book before leaving the house.

Then she remembered Ted saying there were six more Harry Potter books.

She put a hand to her throat, feeling sick. But she dropped her hand and lifted her chin. She would not be seduced by Harry Potter into staying human.

She hurried out of the room. Busy reading Harry, she'd missed her usual naps today. No wonder she was unsettled. She needed to sleep.

In the bedroom, she stripped off her clothes, climbed into the bed, pulled up the covers—and knew immediately something was wrong. It smelled different, like spring when buds popped out of trees and birds flew outside the window. Not a horrible smell, but not the right one.

She turned her head into the pillow and breathed.

Max. It didn't smell like Max anymore.

Bonnie had done this. When she'd cleaned the house this morning, she'd changed the sheets and the pillowcases, taking away the old ones with Max's scent.

Belle rolled onto her back, closing her eyes tightly, willing sleep to come. But nothing was right without Max's scent. No matter how many places she'd slept in the house during the last four years, it was Max she'd cuddled against every night.

Her eyes opened. Hissing through her teeth, she flung aside the covers. After flicking on the light, she stalked to the walk-in closet and stepped inside.

She started pulling shirts to her nose, one after another. But they smelled like the sheets and pillowcases. Like spring.

Bonnie again. Did she have to wash everything? Belle didn't want spring, she wanted Max.

There must be something in the bedroom he was using that smelled like him. Max was in his office in the other part of the house, working as usual. If she hurried...

She rushed out of the closet and across the bedroom, poking her head into the hall. No Max in sight. She slipped out of the bedroom and hurried along the hall. Thunder boomed outside. A breeze stirred against her skin. She glanced at her jiggly breasts, not stopping her stride. So what if she was naked? Only humans covered their bodies, trying to compensate for being furless.

Anyway, no one was here to see her.

Passing the bathroom, she heard the sound of running water. In mid-stride, she hesitated. Ted was working at the bar tonight, and she and Max were the only ones in the house. He must have left the office and decided to take a shower.

She strode forward. When he was finished, he'd have to dry off and comb his hair. Hadn't she watched the routine many times? She'd be in and out of his room before he put the towel away.

The first thing she noticed in Max's temporary bedroom was the neatness, clothes picked up, bed made. A sound of frustration came from her throat. Bonnie had been here, too. Then something on the floor on the other side of the bed caught her gaze. Afraid to hope, she hurried around the bed.

Max's jeans! Max's T-shirt! She pounced on the T-shirt. One thing she knew after years of lying on clothes was that T-shirts were softer than jeans. Bringing it to her nose, she rubbed her face in it.

Max. It smelled just like him.

Now she could sleep.

A sound made her turn, still holding the T-shirt against her cheek.

Max stood in the doorway, a towel wrapped around his waist, droplets of water tangled with the curling hairs on his chest.

Her breath stopped.

She'd been looking at him naked for four years. He was the human she'd chosen above all others, so of course he was special. But for the first time, she realized how special. For the first time, she realized the magnificence of the human body.

Max's body.

One of his books had pictures of statues. Men with muscled legs and arms, their shoulders broad. Sculpted men, she'd thought, looking at the photos.

Max was a sculpted man.

She wondered what it would feel like to touch him. Would his muscles be hard? Or just firm? Would his skin be smooth? Would he be warm?

For four years, she'd rubbed his skin, but she'd never noticed any of this. Never cared.

Now she cared.

Warmth flushed through her body, on her skin, under her skin.

Between her human legs.

She wanted to rub against him.

She wanted to get her scent on him.

And his scent on her.

The rain drummed on the window. It was dark outside, but inside there was light. Inside there was Max and there was her. They were the only two people in the world.

People.

Not cats. *People.*

Her stomach felt as if giant claws squeezed it. What was she thinking?

The towel wrapped around Max's waist tented out. He gripped it to keep it from falling. Jesus, he wanted her. She stood only a few feet from his bed, slender and soft and gleaming, holding his T-shirt against her cheek. Her eyes were big, her lips parted. Her nipples budded, rose-colored against an alabaster background.

Perfect. She was perfect.

But why was she here? Why was she holding his T-shirt like it was something precious? And why did that make his need all the more urgent?

"We can't do this," he said, the words dragged out of his mouth.

"What?" Her voice was a husky croak. Her lips were pink and lush.

"Have sex."

She shook her head.

"You don't know who you are. You might have a fiancé, a boyfriend, someone who cares about you, someone you love."

She shook her head again. Her green eyes looked bruised, her expression dazed.

He backed into the hall. If he stayed a minute longer... If she came after him...

But she remained standing as if frozen.

"You'll have to leave the bedroom," he said.

She nodded. Finally, she started walking toward him. He backed up another step. If she brushed against him...

But she glided out the door and down the hall like a sleepwalker. The smooth line of her back, her slender shoulders, her curving hips and buttocks moved farther away from him. And still she held his T-shirt to her cheek.

Torture. Watching her was torture. Letting her walk away was torture.

Only when she turned into his bedroom did he exhale a shuddering breath, feeling as if he'd run a marathon. He wiped his forehead and found he was sweating. And he didn't have to look down to see the boner still tenting his towel.

His jaw clenched. Tomorrow he'd demand an explanation. From the look on her face, she'd been as shocked to see him as he was to see her. But if he saw her tonight, he might forget that and only remember the way she'd looked.

Perfect. As if God had made her just for him.

Nineteen

Max woke with a hard-on. Not the usual half-sized, ready-for-action-if-opportunity-comes hard-on. This was ready-for-action-now.

A dream lingered in his mind, misty and fading. Sorcha had been in it. He remembered that much. And he remembered what she wore, too.

Nothing. She'd held his T-shirt to her cheek, but not one stitch of clothing covered her beautiful body.

He jumped out of bed and very carefully pulled on his jeans. He walked stiff-legged down the hall to the bathroom, shucked the jeans, stepped into the shower, and turned it on.

Belle walked along the hall, stopping outside the bathroom, listening to the rushing water from within. Another shower? She didn't remember him taking so many when she was in her cat body. She'd tried the shower, but liked the bath better with the water jetting out on all her body parts.

A picture formed in her mind of Max in the tub with her, the water jetting out at his body parts.

Her face heated, she hurried through the kitchen and out of the house. The sun shone, warming the earth. The air smelled fresh, as if the rain had washed away the last of the winter. Beneath her shoes, the ground squished, the grass a brighter green than yesterday.

Would she find Sorcha today?

She had to. Quickly. If she didn't change back soon, she might give in to the feelings for Max that were consuming her human body. She couldn't do that. She shouldn't. Because she wasn't human, she was a cat.

"I am a cat," she whispered fiercely. "I am."

Reaching the trees, she paused. She'd already searched in both directions. Toward the house that looked like a castle on one side where no one seemed to live and, on the other side, the house with peeling white paint and two unleashed dogs, big and mean, their barks ferocious.

Belle turned toward the mini-castle. When she called Sorcha's name, her voice rang with urgency. Leaving Max last night, step by horrible step, had felt like slogging through mud. Only his T-shirt on her cheek had allowed her to leave the bedroom, taking a part of him with her.

She wasn't used to denying herself. If she wanted something, she took it. If she wanted to do something, she did it. It was her nature.

Now she wanted something in a way she'd never wanted something before.

She didn't know how long she could resist this feeling she had for Max. It was like the rain last night. Relentless, pounding, flashing with lightning and thunder.

"Sorcha!" she called. "Sorcha! Come to me, Sorcha. Hurry."

Hurry before it's too late.

Caroline was in her happy place, a store dressing room, trying on designer clothes that someone else was buying for her. So far she'd chosen a silver Stella McCarthy trench coat, black silky slacks, and a scooped neck purple top. Now she was sipping tea while the efficient store stylist searched for two dresses that would fit and flatter her.

Wanting to purr like a kitten, Caroline took out her cell phone and speed-dialed Max. She got his voice mail. Her mouth tightened, but she glanced at her long-legged reflection in the mirror and the tension gathering in her chest loosened.

"Max," she said, "I'll be in Chicago today and tonight. Perhaps tomorrow. I'm going to a design convention and will be staying with a friend I knew from the pageant circuit." A warning whispered in her mind. *Keep it simple.* "She wants decorating advice, I'm afraid, but she's a sweetheart and I can't deny her." Heels tapped on the floor outside the dressing room and wheels creaked. "If you need me, call and I'll come. You know you're my priority."

She grimaced and hung up before she said anything more. What had she been thinking? She sounded desperate. As desperate as she felt, knowing he was slipping away so soon. In less than a minute, she'd gone from purring to crazy.

It was good she wasn't at Max's house today. She was out of control.

The store's stylist pushed a wheeled garment rack loaded with dresses into the dressing room. Caroline's sinking heart rose to its proper place. She felt like Julia Roberts' character in *Pretty Woman.* Except, of course, Caroline wasn't a hooker. She was just a widow who needed to be spoiled a bit.

The stylist handed her a lacy top, babbling that light blue was Caroline's perfect color. Caroline took the top with a smile. This was the life she should be living every day. She needed a man to give it to her. And she could think of only one.

Not her temporary lover. Before the week ended, he would be heading back to his pianist wife in Boston.

It was Max, of course. Max, who was young and virile. Max, who would always take care of her. Max, who would never throw away his money on unwise investments.

She was so tired of things going wrong for her. If by some chance he didn't succumb, she would talk to her mother. Brenda was good at making wrong things go right.

Like Brenda said, it was amazing what determination and desire could do—if you were willing to go all the way and beyond.

Out of nowhere, a memory returned. She was twelve and a pageant judge had wanted to take pictures of her in his home. His staring eyes had given her a sick feeling in her stomach, but Brenda had insisted she go, that it was just a few pictures and would be worth it.

She blanked the rest of the memories, but her skin became clammy and bile rose in her throat.

"Are you all right?" the stylist asked.

She nodded and swallowed the bile, then grabbed the glass of water the stylist handed her. A real glass, not a plastic bottle.

Her sweating stopped. Like her mother always said, "A girl's gotta do what a girl's gotta do."

And she had won the title, so Brenda was right once again. It had been worth what had happened in the room with the photos and the bed and the judge with his skinny hairy legs and bad breath. She'd just learned the lessons of life younger than most.

She set down the glass and admired a slinky dress the stylist said would look perfect on her.

She stood to try it on. Yes, it would look perfect. And, yes, it was worth it.

Phil's stomach felt like a parade ground for a troop of parasites, stomping and chomping. He sat at the small table in his motel room, looking out the window at the three-quarter filled parking lot, watching cars and trucks speeding on the highway. Wishing he were in one of them, racing far away from his half brother who'd kept him on hold for the last ten minutes.

The phone clicked, Bob back. "Any progress?" he asked.

"I called the area hospitals, with no luck. So I checked car repair places and found out her car was towed. I have the address of the guy who paid for it."

"I knew you'd do it." Excitement energized Bob's voice. "You're the only person I can trust with a job of this magnitude."

The parasites in Phil's stomach doubled. "I have a question. Why did you wear a ski mask and muddy your license plates?"

A sharp inhale came over the phone. There was a pause before Bob replied. "I hate to tell you. You'll think I'm an idiot."

He paused and Phil remained silent, his eyebrows contracting so tightly he could feel his skin creasing.

"She told me she was seeing another high-profile client, and she suspected she was being watched. That was the reason she wanted me to come to her instead of her coming to me. And if someone was skulking in the bushes taking pictures, she thought it would be wise for me to wear a ski mask."

Phil didn't reply, running Bob's words through his mind, looking for holes, for chasms, for the feeling in his gut that it was wrong or right. Not finding any of it or anything at all. Just a blank wall.

"It's the truth," Bob said. "I swear on Danny's and Lorna's lives."

"Okay," Phil said. "Okay."

"Okay, you believe me? Say it, Phil, say it."

"I believe you." The words wrenched out of his throat.

"Good. You're doing the right thing. I know you'll do whatever you can to help me. We're family. Blood. And so are Lorna and Danny. You wouldn't want to see anything bad happen to them."

"No," Phil said, but it was a whisper of a word. He cleared his throat and said it louder. "No, I wouldn't. Not if I can help it."

"You can. Only you. No one else but you can do it. And not for the money, though I'll keep my part of the deal and give it to you. It's good for me to know that you're doing it because it's the right thing to do."

Phil nodded. They said good-bye and he hung up.

He buried his head in his palms and hoped to hell that Bob was right. Because he wasn't sure he would have agreed to do it if the money were out of the equation.

Do *it*. Kill.

If he couldn't even name the act of murder, how could he do it?

Sweat prickled under his armpits and his neck. He would do it. He had to do it for Lorna and Danny. It wasn't as if he could go to the police. They would never believe him.

And the money... He couldn't turn down that either. His mom and dad needed it too much.

He grabbed his jacket and strode outside. But even though he gulped in fresh air, the parasitic troop continued its march through his stomach, chomping and poking his stomach lining with baronets, inflicting pain that he knew he deserved.

"You can't go outside," Gwen said to Sorcha at the back door.

Katie honked the horn. Sorcha jumped. Everything Katie did made her jump. What parent hired someone like Katie to be their only child's nanny? Then left her with them for months at a time? The robots in the Star War movies had more compassion than Katie.

"You have to stay in here." Gwen squeezed through the back door, blocking the opening with her foot. "We're just going to stupid dance lessons. I won't be too long."

Sorcha leaped over Gwen's outthrust leg.

"No!" Gwen called. "Come back!"

The horn honked again. Sorcha sprinted across the backyard, away from the house and the car...and one small girl who already loved her too much.

Twenty

Sorcha heard a backpack thump on the stone path, then running footsteps.

"Don't run away. Come back!" Tears thickened Gwen's voice, but Sorcha kept running. She had to. If she stayed, she'd be trapped in this cat body.

The car honked three times, blaring impatience through the country air.

"I love you!" Gwen called.

Sorcha reached the line of evergreens that edged the green lawn. She swiveled and crouched, peeking through the tall blades of grass. Gwen was picking up her bag with her ballet shoes, her shoulders slumped. She crossed the yard toward the driveway as the car horn blasted angrily. At the corner of the house, Gwen glanced back. Her face was to Sorcha, too far away for Sorcha to see clearly, but she imagined tears made tracks down the thin cheeks.

I'm sorry. Sorcha tried hard to send her apology, picturing her silent words flying through the air, from her mind to Gwen's.

She should never have comforted Gwen yesterday. Fletcher had always said she was too soft and that's why she needed him to take care of her. But how could Sorcha resist Gwen's cry for affection? Especially since she understood how it felt to be rejected by the people who were supposed to love her most.

The car door slammed shut. A second later, the car took off along the long driveway.

As if freed from a spell by an evil witch who looked just

like Katie, Sorcha sped toward the road, away from the trees where dangerous animals might be lurking. What if she saw a skunk? Even worse, what if it saw her and sprayed her? Did raccoons dislike cats? She had no clue, but it wasn't something she wanted to find out up close and personal.

Just as she reached the edge of the road, a car sped around the bend. Her heart thumping, she jumped into the ditch, cowering until the car passed. She started to climb up when she heard the roar of another car.

Making a snap decision, she changed direction, leaping into the thicket of trees lining the roadside. The tall branches cut off the sun, making it ten degrees cooler. Even so, it was warmer than just a couple days ago. The air smelled different, too. It smelled green, as if buds were popping out and grasses were growing. Spring had sprung, she thought, the world reborn for another year.

She was reborn, too, but in another body.

The way back seemed shorter than the other day when she'd been scared, exhausted, and grieving. She hadn't cared what happened to her. After all, Fletch was gone. Why should she go on living?

Yet she had run from Deavers, clinging to her life, miserable as it was. She'd run because she was frightened of dying, because she was as wicked as her parents said she was.

At every rustle, her heart pounded like a percussion drum. Time didn't matter in the cat body and neither did miles. But it seemed as if she ran too long and too far before she stumbled onto a piece of a fender. Immediately she knew it was from her car. She stopped and sniffed it, rubbing her cheek against it, compelled to mark it with her scent.

This was where the accident had happened. The spot where she and Belle had changed bodies.

Her spine shivered, the pads of her paws numbing. She wondered what had happened to the cat inside her body. She glanced around. Through the trees, she spotted a ranch house set back in a clearing. That was it. Where Belle must be from. Where she would return to.

The rumble of a car engine made her glance back at the

road. Instead of zipping past, tires rolled over gravel and a car, white and anonymous-looking, pulled onto the shoulder. The car door opened, a loud click that made Sorcha leap backward. As she searched for a place to hide, shoes crunched over twigs and leaves. Her claws extended. Acting by instinct, she raced up a tree trunk.

The footsteps stopped beneath the tree. Sorcha hugged a branch the size of her thigh when she'd been human. She stared straight down at a man's thick brown hair, no receding hairline, no bare spot on the crown.

Not Deavers.

Her frantic heartbeat slowed. This man wore a dark shirt, jeans, and a light jacket. Even as a cat she noticed his muscles, the straight spine, and the tightness of his butt. At least a dozen years younger than Deavers, she thought, relaxing even more. Then he looked up.

A stab of fear pierced her. She knew that face. She'd seen it in Deavers' office, in a four-by-six-inch frame, an aw-gosh-ma'am smile on his face. She'd wondered why the photo was stuck away in the corner of his desk, as if Deavers was distancing himself from the connection. Compelled by a feeling this might be important, she'd asked Deavers who it was.

"My half brother," he said. Usually Deavers acted like he was up for the Mr. Congeniality award, but that day he'd given her a dark look and changed the subject.

She hadn't delved into the strange vibe. She avoided knowing anything more than necessary about her clients, wanting her readings to be unaffected by her knowledge. And now it was too late to find out anything more.

But she didn't need a return of her psychic powers to guess why Deavers' half brother was here.

To finish the job Deavers had started.

To kill her.

She made herself smaller, flattening her body on the branch while digging four pairs of claws deeper into the rough bark. He continued walking away from the car. Stopping at the edge of the tree line and looking past the expanse of wild grasses to the sprawling house, he pulled a small pair of binoculars out of his jacket pocket and raised them to his eyes.

Fear closed her throat, her heartbeat thundering in her small body, though she knew he wasn't looking for Sorcha-the-cat but Sorcha-the-woman.

"Ready for action," he murmured and hiked toward the road.

She'd never made demands in her human body, but felt compelled to send demands to his back: *What are you going to do? Say something! Right now!*

He glanced over his shoulder, his expression puzzled. "I don't want to do this. But I have to."

That wasn't what she'd hoped he would say. She'd wanted him to say he was leaving and never coming back.

She remained in the tree and watched him climb up the ditch to his car. After he drove off, she waited long moments before retracting her claws from the branch and scampering down the trunk.

On the ground, she hesitated. She couldn't go to the house and look for the cat in her body. Belle, that was the name the two men had called her the day of the accident. The same name the one man had been calling every day, looking for his missing cat.

If she went down and found Belle and they switched bodies, Deavers' brother would find her and then he'd kill her.

She took a longing look at the house. What if Deavers' brother killed Belle, believing Belle was her? Belle's death would be on her conscience. Her cat conscience. Because if Belle was dead, they couldn't change bodies.

Being a cat for the rest of her life would be her punishment for being too frightened to act.

"Sorcha," a woman's voice called. "Where are you, Sorcha? You know you have to come to me."

Sorcha froze. It was Belle looking for her again, the way she did every day. She should go to Belle so they could change bodies. It was the right thing to do.

The sound of crunching leaves carried to her sensitive ears.

Making an involuntary screech, Sorcha jumped, her fight-or-flight response kicking in. Or maybe it was her new body's feline survival instincts.

"Sorcha!" Belle called.

Shoes crashed over twigs and branches that had broken off during the storm. Looking toward the noise, Sorcha saw a slender female running straight toward her. Her own image as a human.

A silent alarm blared in her mind, loud and scary, impossible to ignore.

"Sorcha!"

Her heartbeat jackhammering in her ears, Sorcha pivoted and darted between trees, leaping gracefully over rocks and fallen branches, going back to the one place she felt safe.

"Come back." Belle's voice sounded more distant with each word. "We have to switch before it's too late. You have to come back."

Sorcha kept running. She should stay but all her instincts screamed at her to run, and she was listening. Danger was behind her. Safety was in front of her. Fletcher always called her a fraidycat, and he was right. Besides, she didn't *have* to do anything. When she was a human she had to do what she didn't want. But right now she wasn't a human.

She was a cat.

Twenty-one

A young woman with a smile like a sunbeam and bouncing red hair danced into the great room where Belle sat with a Harry Potter book on her lap. Tory! It was Tory! An "eep" came out of Belle's throat, and she slapped both hands over her mouth.

She stood and the book tumbled off her lap onto the carpet. With a swoop, she bent and grabbed the book, then smoothed out a crumpled corner instead of dashing over and rubbing her head against Tory's shoulder. She suspected Tory wouldn't understand.

"You must be Sorcha." Tory sprinted across the Oriental carpet.

As Tory's arms curved over her shoulders, Belle's breath caught. Did Tory know she was really Belle? Was that why she was hugging her?

It didn't matter. Belle squeezed her back. She missed being petted and hugged.

Tory drew back. "Did you really lose your memory? That must be horrible. And my mom's freaking. Jeez, sometimes I don't think she ever heard of the feminist revolution. The way she acts, you'd think she's seventy-five instead of fifty-five."

Belle blinked.

"I can't believe Max is letting you stay here," Tory went on. "It's like him to think he can fix the world, but even he has his limits. I think he must be hot for you. How do you feel about him? You like him?"

I love him. He's my Max. "Yes."

"He's pretty hot, huh?"

Belle thought of him last night with the towel wrapped around his hips and the bulge poking at the towel. As if she didn't know what *that* was.

She nodded vigorously. Max was very hot.

Ted sauntered into the room. "Getting personal, aren't you?"

"Who asked you?" Tory glared at him like he was a disgusting bug. With a sniff, she turned back to Belle. "Max says he's going away. Are you going with him?"

Leave home? Belle shook her head. *Never.*

"First she has to be asked." Max stood in the entryway, his voice dry like the inside of the house in winter. "What are you doing here?"

"Max!" Tory flew across the room and hugged him.

"Well?" His lips didn't smile, but the skin around his blue eyes crinkled and a glow sparked in his eyes.

"It's Mom. She called last night and ordered me to come home."

"Ordered? Since when did you start listening to Mom's orders?"

"She paid for my plane ticket."

Ted whistled. "When Mom shells out money, you know it's serious."

Tory rubbed her thumb and fingers together. "Dimes squeak when they leave her clutches."

"Why?" Still standing in the entryway, Max crossed his arms over his chest.

"To talk you out of leaving."

"Will you?"

She beamed at him. "I think you should do whatever you want."

"'Atta girl." Ted slung his arm around her shoulder and gave her a one-armed hug. "You've got style."

"You could've told me that over the phone." Max lowered his head, the way he did when something bothered him. "Why aren't you busy being the next Broadway star?"

Belle stared at Max, who looked away so fixedly she knew it was on purpose. This was the first time she'd seen him since last night. She'd been outside most of the day, searching for Sorcha until the soles of her feet were sore and her calves hurt. When she'd finally returned to the house, she'd eaten tuna and an ice cream sandwich, drunk water, napped, and took a bath. She'd been reading the second Harry Potter book for only a few minutes when Tory had come in.

Why didn't Max want to look at her? He'd looked at her last night. And she'd looked right back.

She knew it was wrong, the way she'd felt. The way she still felt. Like a woman, not a cat. But Max didn't know she was a cat. How did he know this feeling was wrong?

"Someone has to be on your side," Tory said, her voice strained.

Ted grabbed her suitcase. "You're getting the room in the back. If you complain about how small it is, I'm taking you to Mom's."

"It's still bigger than my studio." Tory made a face. "I hate it. I really hate it."

Max became still. Then he nodded. "We need to talk. Come into my office."

A half laugh, half sob came out of Tory's throat, and she rubbed her hand over her eyes. "Not now. I'm tired and might say things I'm sorry for later."

"Good. Maybe you'll tell it to me without the bullshit."

Her lower lip trembled. "Please, Max."

He stared at her for a long moment before nodding. "Okay, later."

With another sobbing laugh, Tory dashed after Ted, leaving Max and Belle in the living room.

Now he looked straight at her, and he kept looking.

She looked back. If he wanted a staring contest, he'd lose.

His eyelids closed and opened. "How's the book?"

"Wonderful." She glanced at the book and swallowed. When she was a cat again, she'd miss Harry. Maybe she'd skip searching for Sorcha tomorrow and stay home and read the next book instead.

No, no, no! What was she thinking? She needed to find Sorcha and switch bodies.

"Harry's in big trouble," she said.

Max nodded, his arms still crossed, his shoulders hunched. The thought came to Belle that he was holding himself back. But back from what?

"You can read any of my books." He nodded at the shelf. "One of the books about other countries might jog your memory."

"Oh no." Stepping back, she shook her head. "I don't like other countries. I like it right here."

"That's a strong reaction."

"This is my home." She jabbed her pointed index finger at the floor. "I don't ever want to leave."

"This isn't your home," he said, his voice low, his blue eyes darkening with emotion as he watched her face. "As soon as we find where yours is, you'll have to leave."

She closed her mouth in a tight line. *I'll never leave.*

A thought slammed into her mind. What if Sorcha felt the same way about her home? What if she returned to the place she loved? Although that didn't make sense. If Sorcha wanted to switch back to her old body, she should stay instead of leave. But even though Sorcha was inside a cat body, she was still human. Who knew why humans did some of the things they did?

Belle's eyes burned. She felt something she'd never felt as a cat—uncertainty.

Max was watching her, the expression on his face hard, and she jutted her chin. She didn't need *hard*. She needed *petting*.

"Will you hold me?" she asked.

His muscles tightened and his face turned even harder, like one of the stones on the fireplace. "I might not stop at holding."

She knew what he meant. Kissing. Touching. Rubbing body against body.

The burn traveled from her eyes down to the warm place between her legs. She stared into his blazing eyes.

He swore under his breath and stomped out of the room. She swallowed, then sat, picked up Harry's book, and started reading again.

But inside her, the human body itched with an odd emotion that made her throat clog, her shoulders hunch, and her heart feel as though a giant claw reached inside her chest and squeezed.

She didn't like it. Didn't like it at all.

"I'm too busy," Max said into the phone. The spreadsheet on his monitor caught his attention. He should've finished yesterday. This was supposed to be his time for knotting loose ends and training Ted. Between searching for Belle and trying to find a safe place for Sorcha, he was falling behind schedule, his normal tightly held control slip-sliding away.

"Tory's only here for the weekend." Rose had a stubborn note in her voice. "If you have a date, you can bring her along."

"It's not a date, it's work." Max decided not to tell her Tory was extending her visit. Let Tory do her own dirty work.

An exhalation gusted over the phone. "I'm not asking for the sun." Rose's imperious tone changed to a wheedle. "I'm asking for one dinner. When was the last time we got together as a family?"

He swore silently. She had him, dammit. "Okay, okay, I'll go." But it wasn't changing a thing.

"Wonderful! I made reservations for seven tonight at Morrie's."

He glanced at his watch. Two hours away. And Morrie's, the most expensive restaurant in the county. For which he'd be expected to pay.

"I made reservations for four," she continued, "but Ted has to work. I'll be pleased when he starts working exclusively for you. Bartending is no kind of job for a college graduate." Her voice raised an octave. "I know! I'll call Caroline. She can take Ted's place. It makes sense. She's already one of the family."

"Caroline's visiting a friend in Chicago. But don't worry. It'll be four without Caroline."

"You're not bringing *her*."

"Sorcha is my guest."

"But, Max—"

"See you in two hours." As he hung up the phone, he realized with a sense of sadness that he didn't like his mother. She was manipulative, clinging...and frightened.

"Promise me you'll take care of them." His father's voice murmured weakly in his mind. He was fourteen again, looking down at his father lying on the floor, the microwave that had slammed into his father's head turned on its side, debris all around them. A jagged branch from one of the trees outside sticking into his right thigh. The air eerily still after the giant roar of the storm.

"I promise," he said, half crying, tears streaming down his face. "I promise."

"Your mom, too." The three words came out in a thin whisper. Blood pooled out of his leg. Twenty years later, Max could smell the coppery blood, taste his own fear, see the life force fading from his father's eyes.

"I promise," Max said. "I promise."

The voices vanished. The image faded and disappeared, and Max was looking at the spreadsheet on his monitor again, his teeth clamped so tightly his cheekbones hurt.

He'd kept his word. For twenty years he'd kept it. When was it going to end?

"I won't go." Belle shuddered. Why was Max trying to make her leave?

She stood in the middle of the back room where Tory was throwing clothes onto the pulled-out sofa bed.

"We look about the same size," Tory said. "Do you diet like crazy, too? Oooh, this top will look terrific on you. It'll bring out your green eyes."

Belle clasped her hands together in front of her waist and braced her feet. "I'm not going."

"You will." Max stood just inside the doorway, blocking her route of escape, his thumbs looped inside his belt.

Tory laughed. "You may as well give in. The only one who doesn't let Max get his way is Belle."

For the first time since Max had hauled her in here, saying Tory was going to dress her so they could go out to dinner, Belle smiled.

"No," she said.

"Yes," Max said.

"Every woman likes to dress up and go out to dinner." Tory plopped onto the bed, the mattress bouncing. "We can share a dessert. Something chocolate."

"No."

"I get it! You're afraid someone will see you."

"I'm not afraid of anything."

"Then stop arguing and go," Max said.

"Your mother doesn't like me."

"I won't let her make you feel uncomfortable."

Tory laughed, a sound like music. "Who do you think you are? Superman? You'd have better luck stopping a speeding train and jumping tall buildings."

"Sorcha is coming. She can't stay cooped up here."

"I was out all day," Belle said.

Max watched her closely, the way she would watch for a mouse she was waiting to catch. "You are afraid." His voice and his expression softened. "All right, I won't force you." He nodded at Tory, the softness disappearing. "Get dressed. We don't want to be late." He strode out of the open door without glancing back.

"Wow!" Tory stood. "Max backed down. That never happens. How does that make you feel?"

Belle bit her lip. She should be feeling smug. Why wasn't she? Was this human body changing her already?

"I'm going." She reached for the green top. She was Belle. She wasn't afraid of anything.

Phil tramped away from the one-story house, his shoulders hunched to shield him against the biting wind. The sun was lowering and no one was answering the door.

He should have gone to the house earlier today when he'd seen the garage door open. Should have given them the brother-looking-for-his-scatterbrained-sister story that he'd made up. But he knew what had held him back.

They might tell him where Sorcha Anders was. He had the kind of face people trusted. A boy-next-door openness that matched his character. No one looking at him would think he was a murderer.

But that's just what he would be.

He shuddered, colder inside than out, cold all the way to the marrow of his bones. All the way to his heart.

He slid into his car and pulled the door closed, shutting out the chilly wind. But his heart still felt cold. Encased in ice while his stomach burned.

Putting his elbows on the steering wheel, he dropped his head into his hands, his palms pressing against his forehead. "Help me do what's right, God," he whispered. He wasn't particularly religious, but he believed in emergency prayers, and this one was life-or-death. "Help me."

He waited for long moments, but no answer came, no insights, no visions. Just the eerie whistle of the wind that reminded him of a sound bite in an old horror movie, just before the monster stomped on scene and ate the village natives.

Twenty-two

Another woman would have been nervous sitting in the restaurant, eating strange food with implements she'd never used in her life and wearing clothes she'd never thought of putting on. But another woman wouldn't have been a cat in a woman's body. And another woman wouldn't have seen more scenes like this in *The Love Chronicles* than she could count.

Belle glanced down at the clinging green top and black pants that Max had looked too long at when she'd walked out of Tory's bedroom, staggering a bit in Tory's impossible shoes and wondering what was wrong with humans that they did this to themselves.

"Aren't you eating your salad?" Rose asked.

Since she was the only one not eating her salad, Belle glanced across the table at Max's mother. This was the first time Rose had spoken to her tonight.

"No," she said.

Tory laughed.

"Vegetables are your most important part of the meal." Rose stuck her fork in the green stuff on the plate in front of her. "They give you most of your vitamins and antioxidants."

Belle let her sniff tell Rose what she thought of her opinion.

"Puhlease." Tory made a face. "No lectures tonight or I'll gag."

"You'll appreciate me when you're a mother," Rose began.

Belle zoned Rose out, glancing around the restaurant.

People sat around tables covered with white linen, everyone talking and drinking and eating in groups. Just like in *The Love Chronicles* when Maureen caught Jake with her identical twin, Darlene, and threw wine into their faces.

Rose picked up her glass of wine. Belle sat back so if Rose threw it at her, the wine would hit Max, who sat on Belle's right, eating his salad. But Rose lifted the glass to her lips. Belle picked up her own glass and sipped.

"Ptewy!" She spat it back into the glass, but the bad taste still filled her mouth. "Ptewy, ptewy, ptewy."

Rose sat back in her chair. "Oh my God. I'm so embarrassed."

"Are you okay?" Max leaned over her, his hand on her back.

"Here, have some water." Tory picked up Belle's water glass and handed it to her.

Belle gulped it down. Maybe she wasn't as ready for this new experience as she'd thought. From now on, it would be tuna and ice cream sandwiches, nothing else.

She wiped her lips with the back of her hand. "That was awful."

"You obviously know nothing about wine." Rose tilted her glass. "It's smooth, it's fruity, it's—"

"Sour and yucky," Belle said.

Tory giggled. Max chuckled.

"You may be a philistine," Rose said, her nostrils quivering, "but at least you're not an alcoholic."

Max's chuckle stopped. "You're being rude to my guest."

Rose set down her fork. "I don't know what you're thinking. Taking a stranger into your house is irresponsible and impulsive, not like you."

"It's exactly like Max." Tory waved her fork like a tree branch in the wind. "He took in Belle when she was a kitten."

"This is a woman, not a stray cat."

A strangled laugh came from Belle's throat. Max's face turned hard, his eyebrows lowering in a way that Belle knew was not good for Rose. Tory stabbed the fork into her salad like she wanted to murder it.

"You're so full of baloney," she said.

"Tory!" Rose raised her hands to her cheeks.

The groupings of people sitting around tables at either side of them shifted, heads swiveling toward them.

Their server trotted over. "Is everything all right?"

"Just fine." Max nodded at Belle. "Could you bring her a glass of milk?"

Max had expected that his mother would restrain herself in the restaurant. It wasn't the first time he'd overestimated her good sense.

"Mom," he said, his voice low, "you taught me better manners than the way you're behaving toward Sorcha."

Her cheeks flushed pinker than the four carnations in the vase on their table.

"Yeah." Tory grinned. "Especially when Max is paying for dinner."

Rose gave Max a pained look as the waiter came with Sorcha's milk. Sorcha thanked him, picked up the glass, lowered her nose, and sniffed. The tip of her tongue came out. Tilting the glass against her lower lip, she lapped the milk.

Max averted his eyes and tried not to imagine her tongue lapping at his body, starting high and going lower, lower, lower...

He blanked his mind and instead thought of Australia, the Indian and Pacific Oceans he longed to see, the Great Barrier Reef, Ayers Rock, the Melbourne Opera House. The adventures ahead of him.

"I'll have you know I consulted my doctor this morning," Rose said. "He told me cases of true amnesia are very uncommon."

"But it does happen," Max said.

"Not as much as it does on the soaps Tory likes to watch. Ow!" Rose glared at Tory. "Did you *kick* me?"

Tory smiled wide enough for her canine teeth to show. "Was that you? Sorry, I thought it was the table leg."

Max thought smoke was going to shoot out of his mother's ears.

"You could cause a serious injury with those shoes," she said.

"Sue me."

"Keep it up, someone will. I'm sorry I gave you the money to come home. I thought you'd be—"

"On your side? Sorry. Max supported me in my decision to be an actress, and I'm supporting his decision to do whatever makes him happy."

"Even if it ruins the family?"

Tory rolled her eyes. "Could you be more selfish?"

Tuning out his mother's reply, Max glanced at Sorcha. He was sorry he'd insisted she come. His mother was snide; his sister was a brat. And they had yet to eat their main course, so there was more to come.

But for a woman with a brain injury that had wiped her memory clean, Sorcha didn't seem to be concerned by their squabbling. Instead, she gulped down the milk, her head back, her throat working.

Any lingering thoughts of his adventures wiped out of his mind as the napkin on his lap inched up. He wanted to press his mouth against her exposed throat, run his tongue down the smooth column, leaving a wet and warm path down, down, and way down.

He sat back, his spine pressing against the back of his chair. This was wrong on many levels. She was a guest in his house. Convalescing from an accident. She didn't have her memory back and might be engaged. He shouldn't feel like this and he sure the hell wouldn't give in to it.

He'd always been the responsible one, and he wanted that to change. But this was the wrong time, wrong place, wrong woman.

The waiter took away their salad plates and replaced them with their dinners. The bickering stopped while they took bites of their steak, chicken, fish, and pasta. A collective "mmm" went around the table, the reason Morrie's got away with charging twice as much as any other restaurant within a thirty-mile diameter.

It was worth the cost to keep his mother stuffing food into her mouth for the next half hour instead of insulting Sorcha, arguing with Tory, or disparaging Ted's business abilities and maturity. But as soon as Rose swallowed the last crumb of her caramel chocolate cake, she tapped Max's sleeve. He finished off his key lime cheesecake before turning to her.

"It's time to talk about your plans." She held up her hand to forestall him from cutting her off. "We've always talked over the important decisions. It's what's kept the family glued together. We don't act selfishly and do what we want when we want."

Out of the corner of his eyes, Max caught Sorcha stiffening. He conquered an urge to reach out and curve his hand on her shoulder. This dinner had been a drawn-out torture of his senses. Every time she nibbled on something, he imagined her nibbling on him. She was giving him an ache in the groin, his mother was giving him an ache in the head, and he didn't know which was worse.

And he still missed Belle. This afternoon he'd called the sheriff's department and then the humane societies in three counties with no luck.

He faced his mother, pushing thoughts of Sorcha and Belle out of his mind. One problem at a time. "You're all being taken care of. I'm not leaving anyone destitute."

"But you're *leaving*." Rose's voice grew shrill. "What if something goes wrong? Who am I going to turn to?"

He glanced away from her crumpled, pleading face. Across from him, Tory sipped her wine, gazing determinedly over his head. Then he looked at Sorcha. She was staring at Rose, her nostrils flared and her lips peeled back, like an animal about to attack.

"Maybe," she said, her voice harsh, her expression disapproving, "you should turn to yourself."

His mother gasped. Glasses left lips and the eyes of Rose and Tory turned to her as she continued. "Mothers should take care of their children, not the other way around. Kittens leave—" She frowned, then her brow cleared and she continued before Rose could gather her venom and attack. "Baby birds leave their nests. Max isn't a baby, and it's time for you to let him fly. He should do anything he wants and you should be happy for him."

He hadn't thought his mother would screech while sitting in the county's most expensive restaurant, surrounded by candlelight and clinking glasses and well-dressed diners.

He was wrong.

But as she screeched, Sorcha calmly drank her milk and didn't glance at her, leaving it to Tory to whisper sharply to Rose that she was making a scene and embarrassing them.

But Max... He sat with his hands clutched on his lap. Sorcha was selfish and lazy and he suspected she was a liar, but despite all that, she was the truest woman he'd known. She had no pretenses, no hidden vices or quirks. If she wanted tuna for breakfast, she had tuna for breakfast. Lunch, too, along with an ice cream sandwich.

If this were another time and another place, he would suspect he was falling in love with her. But this was now and in this place. And he wasn't ready to give up his dream for her or his family.

A quick affair crossed his mind, but he rejected the thought. It would be wrong, wrong, wrong.

Too bad the image in his mind felt so right, right, right.

Twenty-three

It was a new day but clouds gathering above Phil seemed a portent that life was sucking and not getting better. At least it appeared someone was home this morning, the garage door up and a Jeep in the driveway. The front door creaked opened, and he braced himself to look trustworthy and innocent, though he was here to commit the worst evil a man could do.

The next instant his thoughts flew from his mind as he gawked at a knockout redhead wearing a tight T-shirt and jogging pants that showcased a slender figure with the greatest arms he'd seen on a woman, firm and sleek, with only a faint definition of her biceps. She blinked then stared. Her lips opened a space, giving a glimpse into the dark moistness of her mouth, as if she were about to receive a kiss from a lover.

His testosterone rose, and his irritation sank. He smiled.

She smiled back.

The clouds rolled back from the sun. Rays beamed down on her like a spotlight from heaven.

"Hello," she said.

"Hello back," he said.

They stood like that, staring and smiling. He didn't forget why he was here, but he pushed it back, stomped it into quietude, and focused on the pretty girl in front of him, as fresh and sweet as a strawberry smoothie.

"Who is it?" a man's voice called behind her.

The redhead laughed, still looking straight at him. "Good question. Who are you?"

"Um...um." What was his cover story? Oh yeah. His smile sagged. "I'm Phil Hern. I'm looking for Sorcha Anders."

"Sorcha? Oh my God. This is wonderful! Finally someone who can help fill in her memory gaps. Are you related to her?"

A man loomed behind her. The redhead's husband? Phil's chest constricted. He glanced at her left hand, and the vise on his heart eased. No ring. Then he noticed the man's eyes, the same color as the woman's, a blue as bright as the painted lockers in Joe's Gym. A brother. Had to be.

His gaze shifted to the redhead, who watched him with those bright eyes. He blinked and plowed ahead. "Sorcha's here? She has memory gaps?"

"Yes and yes. It's amnesia." The redhead's lips turned down. "She has to relearn everything. She even forgot how to eat and read."

"Who are you?" the man demanded.

Phil looked over the woman's red hair into the man's blue eyes, sterner and more judgmental than hers. He swallowed. Caught. The brother identity wouldn't do. Not now when he had an example of a real brother and sister in front of him. Neither would his story of being with the press or the FBI. The brother would ask for identification and Phil had a sudden fear that with his sharp eyes he'd realize his badge had been printed by a two-year-old inkjet that cost less than forty dollars.

Brother and sister waited expectantly as his underarms prickled with sweat. Seconds passed and the redhead stopped smiling, a frown forming on her forehead. Quick! He needed to say something quick.

Only one solution occurred to him.

"I'm Sorcha's fiancé."

Max marched into the family room, and Belle wrenched her gaze from the book she was reading. In four years, she had never seen him look so grim. She was curled in his roomy recliner, even though the smaller chair fit her human body more comfortably. But if she sniffed deeply she smelled his scent in the rich brown leather. Besides, this had always been one of her favorite resting places, especially stretched out on his lap while he rubbed her back and ears.

But now she was human. She sighed and lowered the Harry Potter book onto her knees, leaving her finger on the page. Reading books almost made up for not being petted. Hermione was in great trouble, and Belle hoped she wasn't going to die.

"Someone's here for you."

Searching her mind, she found one human word to fit his announcement. "Huh?"

"Your fiancé."

She knew all about fiancés. Julene on *The Love Chronicles* was engaged to Ben, who was married to Shannon, who had two other fiancés. She shook her head. "No."

"You don't remember. You have the ring—"

"I took it off." She held up her left hand and wiggled her naked fingers.

"You were wearing a ring. It must've meant something."

She shook her head, her mouth set.

"You have to see him."

Her head shook again, hair whipping out. She didn't have to do anything she didn't want to do.

He planted his legs apart, crossed his arms over his chest, and stared down at her. "I insist."

"No."

"I'll bring him in here."

"Go ahead." Wishing she could show her unconcern by lifting her leg and licking her thigh, she settled for giving him her I'm-a-cat-and-you're-not look. "But I won't leave with him."

His arms came down, his expression softening. "I won't make you leave. Not until you're ready."

She blinked. What was wrong with her eyes? Why did they burn? Why were tears welling up?

"You're going away," she whispered.

"In nine days. By then your memory will have returned and you'll be somewhere else."

Never. Never, never, ever.

"Are you coming with me? Or should I bring him here?"

She stood and put the book facedown on the chair, the pages open. "I'll come. You won't leave me alone with him?"

"Are you frightened?"

"No." Frightened of a human? Ha! But on *The Love Chronicles*, fiancés hugged and kissed, and she didn't want a strange man to kiss her.

Max headed out of the room. She followed him, looking at his hair the color of the sun going down, the broad shoulders, the lean hips, the curve of his buttocks, and the long, muscular legs.

He wasn't a strange man. If he wanted to hug and kiss her...

Voices came from the great room, Tory's light laugh and a man's deeper tones. Max's stride lengthened and Belle skipped to catch up. In the middle of the room, a man was touching Tory's upper arm. His dark brown hair was cut short and he was almost as tall as Max, the muscles on his arms straining against his shirt.

"Feels good," he said to Tory. "You're doing something right."

"I'm afraid my muscles will turn to soggy oatmeal now that I'm away from my club."

"I can give you a few exercises to—" He broke off, his gaze settling on Max and Belle. He released Tory and strode toward Belle, raising his arms to hug her. "Sorcha! I've been worried about you."

She hopped behind Max, putting her hands on his back and poking her head out. She didn't want the stranger to touch her. She wanted to kick him.

"Slow down," Max said, his voice like the first rumbles of thunder. "Slow way down. Sorcha has no memory of you."

"I'm Phil." He put his hand over his left shirt pocket and took another giant step toward her. "Your fiancé. You remember."

"Keep back." Max's muscles tensed under Sorcha's hands. "I warned you. You're moving too fast."

Phil stopped and put his hands together, as if he were begging. She sniffed. Dogs begged.

"You want your memory back, don't you? Come with me and it'll start coming back to you."

"No." Belle lowered her hands, gripping Max's ribs. He started, and her fingers tightened. She pressed her breasts against his back. If Phil tried to drag her, he'd have to drag Max, too.

A muscle in Phil's cheek twitched, his face looked pale, and he clutched his stomach. Belle wondered if he was going to throw up on the rug. If he did, Max wouldn't like it.

He looked at Max. "She doesn't remember now, but it'll come back soon enough. Thanks for all you've done. I'll just take her off your hands and—"

"She doesn't want to go," Max snapped. "You're a stranger to her."

"I can't believe this." Phil smacked his fist into his palm and glared at Max like he was an enemy. Color returned to his cheeks. "Her memory's got more holes in it than the ozone. She doesn't know what she's saying. You can't want to keep her here." His eyebrows rose, and his voice lowered. "Or do you?"

Max stiffened even more, and Belle wished she could see his face.

She didn't breathe. She wanted him to say yes.

But that was silly. Being human was temporary. As soon as she found Sorcha and traded bodies, she'd be a cat again and everything would be the way it was supposed to be.

"Yes," Max said.

Belle's breath whooshed out, her knees weak.

"I'm not forcing her to do anything she doesn't agree to do. When she's ready, she'll tell me."

"And me," Phil said.

Max jerked his head in a nod.

Belle wondered if anyone else thought it was odd that Phil looked at Max instead of her. If he wanted to impress her, shouldn't he pay attention to her? Instead, he and Max were glaring at each other as if they were two tomcats ready to attack.

Tory sniffed. "I smell something," she said, looking around.

Belle sniffed. In front of her, she heard Max sniff, and three feet from him, Phil sniffed, too. Belle frowned. All she smelled was Max.

"What?" Max asked.

"Testosterone." Tory grinned. "The room reeks of it."

Phil whooped with laughter. Looking at him, Tory giggled, her nose wrinkling.

Phil's laughter stopped and he swallowed, his Adam's apple jerking up and down. He turned toward Max again. "Okay, she can stay."

"Her staying here or leaving was never your decision," Max said.

Belle raised her chin and stepped around Max to his side, so close their arms brushed. Why was she hiding behind him? She didn't need to hide behind anyone. "That's right. The decision is mine."

"I'm not giving up my claim." Phil's jaw jutted. "I get to visit her."

Max looked at Belle. "What do you think?"

She shook her head. If she was alone with Phil, he might try to kiss and hug her. Then she'd scratch out his eyes and there'd be a big mess. The smart thing to do was not to see him. Humans didn't like big messes.

"You should see him," Max said. "It might jog your memory."

She started to clutch at his arm, but pulled back and put her hands behind her back. She was a strong feline, a huntress, not a weak human. "I don't want to be alone with him."

Tory ran to her and threw her arms around her, hugging her. "I'll stay with you when he comes. You won't have to be afraid."

Belle nodded her head against Tory's shoulder. Being hugged by Tory felt good. But she didn't feel like rubbing her body against Tory the way she wanted to do with Max. "Okay." She wiggled out of Tory's hold and added, "I'm not afraid."

"You remind me of Belle," Max said.

"Who's Belle?" Phil demanded.

While Tory explained to him, Belle beamed at Max. That was the best compliment she'd had since she turned human.

Caroline drove to Max's house, energy and confidence humming through her. She'd needed this two-day vacation to clear her head and remind herself of the valuable commodities she possessed in her face and her body.

Max had to see the difference and realize he couldn't leave her behind.

The sun was a red ball sinking into the horizon, no longer blinding, and she took off her sunglasses. On the radio, a woman sang about killing her cheating lover, and Caroline sang along with gusto.

A dark blue Jeep swept around the bend, and in the middle of a word she snapped her mouth shut. *Max*. Too dark to make out details, but she recognized his height and the shape of his head.

He sped past her.

She cried out and hit the steering wheel with her fist. The car veered toward the edge of the road. Her breath gasping, she grabbed the wheel with both hands and steered left. The car straightened and slowed, and so did her agitated thoughts. She peered into her rearview mirror, but the Jeep was gone, the road empty.

She shifted her gaze to the road. A driveway was ahead, and she pulled up to the grassy verge, then backed into it. Might as well go home, pour a glass of wine. Better yet, a liter of wine.

But she lingered in the driveway. Her hands shook. Her breath came out in puffs that hurt her chest. Her fingers clenched the steering wheel. The hunger that had driven her to the restaurant two nights ago was back, gnawing at the pit of her belly. She leaned her head onto the steering wheel, sucked in air and remembered what happened the first time she'd felt the gnawing.

She'd spilled a bottle of nail polish on the dress of a competitor.

She was seven years old.

She thought of the last time she'd felt the gnawing.

She'd pushed her husband to his death.

Twenty-four

"Hey, your problems are solved." Ted slid a beer across the gleaming bar top to Max.

Max scowled at Ted. The last time he'd been at the downtown Milwaukee bar where Ted worked, he hadn't been able to get a seat, but that was a Saturday night. This was Monday night and only a half dozen other customers hung around. At the end of the bar, a blond and a brunette talked in low voices. Three barstools to Max's right, a middle-aged man stared into his vodka and tonic.

"I didn't like him," Max said.

"You feel responsible for her." Ted grinned. "Like a father. Fathers never like their daughters' boyfriends."

Max's scowl deepened. Any father who felt like this about his daughter should be shot. That was part of the problem. Hell, it was the problem. He should be glad Phil wanted to take responsibility for Sorcha. He was leaving soon, after all. Someone had to be there for her.

But not Phil. Not with Sorcha's instant aversion to him.

"Remember how you acted when Tory went out with that guy in her senior year—what was his name?" Ted asked. "Craig, Greg, something like that?"

"The punk with the nose ring and the tattoos?"

"You judged him on his outside. He was a cool guy. The nose ring and tats were the outer manifestations of his inner turbulence."

"Why don't you come a little closer?" Max asked. "I'd like to show you some turbulence."

Ted laughed. So did the guy with the vodka.

"You two brothers?" he asked. "My brother and I used to talk that way. 'Course, he's dead now." He sniffed and looked down at his drink again.

Ted's lips quirked, laughter sparking in his eyes. Max gave Ted the glare he'd been using to quell him for the last twenty years.

"Sorry about your brother," Max said, and turned back to Ted. "He's a phony. He was drooling over Tory, for Christ's sake."

"Well, yeah, he was going out with her."

"Not the punk from high school." Max gritted his teeth. "Phil what's-his-name. Sorcha's supposed fiancé."

Ted wiped a wet ring off the bar top. "A man can be taken but still look."

"I look," the guy with the vodka said. "I look a lot."

"Jesus," Max said under his breath.

One of the women called to Ted for a refill. Ted grabbed a bottle of Zinfandel and stepped down, his leer telling Max they were good looking.

"I think you like her." Vodka guy nodded like he was Isaac Newton discovering gravity. "I think you like her a lot."

Max glanced at him. Vodka guy grinned crookedly; his moroseness melted away. Max gulped down his beer from the bottle, finishing it. Time to leave when drunks could tell he had a hard-on for Sorcha like a teenage boy.

She was arrogant and lazy, qualities he'd never admired in a woman or a man. Okay, she also searched hours every day for his cat and made him laugh. That he admired. She didn't give a damn what anyone thought of her—and she didn't cling. As vodka guy would say, he liked that a lot.

But that didn't explain the way he felt when he was near her. She was special. He'd never met another woman like her and feared he never would again. Every day his attraction to her grew stronger and harder. As though she touched something deep inside of him. Something primal and necessary.

And when she was near, he heated from the inside out,

wanting to slide his hand under her blouse, over the smoothness of her skin. He wanted to kiss the curve of her neck that joined with her shoulder, to inhale her honey scent. He wanted to lick her skin and see if that tasted like honey, too. He wanted to hear her breathing quicken. He wanted to—

"Another beer?" Ted asked.

Max thumped the bottle on the bar and stood. What the hell was he thinking? After seeing her naked, any straight man from eighteen to eighty would think about her and feel primal.

"Better not. I've got a long drive ahead."

"You leaving?" Ted glanced toward the end of the bar. The brunette waved at him.

"Don't miss me too much," Max said.

Vodka guy guffawed. Max nodded his good-bye and started off.

"Hey!" Ted's shout stopped him.

Max turned but didn't go back. "Yeah?"

"I almost forgot. I found Sorcha's parents."

"What search engine did you use? I couldn't find anything."

Ted's grin showed his white teeth. "It's called the Milwaukee phone book. I got in a few minutes early, looked up Anders, made a few calls, and on the fifth I hit the jackpot. Her father said they were going to church tonight and to stop off tomorrow morning." He scratched the top of his head, his hair ruffling. "I didn't get a chance to tell him she's safe with us. Just asked if he was Sorcha's father, and he was inviting me to his home as if he was expecting my call. Hell, maybe he's psychic, too. I'll drive over tomorrow."

"No," Max said. "*We'll* drive over." He gave a firm nod, then strode out. First a fiancé, and now parents. She'd be out of his house soon, his Eve, his Delilah, his Siren. He had his plans mapped out for him, his freedom only nine days away. He wasn't going to give it away for a pretty face and a body he wanted to bury himself in.

This wasn't love. It couldn't be. Just normal, everyday

lust. When he was ready, love would come. And he wasn't ready now.

"You don't think Phil's cute?"

Her hand in the bowl of popcorn, Belle looked at Tory curled on the other end of the sofa, her legs curled beneath her butt, a dreamy expression on her face. On the TV screen, men and women were eating bugs and making faces. Belle didn't know what the fuss was about, although she never ate bugs herself. She just batted them around until she tired of the game or they died.

Mice, now... That she'd eaten. Well, chewed a bit.

Ice cream was better.

"I think Phil's..." She frowned, trying to think of something cutting to say. "Like a dog."

"Oooh, dogs are cute."

"Dogs are stupid."

Tory sat up. "If Phil was stupid, you'd never have gotten engaged to him."

"I'm *not* engaged."

"You've got the ring." Tory's nose wrinkled. "Even if you're not wearing it."

Belle pulled out a handful of popcorn and shoved it into her mouth. When she was eating, no one expected her to answer questions. Tory talked to her much more than Max or Ted, asking what she felt and thought about everything. Belle wasn't sure if she liked it.

"Maybe you don't think Phil's cute because you think someone else is cuter." Tory slanted her head closer to Belle's, the corners of her lips curling up. "So, who do you think is cuter? Max or Ted?"

Belle spat out kernels of popcorn.

Tory fell back laughing. "I knew it! I just knew it. You like one of my brothers."

Belle wiped her mouth with the back of her hand, then brushed the kernels off her slacks, another pair of Tory's.

"Which one?" Tory pushed up on her knees, facing Belle. "C'mon, you can tell me."

"I like them both." That was true. She'd always liked Ted. But Max was her chosen companion. The one she preferred to sleep with and play with and live with. The one she chose to feed, shelter, and pet her.

Her body had changed, but that remained the same. Well, not exactly the same. Not *everything*. Now, though it was a very, very, very bad idea, she wanted him to pet her differently. Like a woman with a man.

When she was with Ted, she didn't want Ted to pet her like a woman.

Was this feeling what humans called love?

She glanced out the window into blackness and saw her reflection—no, *Sorcha's* reflection.

Sorcha, where are you? Hurry up, so we can change bodies. I think I'm getting into trouble.

Cats and humans weren't supposed to do what this human body wanted to do with Max. The thought wiggled into her mind that if she did *that* with him—"made love," they called it on *The Love Chronicles*—that might trigger something and make her stay human forever.

But what if she were wrong? What if she could make love with Max and still be a cat again? Should she take that chance?

"You're no fun." Tory shifted, her reflection joining Belle's.

Blinking, Belle grabbed another handful of popcorn. "Do I have to like one or the other?"

"You're pretty and they're good-looking. You're living in the same house." Tory sat back on her butt again. "It's like putting a magnet together with two nails."

Belle knew what magnets were. You put them on refrigerators. She glanced at her fingernails. What did they have to do with magnets?

"My girlfriends were always gooey over my brothers." Tory made a face. "They used to make up excuses to come here. It drove Max crazy."

Belle had never liked Tory's girlfriends. She chewed her popcorn.

163

"I think it's Max," Tory said.

This time Belle swallowed her popcorn instead of spitting it out. Another lesson learned. Don't spit food.

But would it hurt to tell Tory just a little? When she was a cat, she used to meow and meow and meow, and they'd pet her or give her a treat. Or laugh and wonder aloud what she was saying. No one understood her. This chance to explain her feelings and thoughts might be her last.

"I don't like Max." She bit her lower lip, then the next three words poured out, "I love him."

Tory's breath puffed out of her mouth, and she sat back against the couch cushion, her eyes flared wide. "Love? He's leaving in a week and a half. Do you want to go with him?"

A chill invaded Belle's bones, and she crossed her arms over her chest. "I'll never leave." People kept talking about her leaving. This was her home and people shouldn't leave their homes.

Tory shook her head. "Max has made up his mind. Once he decides something, it's as good as done. He's like... I don't know, a rock. He can roll, but he'll still be a rock. You know what I mean?"

"No." Rocks were rocks. Humans were humans. Except when they were cats. Belle unwrapped her arms and reached for the bowl.

"Honey," Tory touched the hand Belle was digging into the popcorn, "if you think you can change Max's mind, you're going to be hurt."

Belle stared at Tory's hand on hers. If she were in her cat body, she'd hiss at Tory for touching her when she was eating. But she was human—for now—and she just pulled her handful of popcorn out of the bowl. "I won't try to change Max's mind. He has to do whatever he wants to do."

Tory shook her head. "Honest to God, you're like no woman I ever knew."

Chewing her popcorn, Belle nodded. She was like no woman at all.

Sorcha huddled beneath the bushes by the oversized house, waiting for Gwen. For two days and one night she had survived in the woods. But despite the fur coat and a blanket of damp leaves, she'd shivered all through the interminable, dark hours of the night, snatching moments of sleep before the cold woke her again. Or maybe it was her empty stomach that wouldn't let her sleep, needing to be filled. Yesterday, she'd seen a gopher and for an instant her muscles had bunched, as if she were going to pounce on the small animal.

Then she'd come to her senses. Her *human* senses that said killing and eating small animals was icky. Her cat senses argued that if she gave it a try, eating small animals might be a culinary treat. But if she did that, she'd be as evil as her mother and father always said she was.

She lay back on the cold ground and tried to nap, but hunger gnawed at her, keeping her awake.

A tiny sound made her ears perk up. An instant later, the door opened. "Princess," Gwen called softly. "Princess, where are you?"

Sorcha meowed and leapt toward the light and warmth and one coltish girl who held out her arms. Gwen beamed so widely all her teeth showed, happiness radiating from every pore.

"You came back," she whispered, hugging Sorcha to her slight chest. "Oh, I missed you so much."

A purr rumbled out of Sorcha's throat, and she rubbed the side of her mouth against Gwen's chin. Tears splashed down Gwen's face onto the top of Sorcha's head.

"I love you," Gwen said.

Sorcha purred harder. This was what she'd always wanted—to be loved. But not as a cat—as a human.

This was wrong, so wrong.

Her father and mother were right. She was going to hell for sure, because now that she was wrapped in Gwen's arms and Gwen's love, she didn't know if she could force herself to leave again.

Twenty-five

To: Phil Patterson
From: Mike and Jody
Subject: re: money

we got the check in today's mail. as soon as i read the note, i went to my email. it's been a couple days since i checked. had a few problems but i'm okay for now.

what the hell are you doing that bob gave you 25k? and you're expecting more? if he wants you to kill his father so he can inherit everything, go for it—ha ha, just kidding. but the man is a #1 dickhead.

i got one thing to say about you working for your brother. GET ANYTHING HE SAYS IN WRITING. and don't turn your back on him. it hurts your mom that he still blames her for leaving him. she wanted to take him but dickhead wouldn't let her. bob knows that too. i think he enjoys acting like the little boy left behind. i know he was only 12, but that was 26 years ago. man up. get over it.

lucy's been moping ever since we put desi to sleep. when I go to heaven, i'm gonna ask god why dogs have to die young. Dad

———

To: Mike and Judy
From: Phil Patterson
Subject: re: brother

Don't worry about Bob. He won't back out. Desi was the best. I miss him too. Let me know when you're having the operation. I'll try to get back for it.

Phil

———————

To: Phil Patterson
From: Mike and Judy
Subject: re: money

>Don't worry about Bob. He won't back out.>
I worry a lot. you know how those rich bastards are. they only about themselves. he and his dad are the worst of the bunch.

hey, i was just kidding about killing bob's father. i'm telling you this, because the more i think about it, i can't think of anything else he'd pay you this much money to do. if he asks, tell him no. i'd rather die than my son be a murderer.

i made an appointment with mom's surgeon. she goes first, then me. she says she loves you and you should call. Dad

———————

Phil bent over his laptop on top of the square table in his motel room. Tears burned his eyes and pain burned his stomach.

He didn't know what to do now that he'd met Sorcha. He couldn't see her murder a boyfriend, he couldn't see her connive to blackmail Bob, he couldn't see her killing his niece and nephew.

It wasn't that she was sweet. Tory was sweet, strawberry sweet. Sorcha was the opposite, suspicious and glowering. But she was honest and open in her aversion to him, not bothering to hide it. She presented no mask at all that he could see. One of the few what-you-see-is-what-you-get people.

But if she wasn't lying, that meant Bob was the liar.

That meant he was a fool for believing Bob.

Phil groaned. What the hell had he done? What had made him agree to kill someone? Hell, he couldn't even kill bugs. He scooped them up with a piece of paper and shook them off outside his apartment.

"Christ." He pressed his hand against his abdomen. His stomach felt as though a master pretzel maker was experimenting with his intestines. He wondered what would happen if he packed his clothes, hopped in his rental, and went home.

Instead of answers, questions flooded his mind. What if he were wrong? What if Lorna and Danny were in danger? Two pathetic rich kids, always happy to see him the few times he visited, knowing he'd play with them—tennis on the Wii with ten-year-old Lorna, hide-and-seek with four-year-old Danny.

They didn't deserve it. Even Melanie, who ignored them most of the time and blatantly flirted with him, getting a kick out of making him blush from his neck to his earlobes, didn't deserve it.

And the money. He didn't want to think about it, but it was insidious. He'd worried about money every day for the past twenty months. It was an impossible weight on his shoulders that had finally eased.

And there was Tory. He liked her. They'd clicked the instant they'd seen each other. If he weren't pretending to be Sorcha's fiancé...

The pain in his stomach gave a mean twist. He bent forward, his elbows on his thighs, and buried his face in his hands. And he did something he normally didn't do. He thought. Long and hard, his brain under pressure with all his thinking, he put together everything he'd witnessed and heard, examined every line and every expression, and added up two plus two plus two.

Until finally, his stomach stopped aching but his head felt heavy, as if he were lifting weights with his mind.

Somewhere in that unaccustomed introspection, he'd found it, the brain cells that contained the two facts he'd tried to ignore, tried to bury, never completely buying Bob's explanation.

The ski mask and the muddied license plate.

An innocent man didn't do that. Bob wasn't a woman's, tool. He wouldn't put his hands in mud because of a psychic's instructions. Nor would he dress like a bank robber.

Phil's dad had been right. Bob was a liar and a user.

Now what was he supposed to do about this? Turn in his brother?

And there was the money. Of course he wouldn't see any more money, but what about the twenty-five K? He supposed he should call his dad and tell him not to use it.

But how could he? His father had already scheduled an appointment for his mom with her surgeon.

"Tell me, God, what do you want me to do?" His voice ragged, he looked up at the ceiling. The last time he'd asked, nothing had happened. But perhaps God wanted him to figure a few things out by himself. Perhaps God had spent millenniums telling everyone what to do and was sick of them not listening. After all, he'd given them the Ten Commandments, and look how well humans were doing with that.

Quieting his thoughts, he listened for an answer but heard only the blood pulsing through his veins. Finally he got down on his knees and leaned his head against the bedspread. The smell of bleach stung his nostrils, the cotton material starchy on his forehead.

Time passed while he waited for a voice, a sign, even the buzz of a bug. He listened until his knees hurt, but nothing came but the muted roar of a passing car and a woman laughing loudly in the next room. All the world was a comedy...only instead of laughter, tears tracked down his face.

Moonlight streamed into the bedroom. Belle lay with her eyes open, staring at the ceiling. What was the matter with her? She'd never had trouble sleeping before.

She'd never been a human before.

She threw off the covers, the air cool on her bare, unfurred skin. Maybe she was restless because she was alone and not cuddled against Max's back. An image of her woman self curled against Max heated her body, especially the place between her legs. She jumped out of bed.

What was happening to her?

Her feet on the carpet, she stood in the moonlight and shivered. Because she knew exactly what happened to her. The same thing that had happened to Annette with Brad on *The Love Chronicles*. And before Brad, Jack, and before Jack, Ethan.

For Belle there was just Max. At lunch today, she'd had a bite of Tory's sandwich, cheese melted against bread. That's how she felt looking at Max, like she was melting inside. She was the cheese and he was the bread.

She padded out of the bedroom, though she kept thinking this was wrong. Her bare feet made no noise. Quiet as a cat, she thought.

Huffing snores came from Ted's room. She kept going. She needed to see Max. To breathe the same air as him. Then she could go back to bed and to sleep.

Max lay on his back, his mouth open. Every time he exhaled, he went, "Hahhhhhh." Moonlight spilled through the window, illuminating the strong lines of his face, his firm chin, his parted lips. She moved closer, noticing how soft his lips looked, when everything else about him looked hard.

One arm was flung out. She could see his dark-colored T-shirt. Down below, she knew, he wore boxers that gave his penis room to flop around in.

It hadn't flopped when he'd seen her naked in his room.

The thought made her melting parts hotter.

She bent over him. What would it feel like to touch him in this new body? What would it feel like to be touched? What would it feel like to put her lips against his, her mouth open, the way Annette on *The Love Chronicles* kissed all her men?

Would he like it?

Would she like it?

She reached forward. What would it hurt?

Don't do it. This is a line you shouldn't cross.

Her mind was giving her one message. Her body another.

You know where this might lead, her mind said. *If something happens—and you know what I'm talking about—you might be stuck in this body for the rest of your life.*

Her body sneered. *What are you, a chicken dog? You're just curious. Exploring. It's okay if you want to touch. Go ahead. When did you start denying yourself? He's asleep anyway. He'll never know.*

Her hand lowered. One finger touched his bicep just below his T-shirt sleeve. Warm. Vital. Reverberations of his beating heart moved against the soft pad of her fingertip. Blood pulsed inside a vein.

"Mmmm." The wordless sound escaped her closed mouth.

She snatched her hand away, jerked it behind her back, and stepped into the shadows.

His eyes opened. "Belle?" he muttered. "Is that you, Belle?"

His arm came out, his hand groping the cover, patting the empty spot by his side. "I thought I heard you," he said, his voice thick with sleep. His eyes closed again. His breathing deepened.

Belle tiptoed into the hall. This body was getting her into trouble. But that figured. After all, it was only human.

Twenty-six

Max stood in front of Belle with his legs apart and an expression on his face that she'd last seen when he'd caught her eating his plants. "We're going to see your parents. You need to come along."

Belle shook her head, her lips clamped together. She sat next to Tory on the carpet in the great room. Tory had been teaching her yoga, impressed by how quickly Belle took to the stretching exercises, when Max came and stomped on her good feelings.

Why was he trying to make her leave? Didn't he see this was her home? She glared at him and frowned at Ted. He stood behind Max, a half smile on his face, going along with Max like a puppy after a treat.

"I'm staying here."

"What are you afraid of?"

"If she remembered that," Tory said, "she'd remember everything."

Max's gaze didn't flicker from Belle's face. "Shut up, Tory."

Ted laughed. "You may as well tell the sun to stop shining."

"You shut up," Tory said, and Belle wasn't sure which brother she meant it for.

Belle wished they would all shut up. She pushed up to her feet.

"Are you coming?" Max asked.

She glided past him, out of the room. "I have important things to do." She glanced back to make sure he wouldn't

172

pounce and grab her the way he did when he wanted to take her to the vet.

Even Max wasn't perfect.

Max crossed his arms over his chest. "You're going to look for Belle, aren't you?" She turned her head away from him. "Maybe I'm going to look for Sorcha."

Then she headed toward the kitchen.

Max turned to Tory. "What the hell did she mean by that?"

"You got me."

"One of those woman things," Ted said.

Tory slugged his bicep. He grunted and grabbed his arm. "What's that for?"

She batted her eyes. "Wasn't it a manly thing to do?"

"That's enough." Max gave them a stern look. Times like this he felt like their father instead of their older brother. He reminded himself he had a week and a day left, then he'd fly out of Wisconsin, half a world away from his responsibilities.

"You coming?" he called to Ted over his shoulder as he strode along the hall. From the back of the house, a door thudded shut.

"Couldn't keep me away." Ted followed him, his footsteps clomping on the hall carpet.

"I want to come, too." Tory's footsteps were lighter. "I like Sorcha. I want to help her."

"You'll help by keeping an eye on her," Max said. "I don't trust her so-called fiancé."

Tory's face flushed. "He seemed nice to me."

"Then you'll be happy to stay," Ted said. "He'll probably be here soon."

While she bit her lip, mulling this over, Max and Ted escaped into the garage, not bothering to grab a jacket. The sun shone and there was no wind. Max wondered if spring had decided to stop off at Wisconsin after all.

As they drove down the drive, he saw Sorcha tramping to

the thicket of trees, her jacket tied around her hips. His foot on the gas pedal eased.

"I'm getting used to her," Ted said. "I'll miss her when she's gone."

Max grunted and pressed down on the gas pedal again. "She's stubborn and arrogant and expects to be waited on."

Ted laughed. "Maybe that's why I like her. She reminds me of Belle."

"What's cute in a cat isn't tolerable in a woman."

"You're just pissed 'cause you can't boss her around like you do us."

Max shook his head. "In eight days the only one to boss you around will be yourself."

"Yeah," Ted said. "And it scares the hell out of me."

But he didn't sound like he was scared. His voice was cheerful, and he sat taller and seemed to be more present. No longer an observer watching with the intent to be amused, but a participant.

It dawned on Max that maybe if he hadn't been there for Ted, steering him away from trouble every chance he had, Ted would have found his way on his own.

"You'll do just fine," he said, and to his own ears, his voice sounded wooden. "Just fine," he repeated. And so would he be fine, enjoying his travels without a care about another person. Just himself.

But first he had to solve the mystery of Sorcha.

Judy and Jim Anders looked like sister and brother, their bodies so thin they could've been starvation victims, lines bracketing their down-turned mouths and between their eyes. The big difference was Judy's thick curling hair, gray threading through brown, while a thinning gray fuzz topped Jim's scalp.

Jim nodded at the brown couch with the picture of Jesus bleeding on the cross above it, and invited Max and Ted to sit. Jim and Judy perched on two matching brown wing chairs, neither of their stiff spines touching the chair backs.

Max and Ted sat straight, too, the rigid couch not allowing any slouching. Max studied the couple and saw a resemblance between Sorcha in Judy Anders' small, close-set ears and Jim Anders' straight nose. As eager as Max had been to see them, he was already more eager to leave.

"About your daughter—"

"I told you two days ago," Jim interrupted. "We don't know where she is. She chose Satan over us, and now she has to take the consequences."

Ted shifted on the other end of the couch. Max felt his unease but didn't turn, keeping his gaze focused on Jim.

"Why don't you tell us everything you know," he said, wondering who Jim had talked to two days ago and what he'd said.

Jim's jaw clenched and unclenched. "All I know is what your people already told us, Detective."

Detective? Ted made a strangled sound. Once again Max didn't turn his head.

"And what is that?" Max kept his voice neutral. Out of the corner of his eye, he saw Ted whip out a notebook and a pen. Max glanced at him and nodded approval.

"I know she was living in sin." Jim's brows met above his nose. "I know her seducer was murdered. I know she drove away and a masked man chased her. I know you can't find her."

"Her seducer?" Max asked.

"The other officers said he was her fiancé." He gave Max a frigid glare.

Fiancé? Max shared a glance with Ted before turning toward the mother's wing chair. He'd think about the murdered fiancé angle when they left. For now, he'd concentrate on the parents. Surely the mother would stand up for Sorcha.

"Have you heard from her?"

Shaking her head, she glanced at her lap. She wore a baggy black skirt and a white blouse. She muttered, her voice low.

Max leaned forward. "I can't hear you."

Her eyes lifted—green like Sorcha's. But Judy's eyes were

muddied, while Sorcha's sparkled with vibrancy. "She always had Satan in her. We tried our best to chase him out, but she resisted. This is God's way of cleansing her."

"Exactly how is God doing this?" Max managed to speak normally when he wanted to shout.

"He took her home."

Ted made another strangled sound. Max sat still, his head buzzing. "Are you saying you think she's dead?"

She smiled without parting her lips, her head nodding politely. "God gave life, and God took it away."

Max's breakfast orange juice rose in his throat. He stopped talking and swallowed. His hands clenched on his thighs.

"You think she's in heaven now?" Ted asked.

"Oh no." The mother shook her head firmly. "She'll have to stay on another level until she repents for sins."

"You've mentioned that before," Ted went on. "What sins?"

Max let Ted take over. If he opened his mouth, he might tell Jim and Judy to go straight to hell and not collect two hundred dollars. Even Mr. and Mrs. Self-Righteous might kick him out after that.

The mother's smile didn't dip. "Why, she housed Satan."

Ted turned a laugh into a cough. "How'd she do that?"

"She had visions no godly woman ever had." Judy sat with her hands clasped on her lap, her ankles together, her mouth pursed. "We tried everything we could to cleanse her, but nothing worked."

Jim nodded. "The devil's seed was in her."

Max's fists curled tighter, a muscle jumping in his bicep. "How did you try to cleanse her? What was your method?"

"Prayer," Judy said.

His mouth a thin line, Jim nodded. "Every man and woman in the Church of the True and Only God prayed in turn over her for days and nights."

"How many days and nights?"

"Seven days and seven nights." A light burned in Jim's eyes as he looked above Ted at the bleeding Jesus. "The same amount of time God created our world."

"Seven days and nights? Did she eat during this time?"

"The Bible nourished her," Judy said.

"No food, no drink?"

Jim's manic eyes veered to Max, as if he finally sensed the sarcasm. "We gave her water. She wasn't starving."

"She didn't eat for seven days." Despite his desire to be calm, Max's voice hardened. "I'd damn well call that child abuse."

Judy gasped, her hand over her mouth. Jim jumped to his feet.

"Detective or not, I allow no cursing in this house."

Max stood and stepped forward, bringing his fists up. "You allow no compassion or love. Your daughter is well rid of you."

Jim lifted his arm. A shaking finger pointed to the front door. "Out. Get out of my house."

Max took a step toward Jim. Ted grabbed Max's upper arm, holding him back. Max swiveled toward Ted, but the worried frown on Ted's normally smooth forehead stopped the growl from leaving his throat.

"Let's go," Ted said. "We're not going to find out anything from them."

Max gave the glowering couple a scathing glance of contempt before jerking away from Ted and stalking to the front door. Outside, Max inhaled deeply. After the oppressive atmosphere of the Anders' living room, the air smelled of freedom.

"I don't want you coming back to my house," Jim called after them.

Ted gave him a gesture that wasn't in the Detectives' Handbook. The door slammed shut.

Two minutes later, they drove along the south-side Milwaukee block, past dozens of houses crowded together, barely room for a sidewalk between them. Ted spoke first. "Those two make Mom look like a saint."

"Yeah," Max said through gritted teeth. He clutched the steering wheel, his arms tense. He kept thinking about Jim and Judy Anders praying over Sorcha, refusing to give her food. He imagined them shaking her awake whenever she drifted off to sleep, although he didn't know where that image came from.

He wasn't a violent man, but he wished to hell he'd socked Jim Anders in the jaw.

"They didn't have one picture of her," Ted said.

"They don't deserve a picture of her."

"I'm surprised Sorcha has as much backbone as she does." Ted slouched in the passenger seat. "It's like finding Van Gogh's Sunflower painting in a cold and dark basement. With parents like that, I'd expect her to be timid, uncertain, eager to please."

Max's hands unclenched on the steering wheel. Sorcha was a pain in the butt sometimes, but never timid, never uncertain, never eager to please. From the proud tilt of her head to the fire burning in her clear green eyes, her unbending spine and get-out-of-my-way walk, she was pure spunk. If there was such a thing as being too self-confident, that was Sorcha.

Even when she didn't remember who she was.

Even when a murderer was after her.

A chill sliced through him. "I haven't paid attention to the Milwaukee news lately. We need to look up recent murders in the area."

"I'll do that," Ted said. "I'll start with the day we found her. It must've been the trauma of her fiancé's death that made her lose her memory. Though Phil doesn't look too bad for a dead guy."

"If he's the murderer," Max said slowly while he examined possibilities in his mind, "letting us see his face was a stupid step."

"Maybe he's a stupid murderer. Are you calling the sheriff?"

Max remembered Sorcha fighting to keep from being taken to the hospital. The way she'd planted herself in his home as if she belonged there. If he called the sheriff, they would insist on taking her to a medical facility, maybe to the Milwaukee Police Department for questioning, then to a shelter.

He should welcome that solution, but something inside

him revolted. "Not yet. I'll see what she has to say. Phil, too. He better have a damn good story." The prospect of questioning Sorcha's supposed fiancé made him smile grimly.

"She might be safer with the cops."

"Or she might be in bigger danger." Max set his jaw and his mind. "If we call them, her location's got a better chance of leaking. We can keep her safer than they can."

"There's one problem with that."

Max shot him a look. "What?"

"In eight days you're leaving."

Scowling, Max steered onto the expressway on-ramp.

"Aren't you?" Ted said.

"I'm leaving on schedule. Nothing is changing that."

"Not even Sorcha?"

"If I have to, I'll take her with me."

Ted snorted a half laugh. "She won't even go to Milwaukee with you. What makes you think she'll travel around the world?"

Max gritted his teeth. For the last twenty years, he'd been in charge of his world and the people in it. The only resisting force was one small cat. He'd lost Belle, but Sorcha stood fast against his control as strongly as his cat ever had.

An image of Sorcha flashed in his mind, her hair curling over her shoulders, her eyes sparkling, her slender waist, softly flaring hips, and breasts like ripe peaches.

She was irresistible in more ways than one. If she traveled with him, he knew what would happen.

A sharp gladness filled him. He pushed his foot harder on the gas pedal, eager to reach home and see her.

Twenty-seven

The pounding inside Caroline's head was made worse by the brownish-yellow walls of her mother's doll-sized kitchen, making her feel as if she were stuck inside a giant mustard bottle. But eating takeout shrimp with lobster sauce here was better than being at Max's. Everything there was "Sorcha, Sorcha, Sorcha" when it should have been "Caroline, Caroline, Caroline."

She'd gotten rid of the cat, but the woman would be harder to get rid of.

And none of it mattered. Max was leaving.

She picked at her shrimp while Brenda ate her pork with garlic sauce. Elvis crooned "Love Me Tender" on the stereo, but Caroline wasn't feeling the love. Brenda's shabby apartment reminded Caroline of her failures. The expensive dinette set she'd bought for Brenda before Emery lost his money looked out of place, like a jewel in a mud pie. She'd offered to take Brenda to dinner, but after working all day in the telemarketing center, Brenda wanted to flop around her apartment in sweats and slippers.

Brenda slurped up the last of the garlic pork and rice on her plate. Though Caroline was still chewing on her shrimp, Brenda rose and put the half-filled cartons in the refrigerator. Emery used to say the world would explode into flames if Caroline or her mother finished an entire meal. Then he'd guffaw, not caring that Caroline glared at him. If she had weighed ten pounds more when they met, he would never have looked at her. The hypocrite.

It was a relief not to share a bedroom with a man like

that. Though his biggest offense hadn't been insensitivity but poverty, it didn't matter. The result was the same. His ashes were in a city dump and she was trying everything she could think of to seduce his cousin.

She reached for her purse on the counter and pulled out her pill box.

"Prozac?" Brenda asked. "I hope you're careful with those."

Caroline gulped down the pill with a glass of water. "I'm fine," she said, and patted droplets of water from her lip with a paper napkin. Though she knew the pill's effect was cumulative, reaching a level in her bloodstream and staying there as long as she kept taking the prescribed dosage, her breathing slowed and deepened.

Good. She didn't have the luxury to give into panic. She had a multimillionaire to catch and only a week to do it in.

Perhaps she shouldn't have wasted the last two days being cosseted and admired and spoiled. But she'd needed it. Every second. Drinking it in like an alcoholic drank cheap wine.

But that was play and this was work.

"I have to do something to stop Max from leaving," she said. "He wasn't in his office today when I got there. Yesterday he was outside most of the day, looking for the stupid cat."

Her mother's raised eyebrows fueled Caroline's anger. Things like this always happened to her. It wasn't fair.

She tossed her hair back. Never mind the cat. Or Sorcha, the tuna-eating poseur. Caroline wasn't giving up or giving in. Brenda hadn't raised a quitter.

"I'm running out of time to entice Max. I need a new plan." She gestured at Brenda. "You always have the best ideas. Can you think of anything?"

"Not off the top of my head." Brenda cleared away the dishes. Her forehead wrinkling in deep thought, she rinsed off the plates. "But don't worry, we'll think of something."

Caroline tapped her long fingernails on the table, then picked up her glass of Riesling. Five minutes later, she and Brenda relaxed on the gold velvet couch in the living room while the dishwasher rumbled in the kitchen and Elvis sang "Don't Be Cruel." Brenda put her feet up on the hassock and wiggled her toes.

"There has to be a way you can seduce Max," she said. "He's the kind of guy with a conscience. Look how long he took care of his family. And he's helping you. He's got to feel something for you."

"I thought I was making headway." Caroline's headache throbbed again and she put her hand against her forehead. "But now he's leaving. I don't think seduction would work."

"He's not gay," Brenda said. "And you're a beautiful woman. How can he not want you?"

Caroline set her glass on the coffee table and stood. "I've asked myself the same question, over and over."

As if pulled, she stood and walked to the mirrored wall. No lines on her face, no sagging skin, no hippo hips. Her snug blue slacks and lacy top showed off her curves without shouting, "I'm a ho, take me."

She lifted a hand to her cheek. Was her skin loosening just a bit? She leaned in closer to the mirror, and her skin went cold and then hot. She pressed her palms against her stomach. Yes, it was there. Something on her nearly perfect face that whispered, "I'm not twenty anymore."

The aging had begun.

And she was only thirty.

Unable to look at her image again, she faced Brenda.

"I've been touching him, a hand on his shoulder or a quick massage on his back. Letting him know I'm reaching out to him."

"And he's still not coming on to you?" Brenda looked indignant. "What is he made of? Steel?"

"Muscle and skin." Caroline shrugged, remembering the firmness under her fingers. "Sex with him won't be a chore."

"Emery wasn't bad." Brenda sipped her wine.

"Mom, forget Emery." Caroline decided not to tell her mother she'd eaten hot dogs firmer than Emery. "We need to focus on hooking Max and reeling him in. You're much better at this than I am."

Brenda giggled. "I am good. Remember the time I put itching powder in Gina Fairchild's loose face powder?"

Caroline smiled and sat on her end of the couch. Brenda used to tell Caroline she'd always be there for her, and she had. But she wouldn't be there forever. No one would. That's why she needed money.

"And the time I put the laxative in Teresa Able's hot chocolate." Brenda sighed, her lips curving. "Teresa did like her hot chocolate. Too bad it didn't kick in until after she was crowned."

Caroline remembered Teresa's dash to the bathroom, an expression of distress twisting her mouth, the crown on her head. She liked Teresa, who'd once loaned her a pearl necklace when hers broke. The difference between the two was that hers was fake and Teresa's real.

"Laxative, four dollars. Satisfaction, priceless." Brenda laughed, not seeming to notice Caroline's silence. "Remember when I put a knockout drug in Alisha Brock's diet soda?" Her smile turned to a scowl and she set down her glass of wine. "Then her mother ruined everything, drinking it herself. She deserved to have her stomach pumped."

Caroline frowned. Didn't Brenda remember how frightened Caroline had been? The police had been asking questions. She'd been so afraid the police would find out Brenda had bought the drug from the creepy guy who hung around pageants, handing out diet pills for either money or—

She clapped her hands together. "A knockout drug! That's how we'll do it."

Brenda looked at her with admiration and pride. "You're brilliant. Just brilliant!"

"They call them date rape drugs, but I don't plan to rape Max. Just marry him." Caroline stood, too excited to sit. Nothing could go wrong with this plan. It couldn't. This might be her last chance to snag Max.

"Andy Marshall!" Brenda laughed like a young girl. "That's his name. The one who sold me the pills."

"You know where to reach him? It's been ten years since

we were on the circuit." Ten years of watching herself age, her skin showing its pores and the freshness on her face spoiling, like a tomato left too long in the sun.

"I'll find him." Brenda got to her feet, hurled herself at Caroline, and enfolded her in a hug. "You can count on me."

"Of course." Who else was always there for her?

"We need a plan of action." Brenda stepped back, her breaths shallow and fast, her eyes bright. "This is like old times."

"It is, isn't it?" Not all good times. Caroline had lost too often to girls less worthy, despite Brenda's successes in eliminating the competition.

After she snared Max, her losing days would be over. "I'll wait for a night when Ted's working at the bar. Then I'll stay for dinner. Max always invites me to stay when I work late." She nodded, liking the way it was coming together. "I'll give him the drug in his food or a drink. When he passes out, I'll drag him to his bedroom and rip off his clothes."

Brenda frowned. "I thought you were going to take the drug. How is this going to make Max feel like he compromised you?"

"This plan is better. I'll take off my clothes and crawl into bed with him. In the morning, I'll tell him I love him as much as he loves me and I'm so happy he proposed."

"Perfect! But what about Sorcha and Tory?"

"Tell Andy to get enough for three people."

"Bravo, my brave darling." Brenda clapped. "Bravo!"

Caroline whirled around to look at herself in the mirror again. Was this the face of a winner? Was her luck finally changing?

Standing behind Caroline, Brenda's hand curved over her shoulder. Then she poked out her head so she could gaze at Caroline's reflection in the mirrored panels, too. From where Caroline stood, it looked as if Brenda's head and neck were a growth on her upper arm.

"Max will be so lucky to have such a beautiful wife," Brenda said.

Caroline watched Brenda's eyes glisten with pride. If Emery had ever looked at her with half Brenda's adoration, he'd be alive today.

Then she thought of all the money he'd lost, of his stupidity and his arrogance. Her teeth set and her muscles tightened and darkness gathered in her head, thickening, congealing. She wished with her whole being he was in front of her for one purpose.

So she could kill him again.

Phil's cell phone rang and he jumped off the bed in his hotel room. He grabbed the phone too fast and it tumbled out of his hand. Bending to catch it, he conked his head against the table next to the bed. He swore and snatched the phone, his other hand on his head. It rang once more before he raised it to his ear and pressed the Go button.

"Is it done?" Bob demanded.

"Not yet." Not ever, perhaps, but he couldn't tell Bob about his overactive conscience. "She rarely leaves the house."

"Are you camped out watching it?"

He looked out the motel window at the parking lot, a couple getting out of the car two rooms down, the man scratching his butt. "Yes." Another lie, another twist in his belly.

Muffled voices came from the other end of the phone. Bob's voice ebbed and he said, "Okay, I'm coming." When he spoke next, his voice rose and fell, and Phil guessed he was walking. "I have to board the plane. Melanie and I are off to a golf tournament in Palm Springs. I hate to leave the kids but it's for charity. I'll be back in a couple days."

"Nice," Phil said glumly. "I suppose there'll be celebrities there."

"Clint Eastwood," Bob said, "Kelsey Grammer and..."

Phil tuned Bob out, unable to envy him. The last time he was at Bob's house, Melanie had felt up his buns. He'd met Bob's father twice, and the man had a tongue like a machete. Not a life to be envied, despite all Bob's money.

"I'll be back the day after tomorrow," Bob said. "I hope you'll have this taken care of by then. And don't get caught. You know I'd hate to have anything happen to you."

He clicked off before Phil could reply. In pain and miserable, Phil punched in a number.

"Hansford Sheriff's Department," a bored voice said.

Instantly the pain in his stomach eased. Maybe that was his sign. All along, God had been speaking to him through his stomach.

Where was Max? Kneeling on the couch, Belle stared out the front window, then glanced at her pink fingernails resting on the top of the couch back. Tory had painted them and her toenails an hour ago, ignoring Belle's protests. Saying no to Tory was like saying no to sunlight. No matter what you said, the rays shone down anyway.

Hearing Tory walk into the great room, she shifted.

"Are you looking for your fiancé?" Tory's mouth smirked like Ted's often did. "Or Max?"

Belle crossed her legs, wiggling her pink toenails. "I don't have a fiancé."

"That's not what he says. And he's not the one who can't remember anything."

Belle bit her lower lip. If Sorcha loved her fiancé, why wasn't she hanging around, trying to get her body back so she could see him and hold him? Do all the things Belle wanted to do with Max but knew she shouldn't.

"Max should be home soon." Tory slumped in the chair across from the couch. "I called and he and Ted are looking at some of Max's properties. You want pizza again?"

Belle shook her head. Today she'd discovered something better than tuna. A human delicacy so wonderful it must taste like a piece of heaven.

"I'll have a peanut butter and jelly sandwich."

"For supper?"

Belle lifted her head and looked down her nose at Tory—

just like Sophia on *The Love Chronicles*. Being a human was easy with the help of her favorite TV show. "Yes, for supper. Is something wrong with that?"

"Hey." Tory hunched her shoulders and shrank further in the chair, knees up to her chest, bare feet on the cushion. "I don't care if you eat cereal for supper."

"I don't want cereal. I want peanut butter and jelly."

"Fine. Go eat your sandwich." Tory stayed where she was, not moving a muscle.

Belle sighed. It looked as if she'd have to get up and make her own. Except for painting Belle's fingers and toenails, Tory hadn't done anything all day. Well, besides trying on clothes and throwing them on the floor.

As a cat, Belle hadn't noticed Tory's sloppy habits.

Did that mean she was becoming less of a cat? She frowned. The thought wasn't welcome, but for the first time it didn't want to make her yowl.

A sound came to her ears from the driveway, the hum of a car engine, its cadence familiar. She swung around, her hair whipping out.

"It's him," she said, her voice low and tense.

"Him who?"

Belle rose to her knees, her arms on top of the couch back, sticking her face against the window. "Max," she said, her breath puffing against the glass.

Tory's chair squeaked as she leapt off it. A second later, Tory knelt beside Belle, her elbow poking Belle's.

"Ted's with him," Tory said. The car glided into the garage, and Tory and Belle were left looking at the shade tree in front.

Belle twisted away from the window and jumped off the couch.

"Don't be so eager," Tory said. "Wear your heart on your sleeve and it'll get ripped off."

Belle turned her head. Tory watched her, her mouth turned down, her eyes radiating sympathy. Belle didn't understand Tory. What was wrong with letting Max know she was glad to see him? When she was a cat, he'd liked it when she'd rubbed against his leg and allowed him to pet her. Why should that be different just because she was human now?

Did it have something to do with sex?

Everything about being a human seemed to be about sex.

Her body shivered in a good way, a delightful ice cream sandwich way. Sex with Max didn't seem horrid either.

But to never be a cat again... Her shivers stopped abruptly. That wasn't something she cared to think about any more than she wanted to think about leaving her home.

She heard the sound of the back door opening. Muffled male voices trickled into the great room. Belle hurried to the kitchen.

Twenty-eight

A second after Max sat down, the white bag with the sub sandwiches on the table in front of him, Sorcha swept into the kitchen. He felt a lift inside him and tried to tamp it down. Pulling soda cans from the fridge, Ted asked Sorcha if she wanted one. She told him no, heading straight to Max. Her back was straight, her hips swaying, her slender body radiating a compelling combination of sensuality and vibrancy.

Max braced himself. He'd never known a woman like Sorcha. Sometimes she had the innocence of a child, other times the erotic charms of a goddess. She could sleep half the day, then wake up as energetic as a kitten. She had more contradictions than the English language.

"You were gone all day," she said, her tone not accusing, just stating a fact.

"We had a lot to do." Max shuddered to think what her life might have been like growing up under that joy-sucking banner of fanaticism.

He pulled a wrapped sub sandwich out of a bag before she could ask about her parents. "Want a sub? It's turkey."

She bent forward, her nose almost touching the sub, and sniffed. "I can't tell."

He tore off the wrapping. She reminded him of Belle sniffing anything new before she condescended to eat it—or not.

"Okay." She sat next to him, grabbed it from his hands, and stuffed the end into her mouth. Bits of lettuce fell to the table and she ignored them.

Max wanted to laugh. Ted did.

"Sometimes I think you can't be for real." Ted sat and took a sub from the bag. He pulled off the wrapping, checking to see what kind of meat was inside.

Sorcha didn't answer, too busy chewing with her mouth screwed up and her forehead puckered, as if she were testing the sub to see if it was up to the gastronomical delight of canned tuna. Then her brows rose and she chewed faster. Her eyelids lowered, an expression of bliss flushing her pretty face.

A tightness in Max's belly eased and he realized how much he liked seeing her happy. That wasn't good, not when he was leaving. Not with the mystery surrounding her life.

Tory strolled into the room. She was dressed in black slacks and a red top, her ankle-high red boots tapping on the wood floor.

"Going somewhere?" he asked.

"Just shopping. But let's not talk about me. What did you find—"

The front doorbell rang and she swiveled toward the front of the house.

"I'll get it." Max stood.

"No, I'll get it," Tory said.

"I'll get it," he snapped.

She gave him a dirty look. "Who do you think you are? King Max?"

He marched past her. Let her think what she wanted. Someone had killed Sorcha's fiancé and might be after her. His house couldn't be a fortress, but at least he could answer the door.

At the front door, he peered out the spy hole. Phil stood there, his hands in his pocket, his mouth turned down as if his thoughts weren't pleasant, his shoulders slumped. The image of a man on the edge of defeat.

Max jerked open the door. "What do you want?" he demanded.

A muscle in Phil's cheek twitched. "I'm here to see my fiancé. You got a problem with that?"

"A big problem. Sorcha's fiancé is lying in a Milwaukee morgue. So who the hell are you? Is Phil Hern even your name?"

The younger man froze. Max stilled, sensing danger. Then Phil started to slide his hand into his back pocket.

And Max wondered why he'd thought it was a good idea not to call the police.

His defenses up, Max started to close the door.

Phil pulled out a badge. "I'm an FBI agent."

Max laughed. This guy was incredible. One damned lie after another. "Why should I believe you now?"

"I'm investigating a murder." Phil's shoulders firmed, his legs braced, still holding up the badge.

For the second time, Max started to slam the door shut.

"Wait!" Tory called behind him.

Shit. He turned to give Tory a look that should have glued her stylish boot heels to the floor—but she stepped past him, smiling at Phil like he was a producer with the role of her life.

"You're *not* engaged to Sorcha?" she asked.

He shook his head. He smiled at her with his mouth, but his eyes remained sad. The look they shared lasted a couple seconds too long.

Max swallowed a groan. Sweet Jesus, not this. "Tory, you can't believe this bozo. He could be a murderer."

She looked at Max, her lips pulled back, her hands fisted at her sides. "He has a badge."

"I can buy a badge at the party store. He lied before. Why the hell do you think he's telling the truth now?"

"He's a good man." She thumped her left breast. "I know it here."

"How simplistic can you get?" Max ran his hand through his hair. What could he say to get through to her? "Does your heart know someone killed Sorcha's real fiancé?"

Her mouth opened but nothing came out. Max nodded. She was finally seeing the warts on her frog prince.

"He could be the murderer." He jerked his thumb toward Phil.

Her jaw clamped tight, her head shaking. "Not Phil. He'd never kill, would you?"

Phil frowned slightly, looking undecided. Eyes shifted, nose pinched, shoulders pulled in. Then his shoulders squared. "In the line of duty," he said.

"This is a joke. What's your supervisor's number?"

Phil dug in his pocket, his face wooden, as if he slammed down on his emotions. "Here," he said, giving Max a card. "This is your local sheriff's department. Ask for Deputy Olivia Michaels. She'll confirm my identity."

Max jerked his finger at the car in his driveway, a make and model so common it could have been government issue or a rental or just a car bought off a lot. His supply of knowledge covered stocks and real estate, not murder. But he knew enough not to believe a liar. You lied once, you lied again.

"Hit the road. I don't care if you're the Director of the FBI. I want you out of here."

"Max!" Tory's eyes filled with tears.

Max told himself tears came easily to Tory. She was an actress, wasn't she? She cried at commercials, for Christ's sake. Looking into her damp eyes, he shook his head. "He might hurt Sorcha. I can't take that chance."

One tear flowed down Tory's flawless cheek.

"I was undercover," Phil said. "I guess you have the right to feel deceived, but I'm here to protect Sorcha, not harm her."

"Then you should've told the truth. Now get out." He slammed the door on Phil's face, the thump not giving him enough satisfaction.

"Max!" Tory looked at him, her mouth open. Her tears dried but she looked as tragic as if someone had killed her favorite soap opera star. "Please."

"Sorcha's under my protection. I can't take any chances."

"You're so anal. All you need is one look at him and you can tell...tell..."

"That he looks good and has muscles," Max finished.

"Oh!" She jabbed her fist into his stomach hard enough to take away his breath. Then she grabbed the door handle and turned it.

His arm snaked out and he wrapped his hand around her upper arm. "Don't," he ordered. "I can't take chances with you either. If he's a killer—"

She faced him, her eyes tragic. "I know it sounds crazy. I know you're not going to believe me. I know a week ago I wouldn't have believed me either." Her forehead crinkled, her eyes pleaded. "I think he could be the one for me."

"Oh Christ." He shook his head but didn't loosen his fingers.

"It's true." Her eyes blinked and she rubbed her finger below her nose, sniffing inelegantly. "I didn't say anything to him, and he didn't say anything to me." She lifted one shoulder. "How could we? He was pretending to be engaged to Sorcha. But I believe he feels the same way."

"You just met the guy."

She glanced away and swallowed. When she looked back, her gaze was intent on his eyes as if she were trying to peer through them into his mind and read his thoughts. "Didn't you ever look at someone and think, 'She's the one'?"

He wanted to say no, but he thought of Sorcha when he'd first seen her standing in the middle of the road. Frustration welled inside him. "Jesus, Tory. That's lust, attraction, whatever. Not love. I can't let you go to Phil. Bottom line, there's a killer out there and it could be him. He's lucky I don't report him to the police."

"He told you to call the sheriff's department." Her voice was a cry of frustration and anger and want. "Why don't you?"

As if she'd pressed his pause button, Max stood holding her, his mouth slightly open. Why didn't he call them? Why hadn't he called the Milwaukee police yesterday? Hell, why not release Tory's arm this second, walk to the kitchen, pick up his phone, and dial 911?

"You can't give up your control to them, can you?" Tory's chin lifted and her nostrils flared.

"You're wrong." Through the closed door, he heard an engine start up.

Tory's head cocked toward the sound. Her fist went to her mouth and she bit a knuckle.

"Okay, I'll tell you why," Max said. "If I let you go, you promise not to run?"

The knuckle came out of Tory's mouth. "For now."

He released her, his hand dropping to his side. She immediately crossed her arms, her lower lip out, reminding him of how she'd looked as a pouting child. Glancing at her booted foot tapping the floor, he collected his thoughts.

He lifted his index finger. "Number one, Sorcha wouldn't be able to help your friend. She doesn't remember anyone." He lifted another finger. "Number two, it's possible the FBI or the sheriff's people might leak her location, putting her in danger." He lifted a third finger. "Number three..." There had to be a number three. What the hell was it?

Her brows arced.

"The first two are reason enough." He scowled. "Without her memory, Sorcha can't help the police or the FBI or the sheriff. The less people who know where she is the safer she'll be."

"Fine." She reached for the door handle.

"What are you doing?"

"Going after Phil."

He pressed his palm on the door over her head. He'd made it through the drama of her teenage years and had thought the days of emotional lightning and thunder and a few tornadoes were over. How could he have known she was building up to the storm of the century?

She cocked her head. "You can't keep me prisoner."

"I can try to make you see sense."

"You're so..." She lifted her fists and dropped them to her sides. "...controlling. I'm twenty-one. When are you going to let me live my own life?"

"When you make sense."

"Life doesn't make sense." Her booted foot stomped on the floor. "And life isn't always safe. Why do you think I went to New York? It wasn't just to get away from Mom. It was to get away from you, too."

He felt as if she'd kicked him in the head, his ears

ringing. A denial roared in his mind, taking away his breath. She was wrong, all wrong. The family clung to him. He didn't try to control them.

Then he looked at her flushed face and tight lips. And he looked at his hand over her head, holding the door shut. He swallowed a curse, pulled his hand away, and stepped back.

"If you're going after him, you'll need the car keys, won't you?" he said.

She twirled, went up on her tiptoes, and wrapped her arms around his neck. Pulling his head down, she smacked her lips against his cheek.

Tears sparkled in her blue eyes. "Thank you."

"Just go." He gave her shoulders a push.

Max watched her trot toward her bedroom and her purse with the keys in it. She reminded him of a foal bounding out of the stable.

Max headed back into the kitchen slower than when he'd strode out. He couldn't put off telling Sorcha her fiancé was murdered. Too many people knew.

When he turned into the kitchen, Sorcha gazed at him, wiping the last crumbs of her sub from her lips.

Max swore to himself. Unlike Tory, he could rein in his emotions. This wasn't his fate if he didn't acknowledge it.

"What's up?" Ted asked.

Max didn't look at him. "I have to talk to Sorcha," he said.

Ted stood, his chair scraping the floor. "And I've got to work. Man, I don't feel like going. I'm tired tonight."

"You must be getting old," Sorcha said.

Grinning, Ted tapped her shoulder as he passed her chair. "That's the first joke I've heard you make. Is your memory coming back along with your sense of humor?"

She shook her head emphatically, but Max saw her eyes avert. He wondered...

"See you tomorrow." Ted gave a wave before clomping along the hall.

Sorcha looked at Max, her eyes shining. Expectant. Tory's voice came from the hall. Max guessed she was talking to Phil on her cell phone. She laughed, and Max's jaw clenched.

"Let's go," he said.

Belle stood. "Where?"

"Where we can be alone." He started to grab her hand, then pulled back. It might be wiser not to touch her too often.

"The bedroom?"

He looked at her hopeful face and reminded himself he had serious stuff to tell her. Someone had killed her fiancé and might be after her. Plus, her parents made his family look like the Cleavers.

Scratching the corner of his mouth, he wondered again how she'd turned out so normal. Well, not normal, but with a don't-mess-with-me attitude that was as much a part of her as her skin.

"My office," he said.

"I like your office."

She hurried ahead of him, almost dashing along the hall. Again the spurt of energy that seemed at odds with the lethargy that made her curl up and nap a half dozen times a day. She was an enigma, a puzzle he felt compelled to figure out. But some puzzles could take a lifetime to solve and he had only eight days.

Curling her legs under her, she plunked down on the leather love seat along the wall. Although there was room for Max on the other cushion, he pulled up a chair to face her and sat. An expectant half smile curved her lips.

The words didn't come for a moment. He hated to make her smile go away, hated to see her sad. But he leaned toward her. He never tiptoed into water. He always dove straight in.

"Phil isn't your fiancé, but you were engaged. The day your car crashed into the ditch, your fiancé was murdered."

Her smiled flattened, her eyes widening a fraction of an inch. He paused, giving her a chance to say something, to react with horror. She just stared, her closed lips never opening.

Shock. She must be in shock. "You remember any of this?"

Her head shook.

"Eyewitnesses say the murderer chased you. You must've been fleeing him when you crashed your car. He was masked, wearing black. The car was a late-model, mid-sized gray car. Sound familiar?"

Her head shook, her gaze never leaving his face.

"Are you afraid?"

"You'll take care of me." Her eyes were clear of worry, her expression unruffled, as if she never doubted his ability to protect her.

Inside his chest, his heart pummeled against his ribs. He was only a man, not a superhero. And not a monk either. Not the way he was feeling toward her, with his emotions gushing up, along with an erection. "I'm leaving in eight days. I can't protect you forever."

Her head tilted. "You don't have to leave."

"You don't have to stay." He leaned forward another inch, and words he never planned poured out of him, not coming from his mind but from somewhere else in his body. "Come with me. There's time to get your passport if we act now. I'll take you far away from Wisconsin. No one will ever find you."

Her gaze flicked away from his face. She stared at her crossed feet, frowning. He sat back, waiting for her answer, focusing on her, willing her to say *yes*.

"No."

A roar of unexpected hurt gusted through him. He nodded sharply but couldn't talk for a moment. The soreness eased, and he nodded. "Ted will still be here." His voice was thick, and he cleared his throat before talking again. "When I'm gone, you can stay."

Her eyes darkened. "Why do you want to leave? This is your home."

"This is my prison." He got up and walked out before he did something stupid. Like put his arms around her, pull her to his chest, and tell her he'd stay.

That would be fine for the night. Paradise. But in the morning, he'd be sorry.

He was leaving and she was staying. And nothing was going to change that. He'd be living his dream, seeing the world. Once he was gone, he'd soon forget her.

Twenty-nine

Sorcha huddled against the heat register and watched Gwen sit at her desk, doing her homework. From the stereo, a girl with a thin voice sang about being popular. Gwen cocked her head, listening. A sob came from her throat. Then she reached out and turned the stereo off.

What was wrong? Sorcha dashed over and did the only thing she could in this body to comfort her. She pushed the top of her head against Gwen's skinny calf and rubbed.

Another sob came from Gwen. She bent down and her hands wrapped around Sorcha's ribs. An instant later, Sorcha was draped over Gwen's legs, and Gwen was petting her, head to tail, in long sweeps.

Oh yes. This was how heaven must feel.

"You love me, don't you?" Gwen whispered.

Sorcha purred.

"You're the only one who loves me in the whole world."

Sorcha thought of Fletcher. He had loved her. In his way.

"Without you, I'd have no one."

Gwen rubbed Sorcha's ear, using just the right amount of gentle pressure. Sorcha pushed her head against the thin fingers and purred harder, even as her mind told her this was wrong. Without Fletcher, she had no one. She couldn't count Gwen. What she had with Gwen wasn't real or lasting. It wasn't natural.

She imagined what her father would say, and her purring stopped.

"You do love me, don't—" The door pushed open. Sorcha

flew off Gwen's lap and dived beneath the desk, hiding behind Gwen's feet in their Scooby Doo slippers.

Katie stepped into the room, and Sorcha wondered why she hadn't heard her clomp along the hall like a Cyclops. But she had been busy listening to Gwen say she loved her.

This must be how the desert felt when it rained after years of drought. She wanted to suck Gwen's love in through every pore of her cat body.

Katie's brown flip-flops clunked to Gwen's desk. "I thought I heard you talking. What are you doing?"

"My homework." Gwen started typing, the keyboard click, click, clicking, saying, *this user is busy, busy, busy.* "I was just talking to myself. You do it all the time."

"Don't get smart." As Katie stepped closer, Sorcha stared at her ankles, thick with dark hairs growing out of the sides.

Somehow, Sorcha didn't think Katie dated much. She didn't think men liked to date women who looked like prison wardens. *Male* prison wardens.

What parent would hire a woman like Katie as his or her child's nanny?

Even as she asked the question, she knew the answer: parents who didn't give a damn about their child's happiness. Parents like hers.

"Achoo. Achoo, achoo, achoo, achoo, achoo." Katie topped off her sneezes with a honking sniff.

Gwen's wheeled chair inched closer to the desk and farther from Katie.

"Something in here is making me sneeze." The brown flip-flops turned in a half circle.

"There's nothing new." Gwen's voice quavered.

Sorcha sent out a mental command: *Don't let her know you're afraid.*

"Bonnie cleaned today. I shouldn't be sneezing." The flip-flops started to shuffle around the room. Tilting her head to see around the Scooby Doo slippers, Sorcha watched Katie slide her finger over the top of the bookcase. Katie looked at her fingertips and made a huffing sound, as if she was disappointed not to find dust.

She's going to inspect the floor next, and she'll see me. While Katie's back was still turned, Sorcha raced across the room and scampered beneath the bed.

"It's almost spring." Gwen's voice didn't waver, as if she'd heard Sorcha's warning, but her Scooby Doo slippers scuffed back and forth on the carpet. "Isn't there pollen and stuff in the air?"

Hunched to blend in with the shadows below the bed, Sorcha winced for Gwen. Katie wasn't stupid. She was worse: heartless.

"You're hiding something." Katie's voice sharpened.

"No!" Gwen leaped off her chair. Sorcha saw the Scooby Doo slippers point toward Katie as Gwen backed up until she stood at the foot of the bed. Sorcha silently shouted: *No, Gwen! Don't! You're leading her straight to me.*

"I'm not hiding anything." Gwen took one more step back, her toothpick legs smacking against the mattress. "This is my room. Can't I have any privacy?"

"It's under the bed, isn't it? Get out of my way." The flip-flops started toward the bed.

Sorcha scooted back against the wall. She shook like the weakest twig on the tree and wished she weren't so afraid. A fraidycat, that's what she was, even when she was human.

"If you don't move away from the bed," Katie said, "I'll move you myself."

"If you touch me I'll call my lawyer."

"Don't make me out to be a bad guy. I've never laid a violent hand on you."

The reasonableness in Katie's voice made Sorcha feel as if winter blew into Gwen's airy bedroom. Katie didn't have a clue to the many ways her coldness could stunt a young, sensitive soul. She probably thought she was doing a good job. The same thing Sorcha's parents had thought when they'd prayed over her day and night, trying to make the devil leave her small body.

"I'm not moving!"

"You may as well tell me what's under the bed. Don't make me get down on my knees."

"Go to hell!"

"Okay, that's it. No swim class for you this Saturday." The flip-flops turned and started walking around the bed toward the door.

She was leaving? Sorcha was inching away from the wall when the flip flops reached the side of the bed and stopped. She watched, a sinking sensation in her stomach, as the hairy ankles bent and a pair of solid-looking knees dropped to the carpet.

Gwen screamed. Sorcha wanted to move, but her body didn't listen to her mind. The knees scooted closer and Katie's gloomy face peered under the bed, looking straight at Sorcha.

"Eeek! A cat!"

"Yowl!"

"I hate you!"

As if released from an evil magician's spell, Sorcha darted out from under the bed.

"A cat! You know I'm allergic to— Achoo. Oh no, you don't."

Sorcha dashed to the open door. Katie moved like a hippo. Sorcha could run ten times as—

"Woowoowoowoo!" Katie yelled out a war cry.

Jerking her head to the side, Sorcha saw Katie leap toward her in a flying tackle, her arms outstretched.

Oh God, she's going to land on top of me.

Sorcha changed direction, but realized instantly the maneuver put her at the edge of Katie's landing path. Before she could scuttle out of the way, Katie crashed onto the carpet, her hands seizing Sorcha's ribs.

"Yowl!" Sorcha whipped up her front paw, clawing Katie's cheek, then horror rocked through her. *Where did that come from?*

"You frickin' cat." Katie's hands tightened. Holding Sorcha away from her face, she rolled to her feet and shook her.

"Stop! Don't hurt Princess. I hate you!"

"Ow!" Katie stopped shaking Sorcha, but her grip remained unyielding. "You kicked me," she said, looking at Gwen in surprise.

"You're mean. I'm going to report you to the police."

"I think my cheek is bleeding. If the cat scarred me, I'll need plastic surgery. Your parents won't be happy to pay for that." Katie snickered. "Although your mother could probably recommend a good one."

Holding Sorcha at arm's length, Katie marched to the doorway. With each step, her grip tightened on Sorcha's ribs.

"Where are you going?" Gwen's tone changed from angry to pleading. "Don't take her away. I'll be good, I promise."

Over Katie's shoulder, Sorcha saw Gwen's face scrunch, her complexion turning red, even the tips of her big ears.

Sorcha tried to transmit encouragement: *It will be okay. Everything will be okay.* But she knew it wasn't going to be okay at all. She was going to be out in the cold. Alone, hungry, and unloved.

"Impossible," Katie said, each syllable a smashing mallet. "You know how quickly my allergies act up. I'm already feeling the beginnings of a migraine." Katie stepped into the hallway and turned toward the front stairway, her flip-flops purposeful.

"You can get a shot!"

"Even if I liked cats, your mother wouldn't let you keep this one. If she decided to have a cat, it wouldn't be a plain gray one. It would be something special."

"Princess is so special," Gwen said hotly. "Where are you taking her? The animal shelter?"

"I have a calculus test to study for. I've wasted enough time on this creature already."

"I won't let you do this," Gwen said, and the hurt in her voice made Sorcha's insides twist.

Katie glanced behind her. "How are you planning to stop me?" she asked, her voice mocking.

Sorcha watched Gwen stiffen and lean forward, her hands fisted. Then she barreled forward, her arms flailing.

"Don't you—"

A small fist punched into Katie's stomach. Then another, and another.

"Why, you little— Stop that!" Katie's arms dropped, and

so did Sorcha, landing on her four feet on the hallway carpet, her body not even jarring.

"I hate you," Gwen yelled, hitting out with both fists, her punches smacking into Katie's cushioned ribs and belly. "Run, Princess! Run and hide!"

"Oof!" Katie tried to grab a flying fist, and her hand grasped air. She made another snatch, and Gwen's knuckles slammed into her wrist.

Sorcha backed up.

"Run!" Gwen screamed.

Sorcha turned and dashed toward the steps. Yes! This house was so big and she was so small, there had to be a hundred places she could hide.

"Got you!"

Katie's triumphant yell reached Sorcha at the head of the staircase. She skidded down a step, her ears pricked up.

She told herself she shouldn't stop. If she hurried, she could still find a place to hide. Even as she thought this, she turned. Gwen had done something no one had ever done. She'd fought for her.

"Ow!" Gwen called.

A roar like a small lion's burst from Sorcha's throat. She raced up the steps and along the hall, thinking about those hard fingers digging into her ribs. It had hurt. A lot. She knew if Katie caught her, she'd do it again.

Dread dried up her mouth and her running feet slowed. This was stupid. Gwen didn't fight Katie so she could get caught again. This was—

Gwen whimpered.

Looking up, Sorcha saw Katie shaking Gwen.

Sorcha ran faster.

Leaping, she extended her claws, her front legs aimed straight at Katie's face. Still shaking Gwen, Katie must have seen something out of the corner of her eyes, her head turning.

Sorcha slammed into her face.

"Eeeek!"

"You came back for me!" Gwen cried and talked at the same time, snot dripping from her nose. "You came back!"

Sorcha tumbled down Katie's chest, her nails catching on the sweatshirt. Katie lifted her hand and made a fist. Seeing her hand come down, Sorcha yowled and leapt off her. The fist punched her spine and the slam of pain made her yowl again. As she hit the floor, Katie's foot came out, the right flip-flop connecting with her ribs. Sorcha thudded into the wall.

"No!" Gwen screamed. "No!"

While Sorcha lay stunned, Katie swooped down with a grace that shocked Sorcha more than the kick. Just as she'd dreaded, those punishing fingers jabbed into her ribs. When she looked at Katie's face, she saw a thin scratch on the wide forehead.

Her mind scrolled up the image of Katie shaking Gwen, and she didn't regret scratching Katie. No matter what happened to her.

Lifting Sorcha, Katie stomped along the hall.

"I'll call the lawyer," Gwen yelled. "I will."

"Go right ahead. I'll show him my scratch. Who's he going to think is worth more? A vicious cat or an experienced nanny?"

"I hate you, I hate you."

Sorcha looked into Katie's eyes and saw a dull brown, as devoid of compassion as two pebbles.

They reached the stairway. The cruel fingers clamped tighter, and Sorcha yowled.

"You're hurting her!" Gwen cried.

Katie clumped down the steps, not saying a word, not loosening her grip. Then the flip-flops clattered on the tile foyer floor. Gwen trailed after them, her face red and scrunched. Every few breaths came out gasping, and she kept lifting her palms to her cheeks and rubbing hard.

They passed the antique umbrella stand, almost at the door. Sorcha knew what was coming and welcomed it. Harder to bear than the fingers digging into her ribs was the agony in Gwen's water-filled eyes. Katie changed her grip, clutching Sorcha with one hand, her other hand letting go to pull the door open.

Cool air rushed in as Katie raised Sorcha over her head.

Then her hand whooshed forward, her fingers opened, and Sorcha went flying through the air.

Sorcha squealed. Behind her, Gwen wailed as if her heart was broken. Still in the air, Sorcha somersaulted. Right side up, she spread her legs to slow her descent until her four paws slammed onto the sidewalk.

"Go away. If you come back, I promise you'll be sorry," Katie said.

Without looking behind her, Sorcha dashed toward the edge of the property. Her time with Gwen was always meant to be temporary, an interlude. But tonight she felt as if an invisible string attached her to Gwen, joining their hearts.

The farther she ran from the house, the more the string stretched.

She wondered if it would remain when she was human again.

Thirty

Belle tried to read but kept thinking about Max. He was leaving. She didn't understand why. Wasn't everything he needed right here?

She sat in the great room, her Harry Potter book on her lap, almost to the end, but she felt too restless to read. If she had her cat eyes, this would be a good night to go out and prowl. But these human eyes didn't work as well when the sun went down.

One more reason to be a cat again.

She needed to remind herself. Being human was starting to grow on her like these long brown hairs on her head. If she didn't change soon, she'd be one of them, thinking just because she could operate a can opener she was better than all the other species.

Although operating a can opener was pretty special.

The book on her lap started to slide and she grabbed it. Reading Harry Potter was special, too.

Images of Max flared in her mind: sitting at his desk in front of his computer, his expression serious; sprawled on his bed sleeping, his body radiating heat; standing in the doorway of his room with the towel tenting out in front of him.

She closed her eyes. *Where are you, Sorcha? Hurry. Hurry before it's too late.*

Just thinking about Max going away, a hole bored into her stomach, into her heart. In her cat body, maybe she wouldn't miss Max so much and the hole would fill with the joys of naps and watching insects crawl and humans stumble. After all, Ted would feed her, clean her litter box, and pet her when she demanded attention.

She *allowed* humans to take care of her. She didn't need them.

The sound of laughter came closer and Tory walked into the room, holding the cell phone against her ear. "I'll see you in twenty minutes," she said into the phone. Still smiling, she closed the phone and slid it into her pocket.

Tory neared Belle and the corners of her lips turned down. She stopped about four feet away, her hands clasped in front of her, her fingers twisting together.

"I don't know what Max said to you—"

"He said Phil lied. He's not really my fiancé."

Tory's fingers twisted together. "He was undercover and had to pretend. It was part of his job. He was trying to catch the man who murdered your real fiancé."

Belle nodded. Hadn't Evan on *The Love Chronicles* done the same thing when he was an undercover cop, before he'd found out he was the bastard son and heir of the richest man in Thunderbird County?

"You're not angry?"

"No." Why would Belle be angry? She always knew she wasn't engaged to Phil. It was the others who'd believed him. But they were human, and humans put too much importance in words. As if Belle didn't see the way Phil looked at Tory that first day, like a dog drooling over a juicy bone.

"Well, okay." Tory's hands unclasped. She laughed softly and bent forward, hugged Belle quickly, then pulled back. "I wish Max were as understanding as you. He's acting like a guard dog."

Belle shrugged. Ever since she'd gotten into this human body, she'd noticed the resemblance between men and dogs.

"Then you don't mind if I go mountain climbing with Phil?"

"Mountain climbing?" Twisting around, Belle looked out the window. In the distance, she saw hills, but where was the mountain?

Tory's laugh rang out. "Not a real mountain. It's inside a building, a wall with handholds and projections like a mountain. It's great exercise."

A *fake* mountain? Why would anyone... "Go ahead," Belle said. Humans did so many odd things, she hardly noticed anymore.

Did that mean she was becoming human, too?

She shivered as if a cold wind blew at her.

With a wave, Tory bounced out of the room. Belle started to read her book again but stopped when she heard Max's voice in the hall.

Her heart skipped, a happy bounce like Tory's walk.

She was happy because he was near.

When she was a cat, she'd wandered over to Max whenever she'd felt like it, day or night. She missed being with him. She missed him telling her she was a pretty cat. She missed his petting.

She put the book on the table. Humans talked all the time. She could talk to him.

As she stood, he strolled into the great room. Her lips didn't curve up, but a smile grew inside her chest. He'd come to her. He hadn't been able to stay away.

Halfway to her, he stopped.

Her breath caught in her throat. *Keep going, I want to be close to you. Real close.*

A door in the back slammed. Tory was leaving, Belle thought, her gaze not wavering from Max's blue eyes that watched her intently.

"You can change your mind and come with me." He took a step toward her.

"You can change yours." She took a step toward him.

"It's what I've always dreamed of." He took another step.

"Then you have to do it." She took another step. "Just the way I have to stay here."

"You can't stay here forever." Another step.

"Why not? Ted won't mind." Another step.

"It's not what people do." Step.

"I'm not like most people." Step.

"I can see that." Step.

He stood an arm's length away. One more step would take her so close that his breath would touch her face.

The smile inside her was bright, warming every inch of her like the sun. *Max* was like the sun. Drawing her to him even though she knew it was wrong.

She'd always wondered why humans did some of the things they did. Now she knew.

How could anyone resist the sun?

She took the last step.

His arms curved around her back.

Her arms clutched his neck.

"This is a mistake," he said.

"We shouldn't do this," she agreed.

His chest brushed her breasts, his lower half pressed against her stomach. From somewhere inside her came the urge to line up her lower half with his, and she stood on her tiptoes.

He made a sound inside his throat that she'd never heard in the four years she'd lived with him. His head came down, his lips meeting hers.

He *was* the sun!

Rays of brightness and heat spread through her. She clutched him, trying to hold him closer and closer.

"Open your mouth," he muttered, his voice rough.

"What—"

His tongue went inside her mouth. It felt odd, and then it felt right. Nice. Warm. Joining them. Now she knew why the humans on *The Love Chronicles* wanted to kiss all the time.

His hand rubbed up and down her back. His hips moved against hers.

She pressed her hips back against him. Little sunbursts traveled to her center. She pulsed with warmth. With need. She wanted to touch his skin, experience the feel on her fingertips. Put her human scent on him.

She moved her head back, their tongues disengaging. A small sense of reason returned.

She knew what was going to happen. Sex. His body connecting with hers. She'd seen rabbits and birds do it.

The men and women on TV did it all the time beneath the bed covers, especially in *The Love Chronicles.*

I'm not a woman, she reminded herself. *I'm a cat.* But she didn't feel like a cat. Instead, she felt all woman.

If that was what a taste of him did, what would the whole meal accomplish? Would she be able to change back to a cat afterward? Could she take the chance?

She shivered and turned her head away from him.

"Having second thoughts?" he asked, his voice hoarse like the wind rushing through the trees, shaking the branches.

She nodded.

He slid his hand beneath her ribbed shirt and up her back. Blindly seeking, she turned her head to him again, her mouth open, her eyes closed, her doubts sliding away. She wanted to know what it felt like to be with Max. She *needed* to know. She'd never liked to deny herself. Why start now?

She drew away from him. His face flushed and he pulled his arms back, as if he were holding himself from grabbing her to him.

Then her hands lifted to the top of his shirt where it was buttoned. Gripping the material by each collar, she yanked down. On *The Love Chronicles,* Amanda had done this with Jeremy once. Buttons had popped loose, flipping through the air onto the carpet.

Nothing happened. Belle pulled again, jerking the material.

Max's hand lifted and cupped her right hand. "We have all night," he said. "Don't be in such a hurry."

"I want to touch you."

"I want you to touch me. I want to touch you, too."

She tugged her hands away, then started to unbutton his shirt. He wore a blue T-shirt underneath. On *The Love Chronicles,* the men never wore anything underneath their shirts.

"Let's go to my bedroom," he said.

The walk to the bedroom seemed to take forever.

He closed the door, the click loud.

"You can still say no."

"Yes," she said, and smiled. "I say yes."

He jerked his T-shirt up and over his head. Locking gazes with her, he tossed it onto the floor.

She laughed and started to strip off her own top and pants while he unbuttoned his jeans and pulled down his zipper. With his head start, he took off his briefs while she tugged off her socks. Anticipation thrummed through every cell of her human body. She wanted him, she wanted him, she wanted him.

She was going to have him.

She took off her bra and panties faster and tossed them into the air, not caring where they landed. Then she jumped on the bed. He followed more slowly, taking a moment to put something over his penis. Then he was next to her, kissing, touching, holding. And she was kissing, touching, and holding.

Her skin slid against his, and for the first time she saw the benefits of being furless, every slide bringing more bursts of sensation. The lovely, lovely, lovely feelings made her move closer to him, curling one leg over his hips.

She wanted more.

"We're moving too fast," he said in that same funny voice. "I want to make this last. I want it to be a night you'll always remember."

She bit his shoulder, the taste of salt and warm flesh in her mouth. Humans. They complicated everything. Even something that should be the most natural thing in the world.

He moaned and moved on top of her and kissed her, long and wet and warm. The perfect kiss, the perfect man, the perfect place for him between her legs. Her hips moved, rubbing against him. His breath sucked in.

"I can't wait any longer." His voice sounded like it came from his belly.

"Don't wait." Her voice sounded like it came from a place lower than her belly.

Then he pulled away, and all of her internal alarms went off.

No! He was not leaving her. Not like this.

She wrapped her other leg around him to hold him close and keep him from getting away until she was done with him. But he was already coming down, pushing against her, coming inside her, watching her face. Then he was inside all the way, stretching her, filling her. He pulled in and out, rubbing against her at the most wonderful places.

A sound came out of her mouth, a long, "Oooooooooooooooooooooooooooooo." They moved together, her body knowing exactly what to do, and she closed her eyes to savor all the sensations. They were dancing lying down, the best kind of dance.

She pulsed around him, small screams coming from her throat. This was so good, so good, so good, so— Her body shuddered, her hands clutching, her nails digging into his skin.

Then his body was shuddering and he roared out, his head raised, the cords in his neck showing. He collapsed on top of her, weakened, his body still convulsing, his skin sheened with sweat.

She wrapped her arms and legs around him, holding him tightly.

As if she never wanted to let him go.

Thirty-one

The ringing phone jerked Caroline awake. Squinting with sleep, she grabbed the phone and saw her mother's name. Her eyes flared open. Brenda wouldn't wake her from her beauty sleep unless it was a matter of major importance.

"What is it?" she demanded.

"I'm stopping off at Starbuck's on the way to work. Andy Marshall is meeting me."

It took Caroline's sleep-hazed brain a moment to compute the meanings of the sentence: Andy. Knockout drug. Max. Naked. Her. Naked. Them. Married.

The haze swept away, and she sat up. "Did you tell him what you wanted?"

"Oh yes. He's bringing the, er, um, package," Brenda said.

Caroline put hand over her left breast, her heart thudding beneath her palm. She needed something stronger than Prozac, something to take away the feeling that she was about to step off a cliff.

She shook her head. If only Max had responded to her, she wouldn't have to do this. "Aren't you happy?" Brenda asked. "Not every mother would do this for her daughter."

"I love you. You're the best mother in the world."

"Aw, thank you, sweetheart. I know we planned to go to Olive Garden, but after I pay for the package, I'll only have five dollars until my next paycheck."

"I'll stop by the phone center on the way to Max's and pick it up. How much?" Caroline grabbed one of the two teddy bears on her left. Looking down, she saw the ribbon on its head. Mama bear.

"Never mind, I'm paying for it."

"I looked it up on the Internet. The price is only a few dollars, which is why so many teenage boys can afford it. How much is he gouging you for?"

"I'm not a teenager," Brenda said sharply.

Caroline hugged Mama Bear closer and stuck out her tongue. Since Brenda had turned fifty, mentioning age around her was like lighting a fuse on a bomb.

"It's supply and demand," Brenda went on. "Andy's my only contact, and I'm willing to pay more. Don't argue. I want to do this for you. I want everything to be perfect for you. A woman as beautiful as you deserves the best."

Tears moistened Caroline's eyes and she kissed the top of Mama Bear's head. "The first thing I'm going to do after Max and I are married is make him put aside a sum of money for you."

"Not money. Gold bars."

Caroline laughed, the tears fading. Only Brenda understood her. They were two of a kind.

"When do you think you'll do it?" Brenda asked.

Caroline thought of Sorcha living in the house, sleeping in Max's bedroom. Probably trying her hardest to tempt him to share it. Caroline didn't buy Sorcha's amnesia story for a second. Sorcha was lazy, strange and rude. In a beauty contest, the only title she'd win would be Miss Uncongeniality. She wasn't even that pretty. But she slept at the house, and Caroline knew men. No matter what her mother said about men wanting beauty or youth, most of them settled for availability. Sorcha was probably waiting for the right time to entrap Max. An old-fashioned word, but he was an old-fashioned man.

She needed to trap him first. "I'll do it the first chance I can get."

"That's my girl!" Brenda's voice rippled with pride.

Three quarters asleep, Belle snuggled against Max's hard warmth. It felt so right to sleep next to him again, to hear the soft throat sounds as he slept, to smell his scent. She wanted to purr with contentment.

"Ummm," she said.

Ummm? A word, not a purr? Her eyes opened. She was lying next to Max and she was a human, not a cat. Memories of last night poured back.

What had she done?

Her heart rate fluttered wildly. Her fingertips prickled. She'd been right to be afraid to join together with Max, connecting with him in the most intimate way possible. It had changed something in her. She knew because she wanted to do it again. She wanted to reach over and grab his shoulder and shake him awake. No! Not shake him. Kiss him awake.

What was she thinking?

Her breaths speeded to huffs even as she felt the melting between her thighs.

Oh no, she wasn't doing that again. The more she did *that,* the more human she'd become.

Except she felt human now. She'd felt human yesterday, even before she'd coupled with him. Very human.

Max rolled from his side to his back. His soft snores stopped. For an instant, there was silence. Was he awake? Would he want to— Then she heard his loud, even breaths. His arm touched hers, the slide of his skin making her skin warm, making her whimper with desire.

Telling herself she shouldn't do this wasn't working. She still wanted to do it again.

The whimper turned into fear. She'd loved being a cat. Being a human was so complicated. They had so many things to do. Twittering, and not like birds. Watching everything on TV, not just *The Love Chronicles.* Cleaning after themselves.

She scampered out of the bed.

She needed to get away from Max before she leaned over and woke him with her kiss. She needed to find the cat—*oh no, not the cat. Sorcha, the human in her body.* What was she thinking?

Ten minutes later, she walked in the woods. "Sorcha!" she called, her voice urgent. "Sorcha."

As she walked, her panic died and she chided herself for being so worried. She really was becoming like a human. They worried all the time, as if that would change anything. Cats never worried. If something wasn't right, they hissed, they demanded, and when all else failed, they napped.

How could one night of sex change anything? So what if sex with Max was like fireworks of happiness going off inside her? Humans couldn't do it all the time. She knew that, because if they could, they would, and they didn't.

Before Bonnie had scared her away with the vacuum the last cleaning day, she'd talked about a cake she made called Better Than Sex. The next time the urge to have sex with Max hit Belle, she would ask Bonnie to bake her a cake.

"Sorcha! Sorcha!"

Something from her left rustled. Her head tilted. Could it be— A squirrel darted up a tree.

Sighing, she tramped on. Last night had changed nothing. Max was still leaving and she was still staying. No matter what body she was in, this was her home. She knew every room, every piece of furniture, every bush, and every tree. Why would she want to go anywhere else?

A bird nearby sang, but its song sounded like a dirge instead of an ode to the new day. The sky above was cloudy. The gloomy day matched her mood, too dark for the trees to have shadows. Even the air felt oppressive and heavy, thick with moisture.

"Sorcha! Sorcha!"

This time the rustling noises came from her right. She glanced over, expecting to see another squirrel, but instead a small gray cat padded toward her, its green eyes wary.

Belle halted. Half afraid to breathe, she slowly knelt. "Sorcha? Is that you?"

The cat paused and glanced around.

Belle bit her lower lip. How could she tell if it was Sorcha? When she was a cat, had she been smaller than this one? Bigger, fatter, thinner? She'd spotted herself in mirrors, but hadn't paid attention. Only humans looked at themselves for hours on end, trying to find their faults and fix them. Not cats. Cats knew they were unique and beautiful.

"If you're Sorcha, let me know."

The cat's head cocked and it meowed, the sound rising at the end, just like humans when they asked a question.

Belle's heartbeat thumped. It was Sorcha. It had to be.

"I know! Why don't you paw the ground three times? No wait, I've got a bett—"

The cat pawed the ground. Once, twice—it peered up at Belle—three times.

"You are Sorcha." Excitement flared inside Belle. Then it was washed away by a strange reluctance.

She firmed her lips and stepped forward determinedly. Sorcha was here. Wasn't this what she'd waited for? They could change bodies right now.

Stretching out her hand, she knelt down. She swallowed a bitter lump in her throat. "Let's do it."

Gwen slept in snatches, her cell phone next to her pillow. When she woke up, early rays of sun crept into the room and she pressed redial for the sixth time. No one answered again. She wasn't sure what time it was in Greece, but at some point during the last dozen hours it must've been daytime. Didn't the villa her mother and father stayed at have voice mail? What kind of a country was it?

She didn't know what to do anymore.

She'd even tried calling her lawyer but had gotten a machine instead of a person. She hung up, because she knew it wasn't any use. No matter how nice the lawyer's e-mails were, she really didn't care about Gwen. If the lawyer cared, wouldn't she come to see her sometime?

Gwen's eyes burned but no tears came. Last night she'd cried and screamed. Katie had called her spoiled and ungrateful. When Gwen had asked what she was supposed to be grateful for, Katie had ordered her to her bedroom. Katie hadn't taken her phone away, and now Gwen wondered if her parents had left Greece, telling Katie but not her. Or maybe Katie knew if she told them about the cat, they would be angry at Gwen for bothering them.

The only being that showed Gwen affection was gone.

What was she going to do?

The answer came as if it had been lurking in her mind all this time, just waiting to be asked. *Run away.*

Her breath gasped. It felt like hummingbirds flapped their wings in her stomach. Yes, that was it. She'd hide in the woods and the farmer's field. And when Katie called the police, the police would call Gwen's parents. Maybe then they would worry about Gwen and come home to take care of her.

She started to sit, but a gust of dread made her whimper, as if the blood in her veins had turned to a chilled pudding. Maybe her parents would be mad at her for making the police bother them. What if they didn't bother to come?

For long moments, she sat, taking in deep breaths until her blood warmed again. Her mouth set, she hopped out of bed. Her mother and father would be more upset if it got in the papers.

This thought made her stop with one foot raised. She imagined her picture on TV screens and in newspapers. Everyone looking at the girl with the big eyes and Dumbo ears.

Then she put her foot down. It didn't matter what she looked like. It just mattered that she got Princess back.

So what if her parents were mad at her. What were they going to do? Leave?

She rubbed her eyes with the back of her hand. Her head down, she zipped along the hall and around the corner, then opened a closet filled with carry-on bags and suitcases. She grabbed her mother's Gucci bag, shut the closet door, and ran back to her bedroom. Hurrying, she stuffed in her cell phone, laptop, blanket, and a change of clothes into the bag. She grabbed her backpack, too. That should be enough.

After stepping out of her pajamas, she changed into her clothes with the speed of Spider-Girl. In another half hour,

Katie's alarm would go off, so loud the ring reached all the way to Gwen's room. Before Katie was up and about, Gwen needed to go downstairs and get food. Just in case, she'd take some money, too.

In the kitchen she wrote a note: *You're always mean to me and I won't stay anymore. If you won't go away I will. I hate you. Gwen Whitney*

She read it and winced. It sounded like something a six-year-old would write, not the smartest girl in fifth grade. She tried to think of a better way to put it, but kept glancing at her watch and couldn't concentrate. Sighing, she thought sometimes the things that mattered most took less words to say.

The buzz of Katie's alarm shrieked through the ceiling and into the kitchen like angry bees. Gwen left the note on the table, grabbed a banana off the counter, and ran out the door.

Fifteen minutes later, she sat behind the trees and listened to Katie shout her name. Gwen heard the panic in Katie's voice. With the ghost of a smile, she read the e-mail she had typed to her lawyer.

To: Jewel Bernstein
From: Gwen Whitney
Subject: Running away

Hi,

I'm just writing to let you know I'm running away. Katie's going to tell you I ran away because she kicked out Princess, the cat I found. She's partly telling the truth. The other part is that Katie isn't nice to me. I don't think she likes me one bit.

The cat loved me and liked being with me. And I loved her.

I know my mother and father think I'm ugly, and that's why they don't love me. Katie only stays with me for the money. Why can't I have something that loves me?

I won't come back until Katie's gone and I can have the cat.

I mean it!!!!

Gwen Whitney

By the time Gwen clicked on *Send,* her almost smile had turned upside down. Above her the sky darkened, as if it were going to cry for her. Good thing she'd brought her raincoat. She put away her laptop and started walking, Katie's increasingly frantic shouts farther away, reminding Gwen of the caws of a crow.

Thirty-two

The cat crept over a leaf, her green gaze locked with Belle's. Belle remained still, afraid to move, afraid she'd scare away the cat—no, not a cat. Sorcha.

"Sorcha," she murmured. "It's time."

The air around them darkened. Shivering, Belle took her gaze off Sorcha, peering at the sky. Clouds blocked the sun, and the darkness couldn't be because of anything she and Sorcha were doing. Still...

"Let's hurry," she said, looking at Sorcha again.

The cat stared. They were an inch apart. All Belle needed to do was move forward that inch and they'd be touching. *Move*, she told her feet. *Move.*

As if she were a statue, she continued to kneel with her hand out. She'd done all she could. The rest was up to the cat.

Sorcha surged forward, the top of her head touching Belle's hand. A jolt of sizzling energy started at the palm of Belle's hand, coming up through her arm, her elbow, and into her shoulder. The cat stiffened, and Belle knew she felt it, too. And then—

The heavens opened. Rain poured down on them.

Belle shrieked and the cat squealed, both jumping apart.

Her arm tingling, Belle threw back her head and laughed. "C'mon," she said, "we'll go into my house and change there."

She bent to scoop Sorcha into her arms, but the cat skittered away.

What if Sorcha wouldn't go with her?

A danger alarm clanged inside Belle's brain. *Keep calm,* she told herself. She breathed deeply in and out once, then made her voice low and soothing, like Jason, the therapist on *The Love Chronicles* who got all the rich old women to leave him money.

"You don't want to get wet, do you? Come into the nice warm house with me." She took a step forward.

The cat nodded, then scooted next to Belle.

Laughing, Belle started to run. The cat ran alongside her.

In a short time, Belle thought, she'd be a cat again.

Her laughter stopped abruptly, the gray in the sky seeping into her chest, but she kept running, her steps never faltering.

Caroline parked in the driveway. Dodging raindrops, she ran toward Max's back door. Under her breath, she sang, "Don't rain on my parade," a song Brenda never let her sing in her pageant days. "You can't compete with Streisand," she'd say, then smile and gesture at Caroline's face and slender body. "But Streisand could never compete with you."

As she reached the door, something moved in her peripheral. She glanced over her shoulder. Sorcha was running toward her. Caroline's singing stopped. What was that racing alongside Sorcha? Was it...? Could it be...?

They came closer. Caroline's throat tightened. The cat. It was alive.

Her anticipation curdled. A raindrop hit the top of her head and dribbled down her forehead. She shoved the door open and went inside. So the cat hadn't been mortally injured and hadn't crawled off into the underbrush to die. So what? She wasn't going to let it ruin her hairstyle or her day.

She grabbed a napkin off the holder on the table and dabbed her forehead before the drip made it to her eyes and smeared her mascara. The door opened as she shrugged out of her coat.

Woman and cat rushed inside.

They spotted Caroline and skidded to a stop.

"So, you found the cat," Caroline said over the lump in her throat that tasted like ashes. Her intention to stay positive withered under the cat's wary gaze. The cat would get in her way again, hissing when she came near Max. And Max would feel grateful to Sorcha. He'd want her hanging around, making it difficult for Caroline to give him the drug, especially since Andy had misheard Brenda's request and had given her only enough for one person, not three. In a frenzy of inspiration, Brenda had gone home and ground her sleeping pills for Caroline to put in Sorcha's and Tory's food.

Picturing Brenda smashing the pills with a meat mallet between waxed paper, Caroline's spine stiffened, the lump in her throat shrinking. Brenda could have asked Andy to return with the knockout drugs, but Caroline guessed she'd decided to be resourceful and save the exorbitant amount of money Andy had demanded.

Could Caroline do any less than her mother? As Brenda had often said during Caroline's pageant days, "The only way we can lose is if we quit."

The cat squeaked, and Caroline glanced down. The cat stared at her, trembling. Caroline frowned. Obviously it remembered what had happened.

A hissing sound came, but not from the cat. Caroline raised her gaze. Sorcha watched her through slitted eyes, as if she knew what Caroline had done. A chill skittered down Caroline's spine. Impossible.

Then Sorcha's nose lifted in the air and she started to walk past Caroline.

The same impulse that had made Caroline shove Emery on the trail and throw the cat at the speeding car came over Caroline again, too powerful to resist.

She put out her foot.

Sorcha tripped forward and reached out, her palms slapping onto the tile, protecting her face.

"I'm so sorry." Caroline bent over her. "Here, let me help you up."

The look of hate Sorcha turned on her made Caroline back up, her hand against her throat. The cat squeaked again.

Caroline tilted her face down and stared deep into the cat's eyes. Unease made her arms prickle with goose bumps. Why did the cat's eyes look so human? There was a spark inside the green depths, as if the cat knew exactly what she had done and what she was thinking. As if she remembered what Caroline had done to her last time...and planned to do again.

Only the next time, she'd make sure the cat would never walk into Max's life again.

Looking at the beautiful blond woman, Sorcha doubted her eyes. Had this woman who looked like she should be on a magazine cover really tripped Belle? Why would she do that?

The answer came, not in a psychic flash but by adding the leg trip to the cat toss. The reason she was in this four-legged, furry body.

Aware of Belle scrambling to her feet, Sorcha kept her gaze on the blond. The woman bent toward Sorcha, her hands out, reaching for her. Sorcha hissed and backed up, her claws extending.

The door opened. A redhead walked in, laughing, a dark-haired man behind her.

Sorcha scratched the blond's wrist. The blond gave an ear-hurting screech. Jackknifing to a standing position, she cradled her wrist in her palm.

"Belle! You're back!" The redhead's voice gurgled like a fountain. Her arms outstretched, she swooped toward Sorcha.

Sorcha dashed beneath her arms, around her legs, and out the open door.

"Belle!" the redheaded woman cried. "Belle, come back!"

Sorcha ran faster. The redhead seemed happy to see her, but the blond wanted to kill her.

She was halfway to the thicket of trees. Behind her, she heard the redhead wail, "Why? Why did Belle run from..." before her voice grew too distant to hear.

Gwen, Sorcha thought. *I want Gwen.*

She reached the tree line, her body shaking. She'd cheated death twice. Once with Deavers and once after the car accident. But everyone knew what happened the third time.

Rain poured down, pelting through her fur, soaking her small body. She stopped beneath an umbrella of thick branches. After shaking off droplets of rain, she burrowed under a pile of leaves. Even if someone came out looking for her, they wouldn't find her here unless they stepped on her.

She was safe. For now.

Max shrugged into his jacket. In the kitchen around him, Caroline and Tory jabbered. Not Sorcha. She wouldn't look at him and he didn't know why—not after the night they'd shared. He'd woken this morning determined to talk her into leaving with him, but he didn't need to be whacked on the head with a two-by-four to guess that wasn't going to happen. Morning-after regrets were written all over her downturned face.

He ignored the sinking feeling in his chest, as if his heart was drowning in a flood of hurt. Last night he'd been riding the waves, the champion of the world. Today he was going under for the third time.

The hell with it. He had a cat to find.

"I tried to hold her for you," Caroline said. "And she scratched me."

"I'm sorry," he said, glancing at the thin line of blood on her wrist. "Thanks for trying to hold her." He looked at Sorcha. "And thanks for bringing her in."

Sorcha glanced from Caroline to him, her mouth twisted into a sneer. He had no clue what he'd said to get that reaction.

He strode to the door. Women. Rain or no rain, he'd be glad to get outside in the fresh air.

"She's not going to let you find her," Sorcha said, her voice more clipped and deeper than usual. "Not unless she wants to."

"Belle's my cat. Of course she'll come to me."

"Wait until the rain stops," Caroline said. "You'll catch a cold."

"Phil can go with you." Tory jumped for the phone on the counter. "He's an FBI agent. He'll find Belle."

"I don't think finding cats is part of their training," Max said, unable to suppress a flash of irritation.

"Give him a chance. You want to find Belle, don't you?"

"What's up?" Ted said from the entryway, his voice thick with sleep. "Hey, no one made coffee yet?"

Max jerked open the door and strode out. There was a kernel of comfort in their care, but mostly there was a ton of frustration. This morning he would've liked them all gone—except for Sorcha. And Belle.

Why the hell had she run? That wasn't the Belle he knew.

Thirty-three

"Are you sure you don't want to go to the Brewers game?" Tory asked. She stood in the open back door. Standing outside the door behind her, Phil glanced at his watch.

Belle noticed he avoided looking straight at her. Even when he'd said he was her fiancé his gaze hadn't met hers. Was that a guilty conscience? She'd heard of guilt, although she'd never experienced it herself. Unlike cats, humans had something in their heads telling them not to do things they did anyway.

Like what she'd done with Max last night. Though when she was with him everything had been wonderful. Just thinking about it, her human body warmed. Only present company kept her from wanting to do it again.

The questions and doubts had besieged her afterward, like a swarm of fleas.

"I'm staying home," she said.

"The game might jog your memory," Caroline said at the stove where she was warming her soup.

Belle didn't turn her head. Caroline had left this afternoon. Belle had hoped with her gone, Sorcha would return. But even though Belle had gone outside again and called and called, the rain soaking her, Sorcha wouldn't come to her. Two hours ago, Caroline had come back with a carton of chicken soup and brownies, ruining her day even more.

"I'm staying," Belle said flatly. Everyone wanted her to leave. Everyone could go out and get bitten by rabid dogs.

Well, not Tory and Max. Maybe not Phil, because Tory liked him. But if Caroline met a pack of rabid dogs, for once Belle would be rooting for the dogs.

"Have fun." Tory waved and bounced out of the house.

Phil gave Belle a quick glance. His mouth was turned down and his eyes looked sad, like Brad on *The Love Chronicles* when Lorraine had died in the plane accident.

"Be careful," Phil said, then he yanked the door closed as if he couldn't shut it fast enough.

Shaking her head, Belle peered out the square window of the back door. Although the rain had stopped, the sky was still gray and gloomy. She considered searching for Sorcha again, but Sorcha knew where she was. If she wanted to find Belle, she would come, wouldn't she?

Belle sighed. Inside the cat body lurked a human mind, and who knew what a human might do?

Ted poked his head into the kitchen. "I'm going to work."

Belle mumbled good-bye. Caroline waved like a cheerleader Belle had watched on TV. "Don't work too hard," she said, smiling so wide her gums showed.

Belle wished she had hairballs again. She wanted to hack one up on Caroline's shoes.

Max walked into the kitchen. At first Belle didn't want to look at him, then she thought of Phil and his shifting gaze. She raised her chin and her eyes. Max stared at her, his mouth thin as if he weren't happy with her. She lifted her chin higher.

"Just in time for my chicken soup," Caroline said, bringing two bowls to the table. She patted Max's chair. "Sit, both of you. You two were asking for a case of the sniffles, searching for the cat in the pouring rain. I made this just for you. It'll knock any nasty cold germs right on their heinies."

Humming, she went back to the stove to ladle out another bowl of soup.

Max sat slowly, not taking his gaze from Belle's face. Keeping her chin up, she lowered into the chair across from him.

Caroline carried another bowl of soup to the table, still

humming. She sat between Belle and Max. "Eat," she said to Belle. "I guarantee it will make you a new woman."

A new woman? Belle wanted to be the old cat. Didn't she? Doubts lingered in her mind. When the rain had interrupted her exchange with Sorcha, a part of her had rejoiced. A big part of her.

Feeling Caroline's stare on her, she blinked. Something about the blond woman's smile made the hair on her neck lift.

She rose from the table, walked to the cupboard, and grabbed a can of tuna.

"What are you doing?" Caroline's shrill voice hurt Belle's ears.

Belle put the can in the opener and slammed down on the lever. The can opener whirred. When Belle heard the click, she pressed release, grasped the can, and turned around.

Caroline stood in front of her, less than two feet away. Her shoulders were pulled up, tensed. Her eyes looked anxious, like Ted's the time he'd thought he was going to get a bad grade in college.

"I got the soup especially for you." Caroline lifted her hands like a begging dog. "The least you can do is try it."

"I don't like chicken soup."

"You remembered that? What else do you recall?"

Instead of answering, Belle tipped the can. Tuna-smelling liquid spilled out onto Caroline's shirt and pants.

Screeching, she jumped backward. She pulled the shirt away from her chest. Her cheeks turned pinker than Belle's painted toenails and she whipped around to Max. "She did that on purpose."

Belle walked past her and sat at the table. She pushed aside the bowl of soup and set the tuna in its place.

"You could at least say you were sorry," Max said.

"I'm sorry." She gazed at him and not Caroline. Then she said the same thing Gloria on *The Love Chronicles* said after she'd run over her husband with her SUV. "It was an accident."

His mouth didn't smile, but the skin around his eyes

crinkled with silent laughter. "If you'd done it on purpose, it wouldn't've been nice."

She nodded. Exactly.

"I'll feel better if you try my soup," Caroline said.

"Try the soup." Max shrugged, the crinkles leaving his eyes. "It won't hurt."

"Okay." She used the spoon to scoop up some tuna. "After I'm done with my tuna."

"I have to change my clothes." Caroline grabbed a napkin and patted it on her blue shirt and matching pants.

"Tory might have something to fit you," Max said.

"If I were four inches shorter." Caroline glided over to Max and curved her hand over his shoulder. "But thanks for offering. You're always so caring. Luckily I have a spare outfit in my office. I'll be back before my soup cools." She looked at Belle. "You'll be sure to eat the soup, won't you?"

Belle nodded. Anything to make Caroline hurry and go away.

"You promise?"

"I promise." Since when had Caroline been so concerned with what she ate?

With a tight nod, Caroline hurried from the kitchen.

As soon as she left, Max leaned forward. "You've been avoiding me."

Belle swallowed a bite of tuna. "I was looking for Sor— Belle."

"You waited until I came back and then you went out."

"That's how it is. I go and you stay. Or I stay and you go."

"That's not how it has to be."

"I can't leave my home."

"This isn't your home."

She bent her head and ate. What could she tell him? The truth?

"I understand you're scared—"

"You don't understand a thing," she said, and her voice came out raw and shaking at the edges.

"Then tell me."

"You tell me. What's out there that's not in here?" She gestured toward the window.

"Freedom."

"Maybe my freedom is right here." She tapped her knuckles on the table. "Knowing I'm right where I should be."

"This isn't your home, and you're not agoraphobic." He stared into her eyes. "Considering your background, I can see why that is."

She frowned. "Background?" What about Sorcha's background?

He shook his head. "It doesn't matter. For whatever reasons, the house is more important to you than anything else. I'm not going to try to change your mind. Let's not talk about it anymore."

A cry wanted to work its way out of her throat but she swallowed it. Though she'd lost her appetite, she took another spoonful of tuna. Max started eating his soup.

When Caroline returned shortly, wearing turquoise pants and a pink and turquoise top, their bowls were clean.

"You're done already?" Caroline beamed at them.

Belle stood abruptly. "I'm going to my room to read," she said. A yawn overtook her, and she put her hand over her mouth because that's what people did, even though she didn't understand why. What was wrong with showing her teeth?

"Enjoy yourself," Caroline said cheerily.

Max didn't say anything.

Belle waited until she was in the hall before she replied too softly for Caroline or Max to hear. "Bite me."

Phil was tortured. The dome was closed and Milwaukee's Miller Stadium smelled like beer and brats. Beside him, Tory was yelling louder than the drunk in front of them. Phil didn't know what the score was, because he kept looking at Tory instead of the field. She was beautiful, funny, sexy, loved baseball, and her body was toned sweeter than any piano.

And he was lying to her and her brother and Sorcha. Again. One damned lie after another.

Tory jumped up, slapped him on the shoulder, and shouted. The crowd erupted around them, a roar shaking the stands and drowning out his thoughts. He glanced down. One of the Brewers was running to home, another to first. The left fielder caught the ball. Threw it toward home. The catcher raised his hands. The ball arced through the air toward him.

The runner slammed into home.

Tory grabbed Phil's shoulders. His arms circled around her back, her legs folded around his hips, her laughing face leaned into his. Then she was kissing him. And he was kissing her back.

It was just a kiss, he told himself. A kiss was just a—

Her tongue slid into his mouth, stopping his thoughts. For this moment, all he could do was feel.

A kiss wasn't just a kiss. A kiss was heaven and hell combined.

Thirty-four

The fire crackled to Max's satisfaction. He closed the screen and got up, brushing bits of bark from his knees. Behind him, he heard Caroline entering the great room from the kitchen.

"Hmmm, I love a fire." She met him in the middle of the room, a smile on her face. With her four-inch heels, she looked straight into his eyes. "I brought some special wine." She pressed a half-filled wineglass into his hand. "To celebrate my successful buying trip in Chicago."

"I'm not really—"

"I know you like Merlot. I bought it just for you. You've done so much for me. Buying a bottle of wine to share with you is the least I can do."

"I haven't done anything." He took the glass and started to turn toward his chair. Her hand on his arm stopped him. He hoped to hell she wasn't going to thank him again. Throwing a few bucks at Emery's widow hadn't hurt him. Caroline's effusions of gratitude made him feel like loosening his collar—and it was already loose.

Not like Sorcha, who took everything he did as her due. He couldn't remember her thanking him once.

"Why don't you sit on the sofa? I'll get my swatches and show you what I've chosen for the new furniture." She slanted her cool fingers over his lips, stopping any objections. "I know you're leaving soon, but this is still your home. You said you'll come back someday. When you do, I want you to love it. It's the least I can do to repay you for your generosity."

He strode to the sofa. Might as well do this. Otherwise he'd just stew over Sorcha.

He watched Caroline leave the room, admiring her tall, slender figure. She was beautiful, gracious, smart. He admired her. He knew she admired him. He wasn't blind or dense to the little touches, the intimate smiles, the breathless laughter. Only the knowledge that he was leaving had kept him from deepening their relationship. He couldn't sleep with her, then leave.

So why forget his scruples with Sorcha? She was prickly, odd, and obviously had psychological problems. She refused to leave his home.

Even after last night.

He took a gulp of the wine.

God, last night. And what a night! He'd thought their lovemaking had changed the situation, but it had changed nothing. He needed to leave and she believed she needed to stay.

Or did he need to leave?

He frowned and tried to follow that thought, but it drifted away. It didn't seem important anymore. Nothing seemed important. He picked up the glass and took another gulp. Not too bad.

By the time Caroline returned, he'd finished the glass of Merlot and was starting to feel tired. But he shouldn't be tired. After making love with Sorcha last night, he'd slept like a hibernating bear until a good hour past his normal wake-up time.

"You drank your wine," Caroline said, her voice gleeful.

He nodded. He wanted to tell her it tasted good. Make some of that wine talk she liked. It had a nice body and was friendly, ha ha ha. But he decided not to. He was tired. So tired. And his head felt as if it were filled with helium.

"I'm just gonna lay my head down for a minute..."

As he slid sideways, he watched Caroline drop her armload of swatches on the coffee table. Coffee table swatches, he thought, and giggled.

Caroline smiled widely, as if she thought he was funny, too. He liked that better than her gratitude. No one thought he was funny. Ted was the funny brother. He was the responsible one who took care of everyone.

She put a pillow under his head and patted his cheekbone.

Nice Caroline. Thoughtful Caroline. Gracious Caroline.

"Go to sleep," she said. "Don't worry about anything. I'm here."

His eyes closed. He didn't want Caroline. He wanted Sorcha.

Sorcha, he cried silently, Sorcha.

Sorcha!

Katie kept looking out the door. She hadn't been able to do any homework since she'd returned from her last class.

Where was the brat?

She went from room to room in the overlarge house where no one lived but her and one small girl. She didn't count the few weeks a year when Gwen's parents stopped off. Usually, Gwen's mother was calling her friends all over the world, trying to see who they would visit next, while Gwen's father went to the golf courses, meeting with CEOs and bank presidents.

Katie wanted to be one of the CEOs. This job was her key to the open doors that were closed to the average University of Wisconsin graduate.

The brat was ruining everything for her. If Gwen didn't come back, Katie would get fired and Mr. Whitney would never write her that glowing reference.

Gazing out the front window, she nibbled on her fingernail, something she'd forced herself to stop doing years ago. The sun was lowering. Gwen had been gone for nearly twelve hours, although she might have returned during the day when Katie went to her classes.

Perhaps going to her classes today had been a mistake. Maybe she should have stayed home. Maybe she shouldn't have called Gwen's school and said she was sick. But how was she to know Gwen would be so stubborn? She had thought for sure Gwen would return.

She went to the front door, swung it open, and strode onto the porch. Cupping her hands around her mouth, she yelled, "Gwen! Come home, Gwen! I promise I won't punish you."

She dropped her hands and cocked her head. Nothing.

A sick feeling dipped inside her stomach. If she called the police, they would eventually call the school and she might get into trouble for lying.

She lifted her hands again. "Gwen!" she called, her voice sharper. "Gwen! Come home this minute!"

Again she listened. Again there was no answer. She glowered at the smooth lawn, the lacy, perfectly placed trees, the graying sky almost beautiful in its gloom.

Slowly, the corners of her lips tipped up. The Weather Channel said it was supposed to get down to the low thirties tonight. Above freezing, but close. If she didn't panic and call the police, everything would turn out just fine. Gwen would give in and come back cold and hungry.

Where else did she have to go? She had no friends.

Katie went inside the house. Let the stupid girl suffer. Katie would be snug and warm, so what did she care?

The phone rang, and she hurried to the nearest one. Maybe Gwen was calling on her cell phone.

She picked up the phone and answered in a monotone. She didn't want Gwen to guess how grateful she was to hear from her. The girl might get a swollen head.

"Is Gwen there?" a woman asked, the voice young.

A cold finger touched Katie's heart. "Who is this?"

"Jewel Bernstein, Gwen's lawyer."

"The Whitneys' lawyer is David Bernstein," Katie said, her heartbeat speeding.

"My father. I'm the third Bernstein of Bernstein, Bernstein and Bernstein. I've been in contact with Gwen for about ten months now."

"No! I would've known."

"Obviously you don't. I believe you were studying the first time I called. By the way, I applaud your ambition. Since then, Gwen and I have been communicating via e-mail. May I speak to her?"

Katie sank onto the armless ivory chair next to the phone. "She can't come to the phone right now."

"She's not in bed, is she?"

Katie glanced at the clock. A little after seven. Too early for Gwen's bedtime. "She's taking a bath."

"Get her out."

"You can't tell me—"

"Now."

Katie's grip tightened on the phone.

"You can't put her on the phone," the voice continued smoothly, "because she isn't there. Isn't that right?"

Katie's eyes closed. How the hell did the lawyer know this? "Yes," she whispered.

"Did you report it to the police?"

"No."

"Why not?"

"I was hoping she'd return."

"I'm on my way. I expect the police to be informed by the time I get there."

The phone clicked. Katie punched in 911 and wondered what to say that would be close to the truth and still make her look good.

Thirty-five

"They won! They won!" Tory screeched, jumping up and down. Though Phil was a White Sox fan like his dad, he cheered with her. All around them the crowd went crazy.

Then Tory jumped on him and kissed him.

The roars faded into white noise.

The people around them disappeared.

They were the only two people in the universe. Phil and Tory. Her lips were locked on his, her tongue playing ring-around-the-rosy with his, her arms clasped around his shoulders.

He groaned into her mouth.

She lifted her head. "I know you'll say it's too early and I'm doing everything a girl isn't supposed to do, but I could be falling in love with you."

For one second, he felt a great joy. The next, he felt a greater sorrow.

He pulled away from her. "I can't, Tory. I'm sorry. I can't. Not now."

Her brow furrowed. "I didn't say I was, I said I could be." Her face scrunched. "Oh God, I shouldn't have said anything. I'm an idiot."

"No! I do feel the same as you." Even as the words exploded from his mouth, he wished he could stuff them back in. He didn't deserve her. He had planned to kill her friend for money. What kind of person did that make him?

Her gaze lit up. "It's your job. That's the problem, isn't it?"

"I can't talk about it. I'll take you home." How the hell

had he messed up so much? He'd screwed up everything.

As he turned away, she grabbed his hand. He should pull away, but he left his hand in hers. His body was strong; his willpower was jelly.

The deputy Katie talked to on the phone completely understood Gwen was a spoiled rich girl. When Katie told him she would've loved a cat if not for an allergic reaction that imperiled her breathing, he told her about his allergy to peanuts. He even suggested Gwen had run away as a form of extortion.

"But she's only ten," he said. "I'll have to send a couple of deputies out there. If they don't find her, we'll put together a search party."

Katie commiserated with him about the trouble Gwen was causing the sheriff's department. He told her no one ever thought about that. She wondered if he were single, how old he was, and what he looked like.

After hanging up, she closed her eyes and slumped against the counter in relief. That hadn't been too bad. He'd believed her. After all, everything she'd told him had been the truth. She straightened and was smiling as a car drove along the driveway, the headlights shining into the house.

The lawyer, she guessed. Even if there were a sheriff's car close by, it would take a few minutes to drive over. Wiping the smile from her face, she hurried to the door. She decided to wait on the porch. She'd wring her hands and look anxious.

"Gwen!" she called. "Gwen!"

A red, luscious Jaguar rolled to a stop at the foot of the wide driveway. The woman who stepped out of it was young, tall, slender, and black. She strode toward the porch like she was the Queen of the Nile. "Is Gwen back?" she demanded.

Katie stopped wringing her hands. "Who are you?"

The woman stopped two feet away. "Jewel Bernstein."

Katie looked the woman up and down, taking in the sage-green trench coat and scarf that screamed designer. Her eyes dipped to the shoes that definitely hadn't come from Payless, the leather briefcase, and, above all, the smooth caramel-colored skin. "May I see some identification?"

The woman stilled and something in her gaze made Katie feel like taking a step back. Katie resisted the urge. Without a word, the woman dug a wallet from her purse, opened it. She kept the license in her hand, holding it for Katie to read.

"Are you satisfied?" she asked, the consonants bitten off, her voice icy.

Warmth flushed Katie's face. "I have to be careful. You said you were e-mailing Gwen without my knowledge. There are pedophiles on the Internet looking for girls like Gwen. Would you care to tell me how you knew she was missing?" She stood straighter. Taking control made her feel empowered. Defense was the best offense.

"She e-mailed me."

"May I see it?"

Jewel smiled silkily, her teeth shining whitely in the dim light. "Any communication between me and my client is privileged."

Katie held back a scream. Gwen wasn't a client. She was a ten-year-old girl. A runaway.

"I'm her guardian."

"No, you're her nanny." Jewel patted the briefcase. "While her parents are out of the country, my father and I are her legal guardians."

Gas built inside Katie's intestinal tract and she put her hands over her belly. Even if Gwen had all the money in the world—and that had pissed Katie off from day one—maybe she should have been a little nicer to her.

"Now, what have you been doing all day to find Gwen?"

The pressure got worse, traveling to her butt. She shouldn't have eaten the quart of mocha chocolate chip ice cream, but stress always sent her running to the freezer. She squeezed her buns together to stop a loud eruption.

Jewel's gold-flecked brown eyes stared into hers, as if waiting to catch her in a lie. Katie began to shake.

"I'm so worried," she said, using her fright. "So worried." She started wailing, putting her hands over her eyes so the lawyer couldn't see they were as dry as week-old bread. Under the cover of her fake cries, she farted.

A second later, the lawyer stepped back.

By the time two sheriff's units rolled toward the house five minutes later, Katie had worked herself up to crying real tears. And she still hadn't answered Jewel's question.

Every time her flow of tears slowed, Katie thought about being fired from her cushy job and she cried harder.

Clinging to a branch in a tree that bordered the back of Gwen's home, Sorcha heard Gwen calling, "Princess, Princess." Sorcha wanted to meow and go to her, but she held back. Gwen was too attached to her already.

And she was too attached to Gwen.

When she'd fled the house where Belle was staying, her fear was submerged by a giant wave of relief.

She didn't have to be human. The blond woman tripping Belle was an excuse to run.

Not that she had to justify this to anyone. After all, she was a cat. Cats, as far as Gwen had observed, didn't explain or defend.

Except she wasn't really a cat. She was a human in a cat body. Humans knew wrong from right. And it wasn't right to remain in the cat's body. Every day since the switch she'd heard Belle calling her, wanting to switch back to her old body. If she ignored Belle and remained a cat, everything her parents said about her would be right. To be so selfish would prove she really was Satan's handmaiden.

And what about Fletcher? She didn't want to avenge his death, but she should at least try to tell the world what Deavers had done. Even though no one would believe her, she knew the truth and he knew the truth. And in heaven, God was making good and bad lists like a toga-garbed Santa.

If she didn't do the right thing, God would know.

"Please," Gwen said, her voice throbbing with tears. "I need you."

Sorcha dug her claws into the tree branch. She looked at the sky, a brooding gray. *This is breaking my heart. Should I go to her? Give me a sign, God.*

Beams from flashlights came around the back of the house. Men's voices drifted to her. Sorcha heard Gwen gasp and run toward the farmer's field. Turning her head 180 degrees, Sorcha watched Gwen flee, one large bag bouncing at her side, one on her back.

Sorcha looked at the gray sky again.

Thank you for your answer.

Even if it wasn't the one she wanted.

Max was naked. Caroline stepped back to admire her handiwork. He looked even better without clothes on. Wide shoulders, broad chest, muscular definition without unattractive bulges and veins sticking out. Her gaze slid down. Flat tummy, though no six-pack. Well, he was a multimillionaire. If she wanted, she could afford her own boy toy after they were married. Although she didn't think she would. The best sex she'd ever had didn't halfway match the raw excitement of the worst candy bar.

Which brought Caroline to Max's limp penis, looking so innocent. She clapped her hand over her mouth and stifled a laugh. Right, like a sleeping snake was innocent.

Her gaze swept down his long legs and muscular calves. His feet were too wide. He had a two-inch scar on his thigh, but otherwise she saw no imperfections. He would do wonderfully as the father of their children. Two, she decided. She hoped the boy would get her blond hair, and the girl his red-gold curls.

She picked up the phone by his bedside, sat on the edge, crossed her legs and called her mother. "I did it," she said.

"Oh, my God!" Brenda shrieked. "I'm so excited. My daughter's going to marry a millionaire."

"*Multimillionaire,*" Caroline protested. Marrying a

millionaire was nothing. Emery had been a millionaire and look what had happened there.

"Tell me everything," Brenda said.

"It was almost too easy. I already knew Ted was working, but Tory went to the Brewers game. I put your crushed sleeping pills in Sorcha's chicken soup. More than enough to keep her knocked out all night."

Brenda laughed. "It's as if this was meant to be. You married the wrong cousin."

"I didn't meet Max until Emery and I were engaged. When I did, I had no idea how rich he was." She glanced around the plain room. It didn't even have its own bathroom. Of course, it was a guest room and Sorcha was occupying the master suite—Max was too generous, which would stop after they were married. Even so, was this a way for a wealthy man to live? "Things will change after we're married."

"Of course. What's the use of being rich if you can't show it off?"

"It's getting late. I just wanted to let you know our plan worked. Tomorrow I'll guilt him into marrying me."

No shriek came over the line. Caroline's excitement shriveled. "What?" she whispered ferociously, as if Max could hear her. "What's wrong now?" Something always went wrong, dammit.

"It's nothing, baby."

"Mom! Tell me. I can tell you're having second thoughts. I can hear your doubts."

"It's silly, but I was waiting to hear from you and started to wonder... This isn't Victorian times. Men don't think twice about sleeping with women."

"He's not like most men." Caroline spoke through her clenched teeth. How could Brenda turn on her like this? "He's been supporting his family practically since he was a kid. Rose has been working the guilt thing on him like a stripper works a pole. It's ingrained in him."

"You're right, you're right." Brenda laughed a bit shakily. "It's just this waiting got on my nerves. You know I want the best for you."

"Max is the best. And stop worrying." She heard her own voice, as hard as her determination. "I have it all planned. First I'll tell him how happy I am that he proposed. Before he can reply, I'll tell him that Emery would be thrilled that we're getting married, almost as thrilled as I am."

"You know what else you should say?" Brenda's voice trilled with excitement. "Tell him that you're so happy he wants to start a family right away, and you hope last night did it. That it's your fertile time."

Caroline sucked in her breath and put her hand over her breastbone. "That's brilliant! Just brilliant."

Brenda giggled and she joined in. She was still smiling when she hung up a moment later. She considered Max's nude body again, admiring her handiwork before she rolled him to the side. His arm and hip were warm and firm under her hands. His color and his breath were okay, and she was relieved he didn't appear to be adversely affected by the drug. She didn't want to hurt him, she just wanted to marry him.

She pulled the blanket from under him, rolled him onto his back, and tossed the blanket over him. Then she unbuttoned her blouse.

For once in her life, everything was happening just as she planned. After all these years of rotten luck, it was finally *her* turn.

She began to sing. Max was unconscious, Sorcha was in a deep sleep, Ted and Tory were both out. No one was there to hear her.

"Tomorrow, tomorrow," she sang the song from *Annie*, her favorite from all the beauty contests. Unfortunately, it had been the favorite for a lot of contestants. But she was the only one competing in this contest, so she belted it out.

"Tomorrow, tomorrow."

Tomorrow she'd be engaged to a very rich man.

Belle had been sitting in the chair in Max's bedroom too long. She put down her book and rubbed the small of her back—something else she'd never had to do as a cat. She should have stretched sooner, but she hadn't wanted to stop reading about Harry, Ron and Hermione. Every chapter took them deeper and deeper in trouble. How could she put it down until she reached the end?

For now, all three wizards-in-training were safe, though she wondered what would happen in the next book.

A thought hit her. She wouldn't have time to read the next book. Not if she changed back into a cat.

She closed her eyes tight and her human insides went tight, too. Finally she breathed and her muscles loosened. She stood. She would think about this later.

Her stomach gurgled, telling her to get something to eat. Of course. She'd only eaten one can of tuna. When Caroline had left the room to change clothes, Belle had thrown Caroline's soup down the sink. Why eat soup when there was tuna and ice cream sandwiches? Peanut butter and jelly, too, though she'd used up the peanut butter and someone needed to buy more.

She opened the door to the hall, a vision of ice cream sandwiches in her mind. Whoever had invented ice cream sandwiches was a genius.

The sound of singing came from the room Max was using. She stiffened, then started toward the room. "Tomorrow, tomorrow!" the voice sang. Something about the voice made Belle frown. Max usually didn't have the stereo turned on so loud. And why did this song have no music?

The truth hit her as she reached his door.

Caroline was in the bedroom with him.

She grabbed the handle, turned it, and burst inside. Caroline looked at her, her mouth open, one leg in her panties and one leg out.

Thirty-six

Clinging to an upper tree branch on the farmer's land, Gwen watched the bobbing circles of light converge on the driveway. The sun had gone down, and if a moon was out tonight, dark clouds blocked its rays. Gwen had watched enough TV shows to guess the deputies were going to search tomorrow when it was light.

They'd probably bring a dog. She remembered watching a TV show where two bloodhounds sniffed out a lost child. Gwen unwrapped her arms from the branch and carefully climbed down. This was the one time in her life she didn't want to be sniffed by a dog.

She felt around in the tall grasses for her two bags. Clutching them, she started to run—straight back to the house.

Her legs wouldn't go as fast as she wanted. She was tired and hungry and cold, and her idea wouldn't work unless she got home before the deputies left.

A car engine revved, then another. She heard the faint sound of Katie's voice and the deeper tone of a man's voice answering.

She ran faster. She heard the cars cruise down the driveway. Another engine revved up, then took off.

She was about a hundred feet from the garden. A car door slammed. Someone said, "We'll be back tomorrow."

Huffing, she slid to a stop in front of the naked statue of the goddess Athena. She fell to her knees on the grass and slipped her hand into the dip below the base. She got almost as far as her knuckles when she got stuck. She'd grown too much, her hand too big. Panicking, she shoved her hand into the tiny dip. The statue's marble stand scratched the top of her hand, and she pulled back, putting her knuckles to her mouth.

She was never going to get it out in time!

From the front of the house came Katie's voice, and this time a woman answered her. Gwen shoved her hand in again. She had to get the key before Katie was inside. She had to!

She shoved her hand through. When the marble scratched her hand again, she didn't pull out, but her breath sobbed and she choked it back.

Shut up, she ordered herself. *Just shut up.* She squashed her cheek against the cool marble and wriggled her fingers through the dirt and stones until they brushed against smooth metal. Not close enough to grab it. She strained forward, her teeth gritting. One more inch, that's all she needed.

"Oof." Her hand jerked forward, and her breath rasped loudly. She gripped the key between her index and middle fingers, then started to slide her hand out. The key caught. Setting her mouth, she twisted her hand so the key would lie flat. Her teeth mashed together, she pulled again.

At first she thought the statue was going to win and eat up her arm like a monster in a scary movie. She pulled harder and her hand popped out, the key safe. She fell to the ground with an "oomph." Slapping her scratched and stinging hand over her mouth, she scrambled to her feet.

A door slammed in the driveway.

She grabbed the two bags and raced to the door. As she heard the car drive off, she fit the key in the keyhole. Her hand shook and the tip of the key kept missing the slot. She tried again, but it was like putting shoes on during an earthquake. The third time, she wrapped her left hand around her wrist, but instead of steadying the key, she now had two shaking hands.

Any minute Katie would be inside and it would be too late. *Do something!*

She jabbed the key forward and this time it slid in. She

didn't take a second to exult but tumbled inside and closed the door carefully behind her. She crouched but couldn't hear any Katie noises. Taking a deep breath, she ran out of the kitchen, down the hall, and up the staircase. As she reached the second floor, she heard the front door open.

She shook so much she wouldn't have been surprised to hear her bones rattle. Her breaths rasping, she tiptoed up another staircase to the attic, tensing at every creak. She'd seen the lights on in all the rooms earlier and the silhouettes of the deputies as they searched the house for her.

Maybe they wouldn't search the house again tomorrow. She could hide here forever and no one would find her.

As she lay on an old carpet, she wondered if the police had gotten in touch with her parents. If her mother and father knew she'd run away, would they return?

Probably not. She curled onto her side, her legs folded against her stomach. "Princess," she whispered. "I miss you."

Even though she hated crying, hot tears dribbled down her cheeks.

Phil parked in front of the house and took the keys out of the ignition. "Well, here we are."

He felt Tory's gaze on him but was afraid to turn. If he looked into her blue eyes, he'd be pulled to her, like a drowning man caught in an undertow.

"It's getting late."

She shifted her body. He tensed his.

A sigh came from her side. He held his breath.

She moved toward him. He smelled her coming closer. He grabbed the door handle. "I'll walk you to—"

One slender hand grasped his jacket sleeve, pulling him to her. He should resist, but how could a thirsty man back away from water?

He grabbed her and his open mouth met her open mouth.

The next second they were lying across the seat of the car, necking like horny teenagers, which exactly fit the way he felt.

Belle looked at Caroline, hopping on one leg with her pants half off, her bare breasts bouncing. Belle's gaze shifted to the bed where Max lay sprawled on his back, his mouth open, his eyes closed. A blanket was draped over him, one naked leg and one naked arm sticking out.

Inside Belle, a cold feline anger unfurled, growing and growing and growing...

"Well, I guess you caught us," Caroline said with a laugh. "When Max wakes in the morning I'll tell him— Stop! What are you do—"

Belle lunged at Caroline, her arms raised, her fingers bent in the claw position. The huntress was out and was in control.

Caroline screamed and put her hands out to ward her off.

Headlights streamed into the car. A horn honked.

"Oh shit." Phil pushed up from Tory, propelling himself back to the driver's seat. She giggled and struggled to a sitting position. Phil ran a hand through his hair, then opened the door and stuck his head out. He felt like he had a fire hose in his pants. From the passenger side, he could hear material rustle as Tory shoved her top into her jeans.

Ted's head poked out of the open window of his car. "You're blocking the driveway. Did you want to get interrupted?"

A scream ripped through the night air, snapping Phil's gaze from Ted to the house.

"What the hell?" Ted's car door crashed open.

It took Phil a second longer to react. He ran stiff-legged after Ted, not all of his blood returned to his brain yet.

"Wait for me!" Tory yelled behind him.

"Stay back," he yelled, and kept running. He heard her rushing after him, ignoring his warning.

They piled together on the front porch while Ted tried to unlock the door and swore when the first try didn't work. "Get back!" he snarled.

Phil gave him room, forcing Tory to move behind him. Ted slid the key in the keyhole and shoved the door open. As the three of them stormed into the house, another scream shattered the air.

Ted ran toward the lit hall. Phil turned, his arm out to hold Tory back.

"I can't let you go."

She put out her palms and shoved him in his chest. While he stumbled into a side table, she raced past him. The table toppled to the floor. Glass shattered behind Phil as he leapt after Tory. From the end of the hall came the sound of something smashing, too.

"Shit," he said, and pumped his legs faster. No telling what they'd find.

Though still in her human body, Belle felt more like a cat as she watched Caroline fall onto the bed, holding her hands over her face.

Belle was on her in a second. Her jaws clenched, her breaths coming out in hisses, she dug her claws into the back of Caroline's hands and scraped down. Screaming again, Caroline tried to swat Belle. She kicked out her leg, thumping Belle's thigh. Her flailing hand swatted the bedside lamp, sending it crashing to the floor.

Behind Caroline's hunched body, Belle saw Max lying on the bed, not moving. He looked like one of Tory's old dolls. Another kick landed on Belle's leg. She barely felt it, all her senses concentrated on hurting Caroline and saving Max.

She grabbed Caroline's hair with both hands, jerking her head up. "What did you do to him?" she shouted.

Caroline lifted her hand from her face and screamed.

Pulling handfuls of hair so tight she could see Caroline's scalp stretch, Belle shook the blond woman's head back and forth. "Tell me. What did you do to him?"

"Nothing!"

"You lie."

Releasing one hand, Belle whacked Caroline's face just as Ted burst into the bedroom.

"What the hell is happening here?"

Belle turned, her hold loosening.

"She's crazy!" Caroline shouted. "She drugged Max, and now she's trying to kill me. Max should never have let her stay in the house."

Belle slugged Caroline again.

Caroline screamed.

"Sorcha, stop!" Ted leapt behind Belle and wrapped his arms around her, his hands below her breasts. His arms pinning hers, he pulled her back from Caroline.

Belle bit back a scream of anger. She wasn't finished with Caroline yet. Not until Caroline was crawling on the floor, pleading with her to stop.

"Look at me!" Caroline held her hands out. "I'm bleeding."

"You're also naked," Tory said, standing inside the bedroom. Phil stood behind her, his hand cupped on Tory's shoulder.

Caroline gasped and scooped up her clothes. She held them over her breasts and ran out of the bedroom. "I'm leaving," she said. "That woman is a maniac."

Belle struggled to free herself from Ted's hold, but his arms tightened.

"Let her go," he said. "I don't know what's gotten into you. You're lucky if she doesn't call the police."

She slammed her heel on his shin. He yowled and hopped, but since she wore no shoes it didn't hurt enough to make him loosen his hold. Bending her head, she bit his hand.

He yowled again.

This time he released her.

"You idiot!" she shouted. "If Max is drugged, she did it, not me."

"I think she's right. Caroline's the one who's naked." Tory leaned over Max and shook him. "Are you all right? Wake up, Max. Wake up."

Belle hovered, wanting to stay to see if Max was all right and wanting to chase after Caroline and bat her around, making her suffer more with every swipe.

Ted clasped Belle's upper arms and turned her around to face him. She'd never seen his face so serious.

"You swear you didn't do that?"

She punched him in the stomach.

"Ouch." He bent over, grabbing his stomach.

"I think we should get Max to the hospital." Tory was lifting one of Max's lids, squinting into his eyes.

Belle felt as if Tory stabbed a knife in her heart. Tory wanted to take Max away. To the hospital! Tory of all people should know better. Hadn't she seen the man in the doctor's jacket sneak into the room of Amanda's twin sister and strangle her with his Latex-covered hands?

She lunged for the bed and pushed Tory from Max, shoving her to the floor. From the corner of her eye, she saw the shocked look on Tory's face. Belle ignored her and flattened her body on Max's. Holding out her hands to warn everyone to get away or get mauled, she glared at Tory.

"You're not taking him to the hospital."

"Huh?" Sitting on the carpet, Tory bent her legs, knees in the air and feet on the floor.

"People die in hospitals." Why was Tory looking at her as if her brains were leaking out of her head?

"And people get better," Tory said.

"She has a hospital phobia." Ted looked at Max, then toward the hall. "I better find out if Caroline gave Max anything."

"Of course she did." Tory heaved herself to a standing position. "Go find out what she gave him."

"I'll go." In an instant, Phil dashed from the bedroom.

Ted raked his fingers through his hair. "I should go, too."

"Face it, Ted," Tory said, "what you're best at getting from women is telephone numbers. Phil's an FBI agent.

He's trained in interrogation. He'll find out what she gave him."

Max's warm breath puffed against Belle's cheek. She put her hand on his forehead. It felt cool beneath her heated palm. She laid her cheek against his.

"No one's taking Max away. No one."

Thirty-seven

Phil caught up to Caroline in the foyer, where she was pulling on her pants. She was fully dressed, except for the lacy bra hanging over her shoulder. When she'd run from the bedroom, he'd gotten an eyeful of her breasts, bouncing the way only the real ones did. Then her ass, rounded and firm. Now he kept his gaze on her face. An FBI agent wouldn't look below her neck, would he?

Maybe he wasn't a trained investigator, but he knew a little about human nature from the gym, working one-on-one with men and women desperate to get in shape. In his experience, give people a little sympathy and you couldn't stop them from talking, even when you wanted them to stop.

"Don't worry," he said, his voice soothing. "I'm not blaming you for what you did."

She glared at him. "I didn't do anything."

"C'mon, we know that's bullshit. You wanted Max and decided to go after him before he left. As simple as that. To tell you the truth, I admire you for that."

"You're playing the good cop." She took a step backward, her butt almost touching the front door. "You're trying to charm me. I won't admit to anything. It was Sorcha who drugged Max and attacked me. Why don't you believe me? She's the interloper. She's the one you should be talking to."

"That's not going to fly. You were naked. She was dressed. It only fits if you did it."

"It's not fair, not fair." Caroline twisted around and pounded her fists on the front door.

He stepped over to her. Should he put his hand on her shoulder, or would that make her—

She shrieked.

He jumped back.

Her hand in the air, she turned slowly. "Look," she whispered. "Look what she did to me."

Her eyes stared at the long scratches on the back of her hand, blood seeping out of the welts.

He winced. That must have hurt.

Her desperate gaze transferred to his face. "You have to arrest her for this."

Only a thin strip of blue showed around her widened pupils. Spit dribbled from the corner of her mouth down her chin. Looking at her feral eyes, Phil felt like making the sign of the cross and running to the kitchen for some garlic.

Whatever edge of sanity she'd been standing on, she'd leapt off.

He firmed his shoulders and reminded himself of his promise to Tory to find out what Caroline had given her brother. At least he could do something good for Tory before she found out he was scum.

"They're scratches. They'll heal." He grabbed her hands and pulled them down.

She didn't fight him. Instead, she bent her head to see them better, her fixation with the scratches making him nauseous.

"Oh God, look how deep they are. I'll have scars!"

He was opening his mouth to tell her not to be ridiculous when a strobe light went on in his head. "I've had experience with deep scratches. They heal usually if..." He stopped and rubbed his jaw.

"Yes?" Her body rigid, she fastened her gaze on his face as if he were the wise man on the mountain with the answer to the meaning of life.

He continued to stroke his jaw. One of his buddies, a real estate broker, said the more you made them wait, the more they wanted to buy it. When she started to shake, he decided he'd left her hanging long enough.

"If they're cleaned and taken care of right away." He

pictured the little bottles crammed together on his mother's bathroom counter. "Our secret weapon against scars is aloe lotion and Vitamin E oil."

A moan came from her throat and she started to turn.

He grabbed her wrist. She'd accused him of playing a good cop. *Bad cop, here I come.* "Too bad they don't keep any lotions and oils in the local jail."

"Let go of me." She tried to tug away from him. "I'm not going to jail. You can't prove I did anything."

He tightened his grip. "You're right. You'll probably be let loose in the morning. But first you'll be locked up all night. What do you think is going to happen to these scratches during that time?"

She stopped struggling. "Please, don't do this. I'll do anything." She stepped closer to him, her breasts brushing his chest. She tried to smile and it came out a grimace. A scent emitted from her skin, overpowering her flowering perfume. The stench of desperation.

He stepped back, his neck and hands clammy with repulsion. "I won't call the police. I'll let you go home and take care of your wounds."

Her body sagged with relief. "Thank you," she said. "Thank you, thank—"

"*If,*" he said, and she stopped talking, her mouth open, "you tell me what drug you gave Max."

Her mouth snapped shut. She stared at him with loathing.

He shrugged. "I mean it."

"You're a son of a bitch."

"I'll take that as a compliment. Are you going to tell me? Or am I going to call the cops?"

"It's the date rape drug. Does that make you happy?" She glared at him, as if the only way he'd make her happy would be to collapse onto the floor with a massive coronary.

"Which one? And what's the dosage?"

"How do I know?" She jerked her hand back, and he clutched her wrist tighter. Her glare intensified, shooting hatred at him. "I used one pill. It's all I had. I was told he'd sleep a few hours and be fine in the morning."

"And you believed it?"

She made a scornful noise from her throat, her mouth sneering. "Thousands of women have taken it without harm. It shouldn't hurt one big man. Now let me go. I don't know anything else."

He held her for another moment, searching his mind for any other questions. None came and he uncurled his fingers from her wrists.

"Don't come back," he said. "You won't be welcome."

A sob erupted from her throat and red spots blotted her face. "It's all Sorcha's fault. She ruined everything." She wrenched open the door and gave him a wild look, her lips peeled back from her teeth. "I'll get her back for this, I will!"

Phil watched her storm out of the house, leaving the door wide open. Cold air blew in, laden with moisture. He stepped forward to shut the door, his mind working, his stomach churning.

When he went back to the bedroom, he'd tell the others about Caroline's vow of revenge. But wouldn't it be ironic if Caroline killed Sorcha instead of him? Michaels had told him that without more evidence they couldn't prove anything against Bob.

If Caroline killed Sorcha, it wouldn't be Phil's fault. The FBI would arrest her. Bob would pay Phil. He'd have plenty of money to pay for his dad's and mom's operations. And he'd save the gym. Everything would turn out for him.

Instead of going down the hall, he ran to the bathroom across from the kitchen and threw up.

The front door slammed, but Belle didn't roll off of Max. The second she did, Ted might take him away. And Tory—the traitor—would help him. They both perched on the side of the bed, watching her, waiting for her to get off Max so they could grab him.

She glared at Tory, who shrugged and said, "I don't know what's gotten into you."

If she didn't know, Belle wasn't going to tell her. A hospital. What was Tory thinking?

Max stirred, his arm angling around Belle's back. "Sorcha," he said, his voice slurring.

Ted laughed.

Tory giggled.

Belle wanted to hit both of them, but she'd have to get off Max, so she didn't. What was wrong with them? She answered her question: they were people.

"What's taking your boyfriend?" Ted asked, looking at Tory.

Her cheeks turned pink. "You think he likes me?"

"Does Mickey like Minnie?" Ted asked.

As Tory laughed, a toilet flushed.

"C'mon," Ted said, "you know the guy's hot for you. He looks at you like you're a goddess. I'll bet he even listens when you talk. Enjoy it now. It's not going to last."

"'Course not, he's a man. The Y chromosome comes with a defective listening gene."

"The double X chromosome comes with a talking gene."

Tory snorted and opened her mouth to say something, but footsteps pounded in the hall. Her face changed, her mouth softening. "He's coming."

"It's not the Pope," Ted said.

Tory kicked out, but he jumped back and laughed. They were like kittens, Belle thought. Then Phil hurried into the bedroom.

"What'd you find out?" Ted asked.

He shook his head. "She didn't know much. It's a date rape drug that's supposed to knock him out for a few hours. She said he'll be fine in the morning."

"That bitch," Tory said, her voice fierce. "I can't believe she did this."

"Makes me wonder about Emery," Ted said. "He'd just lost his money when he fell off the trail. No one questioned her when she said he slipped and fell."

Tory gasped. "Wow! I never thought of that."

Belle bit her tongue to keep from blurting out she'd thought of it long ago.

"Is there anything you can do to prove it?" Tory looked at Phil as if he knew all the answers.

"Unless she confesses, I doubt it."

"Ooh." Tory shivered.

"But I think you're on the right track," Phil said, emotions flickering across his face. Then he took a breath and his mouth firmed, as if he'd come to a decision. "Before Caroline left, she blamed Sorcha for ruining her plan. She vowed revenge."

"I'll protect you, Sorcha." Tory threw out her hand to clasp Belle's arm.

"Me, too," Ted said. "We won't leave you alone."

"I'm not afraid of Caroline," Belle said. "She's afraid of me. I don't need anyone to be with me all the time." If they didn't go away, how could she change bodies with Sorcha?

The thought of changing bodies set off a war inside her. She wanted to be a cat. She wanted to be a woman. But she couldn't be both at once.

And now this. It was getting too complicated.

Or maybe it wasn't complicated at all. She loved Max. She'd always loved him.

But now she didn't love him like a cat. She loved him like a woman.

Phil cleared his throat. His face was stiff, his voice strangled. "I'll contact the sheriff's office. See if they'll send someone to watch over you."

"Max would hate that." Ted gestured, his thumbs down. "And I can't imagine Caroline coming here with a knife or a gun."

"Unless it would coordinate with her outfit," Tory said.

"I bet she has an outfit for every occasion." Ted smirked, then his expression turned sour. "At the bar, people make threats all the time that they never keep."

Belle nodded. People on *The Love Chronicles* made lots of threats. "Yes, go away, all of you. I'll be fine. Max will be fine."

"Maybe you're right." Tory's hand slid off of Belle's arm.

"I'd better go." Phil looked at Tory yearningly, as if he

wanted to go to her. But he shuffled his feet instead, moving backward.

Tory jumped off the bed. "I'll walk you to the door."

He held out his hand to ward her away and backed into the hall. "Don't bother. I'll see myself out." He gave her a yearning look, then turned and rushed away, out of Belle's sight.

Tory's mouth fell open. "What was *that* about?"

"A severe case of a guy running like hell from temptation," Ted said.

"*Moi?*" Tory smiled widely. Then her smile slid away, her eyebrows pushing inward and up, her face one big question mark. "But why? Is he afraid of commitment?"

"Beats the hell out of me." Ted stood and glanced around. "Do you remember where Max's sleeping bag is? It's not going to be a comfortable night on the floor."

Confident no one was taking Max to the hated hospital, Belle rolled next to Max, his arm curling beneath her shoulder, his hand on the side of her ribs. "You go away. I'll stay with him."

"In case anything happens, I need to be here," Ted said.

The door downstairs shut. Belle glanced at Tory. Tory's eyes blinked fast like a hummingbird's wings, and she looked as if she was going to cry.

"I'm staying, too." Tory sniffed and stopped blinking, her chin sticking forward in a way that said she was going to do something and no one better try to stop her.

Belle had always thought Tory would make a good cat.

Less than twenty minutes later, Ted lay on the sleeping bag on the floor and Tory was curled next to Belle. Brother and sister fell asleep within moments, their breathing slow and even.

Not Belle. She lay with her eyes open, her ears attuned to Max's slower, deeper breaths. She had to stay awake and make sure he was okay. Because she loved him.

He was her Max.

Thirty-eight

Max woke up puking.

The unmistakable sound of food hurling the wrong way out aroused Belle from a light sleep. It took a moment for her eyes to adjust to the darkness and see Max with his head over the side of the bed. A figure jumped up from the sleeping bag on the floor near the door and the overhead light went on.

In the sudden brightness, Belle watched Ted's face turn an ugly shade of green. Slapping his hand over his mouth, he ran into the hall.

Belle looked over at her other side to see Tory sleeping with a smile on her face. The next instant, she heard puking sounds come from the bathroom.

Five minutes later, Ted was helping Max to his old bedroom. Ted was telling Max he needed to go to the emergency room. Max was insisting he was okay.

While Tory slept, Belle got on her hands and knees and cleaned the mess in the bedroom. Silently she fumed. This was so wrong. Humans cleaned up after her. She didn't clean up after them.

She wished Caroline were there. Belle wanted to push her face in the puke until she choked on it.

The ceiling creaked, waking Jewel. In an instant, she switched from sleep to consciousness. She knew she was in one of the guest bedrooms in her father's richest clients'

house, and she knew their daughter was missing. She remembered informing the nanny that she was staying until Gwen was found, disregarding Katie's lack of enthusiasm.

"You can't stay," Katie had said.

Jewel had raised her eyebrows. As a lawyer, words were an important part of her profession, but sometimes silence brought the best results.

"I mean...of course, you can stay. I'm sure you're concerned. If you don't have anything to wear—"

"I have a bag in my trunk," Jewel had replied, her voice stern and her spine unbending. Bullies like Katie pounced on any hint of weakness.

Now she slid her feet over the side of the bed. She had thought the noise that woke her came from the ceiling but it must have come from the first floor. If she remembered correctly—and she normally did—the kitchen was below her room. Perhaps the non-svelte nanny's guilty conscience was sending her on a search for comfort food.

Barefoot, she padded out of the bedroom and along the long hallway that led to the curving staircase, which would take her to the first floor, where, eventually, she'd pass go and find the kitchen.

Walking toward the recessed light at the end of the hall, she assessed her feelings. She'd enjoyed the weekly e-mails the girl had sent her and wondered why she hadn't detected the desperation. She'd known the facts, after all. Gwen's parents were selfish hedonists who didn't want to bother raising their own daughter. She'd guessed the nanny was cold—although she hadn't known the half of it.

She was angry as hell at herself. Even though the firm's instructions from Gwen's parents were to be the contact in case of emergencies only, she should've checked on the girl physically, not just with e-mails.

Turning into the kitchen, she switched on the light. She hadn't passed Katie, so the creak or whatever woke her wasn't from the nanny. Just as well. Jewel felt bitchy enough to do or say something unprofessional. She might even be tempted to smash her fist into Katie's nose. And then she might get sued.

The fantasy she'd built in her mind evaporated. She turned toward the refrigerator. She'd drunk a glass of milk before bed. Maybe another glass would lull her to sleep.

She opened the refrigerator, cool air spilling out, and grabbed the half-gallon container of milk. Funny... She frowned, and looked at the level of milk through the plastic.

When she'd put the milk away earlier, she'd noticed it was more than half full. Now it was less than half. And hadn't the nanny mentioned being lactose intolerant?

She gazed up at the ceiling, remembering the creak that woke her.

Slowly, her frown changed to a smile.

As Max's eyes squinted open to bright sunlight, he heard Ted say, "You're finally up. How're you feeling?"

Max glanced around him and saw he was in his bedroom, not the guest room. What was he doing here? Where was Sorcha?

"What happened?" His voice came out in a croak, his mouth tasted like puke, and he felt like a tractor had rolled over him, and then another and another. "What the hell happened?"

"You don't remember anything from last night?"

Max sat up. His stomach churned. As he clutched his abdomen, he realized he wasn't wearing his T-shirt and boxers.

Ted grabbed the wastebasket by the dresser and hurried to the bed.

"Get that away, I don't need it."

Ted set down the wastebasket. "You're as bad as Sorcha."

"What's wrong with Sorcha?" Max swung his legs over the side of the bed. Had something happened to Sorcha? He had to make sure she was okay.

"She's fine. Chill down, keep cool. Slow your roll."

Max glared at him. "When you make up your mind what

decade you're in, maybe you'll tell me what the hell happened."

"Don't get pissed at me because you're a control freak. I'm not the one who gave you a knockout drug."

"What?" He pushed off the mattress, onto his feet. "Are you insane?"

"Sometimes, but not last night. I know, beats the hell out of me. Caroline did it."

"Caroline? That's...crazy. Why would she do something like that?"

"You're rich and she likes nice things. I told you she was after you. Maybe you know stocks and bonds, but I know women."

Max sank back on the edge of the bed and wiped the heels of his palms over his burning eyes. "I don't believe this."

"Me, neither, not at first." Ted perched on the chair by the dresser. "Tory and I were outside when we heard Caroline screaming. We raced up to the guest room you've been using and found Caroline naked and fighting with Sorcha."

Max's head lifted. "She didn't hurt Sorcha?"

Ted laughed. "You kidding? Sorcha was beating the shit out of her. Caroline was bleeding like a pig. She told us Sorcha was the one who gave you the knockout pill. But Tory noticed Caroline was the naked one, not Sorcha."

"It's still crazy. You're sure?"

"Phil followed Caroline and talked to her. She admitted it to him and left. She promised to get even with Sorcha for catching her."

The muscles in Max's body jerked. "Where is Sorcha? I want to see her. Now."

Ted gave Max an evil grin. "Not everything is under your control. Especially not Sorcha. I think you should've noticed by now, Sorcha comes when Sorcha wants to come."

Max felt as if the top of his head would fly off. He stood, swayed, and sat again. "I'll have to get her." He pushed to his feet again.

"Don't be stupid." Ted jumped off the chair, his hand out to stop Max. "You're not ready to run a marathon. Plus, you've been puking your guts out. You need to brush your teeth and take a bath."

"Get my clothes," he ground out.

"You're as stubborn as... I don't know... Mom?" He laughed at Max's glare. "Tell you what. You take a bath and I'll fetch Sorcha. What do you say? About fifteen minutes?"

"Ten," he said as Ted walked out the door. He needed to see that Sorcha was safe and unharmed in the next ten minutes, or he didn't know what he'd do.

Max's muscles felt atrophied, his bones creaking like an old man's. He forced his sluggish body to move, taking less than ten minutes to shower while his mind shot out thoughts faster than the showerhead gushed water. Whatever he'd taken last night hadn't damaged his brain, for which he was grateful. If Sorcha agreed, he wouldn't prosecute Caroline.

It was embarrassing and would bring him unwelcome publicity. Imagining his picture on the cover of a tabloid, he fought an urge to throw up. His heartbeat thumped against his rib cage, and moments passed before his rapid breathing slowed.

Sorcha. It all hinged on her.

Brushing his teeth, he looked in the mirror and saw a man who needed a shave and had a hard glint in his eyes. He wanted to make the decisions. He didn't want to leave it up to Sorcha. But if Sorcha had fought Caroline for him, letting her make the call was the right thing to do.

She had fought for him.

His mouth foaming with toothpaste, he stopped brushing and stared at his image. The glint in his eyes softened as the realization hit him.

Sorcha loved him.

The independent and sometimes self-centered woman would not have put herself in danger if she didn't love him.

He spit out the toothpaste and rinsed his mouth. From the hall, he heard the door open. He set down the glass and strode out of the bathroom, his shirt unbuttoned and his mind made up.

She stood by the dresser, watching him with her inscrutable green eyes. It didn't matter that he couldn't read them. He knew how she felt—and he felt the exact same emotion.

Thirty-nine

Gladness filled Belle. Max was unhurt! Lucky for Caroline. If Max had been hurt, Belle would have hunted Caroline down and killed her. She knew where the sharpest knives were kept, and she knew how to use them.

"Yes," she said. "I do." Why would she lie about it? People on *The Love Chronicles* lied all the time and it never made sense to Belle. If you loved, you should say so. If you hated, you should never talk to the other person. Although, she admitted, if people never talked to people they hated on *The Love Chronicles*, no one would talk to anyone else.

She hated Caroline, and she would be happy to never talk to her again in her life.

Max took two strides and scooped her against his chest. The next second, his head bent and his lips captured hers.

She gave in to the heat. Max. This was the man she'd loved for four years. The man who'd taken her in as a kitten, then later as a woman with no home. The man who'd always been strong for his brother and sister and everyone else, even wicked Caroline, who didn't deserve him any more than a plant filled with poison deserved the sun.

Her tongue slipped into his mouth. Was he going to make love to her again? Should she let him? But how could she stop him when she wanted him so much she burned?

He lifted his lips from hers.

No, put them back. She flattened her hands on each side of his head and tried to pull his mouth back to hers, but he resisted.

"I love you, too," he said.

"I know."

He threw his head back and bellowed with laughter. She didn't know what was so funny, but the sound of his laugh made joy bubble up inside her.

Looking down, he smiled, happiness gleaming in his eyes. "I feel as if a smoke screen was blocking my vision. Now it's gone and I can see clearly."

She wished he'd stop talking. She could think of better things to do. "Are you going to kiss me again?"

"Soon enough," he murmured. His hands came up to the sides of her head, his thumbs drawing circles on her temples. "I need to tell you something."

"If you must."

His mouth quirked, but his eyes grew sober. "I've been dreaming of traveling since I've been a kid. I want you to go with me." He put his palm lightly over her lips. "Hear me out, then you can talk. If you can't bring yourself to travel, I'll stay here. With you."

He drew his hand back from her mouth. "Will you come with me, or should I stay with you? Tell me and I'll do it. I'm being honest and open, and I want you to be the same."

She became very still. Inside her, she felt her heartbeat slow, like at a funeral she'd seen on TV. Sad, her heart said, sad, sad, sad.

"I can be honest," she said, but she swallowed and stepped backward.

He held out his hand, as if to stop her. She shook her head.

"I'm not Sorcha."

His brow furrowed. "I talked to your parents and your neighbors. What are you talking about?"

She lifted her chin. Even for a cat, saying this was hard.

"I'm Belle."

"What?"

"I'm your cat, Belle. I've been living with you since I was a kitten. That day you left the house because your mother's car broke, remember? The day you thought I disappeared? That's the day Caroline tried to kill me. She threw me into the windshield of a car. The car went into the ditch. The driver of that car was Sorcha. She fell out and we changed bodies."

He shook his head, as if trying to shake her words out of his brain. "I should've taken you to the hospital after all. You have brain damage."

"Ask me anything." She grabbed his arm. "Ask me something Belle would know and Sorcha wouldn't."

He pulled away from her and stepped back. "You need to see a doctor. This time I'm insisting."

"Ask me." She wanted to slap his face. Were all humans this thickheaded? Or just men?

He stared at her, shaking his head.

"Okay, I'll tell you how you found me."

A muscle ticked in his cheek. "I heard meowing outside. It was winter, just over four years ago. You were shivering on the back porch. Everyone knows that."

"Everyone knows a lie."

His face went still, his shoulders stiff, his eyes guarded.

"I was living with a lady in one of your apartments. She never played with me or petted me. But every time you came, you petted me and talked to me. One day, you came to look at the carpet. When you left, I snuck out and followed you into your car. Instead of returning me, you kept me."

"No one knows that." He stared at her with disbelief, shaking his head. "No one."

"Except me. I chose you then, and I choose you now."

"Don't say that. Tell me it's not true."

She stepped toward him.

He put out his palms, holding her away from him. "Tell me you're lying."

"I'm not. I'm Belle."

"You're Belle, my cat." He looked as if he'd received a blow to his head.

"I'm Belle but not a cat anymore." She held out her hands to him. She was human now. Couldn't he see?

"So all the time you were looking for Belle, you were really looking for—"

"The real Sorcha." She nodded. Finally he was getting it.

"Why? What were you going to do when you found her?"

"Change back."

He made a sound in his throat, as if he wanted to throw up again.

"That was before I loved you the way a woman loves a man," she said quickly. "I didn't think I could ever be a human, but for you I will."

Without another word, he turned and left the room.

"That's all right, darling." Melanie Deavers sat up in bed and patted her hair, looking in the mirror across the room. "I know you've been under a lot of stress lately."

Bob stiffened, looking at his wife's perfect profile. It should be perfect after all the money she'd paid her plastic surgeon. He pulled on his boxers. "What do you know about my stress?"

She dragged her gaze from her reflection. "Don't be that way. Of course I know you've been having a little trouble choosing a new hotel. No one blames you. After selecting a string of winners, it's natural for you to be hesitant. The entire world is waiting to see what your next move will be."

His knees didn't want to hold him. He gripped the bedpost at the foot of the bed. "Who told you?" he asked, his voice strained. "What else do you know?"

Her eyes widened. "I heard you talking to your father."

The tension eased only slightly. She didn't know about the psychic. Of course she didn't. Melanie had merely overheard Bob's father calling him a coward and insinuating in his usual icy tones that he'd lost his nerve.

Only three people knew the truth. Himself, Phil...and Sorcha.

No wonder he couldn't complete the act of sex.

No wonder he couldn't choose a new hotel.

Sorcha was still alive. Any day, he'd see her face in the tabloids. Maybe even on one of the sleazier TV shows.

He'd be humiliated. His children would be confused. His

father would look at him with scorn. He'd be charged with murder. Go to prison. After all, he'd killed before.

He needed to stop her. Now.

He reached for his pants. If Phil wasn't getting the job done, he'd do it himself. It should take an hour and a half to drive to the motel where Phil was staying. With any luck, he'd be home before rush hour, everything taken care of.

"Where are you going?" Melanie asked.

He wondered what she would say if he replied that he was off to kill a woman. *That's nice, just make sure you wash your hands and don't get caught.*

"To the office," he said.

"You work too hard." She slid out of bed, so slender each one of her ribs showed. Instead of dressing, she looked at herself in the full-length mirror, turning from side to side. Bob knew she wasn't admiring herself, she was searching for imperfections that needed to be taken care of.

"I would hate it if you worked yourself to death," she said.

She looked surprised when he laughed wildly.

Forty

The scratches on Caroline's hands mirrored the way she felt inside, scraped and scabbed over. And the bruise on her cheek... She dropped her hands and peered into the mirror on her living room wall and felt ill. Her face, her precious face. She stared at her flawed image, enthralled and horrified. And, above all, enraged, her body shaking with a fury so big that the state of Wisconsin was too small to hold it.

On the couch behind her, Brenda held her cell phone to her ear, telling her boss she had to take care of her sick daughter. She wasn't lying, Caroline thought. She was sick. Sick to death of things going wrong.

The instant Brenda dropped her cell phone into her purse, Caroline whipped around. "You should've gone to work. I'm not changing my mind."

"Let it go." Brenda stood. "It's over. We'll find another multimillionaire. Maybe we've been setting our sights too low. We can look for a billionaire. Someone older. We can go to Florida or Arizona."

"I can't think of that now." Caroline glanced at the scratches again, the memories of her humiliation flooding back.

Ted, Tory, Phil, and Sorcha looking at her with various expressions of surprise and shock. They'd seen her naked and bleeding, and they knew what she'd done.

Max was never going to marry her now.

He wasn't going to let her finish decorating his house and use it for a showcase either.

He probably wasn't going to pay her.

"It isn't fair," she said, and the words didn't come out whiny but like the flow of lava, hot and destructive. "One minute success is so close I can smell the stock certificates in my name. The next I'm rolling on the floor with a crazy woman. This happens to me every time I think I'm onto something good. I'm so fucking sick of it."

Brenda tsked. "Of course you are. That woman should be locked up and the key thrown away. What civilized human acts like that?"

Caroline rubbed her forehead. She'd taken her Prozac but it didn't stop the ringing inside her mind. Didn't stop the whisper that said, *Kill her, kill her, kill her.*

She strode to the cherrywood Queen Anne writing desk in the corner. Feeling beneath the panel, she pressed down and a hidden secret drawer opened. She reached in. When her hand came out, she was holding the gun Emery had bragged about buying from a street person, as if that would impress her.

The gun felt solid in her hand, the coolness of the metal warming in her grip, and at the same time cooling the anger, changing it to an icy anger, a thousand times more dangerous than heat.

Even though she'd loaded it before putting it in the drawer, she double-checked to see if it still held bullets. This time nothing was going wrong.

"Honey, please," Brenda said, her voice strained. "What you did to Emery was one thing. That wasn't about revenge, that was about money. Let's go on with our lives and be grateful they don't charge you with anything."

"It would be their word against ours." She slid the gun into her Prada handbag. She didn't know much about guns, but you pointed, pulled the trigger, and the other person died. What else did she need to know? "I'm tired of people shitting on my parade."

"At least promise you won't let anyone see you."

"Sorcha tramps through the woods every day looking for the damned cat. Today won't be any different." Caroline imagined the surprised look on Sorcha's face when she saw

Caroline step out from behind a tree. Then she saw the surprise turn into fear as Caroline lifted the gun.

She patted her mother's arm. "Of course I won't let anyone see me. Don't fuss. I've done this before, you know."

"Yes, but it seems so...risky. And for what? There's no profit."

Caroline slipped the strap of the handbag over her arm. The bag hit her hip, and she felt the solidness of the gun.

Nice. She liked the way it made her feel. Powerful. Just like when she'd looked down and seen Emery's broken body. Until that instant, she hadn't realized how much she'd disliked her husband.

She glanced out the window, the sun shining on the cars on the street. "It's going to be a perfect day," she said. Perfect for a murder.

A sedan pulled into the parking lot, beige and anonymous, with tinted glass. To Phil, watching out of his motel window, the most sinister sight he'd seen since looking into Caroline's icily beautiful face last night.

Bob, he thought. Just the kind of car he'd rent.

He pressed a number on his cell phone. Bob was early. Deputy Michaels was late. Where the hell was she?

"Hansford Sheriff's Department," a familiar female voice said.

"I need to talk to Deputy Michaels."

"So you told me four times already. I gave her your message and she's on the way. If this is an emergency, you should tell me."

"No! Yes! Maybe! If they—" A car door slammed outside his motel room door. He took two steps to the window and peered out. Parked in front of the room two doors down, Bob had exited the sedan.

Parasites inside Phil's stomach started doing a rendition of Riverdance, and he put his hand over his abdomen. "Try her again. Tell her Bob's here right now and if she doesn't get here soon, it's going to be too late." He broke the connection, slipped the phone in his pocket, and hurried to open the door.

Bob stood just outside it, holding a briefcase. Phil's chest tightened. It was like opening door number one and finding a nightmare instead of a dream.

"Where is she?" Bob demanded.

"I don't know. Come in and we'll talk."

Bob stayed outside his motel room, an immovable object. "We've talked too much already. I want action. You should've taken care of this already. I want it done today. Take me to the house where she's staying."

Phil started to sweat, though the morning April air was probably in the high forties. Where the hell was Michaels?

A tan car pulled into the motel parking lot. Phil saw a woman with brown hair and a man with blond hair. Michaels and her partner.

His breath whooshed out and his strong legs felt weak. "I'll get the gun."

Bob followed him into the motel room, the briefcase banging against the doorjamb. "She's still at the house?"

Phil's stomach felt as if it were tied in a sailor's knot. "She's probably walking in the woods."

"Why the woods?"

"She's looking for a missing cat." Phil grabbed his gym bag with the gun and the bullets. "The guy who owns the house where she's staying has a cat that's missing."

"Will she be alone?"

Phil reminded himself that Michaels was coming. Only then could he answer. "Yes."

"Good. The only witnesses will be a squirrel or two. I don't know what you were waiting for. A fucking invitation? Let's get out of here and get the job done." He gave Phil a sharp look. "You know we're doing this for Lorna and Danny, right? It's her or them."

Unable to say anything, his voice choked up, Phil nodded.

Bob headed toward the car, apparently satisfied. "Then let's do it."

Two minutes later, Phil was driving out of the parking

lot. Phil glanced at the rearview mirror. Behind a yellow Volkswagen, Michaels and Brigg's anonymous tan car followed them.

"I've got one, too," Bob said.

"Got what?" Phil stared out the front of the window. The other day he'd barely missed a squirrel dashing to the other side of the road. It had unnerved him.

Bob's briefcase clicked twice. "This."

Phil glanced over to see Bob holding a long-barreled handgun that looked like something an assassin might use.

Holy shit! The car swerved and Bob laughed, an excited note in his voice.

"It's backup." Bob caressed the barrel as though it were a lover. "I'll let you take the first shot."

Phil's stomach lurched. A semi was coming toward them in the other lane and he gripped the steering wheel to keep from swerving again. As soon as the semi passed, he glanced in the rearview mirror.

The yellow Volkswagen was still behind him, but no tan car.

Shit! He felt lightheaded. The couple in the parking lot hadn't been Michaels and her partner, after all. Just a couple renting a hotel room.

He was leading Bob straight to Sorcha.

And Bob had a gun.

What the hell was he supposed to do?

Sorcha crouched in front of a covered rosebush and peered at the mini-castle. She wasn't sure what she waited for, but she kept watching the house. The sun had been in the sky for a couple of hours already, but the searchers hadn't returned. Did that mean Gwen had been caught?

A movement in the attic caught her eye. Someone was pressing against the rectangular window, looking out. The face was a pale blur, but Sorcha was sure it was Gwen. Sorcha wondered if Gwen was looking for a glimpse of her.

Sorcha moved out of the rosebush's shadow, padding into the clearing in front of a white wrought iron bench.

Now Sorcha knew what she'd been waiting for. *This.* The chance to say good-bye before she turned into a woman again.

Gazing up at the pale blur, she sent her a message: *I have to go. I've been scared my whole life, but now I'm going to do the right thing, even though I don't want to do it. Even if it takes me away from you. Seeing how brave you are makes me want to be brave, too. I love you, Gwen.*

Another smaller blur stole up the window. Gwen's hand.

Sorcha imagined it was Gwen's way of saying *I love you, too, Princess.*

Sorcha's soul ached, but she pivoted away. Without looking back, she dashed through the long cut grass toward the neighbor's property and the thicket of trees where Belle roamed every day, looking for her. They'd change bodies with no fuss, like turning on a light switch, and everything would be as it should be again.

The cat would be loved and cared for. Sorcha would be lonely and unloved.

Her dash slowed to a fast saunter, but she kept going. She hadn't realized how empty her human life was until she'd changed into a cat.

Maybe in her next life, God would make her a cat for real.

Forty-one

On hold with his travel agent, Max looked out his office window and watched Sorcha—no, Belle—walk out of the house. Just as she did every day, she strode toward the trees. Now he knew why she exerted herself searching for the cat when she wouldn't bother to toss her empty tuna cans in the recyclable bin.

She was the cat.

The on-hold guitar music stopped and he swiveled in his chair. By this evening, he'd be miles away from Belle and his entire family.

Her voice quivering with curiosity, his agent told him she could get him on a two o'clock flight to San Francisco. She named an exorbitant sum and told him it was nonstop. He gave the go-ahead and hung up. His sanity was at stake, not his bank account.

Ted strolled into the office. He wore jeans and a red Buck's sweatshirt, stubble dotted his chin, and his eyes were half-lidded from getting up a good three hours earlier than normal. Max guessed his lawyer would think he was certifiable when he signed over his real estate assets to Ted.

Too damned bad.

Dressed in stretchy pants, a T-shirt, and her hair in a ponytail, Tory jogged into the room. Tendrils of red curls stuck to her forehead. She slumped onto Max's chair.

"I hate exercising. You guys leaving?"

"You don't know the half of it." Ted gave an empty laugh.

Tory sat up straight. "What's going on?"

"Max is going on his travels early. He's leaving this afternoon,"

"No!"

"We're going to the lawyer's and the bank now."

"No!"

"He's signing everything over to me."

"No!"

Ted gestured, palms up, fingers splayed. "Yes."

Tory turned her blue gaze to Max. "Why? What happened to you and Sorcha?"

He gave her what he hoped was a steely look. "Did I ever tell you to mind your own business?"

"I don't know. Did I ever listen?"

Ted laughed.

Max jerked his chin at Ted. "C'mon, let's go."

"Wait!" Tory jumped to her feet. "You can't leave just like that. You should've seen Sorcha last night. She wouldn't let us touch you. She was like...like..."

"A lioness," Ted said.

"Exactly! So what's going on? You can hardly keep your eyes off her. She's the same way with you. At least take her with you."

Max's fingers opened and closed. His chest felt as if an elephant sat on it. This was torture. He had to get out of here.

"Are you coming?" he asked Ted. "Because I'm going."

Max strode out of the office, hearing Ted's footsteps behind him.

"Men!" Tory called out, a throb in her voice. "You're all the same."

"She's crying," Ted said as they walked into the garage. "She's going to take your leaving hard."

Max hopped into the driver's seat of the Jeep. "She's a better actress than we thought."

He drove too fast along the driveway. At the edge of the trees, a slender woman stopped and peered at the Jeep, her hand shading her eyes from the sun that shone down on her, haloing her in light.

Sorcha. No, not Sorcha. Belle.

He stared straight ahead until they passed her and he turned onto Camel's Back Road. Only when he reached the next property, past the line of trees, did he exhale and realize he'd been holding his breath. His heart must've been beating, but it felt like it had stopped. He was numb inside. Dead.

"Can you slow down?" Ted said. "You keep going this fast, we'll end up in a ditch."

Max eased up his foot and turned on the radio. A song he didn't know and didn't like cranked out. He cranked up the volume, filling his mind with music, drowning out his thoughts.

Twenty minutes later, he was shaking hands with his lawyer, a muscular, freckled man in his thirties. Ted reminded John they'd met last summer, and John did a damn good job of faking his memory of their meeting.

"You're lucky I'm ready for you." John gestured for Max and Ted to sit. "My paralegal started her family leave last Friday, and I asked her to finish your paperwork before she left. Otherwise you would've had to wait at least a day."

Max took a seat. He wasn't waiting for anyone. Not anymore. He glanced at his watch.

"In a hurry?" John asked, opening a folder.

Max opened his mouth to reply, and nothing came out, his throat closing up. Emotion struck him like a lightning bolt coming out of nowhere, fast and vicious. Hurt flared inside him, his numbness burned away. One moment he was thinking of the time, the next he was struggling to speak.

John repeated the question, and Max shook his head. "No hurry," he said, his voice croaking.

He forced back the pain. His hands clenched on his thighs, his muscles tensed, he put up mental blocks to push back the hurt so he could function, an old skill he'd learned from necessity. He'd been through worse after his father died, he told himself, when his life had turned upside-down and everyone else was falling apart. Unlike the soldiers in Humpty Dumpty's time, he'd picked up their pieces and glued them back together.

He needed to pick up his own pieces now. Glue his own life back together.

"Read, then sign," John said.

Max skimmed the document, signed it, then handed the sheet of paper to Ted, who set it on the desk and scrawled his name.

"You're supposed to read it," Max said.

"You read it. I don't have to."

"I hope you'll take better care of the business than that."

"Only one way you can tell for sure. Stick around and watch me."

Max frowned, even as an unexpected wish that he could do just that flashed into his mind. Not because he thought Ted would screw up. But because he thought Ted would do well and he wanted to be there to celebrate his successes. He wanted to watch and feel proud.

John handed Max another document. As he read it, the cell phone clipped on his belt rang. He picked it up, looked at caller ID, then turned off the power.

"Who was it?" Ted asked.

"Mom."

Ted snickered.

Max ignored him and signed the document. He was handing it to Ted when another phone started to ring.

"Yours?" Max asked Ted. "Guess who?"

Grinning, Ted brought up his cell phone and looked at the number. "Mom. What do you bet she talked to Tory and knows you're leaving?"

"Not a penny."

Chuckling, Ted brought the phone to his ear.

"You're not talking to her," Max said.

"I'm not the one who's running away from home," Ted said, still grinning. The next second he was saying hello.

"Ready for this?" John handed him a half dozen or so sheets of paper. "Once you both sign this, it's over, so don't sign unless you're sure this is what you want." His forehead puckered. "I watched you buy the apartment buildings, one by one, saw the sweat and equity you put into them. You're going against my advice."

"No, Mom," Ted was saying. "Yeah, sure."

A prickle of hurt throbbed dully inside Max's chest, slithering under his barriers. He put his palm to his forehead, as if physically pushing the pang back.

"Good," John said. "You're finally listening to my advice."

Max shot him a glance, dropped his hand, and turned pages without making a pretense of reading. Finding the signature line, he scribbled his name. John showed him two more sheets to sign and he scribbled his name on those as well.

Ted held out the phone. "Mom wants to talk to you." He smiled innocently at Max's glare. "Hey, in a few hours, you're out of here. I'll be the one who has to stay and listen to her bitching."

Max grabbed the phone and put it to his ear. "I can't believe you're actually going through with this," she said, her voice screechy with fear. "What about your brother and sister?"

"Everyone is taken care of, Mom. I'm not going through this again."

"What about *me*?" Her voice shook. "I'm not talking about money. Ted's not like you. He hardly visits me. I'll be all alone."

Max closed his eyes. "You're not alone. You have friends. I'll still call you, but you'll do just fine without me. It looks like Tory is staying, and Ted will be there for you if you need him."

Ted's sock on his shoulder stopped him, and he ignored the punch even though it hurt. Just as he ignored a few more prickles creeping under and over and around his mental blocks.

"Maxwell, you can't—"

"Good-bye, Mom. I'll write." He pressed the End button and handed it back to Ted. "I'd advise you to turn it off for at least an hour."

Ted pressed a button. "Done. You handled that well."

Max shrugged and passed the pages to Ted. It was past time for his mother to get a life. "Sign this. Here and here and here. Apparently this is the biggie."

Ted pursed his lips into a whistle. "How's it feel to be a free man?"

A free man. Max sat back. Ted was right. He was free.

But he didn't feel free. He felt...sad.

Even as he admitted it, the mental blocks evaporated, but the pain didn't flood back. Instead, darkness possessed him, filling his mind, his cells, his heart, his soul, drowning him in sorrow. And a cry rose inside him. *Sorcha! Sorcha, Sorcha, Sorcha.*

He pictured her, he smelled her, he felt her. He saw her stumbling toward him in the road, he saw her in his arms after she'd fallen from the tree, he saw her in the bathtub, he saw her eat ice cream sandwiches like a child, not caring that chocolate smeared her face, he saw her naked on his bed and in his arms.

"Something wrong?" John took the papers from Ted. "I still have to sign this. If you want me to rip up the papers—"

"No, go ahead." Max stood, his chest full of emotion, constricting his breathing, and he realized what he hadn't seen in those images.

Belle.

To him, she was Sorcha. Unusual and unique, with no pretenses, no lies. Unlike no woman he knew. And if that came from Belle, he accepted it and even welcomed it and was grateful for it. Just as he accepted his height came from his father and his eye color from his mother. But the man he'd grown up to be was self-made, starting when he was fourteen.

It didn't matter what Sorcha had been before the day she'd stumbled into his arms and he'd taken her into his home. She was a woman now, a woman he loved. He could live without her, but even on the sunniest days life would always be grayer, duller, darker. She made him laugh, made him light up, made him crazy, and he was an idiot for thinking he should leave her.

Exultation hummed through him and he saw her in his mind again, haloed by sunlight as he drove past her. Saw her sad expression, saw the resignation, and in that instant he knew what she planned to do. He stopped himself from crying out, even as shards of fear sliced through his exhilaration, stealing his breath and freezing his heart.

Without a word, he pushed back the chair and strode out of the office.

"Hey! Where you going?" Ted shouted.

Instead of answering, Max ran to the car. His breath gasped and his heart pounded, but was still frozen at its core. He didn't want to waste one second talking.

Ted hurried outside as Max stepped on the gas. "Wait for me!" Ted called.

Max tore out of the parking lot. He wasn't waiting for anyone. He loved Sorcha and needed to get to her before she changed back into a cat.

Forty-two

"Sorcha, Sorcha," Belle called in a conversational voice, not putting her usual energy into it. Instead of marching through the undergrowth like a woman on a mission, she strolled. A squirrel darted up a tree, and she didn't get her usual thought of how easy it would be to leap after the furry thing and sink her teeth into its neck. If she were in her right body.

But which body was the right body?

"Sorcha," she said listlessly. She'd been ready to remain in this human body, but Max didn't want her as a human. So she might as well be a cat. What else was she to do? If he stayed, she might try to change his mind. But he was leaving and she wasn't going to leave with him, that was for sure.

She stopped.

Or was she?

Sorcha ran up a tree to escape a Sumo-sized raccoon. She dug her claws into the thick branch and scanned the woods around her. She hated herself for being such a fraidycat. If she'd been brave, her life might've been different.

But wasn't she being brave now? Searching for Belle so they could switch bodies?

The raccoon kept going, out of sight. The minutes stretched and Sorcha still waited. Since the change, Belle had been walking through the woods every day, searching for her. If Sorcha stayed in the tree, sooner or later Belle would find her.

A rustling noise caught her attention. Her ears pricked up. Another animal?

Looking straight ahead, she saw Belle step over a fallen tree, and a notion struck her. Since her car had crashed and she'd prayed to God to take her instead of the cat, never once had she looked at Belle and thought, "That's me. That's my body."

Why not? Belle was using her body. The image she used to see in the mirror. Yet she'd never felt ownership. The woman she saw in the body was always Belle.

She blinked. If she thought of Belle as being a woman, what did she think of herself? As a cat?

Another noise came from the other direction. Someone walking toward her and Belle.

Stretching her neck out, she looked to the left, straight at the blond woman who'd tripped Belle. The woman she suspected of throwing Belle at Sorcha's car.

Sorcha trembled.

Another noise came from the other direction. Sorcha whipped her head to the right.

Oh God, it couldn't be. Deavers and his brother. What were they doing here?

Her trembles deepened to shudders. Her front legs wrapped around the branch to keep from falling off, her claws digging into the rough bark. Inside her chest, her small heart thundered. A bud on the end of a twig tickled her nose and she shifted.

She should warn Belle, but fear paralyzed her vocal chords.

They were all after Belle. She just wasn't sure which one would kill her first.

Deavers ducked to avoid a low branch. He hated tramping through the woods. When he was a Boy Scout, he'd paid another boy to build a fire for him, then gotten caught and was kicked out of his troop. Every time he thought about it, his ears stung. His father never hit him, but he'd shot words like *stupid* and *lazy* and *coward* at him like they were bullets.

A half step in front of him, Phil strode easily, a regular nature boy. Bob sneered. Phil looked like the original cowboy with his lean physique and even-featured face, but he hadn't been able to shoot Sorcha yet, had he? That made him a coward.

Phil had told him that Sorcha had amnesia. His excuse for not shooting her. Even if Bob believed it—which he didn't—her memory could return. Before that happened, he needed to eliminate her.

Phil's step faltered and he halted. To avoid walking into him, Bob hitched to the side and saw Sorcha. He stopped next to Phil. Her profile was to them and she walked slowly, her spine bent. Defeated.

Yes! Soon she'd be gone and no one would know.

He stepped forward, his shoulder knocking against Phil's hard bicep.

Almost no one. He glowered at Phil, jabbing his thumb in Sorcha's direction.

His eyes dazed, Phil stepped forward, his foot coming down on a branch. It cracked like a gunshot. Sorcha's head swiveled, and Bob could tell she spotted them. But instead of running, she stood still and peered at them, her brows slightly together, as if she were puzzled.

She really did have amnesia. Bob smiled. His luck was in today.

But wait. What the hell was that?

A blond woman, looking as if she'd walked off the cover of a catalog, was coming up behind Sorcha. She stared at Sorcha's back, apparently not aware of Phil and Bob.

What the hell was she doing in the woods, getting in Bob's way?

"You bitch," the blond said.

Sorcha pivoted.

Phil stopped. So did Bob.

They were about quarter of a football field away from Sorcha. Close enough to hit her with a rock.

Or a bullet.

Bob lifted his gun. With his other hand, he nudged Phil. If Phil fired a shot, even if he didn't connect, he'd be just as culpable as Bob. And if Phil ever got the notion to call the police on Bob, he'd be in jail faster than he could say, "Get me a lawyer."

Using both hands, Phil raised his gun. The damn thing shook.

"Go away," Sorcha said to the blond. "You're not welcome here."

The blond's wild laughter splintered up Bob's spine. Apparently Sorcha hadn't spent her time here making friends.

"You humiliated me!" An arm stretched out and she aimed a gun the size of a hot dog straight at Sorcha. "Did you really think I was going to let you get away with it?"

Bob felt his jaw drop. Next to him, Phil tensed. Bob glanced over, saw Phil's finger on the trigger.

You stupid jerk! Let the blond kill her!

Two shots rang out as Sorcha dived to the ground.

The gun tumbled out of the blond's hand. She clutched her chest. Staggering, she dropped to her knees. Then she pitched forward to the ground.

Sorcha made a sound in her throat and struggled to her feet. She was unharmed. With no weapon in her hand.

"You!" Bob whispered, glaring at Phil. "You shot the wrong woman."

Phil shook his head, looking miserable. "I can't kill her. It's not right. All the money in the world isn't worth it."

"You betrayed me." There was a buzzing in Bob's ears, like a thousand bees. He lifted his gun and the buzzing grew louder.

Phil stumbled back. "You can't shoot me. I'm your brother."

"Half brother. And I never liked you." Taking aim, Bob pulled the trigger.

Still staring at Bob, Phil crumpled to the ground.

Bob's excited breaths sounded like a chugging train. *Who was the better man now?*

He stepped over his fallen brother. The blond was dead and Phil was dead. Once Sorcha was dead, all his witnesses would be gone.

Sorcha stared at him, her eyes round, her jaw dropped. "You shot Phil?" she asked. "Why?"

He didn't say anything. Why talk to a dead woman? As he aimed his gun at Sorcha, he planned his next moves. After he shot her, he'd put the gun by the blond woman. The police would think she'd shot Sorcha and Phil, and before he'd died, Phil had shot her.

The perfect murder. Everything was going his way. Even the tree he was standing under shaded the sun's glare from his eyes. He was brilliant. Nothing was going to stop him. Nothing. His children would be safe from ridicule.

And so would he.

Turning his Jeep in the driveway, Max heard the two shots, one after another. He stomped on the brakes.

"Belle!" Instinctively using the name she'd more quickly respond to, he pushed open the door and jumped out.

He ran, leaving the door open and the keys in the ignition, the Jeep beeping behind him.

"Belle!" he cried, his voice hoarse with desperation. "Belle!"

Belle watched the balding man with the pudgy belly aim the gun at her. None of this seemed real. Caroline was shot and so was Phil. Even for *The Love Chronicles* this was a little much.

She balanced herself on the balls of her feet. She wasn't letting this human shoot her without defending herself.

As she jumped, something flew out of the tree and landed on his head.

Sorcha.

He shrieked. Then Belle barreled into him, pushing him backward. He stumbled on a tree root and fell on his ass.

Sorcha squealed, but didn't fall. He shrieked again, and Belle knew Sorcha's four sets of claws were digging into his forehead and skull.

Belle crouched, but before she could pounce, Sorcha yowled an attack cry. Belle's breaths harsh in her ears, she watched Sorcha scratch the man like she was playing tic-tac-toe on his head. He dropped the gun, bringing his hands up to cover his eyes. Sorcha immediately scored her front paws over the backs of his hands, leaving bloody scrapes.

Belle shook with the need to jump on him, too, and start scratching. Still, she held back. Sorcha scratched because she was in the cat body and that's what cats did. Belle was in the human body and humans didn't kill with their own hands.

Humans preferred doing it secondhand.

Bending, she scooped up the gun. Her human nails were too thin and puny to do much damage anyway.

The gun felt too light to be deadly, but she leveled it at the man on the ground. She'd seen this done on TV and knew what to do. She crooked her index finger through the hole by the trigger the same instant the man shoved his arm beneath Sorcha. With a jerk of his arm, he sent Sorcha flying through the air, the small gray body arcing over Belle's head.

Howling like an angry dog, he pushed up to a sitting position, his head, arms, and hands bleeding.

Behind Belle came a squeal and scuffling noises. Good, Sorcha was all right. Not that Belle had doubted Sorcha would land on her feet. After all, Sorcha was a cat.

Stepping forward, Belle aimed the gun at the man's round face. "I don't know who you are, but I'm going to kill you and enjoy doing it."

He paled, his complexion the color of the driveway stones, his eyes on the gun barrel.

"I'll pay you," he said, his voice squeaking. "A hundred thousand."

Belle's grip on the gun didn't waver. It would be so easy to shoot him now. But what would be the fun in that?

Before killing vermin, she liked to play with it first.

"Should I shoot you here?" Her voice cooing, she aimed the gun at the spot between his gaping eyes. Then, with a swift gesture, she lowered the barrel, aiming it at the spot between his legs. All males, no matter their species, valued that part of their anatomy. "Or here?"

His hands clapped over his crotch. "No! I know you, Sorcha. You wouldn't do that."

She laughed. From the tree behind her, she heard the rustle of leaves. Sorcha. Preparing for another attack if needed? Or just watching the fun?

Belle wanted to glance up and share her laughter with Sorcha, but she wasn't done playing.

"Five hundred thousand," he said, his voice desperate.

"How much did you promise *him?*" Belle didn't take her stare off the man, but his gaze darted to the side where Phil sprawled unmoving.

"Please," he whispered. "Please."

"I know! I think I'll start here." She jiggled the gun barrel, and a wet spot started between his legs, growing bigger, the light gray color turning charcoal. With a smile, she swept the gun barrel upward, aiming it at his head. "And end here."

He moaned and closed his eyes, as if waiting for the bullet to shoot into his head.

Belle's lips tightened. This was no fun. The weak human was giving up too soon. A mouse would still be running in frantic circles, trying to escape.

Playtime was over. In all the TV shows she watched, this was when the human woman told the man to get up and she'd take him to the police. The man would get up, grab the gun, and attack her. Sometimes he killed her right away. Other times the hero would come and save her.

Humans were sometimes very stupid.

Belle was shifting the gun barrel a quarter inch higher when she heard her name being called and someone crashed through the woods.

Max!

If she hurried, she could shoot the man before Max reached them.

Forty-three

"Belle!" Max saw her standing, aiming a gun at someone on the ground. She was alive! She wasn't shot! His heart leapt inside his chest and joy pulsed through him.

"Don't shoot," he called as he avoided a football-sized rock. A branch swiped his cheek, and he brushed it away, running as if his life were at stake.

If Belle shot someone, she'd go to jail. She'd lose her freedom. His chest ached at the thought. If need be, he'd go to jail in her place.

"Belle, don't!"

He skidded to a stop. She was glowering at a fortyish man in gray pants and a golf shirt. The man's face and hands were scratched and bleeding, and he reeked of urine.

"Who's he?"

"I don't know. He shot Phil and tried to kill me."

Max glanced around. Instead of Phil, he saw a mound topped with blond hair about forty feet to Belle's left. A groan came from the mound.

"Caroline?" he said.

"She tried to kill me first," Belle said matter-of-factly. "Phil shot her, then this man"—she jerked the gun down and the man on the ground mewled—"shot Phil."

Max looked to the right and saw Phil, another mound. What the hell was this about? Caroline he understood, but— His eyes narrowed.

"He must be the man who killed Sorcha's fiancé."

"No wonder she was so ferocious." Belle smiled and took

293

a quick glance at the tree behind her. "Good job, Sorcha!" she called.

A meow answered her.

The bloodied man shifted. In an instant, Belle pointed the gun at him, her hand steady.

Max started to reach for the gun, but his hand was trembling. She could've been killed. One of these mounds could've been her.

Slamming down his instinct to take control, he pulled back. "I wanted to save you," he said.

"I don't need your protection."

A surprised laugh came out of his throat. "No, you don't," he said. Even as a woman, Belle was independent and arrogant. All she asked from him was love. And just because she had a little, well, oddity in her background, he'd run from her and almost lost her.

He unclipped his cell phone from his belt and dialed 911.

"This woman is crazy," the man on the ground said. "She's the one who killed them, not me."

"I don't think I'll kill you after all." Belle aimed the gun a little lower. "But I wouldn't mind shooting you down there. My finger might slip and it will be an accident."

"Eeee!" The man grabbed his testicles.

The dispatcher came on the phone and Max told her two people had been shot. After he gave her the address and directions, she asked if the shots were fatal.

A grunt came from Phil. Caroline rolled to her side.

"Get her gun," Belle said.

"They're not dead yet." Max hung up the cell phone and hurried over to Caroline. A gun lay on the ground about two feet away from her sporty tennis shoes. He grabbed it by the barrel, careful not to get his fingerprints on the handle.

Caroline pushed up to a sitting position, looking down at her chest. Blood spurted out of a hole in her upper right breast.

She burst into tears. "This is horrible," she said between sobs. "I'll never be able to wear a low-cut gown again."

"No worries," Belle said, her voice cheerful. "Prison uniforms are high cut."

Caroline sobbed harder. Max didn't feel any pity for her. Not after she'd tried to kill Belle.

He strode to Phil, still carrying the gun by the barrel. As he bent forward, Phil opened his eyes, lifting a hand to his head.

"Are you okay?" Max's gaze traced a stream of blood to the starting point by Phil's shoulder.

Phil started to nod and groaned. Wincing, he touched the back of his head. "I think I fell and hit my head on a rock." His voice was faint.

"An ambulance is on the way."

Closing his eyes, Phil winced again. "Shit," he said, the word gasping out. He raised his head. "Could you—"

Bending, Max took away the rock and tossed it to the side.

"Thanks." Phil lowered his head and closed his eyes. Sweat beaded his face, and Max knew he was fighting a boatload of pain.

Max moved back to Belle, standing behind her. Feeling oddly hesitant, he curved his hand on her shoulder, noting his trembling had stopped. He could take the gun, take control as usual, be the man who took care of everyone.

Except Belle. She'd proved she didn't need anyone to take care of her.

He bent his head, his mouth level with her ear. "I don't care what you were before this," he said, his voice low. "But I want to be with you always, not just when I come back from my travels. I'll stay home with you if that's what you want."

She shook her head. "No."

His hand tightened on her shoulder. There was a lump in his throat, and he swallowed. "If you want to trade bodies with Sorcha again, I understand. It's my fault for listening to my mind instead of my heart."

"No."

"No?" His heart thundered in his chest.

From a distance came the wail of sirens.

"Belle? Is there a chance you'll stay with me?"

She leaned back against him. The tension seeped out of his body, and he wrapped his arms around her rib cage.

"I almost died today," she said.

He held her closer.

"Staying here without you," she went on, "doesn't seem as important as being with you."

"This will still be your home."

"Where you are is my home. If you want to travel to those faraway places, I'll travel with you."

He closed his eyes and inhaled her scent. "You are my world." He thought of an old saying, *Home is where the heart is.* They would have it painted and hang it on a wall.

"You sound just like Brian on *The Love Chronicles*," she said.

"Brian," he murmured in her ear, "is a very smart man."

Sorcha peered at the scene from her perch in the tree. Belle wanted to remain a woman. That meant she could stay a cat!

She could return to Gwen, the one person who loved her with all her heart, without expecting anything back. Gwen loved her the way a dog loved. Unconditionally.

She flew down the tree, thumped onto the ground. Belle's head turned toward the sound.

"Sorcha," Belle said, "I'm sorry, but I want to remain a human."

The siren was still moments away but louder, coming nearer. Sorcha stared at Belle, giving her the message: *Being changed into a cat is the best thing that ever happened to me.*

Belle nodded. "Are you going to be okay? I can't let you stay with us. I'd be afraid to touch you."

Sorcha shivered and stepped back. If Belle was afraid, she was more afraid.

"You were very brave tonight," Belle said. "You saved my life."

Sorcha cocked her head. She had been brave. She had

saved Belle's life. Now she had to go live her own. Even if Gwen had to sneak her food and water, she'd be happier being a cat with Gwen than she ever have been being a woman, even with Fletcher.

She meowed a good-bye, then dashed into the woods toward Gwen's house. Behind her, she heard Deavers offer Max more money to let him go. Did he say one million? Max's harsh laughter cut off Deavers' voice, then all their voices faded as Sorcha ran through the woods like an Olympic gold medalist. If the gold medalist were lucky enough to be a cat.

In her mad dash, it didn't take long to reach the mini-mansion. She ran out of the trees toward the house—and slid to a stop on the damp grass.

Three cars were parked on the driveway. A red sports car, a white station wagon, and a brown car with an open trunk that she recognized as Katie's. Katie and Gwen stood by the front drive along with two other women and a bunch of suitcases. Then Katie started to throw suitcases into the trunk.

What was going on? Did Gwen's mother and father want Gwen to go to them? Sorcha's heartbeat hammered inside her even as she discounted that idea. More likely, Gwen's parents wanted to punish her for running away by sending her to boarding school.

It would break Gwen's lonely heart.

It would break Sorcha's.

She needed to hear what they were saying. Scooting low, she dashed to the front bushes.

"Look! A cat!"

A foot from the front bushes, Sorcha froze. She stared at the woman who was pointing at her and laughing.

"Cats are good luck," she said, her molasses voice matching her molasses skin. She was a hefty woman and every time she laughed, her huge breasts jiggled.

A thinner woman with skin closer to the color of caramel said, "We should take it to the pound."

"She's mine!" Gwen ran toward Sorcha. "Princess is mine, and no one's taking her from me."

The next instant she was hugging Sorcha and kissing the top of her head. "I love you," she said. "I love you."

"Aw, that's so sweet," the molasses voice said.

"You're going to let her keep it?" Katie asked, indignant. "You're *rewarding* her for her misbehavior?"

"If you want me to send that letter of reference," the thin woman said, "I suggest you leave this moment."

A tear dropped from Gwen's chin onto Sorcha's head. "You can stay with me, Princess. Did you hear? My new nanny likes you." She kissed Sorcha's damp head and whispered, "She likes *me*, too. Everything is better and it's all because of you."

A car door slammed. Cuddled against Gwen's scrawny chest, Sorcha heard the car speed along the driveway, away from them.

"This is just like the ending of a fairy tale," Gwen said. "The wicked witch is gone, and we're going to live happily ever after."

Sorcha purred and looked at Gwen, giving her a message: *It's not the end. It's the beginning.*

The beginning of her life as a cat. She wouldn't trade it for all the tuna in the sea.

Forty-four

Belle thought it was too bad she had to keep the gun aimed at the man on the ground when she'd rather be having sex with Max. Sirens screamed closer. Belle was glad Max stood behind her, so close she could feel his heat and smell his scent. Not because she needed him to complete her, like Amanda on *The Love Chronicles* needed Brad—at least in yesterday's episode—but because having him near made her feel like purring.

A movement from the corner of her eye caught her attention. Tory raced through the woods from the direction of the house.

"Max! Sorcha! What's going on? I got a call from the sheriff's dispatcher. She said you hung up on her and two people were shot and you won't answer your cell phone. What hap—" She saw the mound that was Phil and gasped. Then she ran toward him, her face contorted. "Phil! Phil! Please, don't be dead."

"He's not dead," Max said.

"An ambulance! He needs an ambulance!"

"Already called," Max said.

"What the hell is going on?" Ted asked, skidding to a stop next to Belle and Max, coming from the same direction as Tory. "Why're you holding a gun at this guy?"

"We don't know his name," Max said, "but we believe he killed Sorcha's fiancé."

"You can't prove it. I have an alibi."

Belle wiggled the gun barrel. "My trigger finger's feeling slippery."

He glared at her, his mouth clamped shut.

Being a human was easy, Belle thought. All she needed was the right accessories. On *The Love Chronicles*, the men gave the women jewelry for a present on their weddings. She decided to ask Max to buy her a gun.

"Caroline?" Ted's brow furrowed. "What happened to you?"

She held up her middle finger.

Even as a cat, Belle had known what that meant.

Ted's eyebrows rose. "Whoa, you're in a bad mood."

Caroline sobbed. She was sitting up, holding her hand over her chest. "This wasn't supposed to happen. Life isn't fair."

"Jesus." Ted turned to Max. "Thanks for leaving me stranded. I had to call a taxi, and the guy drove like he was practicing for the Indianapolis 500. He was dropping me off when I saw Tory run out like a scared rabbit." He nodded at Tory, who was bending over Phil. "What's going on?"

"I'll tell you later. I need you to run to the road and flag down the ambulance."

"Sounds like they're almost on top of us." Ted sprinted toward the road, waving his hand to halt any oncoming vehicles before he even made it out of the trees. Then he was out of sight, and a few seconds later the sirens stopped their high-pitched wail.

In the sudden silence, Belle heard Phil's weak voice say, "I don't really work for the FBI. I'm a personal trainer and work at my dad's gym. Bob's my half brother. He was going to pay me to kill Sorcha."

"But you didn't do it," Tory said.

"No, when I saw Caroline about to shoot Sorcha, I shot her instead. Then Bob shot me."

"You saved Sorcha! You're a hero."

"I'm not. I'm a bastard. Literally and figuratively."

Tory was crying. "Don't say that about yourself. I really like you."

"I like you, too. But after what I did, I don't deserve you."

Voices came from the road along with stomping feet and cracking branches. Belle watched Ted dodge around a tree.

300

A few steps behind him strode two uniformed men, one tall and one short, with guns in their holsters and tense expressions on their faces.

"That's my brother," Ted said, pointing. "He's the one who called 911. And that's Sorcha. She's the one I think they were trying to kill."

The shorter man pushed in front of Ted. "I'm Deputy Olson and this is Deputy Groves. Now, don't make any sudden moves. Very slowly, I want you to put the guns on the ground and back off."

"Gladly." Max set Caroline's gun on the ground and backed off.

Belle didn't feel as glad, but put her gun next to Max's and backed up next to him. Deputy Olson hurried to collect the guns. Belle knew from watching TV what would happen next. A lot of questions, a lot of time wasted when all she wanted to do was kiss Max and decide where they would live now that they knew it didn't matter where.

He put his arm around her.

Deputy Groves was hauling the man on the ground to his feet, putting on handcuffs, the man demanding to talk to his lawyer. Deputy Olson was on his cell phone, telling someone it was okay to come in.

"I almost lost you," Max said, his voice cracking with emotion.

It looked to Belle as if they had a few minutes after all. "I know what's wrong with humans," she said.

He lifted an eyebrow.

"They should talk less"—smiling, she held up her arms—"and kiss more."

His mouth came down. He kissed her roughly, as if he wanted to take her to the bedroom.

She purred.

"I love you," he said, drawing back. "I'll worship you forever."

She pulled his head down for another kiss. He wasn't saying anything she didn't know. She was born to be worshiped.

Epilogue

To: Max Brannigan
From: Tory Patterson
Subject: BOOK!!!!!

Phil's agent sold the screenplay! It's going to be made into a cable TV movie! I think the producer's selling it to Lifetime. And guess what? I'm playing Sorcha! I'm doing the happy dance right now.

As soon as we get the money, Phil wants to pay you back for taking care of his parents' medical expenses. We won't let you say no either. You two are the most wonderful people in the world, and I'm not just saying that because you're my brother and you gave us money and Sorcha said it was okay. Can you imagine what Caroline would've said if the week before you got married you told her you were giving a quarter mil away? I get the creeps thinking about it. Hope they don't let her out of that mental hospital for a long, long time.

Anyway, everything is turning out great. Phil's parents are okay and you and Sorcha are having a baby. I'm so excited about being an auntie! Has she gotten the test to see if it's a boy or girl yet? What do you and Sorcha want?
XXXOOO
Tory

_____

To: Tory Patterson

From: Max Brannigan
Subject: baby

Congrats on the movie deal and the role. I told you not to worry about paying us back. Sorcha doesn't want the test. She's still scared of hospitals, hates seeing the doctor, and is talking about getting a midwife. I don't care what sex the baby is.

Max

––––––––––

To: Max Brannigan
From: Tory Patterson
Subject: Re: baby

That's just like a man. I asked about Sorcha, too. What does she want?
XXXOOO
Tory

––––––––––

To: Tory Patterson
From: Max Brannigan
Subject: Re: baby

>I asked about Sorcha, too. What does she want?

A litter.

– The End –

Love Cats, Dogs, Books, and Readers

I didn't intend to put a dog or cat in so many of my books. They're a part of my life and the lives of so many people I know, and they often they sneak into my books. Sometimes, just as in real life, they want to take over. In other books, they have smaller roles.

Tory's story (Max's sister) is told in the novella, THE FAT CAT. Like CATTITUDE, that was always about the cat, as well as about Tory. The entire novella, MUST WORSHIP CATS, is in the viewpoint of the cat. In A LOVE & MURDER CHRISTMAS, there's a giant cat pooka. There are no pookas or other paranormal elements in the previous two Love & Murder books—but I went for it, and I love the way it turned out.

Thank you for reading my book! To keep up with my latest releases, exclusive giveaways, and special prices, sign up for my newsletter at www.edieramer.com.

Edie Ramer

About Edie Ramer

A *USA* Today bestselling author, Edie is funnier on the page than in real life. Edie has won multiple writing contests. She lives in southeastern Wisconsin with her husband and one important cat. She's happy to be able to do what she loves nearly every day, and she's grateful to all of my readers. You're the best!

Acknowledgments

My heartfelt gratitude to my original critique partners: Michelle Diener for her wisdom and her belief in me, Liz Kreger for her advice and inspiration, and Karin Tabke for always asking "how do they feel?"